THE
WALL
FLOWER

To all the Wallflowers out there. Don't be afraid to step into the light, let yourself be seen, and shine bright. Just don't get the attention of a psychopath. Morally gray men are great but only in books.

AUTHOR NOTE

Thank you so much for picking up a copy of *The Wallflower*. That said, I want to confirm that this is a dark-adult romance novel that ends on a cliffhanger. The hero in this book is a walking red flag. He will piss you off and push your buttons in the worst way. *No* is not a word that is in his vocabulary. He pushes the limits and then pushes them again. This book has numerous triggers, so if you're sensitive to any of those listed below, please use caution when reading. Also, please give Drew a chance. He is a villain, but his heart is pure, and I promise you'll see that in the end if you stick through it.

Triggers:
Virgin heroine, Dubious Consent, Non-Con, Child Abuse, Stalking, Blood Play, Bullying, Murder, Emotional and Physical Abuse, Domestic Violence, Blackmail, Primal Play, Breeding, Child-hood Poverty, Cancer, Psychological Disorders, Marking, Violence, Forced Orgasm/Pleasure.

CHAPTER 1
DREW

IN FOOTBALL, there are two people, winners and losers. Nothing else in between matters, and with my last name and image hanging in the balance, there is absolutely no way I'm fucking losing, not even in practice. I give the asshole trying to stand one more vicious kick to the ribs, then step over his body. He'll be fine. He's wearing football pads.

My friends come up behind me, the men I trust most in the world. Lee, Aries, and Sebastian take my back as I jog slowly toward the training center to clean up after our practice.

The rest of the team, and even the coaches, follow at a healthy pace as if they want to keep their distance.

I'm amped up, as I didn't get nearly enough time to run off my energy. That dick groaning on the ground back there tried, unsuccessfully, for a sack. After his failure, my boys and I taught him a lesson. The coaches called practice over, but I'm still amped up for a fight.

I pull off my practice jersey and start unstrapping my pads as I head into the locker room. It takes a minute to strip them off, leaving me only in my pants and shoes.

1

Once I jerk my locker open, I shove the equipment inside and throw myself onto the bench to strip off my cleats.

Lee plops down beside me, his dark hair standing up in a sweaty mess. "You alright, man?"

I lean back into the locker, letting the cold metal cool me down. "Yeah, fine. Just wish we would have stayed out a little longer today. I have to work off some energy."

Aries leans in, his dark curls equally messy. "Want me to go find you a girl? Give you something to preoccupy yourself with?"

I shake my head and stretch my feet outside the confines of my shoes. "No, I'm saving it for tonight."

"You can go find *me* a girl, Ari," Sebastian says, his tone dark and deep. "I might need a little appetizer before the main event. It's hard as fuck to wait until tomorrow. Just a little thing to suck me off, tide me over. It's always good to get someone to take the edge off."

Aries narrows his eyes at Sebastian. "The last time I found you a girl, you fucked her throat raw, and now I can't go near *that* sorority house ever again."

Sebastian snorts. "She wanted it. She begged me before I let her have it. The only reason she got bitchy about it afterward was because I told her I wasn't fucking a cunt every man on the team has had. She could have my fingers or nothing, and she chose nothing."

Lee snorts from his spot at his locker a few paces down. The room is full now, the entire team filing in and stripping down to shower.

The boys rib each other a bit more, but I lean my head back, clenching my fists, thinking about tomorrow night's big event. I can't wait to sink inside some little doe-eyed beauty who doesn't have enough sense to run when I finally catch her. That's what my body waits for, what my dick waits for. I should have realized nothing else would do.

The guys strip off their own gear, shoving things in lockers and harrying the towel boy as he comes through to hand out the fresh towels.

I snatch one off the stack and shove him faster through the row to get him out of my sight.

"Sebastian, is everything prepared?"

I leave the planning for The Hunt to the most depraved of us. Sebastian always comes up with fun little surprises. He might appear to have his shit together, but he's far from ordinary. The guy makes me look like a gentleman, and that's saying something, given how fucked up I am myself.

Sebastian strips his undershirt off and drops it to the bottom of his locker. "Of course, it's all finished. Who do you think I am? Invitations have been sent out and shared by the guys. Every detail is in order."

I stretch my neck from side to side, thinking. "And the pack this year...anyone who might pique my interest?"

Sebastian grins at me over his shoulder. "What do you think? There are at least a couple of virgins and a few lovely girls who have no idea what they're getting into. I suspect a few of them might bring their own clueless friends along."

Lee and Aries both chuckle at this.

Aries scrubs his hair away from his face. "I want one with a little fight. She might start out clueless, but when I catch her, I want her to make me bleed, and maybe I'll return the favor."

Lee shrugs. "I like surprises. I'll chase, and we will see what I happen to scare up."

I let out a long sigh and stare back and forth between them. "You all know what I want. But this time, I want it to be fucking real. None of this pretends not to want it while her

3

cunt is sopping wet bullshit. I want to see the whites in her eyes. If she fights, fine, but I want it to be out of fear, not pretense."

Lee snickers as he shucks his cleats. "You want what we all want and have yet to find. Good luck, man. I hope when you find her, you're able to keep her."

I shrug. "Maybe, maybe not. That depends mostly on her, I suppose. The more she doesn't want me, I think, the more I'll enjoy The Hunt. That's my goal. The ultimate hunt and the ultimate prize."

I want very few things in life. Given my money and my father's legacy, there is nothing I can't have except this: the perfect chase.

It disturbs me how much I need it. How much I've thought about nothing else recently. Maybe tomorrow will be the night. When you have as little control over your life and the things that happen in it as I do, something as simple as a little chase in the woods can make or break you. It's one singular thing *I* have a choice about.

I clench my fists again and stand, shoving off my pants and tossing the rest of my kit into my locker. Shower first, then I have a nerd to hunt down. I check my phone again, and I'm not surprised when there's no response to my text. The little shit will regret keeping me waiting. I paid him five hundred up front for that paper, and if he thinks he can stiff me, he's sorely mistaken.

It doesn't take me long to shower and throw my wash into the designated bags. I make sure to shoulder-check the glowering teammate who thought he could take me on the way out. Ruckus or Tucker, maybe. I don't remember his name.

The guys watch me go and say nothing as I head out, hair still wet, in my hoodie and jeans. On the way through the training center to outside, I shoot the little asshole a text telling him to respond before I hunt him down and beat the shit out of him.

I stop to fill my water bottle from a fountain on the path while I wait for him to respond. The idiot reads the text but doesn't answer. If that's how he wants to play it, so be it. Unfortunately, some people aren't nearly as intelligent as they think. I don't pay nerds to do the work because I can't do it myself. I pay them because it's easier to have someone else do it. I don't have time to waste on writing papers or doing research. But it only works if the person I hire actually does the work.

I stalk across the quad, heading toward the place I first found him: the library. It's not even a half mile, and the slight chill in the air cools the simmering rage in my veins into something sharper and more sinister as I walk.

A flitty little blonde rushes up to my side, matching my pace to talk to me. "Drew, I heard that tomorrow is the big night."

I give her little more than a grunt of agreement. "So?"

She bats her long, fake eyelashes, now practically running to match my long stride. "Well, I was hoping for an invitation. I have some friends I could bring along for some fun."

I stop, and the halt makes her lose her balance. I wait to see if she falls, but she doesn't. "What kind of friends?"

Out of breath now, her smile widens. "Oh, I have a *lot* of friends. I guess it depends on the type you're after?"

I narrow my eyes and scan down her low-cut top and skintight leggings. She's dressed as if she's ready to go frolicking through the woods at this very moment. "How about someone with a little innocence? Know anyone like that?"

She taps her chin, considering what I've asked, but her eyes have a knowing twinkle. "Well, I have a few who might fit. I'll ask them to come in exchange for an invitation of my own and some tips on how to bag one of your crew."

I tip her chin up gently, towering over her, and lean in. "Sure, come along, but you'll have to figure out how to catch their eye on your own."

Not so gently, I shove her back a few steps. "Meet at the Mill House at sunset, tomorrow."

I walk away without looking back. There's a small chance she might have what I'm looking for, but it sure as hell isn't her.

The rest of the walk to the library is uneventful, mostly because everyone else on the path takes one look at my scowl and doesn't even try to approach me. Good, that's how I like it. I keep up the nice guy image for appearances only, but I'm about as nice as a crocodile that hasn't eaten in months.

I take the stairs to the library entry two at a time and push through the glass doors. It's a big space, being the only library on campus, so it might take time to find the scrawny little fucker. Especially if he's doing his damnedest to hide from me.

I stalk through the stacks first, slowly. My approach sends a few people scurrying out of my way, which is fine. No one catches my eye, and I slow my pace so I don't miss him between a row of shelves.

Once I reach the far side of the library, I move to the other side and begin searching the little study nooks dotting the area. A group of tittering girls spots me in the distance, and I can hear their chatter as they dare each other to come and speak to me. I ignore their existence.

A few other people are spread around, and a professor tucked up into a glass cage in the back. No scrawny little nerd in sight, though. My patience is growing thinner by the second. If he doesn't want me to murder him, he'll make an appearance soon.

Frustrated, I tug my cell phone out of my pocket and shoot off a quick text. It only takes a second to hear the ding in the mostly quiet space. A smile tugs at my lips.

Gotcha, you little fuck.

I scan the space where I heard the sound until I spot him. He's staring at his screen, looking appropriately scared. Good. He should be scared. I stalk around the backside of the stacks and come up behind him.

It takes seconds to grab him by the scruff of his sweater and drag him between the shelves. "Hello, Mark. If I didn't know better, I'd say you're avoiding me. Because you forgot to send me something today?"

He sputters, his phone slipping from his hand to clatter on the worn carpet. Whirling around, he appears baffled. "No, no. I was... I'm not avoiding you. I'm just proofreading your essay. I didn't forget to send it."

"I'm pretty sure it was supposed to be delivered this morning. When I give you a deadline, I expect it to be met. Now, I have to worry about getting my assignment in on time. Which isn't something I should have to worry about, especially when I've already fucking paid you."

I give him a hard shove into the stack of books. He whimpers and turns his head to the side, likely hoping to protect his face.

"I'd love to let you go without any consequences, but that would set a *terrible* precedent for any future nerds I hire." Minding the distance of the shelf behind me, I jerk back to deliver a punch in the gut when I hear a gasp to my right from deeper in the stacks.

It's loud enough to make me pause. I can be as depraved as I like, but I can't risk getting cut from the football team or making my father look bad. It would be unlikely, but I don't need to invite the question, especially not during the season.

It's hard to see what I'm looking at in the dim lighting, but I focus my gaze on a spot hidden in the dark. The gasp came from a little thing in a worn oversized hoodie. Her blond hair is tied up in a knot on top of her head. It's bright blond, a beacon of light in the dim space. She's *very* pretty.

Something dark and sinister swirls in my gut. I can't look away from her. Not for a second.

She steps closer, tentatively, and places a hand on the nearest shelf. "Is everything okay here?" She doesn't sound sure of herself. Not like she's afraid per se... But she hasn't raised her voice at all.

I release my hold on the nerd and let him sink back to his feet. "Yup, everything is peachy."

"It doesn't look like it. If you let him go, I can pretend I didn't hear what you said. No one has to know what you're doing."

I'm a bit shocked at her gall. Is she dating this little nerd? Is that why she's protective of him? The kid doesn't appear to know who she is, not in the least bit, so it can't be that.

"You don't look like the type to blackmail, so what will you give me in return for releasing this little weasel? He's stolen from me. He took five hundred dollars in exchange for services performed, and he's yet to provide his end of the deal. So...where does that leave me?"

She waves at Mark. "If you hurt him, he can't do the work, can he? Think about it that way. Plus, like I said, if you let him go, then I won't have to say anything."

The warning in her words should alert me, but it doesn't. I'm not scared. I lean in and crook my finger. Instead, I'm curious. Who is this girl? I need to get a better look at her. To see the color of her eyes, the shape of her lips, and the slope of her neck. "Come closer."

I watch her intently as she swallows hard. My hand would fit perfectly wrapped around her throat. Like a glove. Yes, I can see it now. My cock grows hard.

Some of the bite she gave a moment ago is gone. "Yeah, I don't think that's a good idea."

"Who says you have a choice?" I hiss.

CHAPTER 2
BEL

THE MOMENT I meet his eyes, I know I've made a mistake. Something dark lurks there, something deep, demanding to come out and play in my presence.

What the hell do I do now that I've caught his attention? His question hangs in the air...*what will I give him?*

I swallow hard and pull on my sleeves to give myself a moment to consider and think. "Just let him go."

The jock smirks and smooths his hand down his former captive's shirt. "Well, the lady says release you, so I guess I'll let you go. I want my paper, nerd, or next time, I won't allow anyone to get in my way. Blood will be spilled. You have twenty-four hours."

The other man hesitates for a moment, his gaze ping-ponging between me and the belligerent bully. I shake my head gently, telling him to leave while he can. This guy won't hurt me, not here in the library or in public...I *think*?

As if the guy can read my mind, he scurries away like a terrified mouse. Unease coats my insides. Without the other guy here, all this jock's attention is left on me.

His gaze sharpens on me as he stalks toward me through

space I refused to cross. He's tall, wide-shouldered, with tousled dark hair and full lips spread into a perpetual frown. Something about him is dark and dangerous, and everything in me says *run*.

I want to back away, but dammit, I don't want to show weakness, especially here, in my domain. This isn't the...sports field...or wherever he gains his admirers and followers. I saw the way he marched in here like he owned the place and how everyone turned to watch him, some even jumping out of the way as he passed by.

He's popular, a jock, and no doubt rich. Two more seconds in my presence, he'll notice my worn sweatshirt and the holes in my jeans from *real* use, not fashion. He'll realize I'm a scholarship student and keep his distance. I don't need to run when he'll do it for me.

Like a bug beneath a microscope, he studies me, his eyes tracing down my body and back up to my face. Worse yet, he's not even bothering to hide the fact that he's checking me out. What a pig. I'm poor, so of course I'll fuck him. That's the look he's giving me right now.

"Come here, my little wallflower. I want to get a better look at you."

I curl my lip in disgust. "I'm not your *anything*, and no, thank you. I need to get back to studying. Unlike you, I have to do my *own* homework."

He takes another step, leaving him only a couple of feet from me now, and *damn,* he is taller than I thought. He's got to be close to six feet two or three. His frame towers over me, making me feel small and insignificant. My gaze trails over his body.

His hoodie strains against his broad shoulders. It's obvious he's a jock because his body alone resembles that of a

Greek statue. I'm afraid to look any lower or take my eyes off him for a second.

A lump forms in my throat, and his lip curls a little more as if he's a cat who's found a mouse waiting to be pounced on.

How the hell do I get out of here? I won't turn my back on that look in his eyes. Like I'm the prey, and he's the hunter.

I move to step back, and he narrows those dark, intense eyes of his. Shaking his head, he says, "Not so fast, little flower. I released your nerd. Now I want to talk to you for a second."

"Umm...I don't have anything to say to you. As I said, I have to get back to..."

What, exactly? The stack of textbooks I contemplated selling to pay for my sick mother to finally go to the doctor? To the chattering girls in the next cubicle talking about some silly little frat hunt thing where they plan to find a hot jock to fuck them in the woods. Yeah, super-a-lot to get back to.

"You're studying, I remember," he finishes for me.

I stand there, feeling awkward as fuck, my stomach in my throat, and I really don't know why. He's not going to hurt me. He can't, not here. I can't help but remind myself that he was perfectly fine hurting the other guy here, out in the open. What's to stop him from doing the same to me? With his size, I imagine not very many people pit themselves against him.

He tilts his head slightly and shoves his hands into his pockets. It's an attempt to be disarming, but it only makes me more nervous.

"What's your name?"

My eyes go everywhere but his face, scanning the area for an exit. If I sprint backward, then I'd be in the main room. He wouldn't push me there, *right*?

As if suspecting my next move, his arm snaps out, and his

hand wraps around my wrist like a vise. "Not so fast, wall-flower. I want to talk to you. Give me your name."

It's not a question this time but a demand.

One I don't appreciate. "No, thank you. You don't need to know my name, and you don't need to put your hands on me either. Now, let me go."

Shifting closer, I catch the smell of mint and something masculine, teakwood maybe. He's only a few inches away now, and I swallow against his intoxicating scent, breathing through my mouth. *Who does he think he is?* Better yet, why didn't I just mind my own business?

Cautiously, I flit my gaze to his and wait. He wants my name, but I won't tell him, so we are at an impasse. It feels like a standoff.

His lip curls again and then blooms into a full-on smile, and suddenly, I see why people stare at him. *Shit.* Something tells me he doesn't use that smile often, only when he thinks it will get him whatever he wants.

"Your name," he whispers, his voice soft and raspy.

"What's the magic word?" I prompt.

He scoffs. "I'm not asking you for anything. You'd better give me what I want."

"Is *please* not a word in your vocabulary?"

Now his eyes narrow, and his grip on my wrist tightens. It's his turn to meet my eyes and stay silent. He wants my name, but he's not going to be civil about it. *Figures.*

I tug on his hold, trying to free myself, which only encourages him to tighten his grip until I stop struggling again. A heat unfurls in my chest, and it takes a minute to realize for the first time in a long time that I'm fucking pissed.

Fighting with my mom all the time about money, about the doctor, all of it has killed something inside me. Has made me squish and bury all my emotions so every twitch doesn't make me say something else that hurts my mother, makes her look at me like I've disappointed her just because I can't watch her die.

How dare he treat me this way? He doesn't even know me? Heat surges through me in a new way, awakening things that have long slept.

I tug at my wrist hard this time, breaking his hold, and clutch my hand to my chest. I resist the urge to rub at the tender flesh there. "Just leave me alone."

"Your name, little wallflower, and I'll leave you alone. It really isn't hard."

"I'm not yours, I'm not a little flower, or wallflower, or whatever the hell it is you're calling me."

"Then tell me your name, and I'll use that instead."

His pensive eyes continue their perusal of my body before dragging those dark eyes back up to my face, trailing a blaze of ice-cold annoyance over my skin. "Tell me..."

I keep waiting for a damn *please*, but he doesn't give it to me. Manners clearly aren't something he was taught. Either that, or he doesn't have to use them often.

"I'm going to walk back to my cubicle, and you can go kick balls, eat dirt, or whatever the hell it is you do when you're not terrorizing people."

His smile widens, and flashing white teeth shine at me in the dim overhead lighting. It's more predatory than comforting. Goose bumps bloom on my arms, and I hunker into my hoodie, although I resist the urge to pull my hood up to hide from him further.

Fast, so fast, his arm loops around my waist, and he presses into me. The breath in my lungs escapes with a shudder, and I'm tempted to kick him in the balls. This close, he's intimidating as hell, and I have to crane my neck back to meet his eyes. Every inch of him presses against me, and all I feel is hard, hot muscle. I shiver, and it seems to delight him, his smile only growing.

He leans in and whispers, "Your name... Plea—"

There's a rustle to the left, and we both freeze, twisting to see who's interrupting.

Professor Stone stares at us with narrowed eyes. "None of that in here. Take it back to the dorms if you want to do *that*."

His tone is just as dark as it was earlier when he warned me about my overdue payment for our class New York trip. At least he's not just a dick to me, it seems.

I take a peek at the jock's face, and it's almost fascinating to watch the genial mask slip across his features. He goes from menacing to mellow in less than a second.

"We're so sorry to disturb you, Professor. It's not what it looks like. I was just helping..." He glances down at my face with a dopey sweet smile, and I realize he's waiting for the professor, who gives him exactly what he wants.

"Maybel?"

He winks at me. "Maybel...she took a little spill. I was just helping her up."

The professor glances back and forth between us, then marches away without another word.

What the *hell*!? Anger rushes to the surface, and I shove at his chest hard, but he doesn't budge. Not even an inch. It's like trying to move a slab of concrete.

"Maybel, is it? I think I prefer wallflower. It suits you better."

He spreads his fingers so he can touch as much of my back as he can. When his hand slides lower to cup my ass, I give him another hard shove to break away from him. "How dare you?"

His mask slips away, and I see his real face again. Boredom, arrogance, and obsession reflect back at me. He's looking at me like he owns me, but I'm too stupid to know it yet. "Oh, this is only the beginning, little flower. You have no idea the things I could do to you. I could hurt you a little. Break you. Rip those petals off that lush little body you try so desperately to hide." He leans into me, and I can smell the mint on his breath, both brisk and biting. "But you've fucked up, miscalculated, because I see you, and you're fucking *doomed*. There's no escaping me now."

Those words should terrify me, and they do, of course, but the tiniest, weird, feral part of my brain throws caution to the wind. There's a dark secret lurking inside me, one I've never confessed to a soul, a fantasy I've never explored, the desire to be taken against my will, to be completely helpless and at another person's mercy, and this man, as terrifying as he is, sparks that reminder, igniting me with new life. The way he looks at me, not like he's looking through me, but inside me, to see all my flaws and broken pieces... He wants me for more than just homework help. He wants me for *me*.

And that's enough fuckery for me. I swallow hard and turn to walk away. Surprisingly, he allows me to go, and I rush toward the stacks, thinking I can skirt the other shelf and get back to the main room as fast as possible. What I don't count on is the prick following me. As if he anticipated a chase, he's hot on my heels, his long legs eating up the distance like it's nothing.

Run, little flower. Run as fast as you can. I can practically hear his voice in my head. What's wrong with me?

I force my legs to move faster, running deeper into the stacks instead, hoping to fake him out, but he's right there, so close. His breath fans across the back of my neck, tickling, stirring the flyaway hairs and shooting goose bumps down my spine.

I don't bother looking back as I speak. "Go away, you psycho."

"'Go away, you psycho,'" he mocks. "I think I want that on my tombstone."

I walk a little faster. "Keep following me, and I'll personally make sure it gets done."

"Which part? The one where you inevitably end up in my bed moaning my name? Or the tombstone?" A soft chuckle reaches my ears. The sound is even more disconcerting than him touching me.

Relief fills my veins when I reach the other side of the stacks. The second I get a foot of distance between us, I take a hard right into the main area and walk straight to my tattered bag. The temptation to turn around and see if he's still following me throbs at the back of my mind, but I don't dare feed into his psychotic game. Instead, I continue forward, rushing toward the library doors which lead outside to my escape.

Once the cool fall air brushes my cheeks, I suck a ragged breath into my lungs, letting it clear my senses. What the *fuck* was that back there? Who the hell *was* that guy? As the adrenaline wears off, my paranoia spikes.

He made such a big deal about learning my name, but he never told me his...

I peer over my shoulder to see if he's still following me, but there's no one. I swear I can still hear his laughter behind me as I push forward. *Fuck.* It would be my luck that the second I meet a hot guy, crazy but hot, he'd be an absolute psycho. I've been so focused on my studies, taking care of my mom, and helping to make ends meet that dating has been pushed to the back burner entirely. Now, the one time there is interest from someone, it's some random guy chasing me around the library, ordering me to tell him my name. *No, thank you.*

I adjust the strap of my backpack and hustle the rest of the way to my car. Fear makes us do crazy things, and with my mind occupied by that jock and his crazy-as-hell antics, I fail to notice the person coming toward me and bump shoulders with them. It takes a second to steady myself, and I nearly sigh with relief when I recognize her familiar face.

"Jackie, what the hell?"

She lets out a small laugh, rubbing her arm where I hit her. "You plowed into me harder than my last date did. What the hell are you running away from?" She flicks her blond hair over her shoulder, tilting her head at me in question. The sun glints off her high cheekbones, shining across her deep blue eyes, making them glow like sapphires.

I don't dare tell her what happened back in the library. Jackie's the type that would tell me to go back inside and get his number. But I'm still glad to see her. Since day one, we've been friends and roommates, and she gives me balance when I need it.

I risk a glance behind me, then shake my head. "Nothing really, just stayed too long at the library. You know how I get immersed in my studies sometimes."

She nods and smiles. "Let's get some dinner, and I can share with you the good news I got. I promise, you'll want to hear it."

I shouldn't, but I take another peek behind me. The feeling of someone watching me lingers at the nape of my neck. When I look back, there are just normal students. No oversized assholes loom in the shadows. *Then why do I still feel his eyes on me?* I shiver and turn toward my car.

"Oh boy, I'm not sure I want to hear this," I joke. "Let me

drop my bag off in the car, and I'll come with you." Her gaze scans my oversized bag.

"Doesn't that kill your shoulder? I mean, there's probably at least fifteen or twenty pounds worth of books in there." She's wrong, there's actually twenty-five, but I don't correct her. I don't want to make myself look any more of a nerd than I already do.

"It's easier to do it this way than having to go back and forth to the dorms or back and forth to my car," I say over my shoulder as I cross the remaining distance to my car. I unlock it and toss the heavy-as-hell bag inside. It lands with a hearty thump, ripping a little more. I sigh. "Oh, by the way, I have to go to my mom's after dinner."

Jackie frowns, and even though she knows I don't have an option, I can't blame her for being sad. We hardly ever hang out anymore, and if we do, it's only for a few minutes. I'm a terrible friend, I know, but I can't do shit about it. Life's got me in a chokehold I can't seem to escape.

Her frown gives way to something mischievous, and she rubs her hands together gleefully as I return to her side. We start walking back in the direction of the cafeteria. "Oh good, that means I can bring any guy I want back to the dorm, and we can run around naked, have sex on the counters, maybe even on your bed too."

I scowl. "Ew, no, that's unsanitary. I don't want your bare ass or any other bodily fluids on my bedding."

"Oh, come on, Bel! It's not like your bed is seeing any action." I know it's a joke, and she's playing with me, but it still stings. She realizes her mistake, and her features pinch with remorse. "Okay, that was mean. I'm sorry. I didn't mean it like that."

"Don't be sorry. It's not like it isn't true." I shrug, and

thankfully, the cafeteria doors come into view. I hate discussing my love life or lack thereof.

"I know, but I also know you're taking care of your mom, and that's your main priority right now. There will be plenty of time for men in the future." She smiles, and I nod, wanting the conversation to end there.

It's bad enough my mother reminds me almost daily that I should be doing other more productive college kid things instead of taking care of her. I want to be there for my mom, but she insists I focus on *my* life. Except it achieves the opposite effect she wants—I worry more and more until my mind becomes a web of inescapable, haunting thoughts that I'm not doing enough for her. That I might lose her. I swallow thickly.

The double doors to the cafeteria open, and we're blasted with warm air as Jackie and I step inside.

The dinner rush is in full swing. The chatter of fellow students and clinking silverware rattles my eardrums. Anxiousness rests deep in my gut. I hate crowds and loud noises. Usually, I come here before lunch or right after dinner to beat the crowds. Mr. Psycho distracted me, and I forgot what time it was. Jackie weaves through the masses, and I follow her closely until we reach the other side of the room where the trays are located.

"Jesus Christ, why are there so many people here today? It's not even Taco Tuesday."

I shrug. "Maybe they're giving away free food."

"Unlikely." Jackie scoffs. "This place is too fancy to give out freebies."

We stand in line with everyone else and wait our turn to select what we want. The cafeteria serves a combination of both hot food and premade items. I grab a yogurt cup, an egg salad sandwich, and water while Jackie goes for a sub sandwich and a slice of pizza.

"Don't you dare judge me." She grins when I give her a raised eyebrow.

"What happened to: *I'm giving up carbs until the new year?*" I speak the words back to her that she said to me just last week after she weighed herself and realized she'd gained five pounds. She begged me to remind her of her diet every time she tried to cheat.

It's not like I don't get it. Carbs are my kryptonite. If I could afford to eat the pizza and pasta here every week, I would. How much I weigh doesn't mean shit. People should love you for who you are, not what the number on the scale says.

"Look, it's that time of the month, and I'm craving something delicious. Bite me," she hisses, and all I can do is shake my head while smiling. Jackie and I are opposites in many ways, but she's the closest thing to a best friend I have.

We pay for our food, and then all that's left is to find a place to sit. If it were me, I'd take my food back to the apartment, but Jackie thinks I need to socialize more. I let her pick a seat, which is the worst idea ever since it's smack dab in the middle of the room. As soon as my ass hits the chair, I start eating. Ugh, it's been hours since I've eaten. I sink my spoon all the way to the bottom of my yogurt and stir it while Jackie leans into my side.

"So remember how I told you that I had something exciting to tell you?"

"Nope. I don't recall you saying anything about exciting news." I shove a spoonful of the parfait past my parted lips.

Letting out a huff, she rolls her eyes. "You're lucky to have such an amazing friend who gets you invited to all the things."

"Invited...invited to what?" I question between bites.

The slightest show of interest from me has her eyes glimmering with mischief. "Oh, now you're interested in hearing what I have to say?"

"Shut up. I was interested before. Tell me more. Not that I'm agreeing to go or anything."

"Of course not. You'd rather sit in your bedroom all night and read."

"Hey, leave my book boyfriends out of it!" I tease and give her a fake scowl.

"You could have a real boyfriend if you would go out and be social."

I stick my tongue out, but she continues like I haven't interrupted.

"Anyway, I got us an invite to the biggest event that Oakmount holds. It's an exclusive invite-only thing that takes place tomorrow night!"

Fear creeps up my spine. "Tom-tomorrow night?" Could she be talking about the same thing those girls discussed in the library earlier? The Chase...or something like that? I was trying my best not to eavesdrop on their conversation, but that's pretty difficult when they're talking loud enough for everyone to hear.

Most of the things she invites me to are planned out beforehand, so I can move things around to have a legit reason not to go if I need to. *Is it mean?* Sure. Have I been spending less and less time with her and more time with Mom? Sure. But truthfully, I'd rather hang out with my books than be hit on by another psycho guy.

She bobs her head and purses her pink lips, the gloss sparkling bright in the overhead lights. "Yes!! Go ahead and provide your words of gratitude. I can't wait to hear how I'm the best and coolest best friend since you know I got us an official invite to The Hunt" She waves her hands like she performed a magic trick.

"I don't know, Jack. It doesn't really sound like my type of event, and if you got an invite, how did I get invited? Do you have a plus-one?"

Jackie rolls her eyes. "The guy who invited me asked me to bring a friend, and since you're the only person I really like..."

"Don't even guilt trip me," I warn.

She gives me her best puppy dog eyes. "Come on, Bel. We hardly do anything together. Please come with me?" I'm tempted to say no and leave it at that, but a nagging voice in the back of my mind reminds me of something I heard the two girls talking about. Prize money. Twenty-five thousand dollars.

"If you aren't tempted to at least go because of me, there is a prize for twenty-five grand. The first person to the cabin gets it."

"So it's a game of glorified hide-and-seek?"

Jackie smiles. "Something like that. Do you want to go? Please say yes. We could both try to win the money, ya know, for your mom?"

I should say no. That's the smart thing, the Maybel thing to do, but when your needs for something outweigh your fears, there's no saying what you won't do.

"Fine, I'll go," I begrudgingly agree, hoping I didn't make the worst mistake of the year. Then again, with that kind of prize money hanging over my head, the only mistake might be not trying at all.

CHAPTER 3
DREW

THERE'S nothing more thrilling than the chase. Actually, no. The chase is exhilarating, but capturing your prey between your bare teeth while they beg for you to release them? *That's* the part that gets me every time. When I was a kid, my dad would take me hunting. He wanted to teach me the fundamentals of life and death and how sacred taking a life was... He had no idea he was setting me up for failure. Maybe he knew how fucked up I was from the start and was trying to curb the problem before it arrived. Either way, it didn't work. It only made me hunger for something real.

Nothing turns me on like the thought of hunting her, of watching the fear fill her pretty blue eyes and her lips part to release a scream of terror. That desire and burning need is only intensified with the knowledge that she's not faking it. She really is scared of me, which makes it all the more exciting. I can see it in my mind, chasing her, pinning her to the wall, and taking what I want. It would be so easy. Would she beg me to stop? Would she fight back? I'd love to feel her nails digging into my skin. Instead of doing what every cell in my body begged of me to do, I let her slip away into the evening.

It's adorable that she thinks she's won just because she escaped. When she realizes I *allowed* her to leave, she'll be pissed, and I can't wait to see that fire crackle in her eyes. She's different, small but fierce, submissive but determined, and now that she's caught my attention, I won't let her go.

I wander through the library's main room, avoiding the gazes of others. This isn't a place I frequent regularly, so I can feel eyes on me. It pisses me off but also pushes me to hurry the fuck up. If I wasn't so preoccupied, I might tell them to fuck off, but I'm interested in something else. As I pass by the study nooks and head for the entrance, I'm struck with an idea. Just on the other side of the circular library desk stands Professor Stone. His gaze is centered on the piece of paper in his hand. He seemed to know who sweet Maybel was. Perhaps he can share some information with me.

"Excuse me, Professor Stone," I greet and tug my phone from my pocket to flash it at him. "Maybel dropped her phone, and I just found it. You wouldn't happen to know which dorm she's in so I can take it over to her?"

Briefly glancing up from the paper, he mutters, "Uh, yeah. I believe she's over in the C building on the third floor. Ask one of the RAs if you can't find her."

Wow. I didn't expect it to be that easy. Just like that, he returns to what he was doing, and I give him a golden-boy smile. Luckily, I exit the main door just in time to see her on the sidewalk talking with the blonde I'd invited to The Hunt earlier. *Interesting.* Maybe it *is* my lucky day?

I duck to the edge of the building, watching as she scans the library entrance, undoubtedly looking for me. Even from a distance, I can tell she's affected by me. The way she keeps peeking over her shoulder and the fearful glimpse I catch in her eyes. I bet she can feel me watching her. The adrenaline pulses in my veins. *Fuck*. The things I want to do to her. It's wrong and fucked up, but I don't care. I never claimed to be a good guy.

From my hiding spot, I watch her toss her ripped bag into her car and head toward the dining hall. Once they're a good distance ahead, I pop around the corner and start to follow them. I tuck my hands into my pockets and plaster on the usual smile. It's nothing more than a heavily placed veil. God only knows what people would think if they knew the real me.

The blood pumps louder in my ears with every step I take. I'm tempted to kidnap the girl and take her back to the estate, tie her to the bed, and lock her in my bedroom, but she's not ready to see that side of me yet. I also need to do all I can to keep my dad off my ass at the moment. It doesn't mean I'll let her slip through my fingers.

When they disappear inside, something close to irritation pricks at my skin. I could go in there, grab a tray, and pile it full of food. I could then plop down in a seat beside her, terrorize her with whispers in her ear, or watch from a distance, letting her know I'm close by and that there isn't a fucking thing she can do about it. It sounds like a fun time, but I do everything I can to limit my time on campus. It's hard enough pretending while I attend classes and even harder when my patience is as thin as it is at this very moment. *Your family name and image are the most important things. Don't fuck it up.* I can hear my father's deep, angry voice in my mind, almost as if he's standing right beside me speaking the words.

You got lucky this time, Maybel.

With the knowledge that I'll be seeing her again real soon, I turn and start the short walk to the other side of campus.

The crisp air carries with it a slight bite of cold. Fall is upon us, and winter will be here soon. I welcome the fresh air and take the time while walking to clear my head. It's only about a mile walk to my family's estate, which butts against the school campus.

Right now, a couple of my closest friends and I live here. Of course we use the old Mill House for meetings, but those have been few and far between with everyone's busy schedules. Every year in October, we hold The Hunt. The one big event has been a tradition on school grounds for over a hundred years. The original hunt was nothing more than a glorified game of hide-and-seek back in the twenties.

It wasn't until ten years ago that changes took place, making the event that much more elusive and popular. Every year, we strive to outdo the year before, and this year will be the first where we have no rules. Everything goes. If you accept the invitation and show up, you agree to those terms. Every year, fifty men and women, mostly Mill members, those members who were inducted into the society the previous year, are picked to be a part of the event. It means the new members, those who are inducted after the start of the year, after The Hunt, don't get to participate, but..tough shit.

In the past, I've grown bored. It's always the same girls and the same fake screams.

This year will be different, though, I know it. I can feel it in my bones. My family has been at the center of The Mill since it was founded three generations ago. I'm determined to make my time as president legendary. Hell, it already is when college students from other damn states beg to come to our public-facing events. If only they knew what happened in the shadows.

For now, I need to focus on the present. All I have to do is ensure Maybel makes it to the event, and then I can let myself go. I can experience the event for what it's supposed to be. Ahead of me is the house. My feet crunch across the packed gravel drive to the old Victorian mansion. Back in the day, the house had been built by the dean of the school, then a couple years later, my great-grandfather acquired the place for his own personal and debauched use.

He wanted a home away from home for his eclectic activities, hosting illegal alcohol parties in the basement for the other high-profile students on campus. My grandfather had specific tastes, and I'd heard a number of stories from my father about the fuck fests that took place on these grounds. Unsurprisingly, it all started during the Roaring Twenties.

The wrought-iron gates open as I approach them, and I jog up the other side of the driveway to the landing and front door. The heavy wooden door creaks as I open it and slip beneath the Gothic arches. Stained glass and polished dark wood greet me, and the spicy scent of cinnamon tickles my nose.

Patty hobbles out of the kitchen and into the main entry, greeting me with a smile and a plate of cookies. She looks as she does every day, wearing the maid's uniform my father provides all the help with. Her thinning dark hair is pulled back into a tight bun at the nape of her neck. Not a single strand out of place. "Andrew, sweetie, take a cookie. They're snickerdoodles, your favorite."

My immediate response is to tell her to fuck off, but I pause. Now don't get me wrong, Patty is a nice lady. In fact, she's the closest thing to a grandma that I have, but small talk with my father's staff is my least favorite thing. I'd rather gouge my eyes out than engage in a conversation that will most likely end up being repeated back to my father, becoming our next topic of discussion. Therefore, I simply smile and snag one from the plate she offers me and then another for later.

With a weathered smile of her own, she pats my arm and walks off, probably to offer the others the same cookies. That seems to be her life mission: stuffing us full of her delicious food. Otherwise, besides laundry, stocking the fridge, and cleaning, she leaves us to ourselves, especially during Mill business.

I climb up the wide circular staircase two steps at a time. At the top of the stairs is a landing that leads down a long hallway. Each side of the hall has numerous doors that lead to a number of bedrooms and bathrooms. And at the very end of the hall is my room.

The first room I come upon is Sebastian's. Sebastian prefers silence to conversation and usually keeps his door closed, so color me surprised when I see it propped open. I pop my head through the doorway and find him sitting on the edge of his bed, a cookie in his mouth as he turns the page of a paperback. One glance at him and you would assume he's all looks, with his perfectly moussed hair, devilish smile, and haunting green eyes, but contrary to popular belief, he's smart as hell. I assume it's from all the reading he does. We've known each other since grade school, and there's never been a time when I haven't seen him carrying around some type of book. If he doesn't understand something, he researches it until he does.

I gesture to the book. "You can read. When did that happen?"

Without missing a beat, he launches the cookie at my face. I catch it midair and shove it into my mouth. His eyes promise murder and destruction, but all I do is shake my head. Sebastian is many things—monster, asshole, crazy son of a bitch, and believe me, he is all those things and more, but he's also loyal, determined, and the closest thing to family I have.

"Thanks!" I say around a mouthful of food.

"If you spent more time spreading pages in books instead of spreading legs, you might be half as smart as me." The murderous look disappears from his eyes, but the usual aura of depraved darkness surrounding him clings to the air.

Everyone thinks I'm fucked up, but no one knows fucked up like Sebastian. While my own childhood has been shitty as hell, it looks pretty damn great compared to his. Either way, showing pity or apologizing for the past doesn't make sense. We can't change it, but sometimes I wish I could tell him it will be okay. That he'll come through all of this on the other side. His attention slips back to the book, and I meander into the room, dragging my fingers across the bookshelf near the door.

"Spreading legs is more entertaining," I quip, tossing myself into an old armchair near his bed. I prop my feet up on the edge of the bed, my dirty boots resting on his gray comforter.

"Seriously? Where are your manners?" He shakes his head and glares icy daggers through me. "You might be my best friend, but you have five seconds to tell me what the hell you want before I toss you out of my room."

Before I can mutter a response, he shoves my feet off the bed and wipes at the comforter like I've ruined it in some way. We have a washer for a reason.

"Sorry, I left my manners at the front door." I laugh and continue. "I'm here on official Mill business. I need to know the specifics of the plan for tomorrow night so I can put some precautionary measures into place."

The muscles in his jaw flex and jump. "Weird. I thought you asked me to plan the events this year. I've made certain everything is done, and you're either questioning me to see if I've completed everything or attempting to oversee my work. In which case, if that's what this is, you can fuck off and jump down the cliffs. I've spent hours planning this event and sending invitations out. Friendship or not, I won't be questioned by you."

The cliffs being the far edge of the property complete with our own personal waterfall. Joke's on him—I've been jumping off that ledge since I was a kid.

"I'm not questioning you or trying to oversee you. Everything is fine, but my inner control freak needs more information. Especially since I found someone worth chasing for the event."

He stares at me, studying me, no doubt seeing the gleam in my eyes that's been dead for a while. "Consider me curious, who is she?"

"Who she is doesn't really matter. She wouldn't even tell me her name. As soon as I'm done here, I'm going to talk to Lee and have him gather some intel for me. I'll use whatever information I can find to keep her compliant. I just need some ammunition first."

"Hmm. Last we talked, you were going to the library to get your paper from that thieving nerd. You couldn't even find the non-fiction books in the library. How the hell did you find this girl?"

Of course the fucker has to bust my balls a little bit. The library isn't my usual hangout spot, nor is it a place I frequent often, which is probably why Maybel stayed out of reach for so long.

I lean back in the chair. "First of all, you're a dick. Second of all, I didn't find her. Funny enough, she found me. It was like fate delivered her to me on a golden platter. Happenstance, really. I can't wait for tomorrow—to see the fear shine in her eyes, and it's the real kind, none of that fake shit we get each year. I want to hear her screams, smell her panic, and feel her cunt squeeze me tight."

His own eyes darken, and I know that look. He's been searching for something similar for a while now, but he won't get a piece of mine. Maybel is mine. All fucking mine.

"Congratulations, buddy. I'm happy for you, and if you decide to share, we could have a hell of a time tag-teaming her. I can already see it now. It brings back fond memories of the one year we took down that shy little deer. What was her name? Vivian?"

Red-hot anger fills me in an instant, and I clench my hand into a tight fist, ready to swing at him. It's sudden and uncontrollable, but most of all, it freaks me the fuck out. I've never felt such an emotional reaction like that when it came to a girl and sharing. Hell, sharing is hot as fuck, and something Sebastian and I have done often, so why am I considering ripping his head off and shitting down his throat at the mention of it?

"I'm guessing by that look of murderous rage in your eyes you aren't interested in sharing?"

I shake my head and swallow down the rage. "Nah, at least not the first time."

Sebastian shrugs. "That's fine. Now in reference to the event and you needing to know shit. All I gotta say is tough luck. You'll find out the same way everyone else does."

"Asshole," I grumble jokingly and push up out of the chair. If I really wanted to know anything, I could easily find out. One phone call would give me all the information I need, but it would mean talking to my father, and I'd rather not.

"Go bother Lee. I have to finish this book."

"You're such a nerd," I say over my shoulder as I turn to walk out of his room.

"At least I can write my own papers," he counters, and I'll give him that. He's got way more patience than me. I'm smart in the academics I need to be smart in. Nothing else matters. At least that's what my father thinks—and ensures.

Wanting information about Maybel more than I want to fuck with Seb, I head straight to Lee's room.

Drake blares from the other side of the door so loud it's as if it's open. I'd knock, but what's the fucking point? Grabbing the brass knob, I twist and shove the door open. I'd like to say I'm surprised when my eyes immediately land on some random girl's pussy, but I'm not. She's on her knees at the edge of the bed, deep throating his cock like a pro.

Standing just inside the doorway, I lean against the jamb, my arms crossed over my chest. The girl's head bobs up and down almost furiously, and my eyes catch on Lee, who's fisting her by the hair. His hands guide her movements, his head tipped backward and his eyes closed. Almost as if he senses me standing there, his eyes pop open, and he leans forward, a smile splitting his face a second later.

Being bashful in this house gets you nowhere. Sex is as normal as doing the laundry. I've seen every one of my friends' cocks, and even a few people who aren't my friends. This is tame compared to most of the things I've seen.

I tap my imaginary watch and yell over the heavy beat to ensure he can hear me, "I need your expertise, so please hurry it the fuck up."

"Leave it to you to ruin a good blow job." He snorts and fastens his hold on the back of the girl's neck, fucking her mouth almost savagely.

She gags, pushing back against him. It's a feeble attempt at escaping, especially since it only encourages him to tighten his hold and thrust faster. He grits his teeth, his eyes becoming half lidded. I stand there watching, unaffected by them. My mind is on someone else entirely. A few more pumps, and he finishes in her mouth. When he's done, she leans toward him, probably asking when he plans to return the favor, but he shakes his head.

"Go downstairs and wait. I'll come find you when it's your turn."

Called it. Her lips part, an argument waiting to slip free, but Lee's cutting glance is enough to make her grab her dress off the floor and walk out of the room. She slips it on as she walks toward me, and I keep my stance in the doorway, forcing her to squeeze by me to pass.

He switches the sound system off. The absence of the ridiculous music is almost an entirely new sound.

"Friend of yours?" I tease.

"You know better than anyone else the answer to that. She wanted my dick, so I gave it to her. If that's considered friendship, then sure. Otherwise, nope."

All I can do is laugh. Lee's father thinks he's never going to give him grandchildren. The homophobic ass doesn't realize bisexuality isn't the same thing as being gay. Of the pack of us, Lee seems the most stable, so he's got that going for him. He's also the first one to jump into any mess, off any roof, and over any bridge. Most likely following one of us assholes on the way down. It also helps his social standing at school that his father owns a billion-dollar tech company. Lee learned to hack while he learned to walk. It's in his blood. If only his father was more supportive of him.

Hopping off the bed, he disappears into the bathroom and comes out a minute later, a pair of basketball shorts hanging low on his hips. "Do you require my expertise?"

"Yes. I need intel, anything you can find." I cross to sit beside his desk as he slips into his office chair and slides up to his computer.

"Of course you do. Good thing you got a friend like me, huh?" He grins. "So what's her name?"

"Maybel. Found her in the library. Well, actually, she found me. She lives over in the dorms. Refused to tell me her name and tried running away. Turns out she's a bigger challenge than I expected. Now I need to know whatever I can about her."

What kind of person does it make me, knowing that I'm excited about the possibility of having something to use against her? Blackmail, white lies, secrets. If I can use it as ammo, then I will. Anything to keep her compliant.

"Ahhh, got it." Lee doesn't ask questions, and why would he? He knows the score and how cruel the world can be.

Don't get it twisted. Lee might appear to be the most normal of us, but he's got his own demons and secrets. His fingers move over the keys easily as he hacks into the university's student database. In less than two minutes, he's got her university profile loaded. I lean forward, staring at the screen a little closer.

It's her, and my heart kicks up all over again. Every muscle tightens, priming me for what's to come. The anticipation is killing me, and I haven't even solidified that she's going to be at the event. It doesn't matter if she goes or not. I'll find a way to get her in the woods. The event would just be an easier way.

"That's her," I announce.

Lee nods and studies the screen a beat longer. "She's cute and a little nerdy but definitely not your type. Is this revenge or something else?"

"It's not revenge, and I know she's not my type. Maybe that's why I'm so compelled to own her. I don't really know, but what I do know is that I need you to send me whatever you can find on her."

"Just invite her to The Hunt. Then you can be the first to catch her and do whatever you want to her."

"That's the plan, genius. However, she's a smart girl. I need to ensure that she'll attend, and that if she doesn't show up, I have proper blackmail in place to use against her."

"This sounds..." Lee narrows his eyes and looks at me hard. "Are you going to make her your girlfriend or something? Because from the sounds of it, you're talking as if she'll be a permanent fixture."

Am I? Fuck.

"No. You know I only fuck, no dating. My plan is to claim her and fuck her until I grow tired of her. She's different, though, and by the looks of it, a challenge. Therefore, I'll need something to use against her."

"Makes sense." He nods, his attention going back to the computer. He scrolls down the screen, clicking on a few more tabs. A moment later, a file containing her exact address, parents' address, her current GPA, class schedule, and information regarding that girl I saw her with who I now know is her roommate, pops up.

Quickly, I fish my cell phone out of my pocket and snap a photo. "Send it all to me."

"Not a problem," he mutters, his eyes moving over the screen as he reads something. "It appears Ms. Maybel Jacobs has gone in to see the school therapist multiple times this year. Looks like she suffers from depression, anxiety, and PTSD. I wonder what she's got going on upstairs. You sure you want to get tangled in her crazy?"

The way he's questioning me right now leaves a bad taste in my mouth.

"No offense, Lee, but I didn't ask for advice. I asked for information, and you've provided me with that. We all have personal shit going on, depression, anxiety, abuse, and trauma. Life goes on. Now, please, don't fucking question me again."

"Look, I didn't mean it badly. I'm just surprised. You've never come to me about a girl before, especially not to get dirt on one, and you have women tossing themselves at you left and right. If you need blackmail, then something tells me this one is a hellion, and taming her won't be easy."

I clap him on the back. "Thank you for the information. Let me worry about that. My interest in her has nothing to do with The Mill, nor is it anyone's concern. All you need to know is that she's not like the others, and I want her. She doesn't know what's good for her yet, but she will soon enough."

"Sure, sure. Just watch yourself." The warning hangs in the air between us, and I know what he's referring to when he says watch yourself: *My father.*

He stares at me a moment, weighing something in his mind. "Take this."

I watch as he reaches behind his computer for a moment and pulls out a black flash drive the size of a piece of gum. "Remember that job I worked on for one of the brothers last year to change the grades in his class and not get caught? You can use that to get more information on this girl if you get access to her devices. It's a simple plug-and-play that will mirror everything for you."

Perfect. He hands me the device, and I slip it into my pocket. "Thanks for this and for the warning, but we both know if anyone can handle my father, it's me."

"It's not about handling your father, Drew. It's about surviving. Shit's getting worse, and it'll only be a matter of time before something happens."

My mood sours in an instant. Conversations about my relationship with my father will do that. "Bad shit happens every day, Lee. You can't save me. Let whatever is going to happen, happen," I growl.

Lee frowns, and I understand his sentiment. I recognize his fear and warning. I comprehend more than anyone, but nothing can change what is already happening. I'm merely a puppet in my father's play, and he's pulling the strings.

"It doesn't have to be this way—" Lee starts, but I cut him off.

"I don't want your advice, so save it for someone else. Thanks for the drive and intel. I appreciate it. You need anything in return, you know where to find me," I remind him and walk out of the room, stopping the conversation from going any further.

Once in the hall, I continue toward my bedroom. The door to Arie's room is closed, and I'd stop to bust his balls as well, but I'm in too much of a pissed-off mood to consider fucking with him. Aries lives up to his name. He's always mischievous and instigating fights. I swear he gets off on other people's pain. Not to mention, one strike of a match, and he'll blow the entire place up. He might be gorgeous, as all the women say, but he's the devil reincarnated.

All the way at the end of the hall is my room, and I practically kick the door in once I reach it. It's the primary suite, complete with Gothic arches and aesthetics. I tried to update the furniture so it doesn't look like Edgar Allen Poe's favorite brothel. The attached bath is completely remodeled, and I let out a long sigh as I cross the threshold. Personally, I think I have the best room in the entire house. Not only does my window overlook the front lawn but my room is also the biggest. Just beneath the window is my bed, and on the left side of the room is a sitting area and walk-in closet. To the right is the en suite bathroom. Gray and black accessories dot the interior. Cold and stark...just like my heart.

I strip out of my clothes on the way into the bathroom. The marble flooring gleams when the sunlight hits it, and I walk into the shower, which is the size of a small closet, and twist the knob all the way to hot. After a moment, the glass-enclosed stall fills with steam, and I step beneath the hot spray.

My tense muscles quake beneath the penetrating blast of water, and it feels amazing. As soon as I allow myself a moment to just stand there and think, all my thoughts turn to Maybel. It's ridiculous how possessive my fantasies have become when I think about her. I don't know a damn thing about her except what's written on paper, and somehow, that's enough for me. Somehow, my brain has justified that she is mine.

Almost unwittingly, I take my cock into my hand, squeezing myself hard while sliding up and down the length. The mere thought of her has me horny and ready to blow my load. I tighten my grip and jerk myself harder. My grip fringes of pain, and I grit my teeth.

Fuck, it feels so good. All I see is her in my mind. She ran so perfectly, without me having to prompt her, and the best part of all, she got away.

Dammit. I stroke myself faster, up and down, up and down. I'm on the edge, close to losing control.

Control. I would've lost it entirely if I'd caught her in the dark abandoned stacks at the back of the library. No one would've been able to save her from me. I'd have ripped her leggings and panties off her body and fucked her raw right there. Would she have begged me to stop? Or would she have begged me to keep going? All I can see is how she tried to hide from me, and the way she pressed her glasses up her nose. How her eyes flashed and her chin tipped up as she attempted to stand up to me.

No matter the cost, I need her body beneath me. I need to feel her trembling cunt as I press deep inside her, fucking her until she's a weeping mess, begging me to stop because the pleasure is too much. I can only imagine how beautiful her pale, smooth skin will look covered in my marks. I can't fucking *wait* to find out. I work myself closer to the edge, my thoughts swirling as I consider everything I want to do to her. Pleasure zips up my spine, and I let out a roar as I explode, splashing ropes of sticky cum against the tile. I let out a blissful sigh, and the frustration I carried from earlier feels lighter now.

I quickly finish washing and rinse off. When I step out of the shower, I'm calmer, my control closer to the surface. I consider the information I have. It's not much at the moment, but there will be more to come. Right now, though, I need to ensure that Maybel makes it to the event tomorrow night, and the only way to do that is to ensure her friend, the blonde, brings her.

I smile to myself as I dress quickly in a T-shirt, jeans, and my university jacket. The package isn't complete without the jacket, the golden child fulfilling his family duties. The gentleman, the charming hero. That's who I want her to see, who I want her to think I am until it's too late for her to get away. I might have already ruined that in my surprise at the library, but it'll be interesting to see how she pivots when I show up at her dorm. There won't be anywhere to escape.

I shove my wallet, keys, and phone into my pockets and head downstairs. I've just passed Sebastian's room when he asks where I'm going.

"Out." That's the only response he gets. Before anyone else can ask me what I'm doing or if I ate lunch like they're my parents, I slip out the front door and walk down the driveway, heading back toward the campus.

I have a car, two actually, but I prefer to walk. It gives me time to clear my head and think through things. Plus, you can be a lot less conspicuous without a car. On the walk, I consider what to say and how I'll lure her out of hiding. Her little roommate is going to play an integral part. If necessary, I will blackmail her too. Nothing stands in the way of what I want.

The streetlamps have just turned on when I reach her dorm. I tuck my hands into my pockets and stand casually outside the building, waiting for the first girl to offer me the opportunity to enter. Obviously, I'll have to see maintenance about making a key card so I don't have to stand out here, flashing a smile every two seconds. It'll be well worth the five hundred dollars.

It takes all of two minutes for a bystander to take pity on me.

"Are you wanting to come in?" the brunette asks, licking her lips. She's pretty, but something tells me she's one of those girls who pretends to be afraid, and that's not what I'm looking for.

"Yes, my girlfriend isn't answering the phone." I shrug.

She bats her eyes at me and holds the door open. "What kind of girl leaves their boyfriend out in the cold like this?"

I ignore her comment altogether and slip inside the dorm. A rush of warm air hits me, and I start up the stairs, heading to the third floor.

"If you get bored with your crappy girlfriend later, I'm in 2B." Her voice reaches me, and the offer hangs there, but I don't show any interest. I'm selective about the girls I fuck, and even more selective about the ones who see the darkness hiding just beneath the surface.

Ignoring her existence, I continue. Once I reach the third floor, I focus my attention on the doors, zoning in on the oh-so-helpful name cards attached to each door. Their dorm room number was in the information that Lee provided me, but the door tags make it way more engaging.

Perfect. Jackie and Maybel are in the third one down. It's nice to have a name attached to the person who is going to become an accomplice to my bad behavior. I lift my fist and knock softly, then pull my hand back to wait, my heart slowly inching up my throat with every passing second.

It's not nerves; it's adrenaline. I can't wait to see how my little wallflower's skin pinkens under my teeth and the sounds she makes as I fuck her into the ground.

A moment later, the door flies open, and the same buxom blonde from outside the library appears. Her eyes light up with recognition. "Oh, it's you."

I give her a smile as fake as her tits. "It is me. May I come in for a second? I just want to make sure you have all the information for tomorrow night. As you know, this event is highly selective."

She opens the door the rest of the way, and I spot the half-empty bottle of wine on her kitchen table. I peek inside, surveying the space like a high-end thief who plans to break into the place later. There are three doors that break off from a large open room—one closed, one open to a mess, and the other open to a bathroom. A small kitchen sits at the left of the door, an old scarred table in the middle of the space.

"Is your roommate here? I wanted to talk to her, too," I ask casually, trying not to appear overly interested.

She waves at the closed door. "Oh no, she had to go help her mom. She's sick right now. Pretty sure it's cancer or something. She refuses to give me any details. Her mom is all she has."

I nod, making sympathetic noises at the appropriate

places while also filing said information away in my brain. "Oh, of course."

I pull out a black envelope and hand it to her. "You'll need this to get through the gate. Do you mind if I put this in her room? Each one is personalized, so..."

It's a lie, but she doesn't need to know that. I had Sebastian make this one special for me when I found the woman I planned to hunt.

Buying my act, she doesn't hesitate and waves at the door. "Yeah, go ahead. She's super excited about the event."

I nod, considering her tone, and head toward the door. "You don't have to wait for me. I'll let myself out when I'm done."

Is Maybel really excited about it, or not? Jackie's tone makes me believe otherwise. Her eyes skim down the length of my body, and I swear I see an inkling of suspicion bloom in her gaze, but as soon as it appears, it's gone. Instead of questioning, she nods, grabs her wine, and heads into her room. *Perfect.*

Taking the doorknob into my hand, I twist it and push it open. I step inside and am greeted with a unique, sweet scent. Sugary sweet. One I hadn't caught over the musty scent in the library. My eyes dart around the room, absorbing every little detail.

It's perfect, each item in its place. I grab the back of her black office chair and take a seat. It squeaks beneath my weight, and I push toward her desk. There's a bag sitting on top, and it only takes a second to fish out her laptop, open it, and pull the tiny flash drive I brought with me out of my pocket. I plug it into the machine and then text Lee. It takes him seconds to get back to me, so his little date must be gone.

I'm in. She's all yours.

His text comes back.

I wait for the software to load onto my phone, then watch as the view from her computer camera mirrors my phone screen. She won't be able to hide a single thing from me. "All mine," I say to myself. "I can't wait until she figures it out."

Once I finish, I put the computer away and leave the black envelope on her desk, a red ribbon wound tightly around the matte paper. I give her room one more glance and leave before I give in to the urge to stay and inspect every inch between these four walls. No, we're going to do things the proper way, and the first step is always...

The Hunt

CHAPTER 4
BEL

IT SEEMS the only person not willing to admit my mother is sick is the woman herself. I spent the night and most of the day there, helping her around the house and trying to convince her to see a doctor.

She can't do her own grocery shopping at the moment and can't go to work, yet she keeps insisting it's just a bug, a flu, and it'll pass.

We've both seen this before, and I understand her not wanting to face the facts, but I'm exhausted and heartsick.

I'm brushing away tears as I enter my suite on campus. It does feel good to be by myself for a moment or at least be able to go into my own room and worry about something else for a bit.

My roommate jumps up and rushes out of her room the second I shut the door behind me. "Where the hell have you been? We're going to be late."

She's got her hair in rollers, and her makeup is already in place.

I tip my chin toward her. "If this thing is supposed to be a hunt, aren't you worried about your face melting off by the end?"

She smiles. "Hell no, I have a bulletproof setting spray. Now get in there and get ready."

My shoulders fall away from my ears, dragging me down. I no longer have the strength to stay upright. "I don't know, Jack. I'm pretty tired. I should probably stay home."

She narrows her eyes and starts tugging pins out of her hair. "Um...excuse me...did you forget about the twenty-five-thousand-dollar prize you want to nail down?"

I head into my room, dropping my overnight bag on the floor and throwing myself back onto the bed. "I may need that money, but what are the odds I'll actually win it? I'm probably just kidding myself."

Something on my desk catches my eye. I lift my head to stare at it, then scoot off the end of the bed to pick up the black envelope, wound with a red ribbon. "What the fuck?"

I rip open the thick, rich paper and spread a cardstock invitation. The details are pretty sparse, only an address and a time. At the bottom is a scribbled note requesting I wear the envelope's ribbon.

Fucking *hell*. I have no doubt it's that asshole jock who is asking this from me, and...fuck him. I'm not about to hand myself up on a platter for him to toy with.

I toss the invitation and the ribbon on the desk and sigh. Even if there's only a slim chance of winning the prize, I have to try. For my mother. Or else I'll never be able to say I tried everything.

Instead of climbing back into bed and staying there for a year, I go to my closet and pull out some clothing. "Jack, what do I wear to this damn thing?"

She comes flouncing in, brushing her curls with her

fingers. "Um...something you move in easily, and something dark to make it harder to see you, if that's what you want." She winks and readjusts her boobs inside her neon pink minidress.

I pick up a slinky black dress, with pockets of course, and lay it out with some fresh underwear. I need a hot shower first. Maybe it'll get me in the mood to go out.

News flash: I'm almost more exhausted after the shower. This is stupid. I'm going to end up lost and walking around in circles. The only thing I'm coming home with is fucking poison ivy.

Oh well, at the very least, I can't let Jackie go alone, so...I really have no choice.

It only takes a few minutes to dress and slip a few essentials into my dress pockets. I lotion up, then twist my hair into a messy bun on top of my head. My glasses go on last, and I step into the kitchen of our suite. "Are you almost ready?"

A minute later, Jack steps out of her room, looking like she's going to a club, not anything even remotely outdoors. "Uh...you sure you want to wear that?"

She glances down at the bright pink minidress. "What's wrong with it?"

"Doesn't it, like, defeat the purpose?"

She smirks, grabs her small crossbody bag, and opens the door to leave. "I guess that depends on your purpose, huh?" With a thwack, she smacks my ass on the way out the door. It earns her a squeal from me as I scurry out into the hall toward the stairs.

It doesn't take very long to cross the campus toward the address. We reach an iron fence, where a man in a suit is posted. As we pull up, he motions at me to open my window. I hold a finger up to ask him to give me a second and lean down to crank the handle to roll down the window in my old-ass car.

Once we show our invitations, he waves us in while he speaks to someone on a radio.

I pull up the driveway, looking for parking. When I see the house, my jaw drops. "Holy shit. I've always wanted to know what was up here, but I never imagined it was this."

Jackie wiggles in the passenger seat. "Isn't it gorgeous? I saw it last year during The Hunt, but it's still breathtaking."

I park with the other cars and climb out, the door creaking loudly through the mostly quiet twilight.

We head up the small hill to find a group of people milling around in front of a small black platform. From the back of the crowd, I lean to Jackie. "So is there anything I should know here?"

She shrugs. "They change the rules every year to keep it fun. Last year, everyone had to wear blindfolds. I wonder what they'll do this year. And where the hell is Sebastian hiding?"

I shake my head as she scans the people, but I don't see any oversized jocks lurking. Only the women and a few men are here, waiting.

It doesn't matter. I have my eyes on the beautiful house. It's huge and so pretty. I scan each stained glass window and sigh. I'll never have anything like this, but it's lovely to look at.

Gravel crunches, and we all shift to look toward the driveway leading to the left of the house. Oh *shit*. I duck behind the taller women in front of me. Oh shit. Oh shit. Oh shit. It's *him*.

I peek over her shoulder, which earns me a glare from her. "Sorry," I mumble. "Just saw my ex."

Her glare softens, but she shifts a few feet forward to get some distance between us.

One of the men who approached steps up onto the platform and raises his arms to call for quiet. "Welcome to The Hunt"

I keep waiting for him to produce a top hat and tug out a rabbit.

Jackie squirms against me. "Oh my god, there he is. Sebastian," she breathes.

He's wearing black on black, his dark hair perfectly settled, his green eyes flashing in the setting sun.

I roll my eyes and glance at the other few men and find the tallest one staring back at me. "Who is that one?" I whisper. He looks like the guy from the library, the unhinged one. She notices where I'm staring and grins wickedly.

"That's Andrew Marshall. Captain of the football team, school golden boy, and millionaire." She waves at the house. "This is his family's estate."

I push my glasses up my nose and force my eyes away. "Of course it is."

I turn my attention to the man speaking and notice the menace in his tone. He doesn't sound angry, per se, but...damn, I feel like I'm in trouble.

He raises his voice over the whispers. "Six miles to the cabin, which is north. First person to arrive wins the trophy inside and the prize money. Simple."

The grin on his face as he says "simple" causes my stomach to drop. Shit. I'm not going to like the next part.

He waves toward the towering woods about a hundred feet away. "This year, we've added something special. If you join the event, there are no rules. You do what you want in these woods...and if you go in, you agree to these terms. If someone catches you...you better learn how to beg for mercy."

Jackie gulps and fans herself next to me. "I'm calling for mercy now, shit."

My chest is tight as I stare out at the dark trees. Fuck, this could be dangerous... What if there are coyotes, or bears, or shit...the tall jock looking at me like I'm his next meal?

Maybe this is a bad idea.

I'm about to suggest we leave when Jackie grabs my arm. "I'm so excited. Even if I don't bag Sebastian, there are a lot of hunters...I hope at least some of them have an imagination."

"You don't want to win the money?"

She laughs, then sees my face and sobers. "Sorry, I don't care about it... But if I get close, I'll try for you and your mom, okay?"

Mollified, I nod and stare at the other participants, all overcome with excitement. I feel like the only downer here. It can't be that bad if these people are so excited and ready to do this, right?

I stare down at my shaky hands. Shit. I need to get myself together. Jackie grabs my hands and stares up into my eyes. "Hey, hey, it's okay. You don't have to do this if you don't want to. Go sit in the car, or come back and get me."

I gulp and shake my head, fending off tears. "No, I have to do this for my mom."

She nods and squeezes my fingers. "Well, if you're sure. Try to relax. It's just a game. I promise you'll have a blast."

Not sure she knows what I consider a blast, but I don't want to bring down the mood even more.

There's some shuffling as the men join another group of men and a couple of women off to the side.

I wave at the group. "What are they doing? Planning their stock exchange heist?"

She rolls her eyes. "Those are the hunters. They give the runners a fifteen-minute head start to make it more fun for them, I guess...give us a chance to get away."

Oh, I didn't know that. If I can sprint this thing, maybe I'll have a chance. I haven't run in years, but hey...I can try. I *have* to try.

I bounce on my feet for a second and try to stretch my legs a bit. My muscles protest, but I ignore the light pain and continue until that man, Sebastian, steps up again.

"Is everyone ready?"

My heart suddenly crowds my throat, and I can't breathe.

He smiles, cruel and cutting. "Set..."

He throws up his hands. "GO!"

As I race toward the tree line with the pack, all I can think about is what the hell did I get myself into?

I risk one glance back to see the jock, Andrew, staring after me.

Fuck.

CHAPTER 5
DREW

THERE'S a tension in the air that I can barely breathe through. My bones vibrate, and my skin, every sense, is on fire. I'm attuned to the footfalls heading into the forest. The sound of the wind in the trees, all of it. An elbow catches my ribs, and I jerk in surprise. Lee stares at me, one eyebrow cocked. "You seem on edge, man. You okay?"

I roll my shoulders back, stretching the fleece of my jacket. "Yes, fine. We've all been on edge waiting for this. I found myself a prize, and I plan to claim her. I can already taste her."

The light is fading fast, and the small crowd near The Mill grows restless. We're all ready for our jet into the woods. Peering through the trees, we can see a few brave souls lingering, choosing not to run. Easy pickings for anyone not looking for a chase.

I can't wait to run down my quarry and hear her scream in fright as she runs and then my name when I finally catch her. Well, maybe, if I don't gag her first... Depends on how much of a fight she puts up.

I shift from foot to foot, staring into the trees. It's easy to know where she's headed. Of all the bunnies running through the forest today, she's likely the only one in it for the actual prize. And the one with the least chance of actually reaching it.

The guys gather up, the few women who enjoy the hunt, too. Sebastian steps in front of us and grins wickedly. "Gentlemen...and ladies..." He dips his head toward Lindsey and Sasha. "Are you ready to find your prize?"

We spend a minute hopping around, stretching, and generally preparing as our adrenaline spikes. I feel like I might vibrate out of my body.

I get a similar feeling for every game, but this is so much more. Every year, it's the same, but I know there's a real prize waiting for me this year. There's a pit in my gut and an ache in my chest. I'm more ready than I've ever been.

Sebastian waves a flare gun around for effect, keeping it aimed at the sky. "On your mark. Get set..."

We all brace, ready to run. He shoots the flare into the air, and everyone takes off like a shot.

Everyone except me. I want to give her a little time to get some distance to make my catching her all the sweeter.

Will she fight? Run? Kick? Punch? Scream?

I've seen it all and more, but I've never heard *her* scream, and I can't wait.

During the few seconds I held her in the library, I knew she'd make the perfect prey.

I stroll toward the tree line. Everyone is already gone. Jackets are discarded at the edge of the forest. Shoes, bags, clothing, and all sorts of accessories were abandoned to be reclaimed later.

I step over a pile of clothing and cut across the tree line. It's darker now, and I close my eyes as I walk slowly to adjust to the lack of light. Once I can see a little clearer, with nothing more than the fading twilight and a few scattered lanterns, I pick up my pace. Not because I need to move fast to get to her, but because I'm losing my grip on my patience. All I want is to catch her, to claim her, and call her mine.

The forest sounds are louder now as crickets and other animals are scared out of the underbrush. More than the natural sounds, there are unnatural ones too. People fucking hard and rough in the fallen leaves. Others scream through the woods as their pursuers give chase.

I smile to myself. There will be a lot of sore, tired people come morning...some who won't even make it that long.

Someone crashes through the trees to my right, but I don't flinch, not when I know it's not her. Even if she's running, she'd do it quietly. Her life is controlled and precise. She might run, but she'd keep to the path, heading in the direction of her goal. All I need to do is follow until my little wallflower gets tired. It won't take long to catch up with her.

The trees sway in a slight breeze, a chill already building in the air. I'm warm enough walking, but she'll be cold eventually. If she behaves, I'll make sure we both have everything we need by the end of the night.

A high-pitched scream sounds to my left, and I spot someone in the dark grab a girl off her feet and slam her back into a pile of crunching leaves.

I stop for a moment and watch, wondering if her scream is for real or if she's just one of the women who pretends to be scared, only to run into one of the chaser's arms the second she's caught.

The man, Nathan, by the look of him, grasps her hips up and ruts against her, both of them still clothed.

She claws at the leaves and the earth, trying to pull herself away. There's no fear on her face, as far as I can tell, but she's definitely trying to get away. At least for now.

I smile and lean against the tree as he clamors after her, his hands easily grabbing her small frame and holding her down. For a second more, she struggles, and he holds her tight, putting more of his weight into her, her hips and legs pinned now.

Once she accepts she's caught, he strips her black leggings down her plush hips, holding her tight around the waist. First one side, then the other. She squeals as her bare ass is exposed to the cold night air, and he slaps it hard enough to make her squeal again.

A moment later, Nathan stops, catching sight of me. "You want some? I'm happy to share my prize with you."

The girl glances over her shoulder at me. A panicked look appears in her eyes but then disappears when she sees who he's talking to.

I shake my head and move along. "No thanks, I have my eye on something else. You two kids have fun."

More sound spills through the forest. Screaming, moaning, fucking...*everything*. The perimeters are mostly blocked off so we have privacy. The gates around the estate ensure no one will wander in as well. We've kept our members and participants as safe as we are able. The rest is up to them.

Leaves crunch under my boots as I continue, the anticipation building. I scan the fields, the leaves, and the small clearings for her, but find nothing. She's not out here for sex. If she's smart, she'll avoid the others and continue to the cabin. What I've learned about her in the last twenty-four hours is that she needs the money. Unlike me, she's here on scholarship. At least most of her tuition is. The rest she pays out of pocket in installments, and she's been late on payments for a while.

I shove my hands into my pockets and pick up my pace. I'm dying to hear her voice again, to speak to her. No doubt she'll fight me like she did in the library. Only this time, she's on my turf. There's no escape. I curl my hands into fists, my pockets tightening across them. I need to calm down, or everything will go too fast.

I walk faster to burn off some of my excess energy. There will be more than enough for her, but I don't want to push her too far too fast.

The leaves swish and fly around my feet. As I enter a small clearing, I catch sight of blond hair and stop short.

The woman is on her back, her blond hair spilled across the ground in a halo around her. I march closer, about ready to snatch her up and fucking destroy the man with his hands up her dress.

But then the clouds part enough to shine some of the barely risen moonlight down, and I recognize her friend, the one who begged me for an invitation.

I still stalk forward and crouch beside her head to stare down into her eyes. There's pain there as the man between her thighs shoves her legs apart roughly and enters her in one brutal thrust.

She stares up at me as pain morphs into pleasure, and I lean closer. "Where is she?"

A moan escapes her lips, and her eyes flutter closed for a moment. "I...don't know."

I catch a stray tear at the corner of her eye and squish it between my fingers, my gaze flicking to the man. "Stop for a moment."

Without a word, he stops, holding himself against her, his fingers clenching tight as he wars with himself.

She whimpers and digs her feet into the dirt to get some movement. He's too snug against her, though, so she doesn't succeed.

"Tell me where she is, and I'll have him start again. Was

she with you for a while, or did you lose her from the outside? Give me a little hint."

She whimpers and tries to move again, and this time, I press on her chest, holding her there, not letting her shift even a tiny bit. "Give me something here. Don't you want her to feel just as good as you do right now?"

She shakes her head, thrashing back and forth on the ground. "She's not like me. She didn't come here for the sex."

I nod. "You're not telling me anything I don't already know. She's here for the money. But sadly, she won't make it to the cabin to claim the prize."

She laughs and struggles between us. "You're in for a fight, then. She's stronger than she looks and *really* wants that prize money."

I release my hold and stand. "Carry on, then."

Back between the trees, I continue my trek. More and more people are fucking now, and their moans of pleasure fill the air. A few lucky ones are still in the race, and I scan the dense forest, watching for her to make her grand appearance. Any whisper or sight of her. Each second that ticks by without seeing her ramps up my anxiety. I'm strung tight like a bow and barely restraining myself. The longer it takes to find her, the harder it will be to stay in control once I catch her.

I trot along, scanning the woods now, peering across couples to make sure someone else hasn't taken what belongs to me. I'm not sure I wouldn't kill any fucker who catches her first. I've finally found the perfect challenge, the perfect girl, and I won't let anyone take her from me.

As frustrating as it is that she's not making it easy for me, I have to give her credit for being quicker and far more clever than the majority. Almost an hour in and she hasn't been caught yet. At least that I can see.

I pick up my pace, my trot becoming a jog now. It helps to work off some of the pent-up energy. An electric current ripples through me when I see the glint of glass off moonlight about two hundred feet up ahead.

Is it her?

I grit my teeth and clench my fists as I transition to a full run. My lips pull into a prideful smile. She's full-on running, hopping over logs and a few rocks that haven't been cleared near the falls.

It doesn't take long to close some of the distance between us, and the closer I get, the easier it is for me to see her and follow her movements. Yes. *Fuck yes.* That all-too-familiar exhilarating rush pulses in my veins. There's nothing like hunting them down, cracking them open, and seeing just how far you can push them before they break. That's what I want more than anything... to own her, to make her see that she doesn't have an option. She's mine, even if she doesn't want to be.

I'm strung even tighter as I watch her run, and the only thing pounding in my head is... catch her. Catch her. Fucking *catch* her.

She's all I need and all I want.

I run faster, my chest heaving. It takes a minute to close the distance, twenty feet now. She's so close that I clench my fists to avoid reaching out and giving myself away too soon.

Faster. Harder. Get there.

I jump over a log and keep crashing forward. I'm so close now I can see the pale length of her hair coming out of the messy bun she'd thrown it into.

Yes.

A shape to the left comes out of the darkness, and I watch as another man rushes toward her.

Oh *hell* fucking no.

I sprint dead out and take him down hard, throwing him across the dirt and grass. When I'm able, I shove off him and catch him in the ribs with my boot. "Stay the fuck down, and don't touch what's mine."

There's a soft gasp, and she's standing frozen, rigid, her hands cupping her face as she watches me.

CHAPTER 6
BEL

FOR A SECOND THERE, I thought I might make it. Everyone else is distracted by sex, fighting, or drinking. I've caught sight of a few campfires with all kinds of things happening around the soft light. Mostly, though, everyone has been running. But I haven't seen anyone for the past twenty minutes, not even a couple of the girls who kept pace with me.

I'm exhausted. When he grabs me, a tiny part of my brain says *thank goodness*...because I'm exhausted.

But what the fuck am I thinking? It's *him*. The one watching me, the football star from the library... Some part of me knows he'll make me pay for getting free from him yesterday.

I kick off and try to squirm free. The other man who caught me is limping in the opposite direction.

He grips my hips tight enough I'll have bruises. "Where are you heading in such a rush, little wallflower? We haven't had the chance to chat yet."

I screech and try to pull free, but he's got me tight. "Fucking let me *go*."

I manage to get out of his hold, but I yank so hard my momentum takes me down to the brush. Then he's there again, behind me, his hands on my hips at a new angle.

"By all means, if you can get out of my hold, please do. It'll make things even more fun. I can do whatever I want to you...but you can also do whatever you want to *me*."

I kick out, and I'm satisfied when my foot lands against his solid thigh, but all he gives me is a grunt. "I don't want to do anything to you. I just want to make you disappear."

He chuckles softly and molds his hands to the shape of my hips, spreading his fingers wider so he can touch more of me. "You think that now, but by the end of the night, you will be begging me to take the edge off."

I roll my eyes and wiggle harder, but he's like iron around me now. "I'll never beg you for anything. Now let me go."

I'm pulling so hard that when he releases me, I skitter forward on my hands, mud caking my nails and between my fingers. I don't even think about why he let me go. I clamor to my feet and rush forward into the dark. He'll catch me. I'm already winded, and he's a fucking football player, but maybe I can get to the cabin first.

I crash through the trees and the bushes, not bothering to stay quiet. What's the point now? No one in these woods is attempting to be quiet.

Leaves crunch underfoot, and I kick them up as I go. They crackle behind me too, and I know he's following, no doubt walking to match my slow-as-hell pace. I'd hoped I could put more distance between us, but shit, I underestimated how many just wanted to roll around and rut in the dirt.

Someone cuts close to my right, and I swerve around a tree and cut west. That's all I can do for now. I'm scared of being caught by him but even more scared of being caught...I guess by a different stranger.

I run faster and faster, trying to get as much distance as I'm able. When I can't run any longer, I slip behind a large tree and brace my back against the rough bark.

Why am I doing this to myself? It's supposed to be a damn game, yet my heart pounds and my blood whooshes in my ears so loudly, I couldn't hear if someone were to sneak up on me. If I think logically about it, a game with a massive prize wouldn't be an easy win.

At this point, I'm regretting joining this stupid race. All of it. It might not be worth it, especially if he catches me. The only one who has been chasing me from the start.

I hear a call in the dark. "Littttllllleee walllflower...where are you?" His low timbre taunts, haunts even.

Shit. I know I can't just pop out and say sorry, made a mistake, I give up. He won't give a shit, and he won't let me walk away. *None of them would.*

I slide down the tree, the rough bark catching against my clothes as I hit the hard ground. My legs tremble from exhaustion, and my fingers are freezing. I hate this so much. I'd much rather be in my bed, cuddled in with a cup of tea and a book.

Who thinks this sort of thing is fun?

I wrap my arms around my knees and listen to the darkness, trying to pinpoint where he is. It's been quiet for a couple of minutes, but I don't trust it.

Up ahead, a woman comes crashing through some small trees, pushing off anything she can find to try to get some distance between her and her pursuer. A man appears only a couple of minutes later, following close. I press hard against the tree, attempting to make myself as small as possible so he doesn't notice me. Then again, I shouldn't be worried. He has his sights on his own prey.

He tackles the girl, and they land in the underbrush. I keep quiet as she fights, rolling onto her back to grapple with him. It takes seconds for him to secure her arms and pin her hips down underneath him.

She screams, a loud wail cutting through the night. I jolt and press against the tree, using it to get to my feet. One more scream like that, and I'll have no option but to interfere. I won't sit here and be a witness to her rape.

She makes another small scream, then it shifts as he drags her underwear down and sinks inside her. I look away, not wanting to see, even as my body grows hot from the grunts he makes and the noises spilling out all around through the night.

What the hell am I doing here? This isn't me. I've never even had sex...and now...the prospect of losing my virginity in the mud is harrowing.

I take another deep breath and start walking again, heading deeper into the woods, hoping for a glimpse of the cabin every second. Even a hint, so I know this is worth it, and I can actually *make it* there.

Maybe the next best option is to bow out before I find myself in over my head. Which might be a viable plan if I had any indication as to which way is out. I'm surrounded by towering pines and underbrush. Every so often, a lantern is on a post driven into the ground. I've been trying to stay away from those light sources to avoid getting caught. I don't even see any lights from the distant estate or nearby campus.

Shit. What have I *done?*

A soft voice filters through the dark. "Bel...come out and play with me! You know you want to."

Fear slithers up my spine, and I cover my mouth with my

hands and press back into the tree trunk, trying to keep as quiet as possible. Why is he hunting me when he can have his choice of any of the girls tonight? I'm nobody. Nothing in his rich, spoiled world.

Maybe he felt like I'd challenged him by telling him no at the library? Now he needs to satisfy his jock-boy ego.

Either way, I fear what happens if he catches me.

The voice in the dark comes again. "This could have been a pleasant experience. Hell, I might have even tried being nice to you."

I fold my lips in and add pressure to the hand at my mouth, all while resisting the urge to scream *bullshit* in the direction the voice is coming from. Nice isn't in that man's vocabulary, and I know that from seeing him for five minutes.

The reality of it is that his taunting is starting to piss me off. If he's going to stand out here and shout lies at me, what's the fucking point? A small part of me knows what he's doing. He wants me to react, and he's trying to draw me out. I just wish it wasn't working because it is, and that pisses me off even more.

What does this asshole want with me, anyway?

The couple in the bushes a few yards away finally finish. She goes out into the darkness alone again, and the guy cuts through the trees, smiling.

Then I hear voices, his and the guy chasing me. *Shit. Shit. Shit.*

If I go quietly while he's distracted, maybe I can put some distance between us and possibly win this thing. Hope blooms inside my chest. Carefully, I slide away from the tree, staying low, my eyes trained on the ground and any objects that might reveal my escape. I can still hear them chatting away somewhere behind me. I hold on to that as I move quicker and deeper into the woods.

Once the voices fade, I stand upright and move as fast as my tired legs will carry me. All I hear is the swooshing of blood in my ears mixed with my own heavy breathing.

It feels like I've been walking for hours at this point. There's a chill in my bones, and my legs and feet ache. Never mind the regret I'm now having for signing up for this stupid event. *What was I thinking?*

You were thinking you needed to help your mom. But if I have no hope of getting to this damn cabin, then why am I still out here torturing myself?

I keep walking for what feels like forever. The forest I cut through feels thicker, with more logs and bushes around. I have to skirt large trees and shuffle through the underbrush.

It's thicker here, and maybe that means fewer people are trampling through this area. It might be a good sign if my legs weren't burning and the extra effort here wasn't slowing me down.

Fuck. You know what? It's against the rules they announced at the beginning, but I pull my cell phone out of my pocket and hold my hand over the screen. I push the button to light it up, but nothing...*shit*...there's no service.

And I can't risk using it for the light either. *Dammit.*

I shove it back into my pocket and scan the woods for any clues I could be going in the right direction.

There's the sound of water from the right somewhere. If I hear the falls and the river on that side, then I'm still going the right way. Maybe the best place to start would be to go to the water and find the cabin up the river bank. It would take longer but likely keep me out of the main hunting area.

Best of all, it's a plan, and a good strategy always makes me feel better about life.

I turn toward the sound of the water and start heading that way. I walk and walk and then walk some more. My heels throb, and my legs burn, but none of that matters if I can keep myself out of the lion's mouth.

Hunting for the water, I miss a log lying in my path and trip, going ass up in the dirt.

My knees hit first, then my palms, and finally, my cheek skids across the ground. *Ugh*.

I hit hard, the breath in my lungs knocked out of me, and for a moment, I lie like that in the dirt. My fists clench tight as my rage boils over inside. Tears leak out of the corners of my eyes, and I swipe them away with my dusty palms.

The urge to scream is almost overwhelming, and I bite my lip to repress it. Allowing nothing but a groan to slip past as I press up off the ground and roll over onto my ass. I don't feel bad for myself often, especially when I know others out there have worse circumstances, but right now, in these dark woods, where I'm alone and cold, I give in to that self-pity. More angry tears fall, and I hate every single one that escapes.

It's fine. I lean my back against the offending log and give myself a second to rest and breathe. I just need a minute to pull myself together and consider my next move. *One* minute.

Crickets break up the silence around me. At least I didn't fall face-first into someone's ass. The mere thought makes me gag. Then again, now that I think about it, it's been a while since I've seen anyone else... I don't know if I should be worried or hopeful. If this is the direction of the cabin, and no one else is headed this way, then I might be on the right track. If it's not, well... I don't allow myself to think further on that.

I sigh and sink against the log a little more, resting fully now. With all the sounds of the night surrounding me, I sink deeper into the calmness, and it's that moment when I fuck up.

It's a fraction of a second before I hear those heavy footfalls pounding through the underbrush, but I'm not fast enough. I've barely gained my footing and am standing when from behind, a hand closes over my mouth while his other arm snakes around my waist, knocking me off my feet.

I want to scream, to cry, to beg him to let me go. To reveal my stupid hope that he'll take pity on me, but I already know how this will end.

With me on my knees before him.

CHAPTER 7
DREW

I'VE LET her run around these woods like a scared little rabbit for some time now. I'm surprised she has any fight left in her. Especially since she spends most of her time in the library and not in the gym.

"I've got you, little flower. Calm down so I can look at my pretty prize," I say, sliding my hand away from her plush mouth.

She lets out a screech, kicking her legs futilely into my knees. I squeeze her tight, letting her continue until she eventually wears herself out. The idea was to let her believe she was getting away and let her push herself to exhaustion. Her fight is intoxicating, but hunting her down, and laying claim to her is far more tempting. Her body quivers in my arms, her muscles already strained and on the edge of giving up.

"Shh..." I whisper. "Relax, I'm not going to hurt you."

She sags abruptly, almost sending us both back down into the dirt. "You've chased me around the forest in the darkness like you're hunting an animal. How can I believe you won't hurt me?"

A chuckle escapes me, and I run my nose down the side of her neck. Beads of sweat make her skin sticky, and it takes every level of restraint I have not to lick the side of her throat and taste her fear. "Well, what if I promise pleasure along with the pain?"

She huffs, and I can't help the smile that splits my face. My little wallflower has some sass. I like that. It just leaves me with more pieces of her to break. "Are you doubting me, little flower? Because I won't lie, that hurts my feelings."

That earns me another snort. I hold her harder against me, wanting her to know who is in control. Without her over-sized sweatshirt, I get a much better feel of her body. *Fuck me.* The softness of her hips and the slim line of her waist... I lick my lips as I gaze down the ample curve of her tits. They will feel so good in my hands. I start to let my mind wander. Will her nipples be tiny or big? A dusky pink or a darker shade of brown?

I slide my fingers up from her waist to cup her in my palm. *Oh yes, perfect.* My cock screams for release. I'm so fucking hard, I could explode right now just rutting against her sweet little ass. On that note, I wonder if she's ever been fucked in the ass? It doesn't matter. There's a first time for everything.

"What do you want?" she whispers.

I give in and lick a line up to her earlobe. *Salty and sweet.* "There are a lot of things I want from you, flower, but right now.... I want you to scream for me *because* of me. I want you gasping for breath. I want you crying, your eyes shimmering with tears. I want you running, doing everything you can to escape me, while knowing deep down inside you'll *never* get away. I want all of it. So I'll give you one more chance to get away."

She wiggles, and I slowly lower her until her feet are

underneath her. The second I relax my hold, she shoves off my chest and rushes away. This time with a little more vigor than before. *Mmm...good.*

I stand my ground, listening to her crash through the brush, keeping an eye out for anyone else who would be stupid enough to try to claim her. The woods might appear empty, but another bigger and badder animal is always hiding in the bushes, waiting to pounce on your prey.

I saunter behind her. Even at her fastest, I can keep up with her pace. It's nothing to keep her in my sights, to watch her try to get away. She's already caught; she just hasn't accepted her fate yet.

"You could give yourself up, little flower," I taunt. "But I'd punish you for that before we could get on with anything else."

I catch a screamed, *"Fuck you,"* from the direction she's running, and my lips tip up into a smile. Oh, she's going to be *so* much fun to break. I knew the moment I saw her in that library sticking up for the nerd that she was exactly what I needed. I adjust my hard-on and keep walking. Only a little longer and I'll have her on her knees and on her back, her tight little pussy squeezing my fat cock.

Once she finally gets a little distance between us, I pick up my step, breaking into a slow jog. *That's it. Give me a real challenge, flower.* Make me work for it.

She cuts to the right, no doubt still hunting for the damn cabin. Her friend might have dragged her out here, but I was thorough in my preliminary research of her. It's my money in that cabin, but no one is getting there, especially not her. I plan to keep her busy for a while.

"Little flower," I taunt, letting my voice ring out so she knows exactly where I am.

I don't get an expletive back this time, nothing but her

crashing footfalls. I can smell the fear and panic rolling off her. When the noise stops, I stop too, letting the forest go quiet around us. Is she taking a break? Or trying to hide from me again?

Either way, she'll fail. "Little wallflower? Where are you?"

Nothing. Silence. Not even the sound of her panting breaths. She's hiding, then.

I step through a copse of trees and listen carefully. Still nothing. A smile spreads across my face again.

Finally, a woman worth my time, effort, and attention. Never mind if she wants it or not, she's got it. I crouch and grab a stick, then throw it out into the trees. Again, I listen.

Sound breaks through the silence, crashing footfalls and muttered curses as she rushes in the opposite direction of my stick.

Aw. She tried. It's so *cute*.

I quickly follow and don't bother staying quiet. I want her to know I'm coming for her. She can run all night if she wants, and I'll stay right on her heels, hunting her like the prey she is.

It would be easier if my cock hadn't been rock hard since the first moment I touched her. My patience is dwindling. Only a little more, and I'll catch her again, maybe toy with her a little more, but soon enough, I'll have to take her.

As I jog ahead, my steps are thundering booms in the mostly quiet space. That's the thrill of The Hunt. I want her to feel me behind her, the tiny hairs on the back of her neck standing on end, her fear of being caught, making her choose her next move. Truthfully, I want her a little more terrified of me before I catch her for real. I want her sweating because she fears what will happen when I capture her, not the fear of being caught. For the next ten minutes, I dodge her steps, grasp onto her slim waist, and release her, letting her rush away, no doubt tiring herself out even more.

Each time I touch her, she shrieks, screaming and cursing at me. I even catch the sheen of tears on her cheeks when she crosses paths with a lantern.

Finally, I'm getting her where I want her. The next time I grasp her hips, she spins hard to the left, rolling out of my grip and rushing off in the other direction.

I falter over a branch and recover quickly. As I give chase, she shouts over her shoulder. "What the fuck do you want? Stop messing with me!"

I laugh and keep up with her, matching her pace now. "I'm not walking away for anything. Don't worry, you'll get tired, or I'll get tired soon enough, and then we can stop for a while."

Her entire frame shivers, and she swipes tearstained cheeks. "Why are you such an asshole?"

I don't answer but grab her around the waist. Again, she twists away, and I laugh, continuing to play with her. She swats at me every time I reach for her. We rush through some trees, and it only takes her looking away for a split second to go down hard in the dirt like she did earlier.

I slow and approach her cautiously, watching her every move. Instead of standing, she lies there, her face pressed to the cool ground, her hand coated in dirt and dust. The crisp smell of nature and the intoxicating scent of fear fill the air.

I crouch near her head. "Playing dead already, little flower? We haven't even got to the best part yet."

"Fuck off," she sneers.

I lick my lips and study the line of her spine and how it curves into the lush globes of her ass.

For a moment, I just look at her through the darkness,

watching the way her back rises and falls in ragged gasps. Once she's had a moment to breathe, I reach down and haul her body up against me. Like I anticipated, she fights tooth and nail, striking out until I spin her and pin her arms down at her sides. Her fight threatens to make me lose control, and if anything is worse than being a predator, it's being an out-of-control predator.

"Calm the fuck down," I snap and loosen my grip on her. "Your fighting turns me the fuck on, but it also makes me want to hurt you in ways that you aren't ready for yet. So keep it up. Either way, I'll end up with what I want."

I barely register her hand pulling from my grasp or that she's slapped me until the sting of it blooms across my cheek. The muscles in my jaw tense. It's not the first time I've been hit, and it won't be the last, but it's unexpected from her. Instantly, she tries to pull back, horror filling her delicate features.

"I'm... I'm sorry..." she mumbles while clutching her face in her hands like she can't believe she did such a thing. It's strange how she apologizes, even when it was an act of defense. I remain silent, letting the emotions roll through her. There's something about her, something real, something that makes me want to bottle it up.

Dropping her hands, she shakes her head in distress, and I notice a trickle of blood rolling down to her full upper lip. There's a scrape on her cheek and the hint of a bruise already forming. I'm not surprised she's hurt herself. I guess I'd be more shocked if she didn't, given the terrain and the fact that she's running in the dark. I gently swipe at the blood, and she belatedly bats at my hands.

"Stop. You've hurt yourself, little flower." She scowls, and it's so damn cute. Her glasses are askew, her cheeks burn pink, and her pretty green eyes shimmer brightly in the moonlight. I straighten them and push some of the golden hair out of her face to get a better look at her. "Let me look at you." Her legs wobble, and I place a hand against her hip to steady her. Even in the dim moonlight, I see her scraped knees and palms. "Maybe if you wouldn't have run, then you wouldn't have hurt yourself."

The remark earns me another scowl. She curls her lip in disgust and tosses another insult at me. "And maybe if you weren't a psychopath hell-bent on hurting people, I wouldn't have had a reason to run in the first place."

All I can do is smile. Her defiance is everything I could've hoped for and more. Her knees knock together, and I rub my hands up and down her arms to warm her. "Let me clean you up a little, flower."

I reach into my pocket for the small first-aid kit I always bring on nights like tonight. Most of the time, they go unused, but fortunately for my wallflower, I care enough to make sure she doesn't end up with an infection.

I take out an alcohol wipe, and she wrinkles her nose at the smell of the antiseptic, her dark eyes watching my every move as I clean up the cut on her face. Maybe it's instinct or something else, but she allows me to clean and bandage the wound, which makes me believe she's not entirely repulsed by my presence. When I kneel down in front of her, she moves her legs like she wants to kick me, but I trap her knees together and swat at the back of her thighs. "Don't do something you'll regret."

She sniffs. "That's rich. You can do whatever you want to me, but I can't do anything to you?"

"No one said that. You can *try* to do whatever you want to me. The rules are the same for you as they are for me, but let me make it very clear. It doesn't matter what you do to me.

Nothing short of fucking death is going to stop me from taking what is mine."

Almost like she's given up completely, she slumps to the ground. I reach down and lift her under the arms, holding her tightly against me. The way her body feels, how it molds to mine... *Fuck.* I've been with a lot of women but never felt such an intoxicating pull toward any of them. When she notices my straining erection against her thigh, she starts to fight again, but I tighten my grasp on her.

"Nope, not happening. You feel that? This little chase you've led me on has me so hard, I can't even think straight."

She lets out a tiny whimper. "I didn't do anything."

"You..." I run my hand down to her hip and slide my hand up her dress to feel her bare skin. Goose bumps pebble her flesh, that is, until I slide my hands between her thighs and cup her sex hard over her panties. Another whimper escapes her, and I love that sound coming from her lips.

"Tell me, flower, will you scream for me?"

She lets out a blood-curdling scream, and like thunder bolting across the sky, the energy inside me becomes electricity. "You're such a good girl, flower. Obeying my rules and doing exactly what I want, but I'm not surprised. I get the feeling you always follow the rules."

"Shut up, and stop touching me!"

I lap at the beads of sweat trickling down the side of her neck. "I can do whatever I want to you. You agreed to that when you entered these woods. Now, I'm just taking what already belongs to me. It's not my fault you haven't realized it yet."

"I didn't agree to anything!" she growls, and I dig my teeth in where I licked her a moment ago. Another squeal erupts from her tender throat.

"Careful, love. I want to hear your screams later, so don't wear your voice out yet."

She swallows hard, and I can feel it against my mouth. The urge to bite down harder beats at me, but I don't give in, not yet. There is so much more I want out of her.

I carry her to a large log and set her down. "Relax for a second. Let me take care of you and make sure you haven't beaten yourself up too much."

She reels back. "Why?"

"Despite what you think of me so far, I want your pleasure as much as your pain. I plan to get it from you in any way I can...whether you want it or not. Wanting it makes this easier, but I'm always up for a fight where I have to take it, too."

Her throat bobs, and she wraps her arms around her middle like that will save her from me. I shove her knees apart, and she tries to pull them back together, earning her another swat on the side of her thigh. "No, flower. If I move you, you stay where I put you, or you'll regret it when I move you into a position far worse."

Tears well in her crystal green eyes and slip through the dirt on her cheeks. Slowly, so slowly that I almost lose my patience and rip her legs apart myself, she widens her thighs for me.

Ducking my head, I run my hands up the smooth skin and press my thumbs along the line of her muscle to the edge of her panties.

"Very good, flower. You're a quick learner. I like that."

"I hate you." The words vibrate out of her.

Mmm. "Tell me more. I want to hear you scream how much you hate it when I'm inside you."

Her eyes go comically wide behind her glasses. "You...you..."

"I what?"

"You plan to..."

"Fuck you into the ground until you scream on several different levels? Yes, that's exactly what I have planned." I look at her scraped-up and bloody knees. "But first, I need to get you cleaned up. I don't want to risk you getting an infection and dying. You can't be a willing... or should I say, unwilling participant if you aren't alive."

CHAPTER 8
BEL

WHAT THE HELL *did I get myself into?*

Not only did I catch the attention of a complete psychopath but I also signed up for one of his fucked-up games. The look in his eyes tells me he's dead serious and not about to walk away *or* let me go...

He mentioned fucking, like all these other people, in the dirt, on the cold forest floor. Something tells me he won't make it easy on me either, and there's no option to say no.

I swallow hard as his thumb brushes over the scrapes on my knee. His touch is tender, the complete opposite of the dark look in his eyes. He's eye level with my pussy, and I don't know how I feel about that. It's dark, so I can't tell if he's actually looking at me. Why spread me open if he's *not* going to look?

"What do you want?" I ask again. "Why me?"

I hate the fragileness in my voice, but he seems to revel in it. Whenever I make even the smallest noise, he closes his eyes as if savoring the sound.

He takes so long to answer that I don't think he will answer me at all.

"I'll be honest. I'm not sure. There's just something...different about you. I'm going to see it through."

"Until...?"

"Until I'm finished."

I gulp. "Finished, like you're going to use me up and throw me away, finished?"

He snorts and rolls his eyes up to meet mine in the dark. "Until whatever fascinates me about you lets go. It'll be easiest if you just give in until then."

"But...*why*? You don't know me. There are plenty of other girls on campus who would go from one end of the quad to the other, sucking you off in public... And you want me...the vir..." I stop myself before I reveal too much.

Thankfully, he doesn't seem to notice I've cut myself off. Would it matter to him if I told him I was a virgin? Probably not. He'd look at it like a consolation prize. He stays kneeling by my feet and lays out his first-aid kit again. He pulls out another disinfectant wipe, and I wince as he cleans the cuts, then slathers on some antibacterial gel. The kindness he's showing me is too much for my fragile mind at the moment, and then you add in the silence, and it's too much to bear. I'd take his filthy words over silence right now.

"You're right. There are plenty of girls, but none of them hold my attention like you do. None of them draw me in and make me want to own them, keep them."

"What is wrong with you? You make me sound like a fucking basketball or a damn coat. I'm a human being, *not* a belonging."

He bandages the cuts, and they feel better without the gritty dirt all over them, even if they sting from the cleaning. My face hurts from hitting the ground, and my hands are cut to high hell from all the times I've fallen, but it's better than lying down and taking it. When all of this is over, I'll at least have some sort of dignity intact.

"I promise you, you do not want to know what is wrong with me. We don't have the time or paper for that conversation, and I'll have you know I prefer football over basketball, in case you didn't know that already. And just so we're clear, you're mine and belong to me, Maybel." He stands to his full height and grabs me by the back of the neck, pulling my face closer to his. I find it impossible to look away even when I know I should. "You belong to me. Every whimper and moan. Every orgasm. Every single thought you have is mine. Your sweet little soul and pussy. Mine as well." His voice is low and husky, and the smell of mint fills my nostrils. A wave of dizziness slams into me, and my knees threaten to buckle beneath my weight. *Fucking hell.* He's serious but absolutely batshit crazy if he thinks I'll go along with this.

I shake my head as much as I'm able with him holding me. "No. I don't belong to anyone but myself."

"Keep telling yourself that, little wallflower." His hold on the back of my neck disappears, and I suck a ragged breath of relief into my lungs to be out of his grasp. It's short-lived when those same fingers move to my throat, his huge hand squeezing the column. "Keep telling yourself that."

I'm momentarily paralyzed, and all I can do is stare at him. Shit. He's huge. Bigger than I remember when he grabbed me in the library. His eyes darken, the green in them appearing almost black. "You'll need to stand on your own because it's time for me to inspect my prize."

"Inspect?" I whisper. "What does that mean?"

He releases me like I'm a burning coal, and I don't bother hiding the fact that my knees shake. I huddle into myself, both from the cold and the fear coursing through my veins.

Like he's got all the time in the world, he just stares down at me. I feel insecure, like I'm beneath a microscope...about to be judged. As he watches me, I take the opportunity to stare up at him. His dark hair brushes his eyebrows, and his dark green eyes see right through me like I'm made of glass.

"We can stand here all night," he finally says. "I'm nice and toasty. You, however, look a little cold."

I gesture at my dress and bruises. "And you want me to take my clothes off, knowing I'm already freezing?"

He shrugs. "The faster you strip, the faster we can move on to warming you up."

I swallow around the golf ball-sized knot forming in my throat. My breathing is faster now, my heart hammering against my ribs. Every fiber in my body prays that he's fucking with me, but I know better. This isn't some messed-up mind game. He's serious, and if I don't give him what he wants, he'll take it from me.

"Strip, flower, or I'll do it for you."

"What if I want to walk away?" I whisper. "Just leave. No money. No bother. I go home and chalk this all up to stupidity?"

That earns me a chuckle. "I'd say nice try, but you're smarter than that. I already told you that you belong to me. I'm not giving you up that easily. Besides, if for some reason I allowed you to walk away, do you think I would let you get away scot-free? You walk away, and everyone on campus will find out that you're a liar and a cheat. Think smart, flower, do you really think I won't use my status to ensure *everyone* turns their back on you?"

As he speaks, my heart rate climbs. "I'm not...I'm not a cheat *or* a liar."

"You said you want to walk away...If you do, that's going against the agreement you made when you stepped foot in *my fucking* forest. You wouldn't think twice about keeping the prize money...but now that you're caught, suddenly you don't want to suffer the consequences. Sorry, love, but that's not how *this* works."

My world shrinks to this very moment. He's really going to force me to strip or ruin my life. No one will go against him or believe me over him. I'm a nobody who can barely make my tuition payments. "What if we make a deal?"

The corner of his lip curls up, and then he licks them and steps forward. "What kind of deal?"

It seems I have his attention. A *terrifying* thing. "If I do this. I don't run and see through whatever you want...you point me in the direction of the cabin and let me still try to get there."

He laughs. "Twenty-five thousand dollars for a quick fuck in the woods? I don't think that is worth it for me. I could take you and keep you until dawn. Ruin all your chances of getting there."

"What do you want, then?"

He steps closer until his heat wafts toward me, causing me to lean in, even against my own will. The smell of peppermint and teakwood fills my nostrils, and I hate that I think he smells good on top of all of this. Especially with what he plans to put me through...

With a look that chills me to the bone, his sultry eyes scan me, from the bruised knees to my messy hair. "Convince me, little wallflower. Is that cunt worth twenty-five K? Show me, and maybe I'll agree to your deal. But right now, as we stand, I have no proof that you're worth it."

Fucking *hell*, of course he has to be crude too. At this point, the only thing I have left to lose is my dignity, but soon enough, he'll have that too. I might as well shred the remaining pieces of it myself... At least then, I know he didn't take that from me, either.

I reach around and pull my dress up and over my head, then toss it down. Anger and pain rip through me. I want to hurt him, to make him feel what I'm feeling right now.

Cold air wafts across my skin, and he stares down pointedly at my bra and panties. "Keep going," he whispers huskily.

With shaking fingers, I unsnap my bra and let it fall on top of my dress on the forest floor.

His eyes scan my breasts, and I reach to cover them almost instinctively. It takes less than a second for his hands to snatch mine down so he can stare.

I don't have big boobs, but big enough to need a bra. His eyes devour them, and he licks his lips again before releasing my wrists. I stay still as he slides his fingers around my waist and pulls my body flush against his.

The denim of his jeans is rough around my legs. I try not to enjoy the warmth of his hips and stomach against me. "Getting warmer, little flower. I want to see it all."

I beg him with my eyes because the words are lodged in my throat. *Please. Don't make me do this.* He levels me with the same blank, heated stare. He doesn't care, and he's not going to cut me any slack.

If I want that twenty-five thousand, he's going to make me earn every single penny.

My hands shake as I grab the edge of my panties. Every muscle in my body freezes. I can't do it. *Fuck*, I thought I could, but I can't.

"Need some help?" he asks. His voice is deep, dark, and I know he's more affected than he's letting on.

I remain quiet, and that must be all the answer he needs as he reaches into his pocket and pulls out a pocket knife.

Instantly, I stumble back, watching cautiously as he flicks it open. "Easy, wallflower."

He slides the cold blade under the edge of my panties and gives a sharp jerk. They slip free down my legs, and I kick them off over my shoes.

"That's more like it." He leans back enough so he can look down at my body. "Oh, little flower, you are *far* more delicious than your wardrobe suggests."

I wince. "Don't spare my feelings. Please. You might not realize it, but I don't dress myself for anyone."

"Hmm...we'll see about that." He releases me and steps back. "Well, get on with it."

I lift my chin and watch his face carefully. "Get on with what?"

"You want that money, you'll have to fucking earn it." He presses one heavy hand onto my shoulder and pushes me down slowly to my knees. I stumble and fall onto my small pile of clothes.

"I...what do you want me to do?"

He cocks his head and crouches down in front of me. "Was it not obvious?"

I'm not about to elaborate on my lack of sexual experience. I can assume what he wants, but I'm not entirely sure. I can't let him know that.

"Tell me, please..." I hate how small and shaky my voice sounds.

He stands again and stares down at me, his gaze flat and cold. "Unzip my pants. Pull out my cock and wrap that sassy little mouth around it. It's as easy as that."

"Is that all you want?" I mock him.

He gives me a cold, cruel smile. "It's the *first* thing I want."

With shaking fingers, I open the button on his jeans and slide down his zipper. He's been hard since the first time he caught me. My hand brushes the length of him behind the fabric. He feels huge, impossibly large. I've never given a blow job in my life, and now he expects me to do it on my knees, here, now, in the middle of the woods? Talk about a first-time experience...

"Suck it," he orders. There's a hard edge to his voice. "*Now*. Show me how much you want it."

I swallow hard and pull his length out of the fly. He's as large as he felt, his shaft long, and the swollen head thick. I wrap my hand around him, and some part of me registers how much I appreciate the warmth of his body. My hands shake as I give him one experimental pump with my palm.

My entire body quakes as I kneel on my ravaged knees. This man terrifies me, and I *know* this isn't all he'll want. Not for twenty-five thousand. Not after all the taunting and torture he's subjected me to.

I swallow hard and shuffle forward. He seems to realize I'm having trouble and closes the distance. His dick bobs closer to my mouth, practically kissing my lips.

Adrenaline and cold fear start to settle deep in my belly.

What the hell am I doing right now? Who the fuck is this asshole to force this on me?

As I kneel there with my hand wrapped around his cock, I realize I've never hated anyone in my life except my asshole father who abandoned us when I was a baby. A man I've never met. Never hated anyone else...

Not until right now.

I stare up at him and the hungry, cruel look in his eyes. He's enjoying this. Every bit of my struggle turns him on, heightening his pleasure. I slide my hand down his length again, sucking up the warmth. It's all I can get right now, and I have a feeling shit is about to get *so* much worse. I can't let him win. At least not without a real fight.

With a sigh, I lean forward and twist my hand hard around his cock.

"Fuck!"

The second he doubles over, I grab my dress and run.

I've either made the biggest mistake of my life or he'll take the hint and leave me the hell alone.

CHAPTER 9
DREW

PAIN SHOOTS through my dick and up into my gut. I double over and brace my knuckles on the ground to catch my breath. Oh, that little brat *will* pay for this.

She's running through the woods naked, and I'm going to bring her down and fuck her until she screams my name *exactly* the way I want her to.

I tuck myself back into my pants and zip them.

It takes seconds to pinpoint which direction she ran off. I'm grinning like an idiot as I jog through the trees to catch up with her. She had a little bit of a head start, but I don't intend to let her keep it.

I chase her through the woods, listening to her run, listening to the sounds of her breathing, and enjoying every little whimper as she hits trees, bushes, and logs. She's not very graceful, and she's too busy watching for me to keep her eyes on the path in front of her. It doesn't take long until she hits her knees again.

Her poor, abused knees are taking a beating tonight.

I easily catch up with her.

I stand over her prone body and stare down. "I thought you wanted a deal, but now, I think you want something else. Why keep running if you didn't want me to chase you, little wallflower?"

She whimpers, and I pull a small flashlight from my pocket and shine it down on her body. All creamy pale skin, covered in dirt and blood from the chase. Oh *yes*, she's the ultimate prize, and like a true hunter, I will enjoy every second of this. Her cuts and scrapes are superficial. Nothing major. Her knees are the worst of it. I strip off the jacket I'm wearing and throw it on the ground, then I haul her up by the hips and position her so her knees are cushioned by the jacket. She makes me want to at least try to be less of an asshole.

"I'm not doing this for you, flower. I'm just making myself more comfortable."

I trail a hand over her bare hip and watch goosebumps bloom from the wake of my fingers. Her skin is soft, silky, and I can't wait to feel how hot and wet she is between her legs.

"Talk to me, little flower. Anything broken?"

She groans and tries to push up, but I keep a firm hand on her lower back to restrain her. "Besides my pride or dignity? No, not really."

Her glasses are askew again, so I reach out and tug them off her face. She swats out to grab them with one hand, and I tuck them into my pocket for safekeeping. "Don't worry. You'll get them back."

Her voice is high and scared. "I can't see much without them."

Hmm..." Good, maybe that means you won't pull a stunt like that again."

"But... I thought you wanted me to run."

I laugh now. "Oh, you are *so* much more than I gave you credit for. Now, scoot closer so I can keep you warm."

I lay the flashlight near my legs so both hands are free to pull her up onto her knees. "Come closer."

She whimpers and groans as she sits up fully. "Just let me go."

"You don't want the money anymore?"

She scoffs. "We both know you were never going to give me *any* money. You just want to fuck with me, tease me, use me, and then discard me like all the others. I'm not stupid."

"That's where you're wrong, wallflower. I *do* plan to do some of those things, but after I use you, after I break you, I plan to *keep* you. You belong to me until I say otherwise. I won't repeat myself again."

She sneers at me. The fight in her makes me crave her that much more. How pretty she will be once she breaks... I let my gaze slide down her tearstained and dirt-streaked face to her neck, then over her shoulder down to her nice round tits, with the blush pink nipples that are hard as diamonds right now.

I keep going, eyeing the smooth flat curve of her belly and then to the soft tuft of blond hair right at her pussy. I lick my lips and grab her ankle to spread her legs enough for me to get access. She kicks her feet out like she might try to scramble away, but I wrap my warm hands around her chilled skin tighter and drag her upper body the remaining inch into my chest. . Then I tug her closer until her legs frame my thighs.

Right where I want her.

I lean until my face is even with hers, cheek to cheek. She moves to pull back, but I grab her by the neck. "You ever make a move to hurt me again, and I'll make sure I deliver that punishment on you tenfold. Do we understand each other?"

She gulps again, tears still falling, and nods.

I shove her thighs apart to take a peek at what I've won. Her pussy opens for me, blooming like a flower. Fuck me, she's ready to take my cock. I can't wait to slide in there and see how tight she is. I'm guessing a girl like her has been with maybe a handful of guys, if that. She moves to press her legs together, and I allow her to do it. When her thighs touch, I pull her up to resettle her knees on my jacket and lean up so she can feel my cock press against her ass. She wiggles, and I dig my fingers into the bones at her pelvis to keep her still. "Not too fast, Flower. I want to savor this."

"I know what you want. Just get it the fuck over with."

I lean over her, pressing some weight on her back so her legs quiver. "Well, now that you said that, I think I will take my time."

She huffs out a breath and goes still in my grasp. That won't do. I slap her ass hard enough to send her scrambling forward and onto her belly. As I predicted, she comes up spitting, scratching, striking, going for my face.

There she is. My little wallflower has more fight in her than she lets on.

I grasp her wrists hard enough to make her whimper, then spin her so her back is against my chest again, her ass pressed *exactly* where I want it. I pump my hips forward so she can feel every inch of my length.

"I can't wait another minute to have you," I whisper against her neck as I gather her delicate wrists in one hand and pin them against her chest with my own fist.

I use my other hand to work my jeans open and pull out my aching dick.

It's finally time to have her. She's lost this fight. She's *mine*.

I tilt her hips up so I can rub myself against her, feeding my cock between her thighs. The heat of her pussy radiates over my cock, beckoning me forward. She lets out a whimper, but I ignore it. In a few minutes, she won't be doing anything but begging me for more. I thread myself through her pussy lips, back and forth, ensuring the head of my cock brushes her clit with each pass. Her whimpers grow into something more, something sinful. A sharp intake of breath. Perhaps shock or surprise? Why would that little movement surprise her?

"Talk to me, little wallflower? Does that feel good?"

She stays silent; not a single word escapes her, so I continue doing what I please. If she doesn't want to give me anything, then I'll worry about myself.

I love how silky and pink she is here. All the blood rushes down to her center, warming us both up. I hug her body tighter against me, then shove her shoulders down so her back arches while she's on her hands and knees. A ragged sob cuts through the night, but I ignore it. She knew the rules when she came in here, yet she tried to make a deal for this exact thing. Now, I'm taking it, and she will enjoy it just as much as I will, whether she admits it or not. I bet she's only crying because she lost. This has nothing to do with pain or being hurt. I've ensured she didn't hurt herself, and I haven't laid a single finger on her that would cause her harm. I have no reason to feel bad. Focusing on the pleasure instead, I rub myself against her opening, holding her hip with one hand and taking my cock into my other hand. This isn't my usual forte...ninety-nine percent of the time, I take what I want with complete disregard for how rough or brutal I am. Every woman knows the score before they throw themselves at me.

But Maybel is different, and because of that gut instinct that tells me to use caution, I lean into it, letting it guide me.

Pushing forward, I press the thick head of my cock into her wet heat and take a breath. Her muscles are tight, tighter than I anticipated, so much so that I have to grit my teeth and push through her body's resistance. She shifts in my grasp, her shoulders angling down, her head pressed against the cold dirt. Every inch of her body is strung tight like a bow. Maybe she hasn't been fucked in a while. At least she's stopped fighting me. If only her body would let me in. As much as I hate it, I slow and ease my cock in a little deeper, then back out.

I notice that she shifts the tiniest bit forward like she might get away. All I can do is smile. Now that she's in my dark web, she'll never escape me. To secure her, I snake an arm under her belly and hold her tight in place.

"Not getting away this time. It's my turn now."

"You don't... I can't..." Her words break up into small sobs. "Wait... you're too big. You'll hurt me."

I've been told that a time or two, but most of the time, the pain that comes with the pleasure of stretching them is pushed to the back of their minds after I thrust a couple of times. It's not the same here. No, the deeper I sink inside her, the more feral she becomes. Her fingers claw at the earth like she needs to get away from me or she might die. I don't know if I should be insulted or thrilled that she's more afraid of my cock than me.

"Shhhh. It's okay, you can take me. Hell, you already are. *Aren't you?* Your tight cunt might be struggling to take all of me, but she's stretching beautifully around my cock. Fuck. Don't worry, babe, you'll stretch, even if I have to make you," I whisper into her ear as I thrust forward. Bolts of pleasure zing up my spine. I'm certain with the way her body keeps trying to fight against me, pushing me out, that she's never been fucked by a man with a cock the size of mine. That explains the need to climb out of her skin and get away from me. It doesn't matter. Her body will adjust, and when it does, she'll be begging me to rut into her.

"Fuck, your pussy is strangling my cock." I groan. A small hiss fills the air, and she inches forward like she might be able to escape, but I keep a tight hold on her, forcing her to take every last inch of my cock. "There's no escaping the beast now that you've awakened him, flower." My heart stampedes in my chest. My cock is being squeezed so hard, her pussy feels like a virgin cunt. Fuck me, so tight and wet. God*damn*. I want to slam into her over and over again, sinking my fingers into her creamy flesh, marking her, making her mine, but instead, I stop. I pull myself free of her tightness and peer down at her delicate folds.

My breath catches. In the dim moonlight, I catch sight of the red sheen that's coating my cock, the inside of her thighs, and her pussy.

Blood. Virgin blood.

This deep primal need to own and claim every inch of her overtakes me. My brain doesn't even have time to grasp what I'm doing. Harsher than intended, I grip her by the thighs and drag her pretty pussy up to my mouth.

She lets out a squeal but doesn't try to stop me as I bury my face between her legs and feast on her. Top to bottom, I lick her pussy clean, tasting the sweet sacrifice she's given me. The coppery tang of blood explodes against my tongue, and I lap at her greedily, wanting more. Other men may find this disturbing or disgusting, but I'm not afraid of a little blood. I flick my tongue against her clit a few times before I wrap my lips around it and suck. Her entire body shudders against me, and I know I have her right where I want her when she lifts her hips, trying to fuck herself on my tongue.

Deeper, she needs more. I know this, but I want her dripping by the time I slide back inside her. Fastening my lips on the bud, I suck harder and flick my tongue at the same time, angling to hit her a little harder and going until she pants.

"Oh god," she moans into the night air.

"Not god, flower, just Drew," I growl against her folds. Fuck, she tastes so divine. I could sit here all day and lap at her pussy, but I need more. If I don't satisfy the beast, there's no saying I won't break her before I have the opportunity to see what she's made of. Tamping down the primal urge building inside me, I swallow hard and lift her so her back is against my chest again. I move her gently as if she's a piece of glass.

Skimming my nose against her throat, I speak, "I think you forgot to tell me something."

"I didn't forget to tell you anything. I was never given the opportunity." The way her voice cracks reminds me that there's a soft, tender part beneath that sassy front she puts up, and I need to be careful not to tear her soft petals.

"That's a lie. You could've told me at any point in time. I just think you wanted me to find out on my own, but that's okay because you have no idea how thrilled it makes me to be your *first*, to know that I'm the only man who's been deep inside you. The only man to fuck you and claim your hole. Your virgin cunt tastes as sweet as it feels too."

The softest of sobs fills the air, and I release my hard grasp on her and trail my fingertips over the length of her body. Soft, creamy, smooth skin. The perfect canvas for my rage and destruction. Trailing lower, I finger her entrance and ease one single finger inside her.

She's so wet and ready, I choose to add a second finger right away. It's a snug fit, but she'll take my cock here soon, so it doesn't matter. I shudder at the feel of her tight cunt squeezing the life out of my fingers. I hear every whimper and sniffle, but I also hear her slight intake of breath. I feel the way her body tightens little by little, and I feel the wetness dripping down my hand and onto the ground. Fuck, she might be afraid and confused, but she isn't saying no. She isn't trying to stop me. *Not that I'd let her.*

"Shhh. It's okay. I know this might feel wrong, but it isn't. Now I'm going to fuck you until you come all over my cock. I want my cum mixed with your virgin blood... And I can't wait to watch it leak out of your tight hole and down your thighs. A true masterpiece of my complete destruction of your virginity."

"I'm not on the pill." The panic in her voice can't be missed. "You can't come inside me."

I lick up the side of her neck and take her earlobe between my teeth, nibbling on it before whispering into her ear, "I can do whatever I want, sweetheart. That's what you signed up for when you entered these grounds. You gave up complete control to me, but because I'm a nice guy, and the last thing this world needs right now is another psychopath running around, I'll get you a Plan B and make you an appointment for the shot."

"I don't need birth control," she growls. "And you should use a condom. I don't want any diseases you might be carrying."

I let out a chuckle. "It might come as a surprise, but I've never fucked a girl without a condom. You're a first for me, and now that I've had a taste of what that's like, I won't be going back. I don't want anything between us, not even a thin piece of latex. So if you're worried about diseases, I can confidently tell you I have none."

"Well, maybe I do." She pants, trying to speak through the building pleasure in her core.

"If you're trying to scare me away, it's not happening. I

don't care. You were a virgin before this. You can't make me believe you have anything, so keep telling yourself whatever you need to. Nothing is going to stop me from sinking deep inside your cunt, again and again. Not even you."

"I hate you."

"Hate me all you want, baby. If your hate tastes this good, I can't imagine what your desire tastes like." I continue to stretch her with my fingers, slowly fucking her, listening as her breaths turn to pants and her hips buck against my hand. I could've been a dick and carried on fucking her, knowing that it was going to hurt no matter what I did, but the tiniest part of me wanted to try and lessen the pain however I could. Now I'm kind of regretting it since my balls are aching, threatening to turn blue and shrivel up. Between the chase and foreplay, I'm ready to explode. Her cunt is a sloppy wet mess by the time I'm done with her, and when I pull my fingers from her tight hole, she lets out a disapproving groan. "No worries, I have something better than my fingers for you."

I guide my cock to her entrance and slide inside her slowly, so very slowly. Every clench of her tight muscles has me gritting my teeth as I force her to take every single inch. The desire to rut into her over and over again grips me ten times harder. I want to hurt her, but I don't want to ruin her just yet. There will be plenty of time for me to take her like the animal I am. Latching onto every last shred of control I have, I fuck her slowly, in and out, marveling each time I see the streaks of blood on my dick. A fucking *virgin. How could I get so damn lucky?* The thought makes me move a little faster, needing a little more friction.

"You feel so good, Bel, *so* fucking good."

I snake a hand back down her belly and continue to massage her clit, my fingers moving faster over the tight bud.

Liquid from her cunt pours over my length with each thrust, and I love the fucking sounds her pussy makes as we connect.

"Drew..." She moans my name, and it sounds so fucking beautiful.

She's close now. I can sense it, feel it in the way her body trembles and her muscles quiver. Even through the pain and stretching she feels, she pushes her ass back against me, chasing the pleasure. Oh *yes*, she wants this. She wants *me*.

"You're going to come for me, aren't you?" I ask.

"Oh god..." Her words are raspy, her breaths coming out more like pants now.

"Do you feel it building? I can feel every clamp of your tight pussy around my dick, and it's driving me crazy. You're going to come with me. That's your only choice here. If you don't, I'll continue fucking you until you do, and believe me, flower, you don't want to know how long *I* can go. I'll leave you a whimpering, cum-filled mess if you don't do what I ask."

A soft cry escapes her lips, and she digs her nails into my wrists. The pain sends bolts of pleasure down the base of my spine. *Fuck me.*

"Say it," I growl.

"What?" she cries.

I thrust harder. I'm so fucking close to coming, but I need to feel her first.

"Tell me you're going to be a good girl and come on my cock." I hiss while bottoming out inside her. My grip on her tightens as I fight off the pleasure. The second the walls of her pussy clamp tight around me, milking me, I snap. Getting the girl off isn't ever my concern, but this girl isn't just anyone, and the idea of not feeling her flutter all around me, sucking my cum deep inside her and holding it there makes me furious.

"Oh *god...*" My little flower groans. "I'm... I'm coming."

She explodes a second later. Her tight pussy strangles my cock and steals the air from my lungs. I abandon her throbbing clit and move my hands to her hips, getting a better grip so I can rut into her as hard and fast as I can. I fuck her through her orgasm. The pleasure is so great, I swear I black out for a moment. All I can hear are her whimpers and the slap of our flesh against one another as I climb higher and higher.

"Fuck, you're doing such a good job, Bel. I'm almost there." I praise her, feeling the distinct tingling deep in my balls. My vision blurs, my chest constricts, and I grip her with bruising force, slamming deep one last time.

Then I explode. The warm heat of my release spreads through her womb, and I smile. I've never experienced something like this before. I gently stroke the spots where I know she'll have bruises tomorrow before I encase her in my arms. Her small body trembles against me, and I'm unsure if it's from the cold air or the aftermath of her orgasm. Either way, I clutch her tight to my chest and do my best to share my warmth with her.

Gently, I nibble her neck and earlobe, attempting to kiss away the hurt. She's so fucking intoxicating. "How did your first time feel?"

She lets out a defeated sob and folds over to catch her face in her hands. Her emotions are all out of whack, but it's not unexpected. "I can't believe I let you touch me. I don't even *know* you."

"You know me a lot better now." I climb to my feet and pull her up with me. Then I wrap my jacket around her naked body. It covers her from knee to neck. "Are you up for another round, or are you done for the night?"

Her green eyes become slits, and her lips tighten, then she does something I never anticipated. She spits in my face.

"How can you stand here and act so casually about what you just did? Taking my virginity. I fucking *hate* you, and if you ever touch me again, I'll go to the police. Do you hear me?"

For a millisecond, I'm shocked, mainly by the size of her balls, but also because with how smart she is, it's safe to assume she understands the repercussions of her actions. Clearly, she does but doesn't really give a fuck. Guess I'll have to fix that. Before she can make a mad dash and escape me, I shed the gentle, kind front and wrap my hand around her delicate little throat.

A squeal escapes her lips when I squeeze, applying ample pressure. She might have been the *first* virgin I ever fucked, and she might be my perfect match when it comes to every-fucking-thing else, but she *will* learn who is in control by the time this is over.

Leaning in, I stare into her frightened gaze. *Perfect.* Exactly what I needed to see. Perhaps she can tell when to close her mouth and open it.

"Understand something, flower. *I'm* the one in control. *I'm* the one with the power. In every sense of the word, you belong to me. If I want to fuck you right here and now, I will. If I want to share you with my friends, I will. If I want to make you lick the spit off my face, you fucking will. Don't tempt me to prove a point because I promise you, I will, and then you'll regret *ever* fucking with me. I've been kind to you when I didn't have to be, and let me just say kindness isn't something I offer everyone, but don't be mistaken. Kindness is not my biggest weakness, and I have no problem breaking you just to piece you back together again as I please. Do you understand?"

Beneath her fear, the anger and rage remain. I can see the

flames crackle and pop. She wants to hurt me, but she knows damn well I'm not bluffing. Her cracked lips part, and I loosen my grasp ever so slightly to allow her to speak.

"Yes," she croaks.

I release her with a satisfied smile and wipe the spit from my face. Next time she does something like that, I'll use it as lube to fuck her ass. "Good. I'm glad we got that out of the way. And for future reference, the police won't help you. No one will."

"You're so mentally unstable. You should be in a psych ward," she growls and tightens the coat around her small frame. "If no one believes me, that's fine. It doesn't matter. I'll find a way to make myself less appealing to you."

I'd laugh if I didn't really think she might do something like that.

I sigh. "Do what you must, but just know... whatever consequences take place are those you've earned."

Sparring with her makes my blood heat. I'm addicted to it. I've never experienced anything like this with any other woman...and now I don't want it to end.

"I don't care about your consequences. You can't hurt me any more than I've been hurt in my life already. All you are is a bully with a chip on his shoulder who thinks he can have anything he wants, but you can't. Not without force. You're pathetic."

I yawn directly in her face. "Are you done yet? I've heard all that and more before."

Bel's rage climbs higher, and I wonder if she's really mad at me or herself for letting things go this far. She didn't ask me to stop, and she didn't say no. The only person she can blame for what happened is herself. Angrily, she turns and stomps off in the wrong direction. I follow her closely because one, it's adorable that she thinks she can dismiss me so easily, and two, I need to make sure she gets back to campus in one piece.

We walk only a few yards before she peers over her shoulder at me. "Stop following me!!"

All I can do is shake my head. "If you want to get out of here, you need to go left. It's only about a half mile back to the cars."

"Fuck you," she yells back at me, her fire making my smile widen. Perhaps I've found something worthy of my attention.

———

Letting Bel return to her dorm alone takes substantial effort, but I manage it. I was tempted to drag her back here kicking and screaming, but thought better of it. Instead, I took the rest of the evening to brush up on everything I knew about her. After a couple of hours of sleep, I rolled out of bed, showered, and changed.

Now I'm in the kitchen, getting ready to discuss the events of last night. It's just me, the boys, and a truly glorious stack of pancakes.

Lee stands in only his pajama pants, scratching up his chest and over his shoulders. Sebastian's in a button-down and slacks but sporting a truly glorious black eye that makes me smirk every time I see it. Aries sits at the counter with his bare feet propped up, his shoulder-length curly hair wet and dripping onto his T-shirt.

I shove them off. "Get your ugly-ass feet off the counter. We're about to eat."

When I take the seat next to Aries, I glance over at Sebastian. "Call it."

He stretches his head to the side, back and forth, like he's amping himself up for something. Then he snags an open bottle of 151 off the counter, takes a long pull, and passes it around.

"I call this Mill meeting to order."

There are very few things we do officially or publicly. Most of them happen during the season, so we have the rest of the year to plan. But we still try to keep some of the old traditions alive. We're the four senior members of the group, and then we have several junior members. It takes a family name and a lot of money to get invited, and of course, everyone wants in before *The Hunt*.

I open my mouth to ask about how the night went when a woman comes walking into the room, completely naked. We all glance at Lee, who seems unconcerned as he pours some of the 151 into his espresso.

"Charity, I told you to stay in bed."

Her full pink lips form into a pout, and I eye the mascara lines on her cheeks before assessing the rest of her. Hell, there is mud caked around her ankles. "I smelled pancakes, and since I'm hungry, I thought you might share?"

Lee's mouth folds into a flat line, and I grin. He rarely gets annoyed, but when he does, it's usually a good show. With all the athletic skill he's built in the ten years of his life, he snags a pancake off the stack and throws it at her. She barely catches it in her hands, a folded soggy mess. She glares icy daggers at him. If she thinks she's mad now...

Grabbing the bottle of hot syrup from the counter, I pour some onto the top of the pancake, smirking as it drips off the pancake and onto the floor.

I point her back in the direction she just came. "Get out. You've got your pancake."

Her eyes skip around the room, and finally, she realizes she interrupted something. "I'll just..."

"Yeah," I prompt, staring her down as she goes.

When I flick my eyes back to Lee, I find him unfazed.

"Before we continue, did any of you other assholes have a sleepover with some unfortunate woman or man who will inevitably be tossed out?"

The two of them shrug and shake their heads. Lee's smug mouth twists up into a smile, and I watch as he looks up at the ceiling.

"What?" I bark out.

"There might be another one up there, but I think he's still sleeping."

All I can do is shake my head. "Of course."

I focus my attention on Seb and Aries, tuning out Lee completely. "Report? How did everything go with the event?"

Seb narrows his eyes and leans forward, bracing his elbows on the counter. "Everything went as expected."

I swirl my finger in the air near my eyes. "And this? Was that expected too?"

His jaw clenches and narrows his gaze. "Some of us were focused on the event and not on chasing down some little library nerd all night."

I shrug, unbothered by the mention of Maybel. These guys are like brothers to me. I have nothing to hide. They knew about my interest in her, and they know I claimed a piece of her soul last night. That's all they're going to know too. I grab a plate and layer some pancakes with butter and syrup onto it.

"Fine, anything we should be concerned about from attendants, staff, police? Anyone actually make it to the cabin?"

Seb snorts. "Of fucking course no one made it to the cabin. Who do you think I am?"

Through a mouthful of pancakes, I say, "Is that how you got the black eye?"

Aries snorts, and Lee hides his smile behind his coffee

mug. Seb merely rolls his eyes, choosing not to go into the specifics on how he obtained such a bruise, and we go over some more details from the event. It seems everything went to plan, which is a miracle in and of itself. We usually get one or two assholes who complain they didn't get the girl they wanted or one girl who complains about how someone was too rough with her. Every year, it's something.

Once we wrap things up, I finish my breakfast and head back upstairs. When I step into my room, I freeze. The sound of running water from my bathroom greets me. Weird, I didn't leave the water running this morning. Suspicion leads me across the room, and I shove the bathroom door open to find a petite brunette standing under the spray, her hair wound up on top of her head.

She bats her wet lashes at me once she notices my presence. "Oh, good. I've been waiting for you. Want to join me?"

I hold the shower door and give her a slow look. "Where did you come from?"

"Lee invited me."

"Well then you should probably be showering in Lee's room and not mine."

She lathers her tits with soap and slides her hand down to her pussy. Whatever she's trying to do, it's not working. "What, no... I only spent the night because I wanted to see you. I looked everywhere for you at The Hunt. Were you even there?"

Was I even there? I give her a once-over. I don't see a single bruise or scratch on her. One of the pretenders, then. I keep my disgust contained to a slight curl of my lip.

"You have five minutes to finish whatever the fuck it is you're doing and leave my room, or I'll drag you out of here by your hair."

"But I thought you'd want some company. Are you

rejecting me?" The huff in her voice makes me laugh. Oh god, the audacity. How could someone possibly not want her?

"Four fucking minutes," I warn and walk out of the room, slamming the door behind me. It isn't like me to turn down free pussy, but I'm only interested in one person right now, and I'm saving every inch for her.

I ROLL over in bed and get a front-face view of my dirt-caked nails. Last night, I wobbled, mostly naked, all the way back to my car. It was dangerous as hell to drive without my glasses since the psycho didn't give them back to me, but thankfully, I made it. And no animals or people decided to jump out at me. It didn't take long to get home, with the heat cranked to the max so I could thaw.

My body is one big ache. Plus, there's an ache down *there* that's new and makes my cheeks heat every time I think about it. My exhale comes out choppy, and reality hits me. What the *hell* happened last night? If it wasn't for my body covered in bruises and dirt, I'd say it was all a fever dream... A hallucination. What kind of person hunts someone down in the woods and then fucks them like an animal?

What kind of person wants *more*?

At the same time, I'm still scared. I don't know why, but some part of me thinks Drew won't be happy with just our little encounter in the woods. He'll want more. He's relentless and spoiled, and rich assholes like him *always* want more. He also probably doesn't hear the word no very often. I can't stop thinking about it. I can't forget his touch. His words. Tears burn at the back of my eyes, and I'm overcome with emotion. I cup my face in my hands and let the hot tears slide down into my palms.

After a five-minute mini-pity party, I swipe hard at my cheeks and scrub my skin to bring myself back. People have sex *all* the time. It's *not* important; it *doesn't* matter. It doesn't *matter* that I feel degraded and abused. That I feel ashamed of how my body responded to him. I can't even blame him, not entirely. It's not like I stopped him. I didn't even tell him no.

I shove the covers off my legs and slowly shift to the edge of the bed. I need a damn shower, some food, and then I want to spend the rest of the day trying to forget what happened last night, preferably with a pint of ice cream and a sappy movie.

I blink my eyes, attempting to clear the blurriness, but that won't happen without my fucking glasses. Ugh, what the hell am I going to do? Then it hits me. I have another pair of glasses somewhere in here. I lean over and pull open my bedside drawer, digging inside for the prescription sunglasses with the cracked lens. It's not an ideal solution, but I can get my glasses back later if I can bring myself to go hunt him down... Maybe I can send Jackie instead. She seemed to like him well enough to drag me out to the event in the first place.

I lumber out to the living room and find Jackie sitting at the table, earbuds in, chowing down on a bowl of Coco Pops. When I stop at the table and lean against the surface, she pulls out her earbuds and looks me over with a slight cringe. "Uh...did you have fun last night?" From what I can see, she doesn't have any bruises, while I can feel my own with each step I take.

"I wouldn't say *fun* exactly." I swallow hard and move to grab a bowl. But then I catch sight of my nails again and decide I have to scrub my hands before I can pour my break-fast. Five minutes later, I sit down beside Jack who decides then to stand and head to the sink. So much for having break-fast together.

"I have a date in a few minutes. One of the guys from the event last night. We're going to study." Even though her back is to me, her tone tells me she just wiggled her eyebrows as she said the word "study."

I scoop up some cereal and shove it into my mouth, chewing slowly to give myself a moment to come up with something to say. I don't want to rain on her parade right now, but mine's been flooded, and I'm not in the mood to discuss what happened last night.

After a moment, I just offer a halfhearted, "Cool," and continue eating.

She turns to face me after setting her bowl on the drying rack. "How was Drew? I know he was looking for you last night. I'm assuming from your disheveled look that he found you."

The mention of his name almost makes me choke on the sugary cereal. I clear my throat and keep my eyes on the dark-ening milk in my bowl. "Uh...yeah, he found me, eventually."

"What happened? I've heard so many things about him." Her eyes widen meaningfully on the word *things*.

"What kind of things?"

She gets down on her elbows and lowers her voice like she's trying to keep our dorm room ghosts from hearing. "He's ruthless in bed, both with his, er...*pleasure*...and his part-ners. He doesn't really date much. He's more of a hookup kind of guy, so all the girls want to try to bag him. But, I mean, look at him. Who wouldn't want that? His father's this billionaire and one of the top alumni at the school. Plus, the whole quarterback of the football team thing makes all the girls and some of the guys, if I'm being honest, drool like dogs." She slaps the table and stands. "Anyway, I gotta run. Get some rest today, girl. You look like shit."

Thanks. I make a noncommittal noise and continue eating as she bustles out the door. In the hall, I hear her giggle, and then the door opens again. I'm about to ask if she forgot something, but the words stick in my throat, clogging my ability to breathe or think.

He's *here*. He's back.

Warning bells go off in my mind, telling me to get the fuck up and move away from the danger, but I can't. My limbs won't move. I'm frozen, a deer in headlights, while Drew stalks closer, shutting the door behind him. "I've been looking for you."

Deep breath. I need to get my galloping heart rate under control. I swallow the bite of cereal I forgot I'd taken and clear my throat. "Well, you didn't check the place I live until now, so I guess you weren't looking *that* hard."

What I really want to say is, go away and don't come back. My body continues to betray me as the sensations from last night return with the rush of looking at him. *Dammit.* He shouldn't be able to affect me like this. I hate him.

He skirts the table and slides the chair opposite me out from underneath. I gulp and point at the door with my spoon. "Do you make it a habit of showing up at every girl's house you terrorize, or is this just for me? I didn't invite you inside, so you can leave the way you came."

There's a smirk on his face as he slowly, deliberately takes the seat across from me, his green eyes studying me. I feel like a bug about to be stomped into the ground. His eyes move to the bowl of cereal in front of me, and like the thief he is, he snatches my bowl from my grasp and starts spooning cereal into his mouth.

Okay, fucker. That's taking things too far. I give him my best glare. "What the fuck is wrong with you? Do you live to annoy me? Don't tell me this is some kind of asshole frat boy revenge scheme because I stuck up for that guy?"

He raises an eyebrow and swallows the cereal—*my* cereal. "Frat boy revenge scheme? First, I'm not a frat boy. Second, I don't do revenge. I like to think I'm more methodical than vengeful. Instead, I just get even."

Fuck.

My mind wanders, and all I know is that I need to get out of here. Away from him and his stupid scent. Something like soap and that damn teakwood wafts off him, and it's just pissing me off now. Something that evil should not smell that good.

"How about we call it even after last night's events, and you leave me alone?"

He continues to shovel food in his mouth, then pauses. "No, I don't think I will. There's something about you, something that draws me in, and until it lets go, I'm afraid you're stuck with me."

"What about what *I* want?"

He shrugs one broad shoulder, his white T-shirt stretching across his chest. Not that I notice. "I don't give a shit about what you want. You're the one who got in my way first, remember? If anything, this is all your fault."

It's not surprising that he continues to put this all on me. "No good deed goes unpunished, right?"

He snorts. "Something like that."

Once he finishes my cereal, he leans down and plops a canvas tote onto the table. I eye it like he's smacked a bomb in front of me. What the hell is in that bag? Do I even want to know? No. No, I don't. I shove away from the table and stand.

"Um...I have to get to the library, er...back to work."

His eyes narrow, and he too pushes away from the table, choosing to stand. Then his gaze drifts to my open bedroom door. First, he chases me through the woods, claiming my virginity, and now he enters my dorm uninvited.

"Remember how you said we don't know each other? I was just thinking, what better way to get to know one another than to spend time together?" He darts off in the direction of my bedroom, as I anticipated.

"Oh no, you don't." I chase him, and damn him and his long legs. "What the hell are you doing? This is *my* room. Do you not have manners? I didn't even invite you into the dorm, let alone my bedroom. Most would take the hint by now, but that's me telling you to leave."

He appears relaxed, uncaring to what I've just said. Meanwhile, I'm burning with rage as he pokes around my bookshelves, pulling a few off the shelf to inspect them. Flipping through the pages, he turns to look at me, his features smoldering.

"Romance? Hmm. I like it. Does she ever fall for the villain or only the good guy?"

"Trying to create your own happily ever after? If so, it's not going to happen. You're far worse than any villain in those books." I growl and grab the book from his hands, gently placing it back on the shelf. I will become murderous if he dents the edges of any of these books.

"Even villains need to be loved, Bel," he says all matter-of-factly. Like he knows a damn thing about love or romance.

Losing interest in the books, he moves on to my jewelry box, thumbing through it like it's his. I step beside him and watch his face as he pulls out the cheap costume jewelry at the top before tossing it back in with blatant disinterest. I swallow thickly when he reaches toward the bottom, like he's making a beeline for my soul... His big fingers grasp onto the diamond engagement ring as he plucks it out from its hiding spot.

His entire demeanor changes in an instant, and he thrusts the ring toward me. "What the hell is *this?*"

His features show so much animosity as he stares into my eyes that I don't even think to lie. "It's my mother's engagement ring."

He shakes it like a bell. "But she's not dead, so why do you have it?"

The old pain of a past that never leaves wells up, and I shove it back into the hole in my chest where it belongs. "First, that's a personal question. Second, it's none of your business."

He gives me a disbelieving look. "You think you can keep your secrets, but they belong to me now. Just like *you* belong to me now. All of you is mine, and that means even the secrets you keep are mine. It's fine, though. I have my own means of figuring things out."

"I suppose money can buy you all types of information," I growl since it's my turn to get angry. Snatching the ring from his fingers, I lob it at the box so hard it bounces up and almost out again. "Now get the hell out of my room."

He leans in close enough that I can feel the heat of his body rolling into mine. He's way too close for comfort. "Make me."

There's so much challenge in that single demand but also a plain-to-see smugness because he knows I'm incapable of making him do anything. No matter how hard I try, I can't physically move this man.

"Did you get dropped on your head as a child? Or maybe you've taken too many hits to the head in football? Either way, I'm not sure why it's not connecting in your mind that I don't want you here. I don't want to get to know you, so why show up here and pretend everything is okay?" I lose some of my steam and deflate, stepping back to put distance between us. "Surely, this all can't be because I stuck up for that kid. If it is, then I'm sorry. I'm asking you nicely to please leave me alone."

He raises his eyebrows and gives me a cocky grin. "Unfortunately, you put yourself on my radar by putting your nose where it didn't belong. Every action has a direct consequence. I am that consequence, sweetheart. Now, do you think you can say please again? I love the way it sounded coming out of your pretty mouth."

I scrub a hand down my face, my own frustration climbing. "There are plenty of other far more willing girls at this university who would bow at your feet for a simple hello from you, but you're choosing to pine over someone who would rather stick forks through her eyes than be in your presence."

He shrugs. "I'd love to see that, and I already told you. I don't know what it is about you yet, but I'm not going anywhere until I figure it out."

"So fucking me in the woods was...figuring me out?"

He snorts. "You mean taking your virginity on that dirt-strewn forest floor? It was on the path to getting to know you, yes, but it's not the only route I plan to take. Not every meeting is conventional or plays out like it does in your romance books." He leans in again, and I wish I could say that his presence only terrified me, but it doesn't. It warms me and makes me feel seen. "Sometimes, things start off wrong or bad. Not every moment is perfect or thought out."

"No, but there's no point in showing interest in someone when the other person already said they don't want anything to do with you. In fact, I think that's grounds for a restraining order, but I could be wrong."

Laughter escapes his lips, and it sounds nice, which is ridiculous since nothing about this psycho is *nice.* "You're something else, flower."

"I don't want to be anything to you."

"That's too bad since I thought about you this morning. I had to jerk off when I saw how your virgin blood stained my skin. Even now, I can still feel your wet, bloody cunt pulsing around my cock. That's all I could think about last night. I had to stop myself from breaking into your dorm and fucking you in your bed."

He knows how to be romantic, doesn't he? I swallow hard against both the arousal and revulsion his words inspire. "I'm glad your memory is better than mine. All I remember is pain and suffering."

He plucks the sunglasses from my face, then reaches into his pocket to pull out something. A moment later, he replaces them with my actual glasses, the ones he took last night. "Suffering and pain? There might have been pain in the beginning, but that can't be helped. I don't remember you complaining, though, when I made you come so hard you saw stars."

"We can agree to disagree, then."

He smirks. "I like this better. I want to see your eyes."

I lean away and adjust the glasses better. What an asshole, bringing up the orgasm I had at his hands. I don't want to be reminded of that, even if I've never experienced something as toe-curling as that. I'd never orgasmed like that before, not by my own hands. Now that I can see, like for real, I think it's time for me to leave. I exit the bedroom and enter the suite, grabbing my ready-to-go backpack off the floor.

"Bel?" Drew calls from the room.

Nope. I'm not doing this with him. The next thing I know, he'll have me on the bed in my room. Wasting no time and wanting to piss him off a little, I grab the sack he left on the table and rush out the door. I flick the lock into place before slamming the door and then race down the hall at a dead sprint. Let him look through my things. He won't find anything, especially since there's nothing to find. I can only hope he'll get bored and realize what a mistake he made in choosing to torment me.

By the time I make it to my car, I'm out of breath. I climb in and sag against the seat, locking the doors just to be safe. The tiny hairs on the back of my neck stand on end. I remind myself that I'm safe as I scan my surroundings. There's no sign of Mr. Psycho.

Thank god. I let out a sigh and cautiously open the bag he brought. I can only imagine the contents. Unfortunately, it's nothing good. Inside are some protein bars, my discarded clothing, the Plan B he promised, as well as the birth control pills he wants me to take, and a slip of paper. I could refuse to take the birth control pills, but then I'd end up in a worse scenario. *Fuck.* I drag my attention to the paper. It's folded, making it unable to be read from inside the bag. I pull it out and unfold it slowly, my hands trembling. My mouth pops open, and I gasp. Is this real? It can't be. Someone pinch me because I think I'm dreaming.

Printed on that paper is a ten-thousand-dollar check, and it's made out to me.

"Oh fuck."

CHAPTER 11
DREW

SHE ESCAPED AGAIN like a mouse barely missing the trap. She's much more than I anticipated, and the challenge she provides only makes me want her more. When I return to The Mill after my shenanigans with Bel, I find Lee curled up in my bed, my covers mussed and tangled around his bare legs.

My eye twitches with annoyance. *What the actual fuck?* I kick the side of the bed, the edge of my boot lands close to his junk, and like a smart man, he jerks away from the edge.

"This whole, I'm quirky and wait in my friend's beds for them to come home like a creepy asshole, might have been endearing the first time you did it, but now it's just fucking weird." His eyes pop open, anger shining bright in their depths before shifting to the playful playboy he shows the world. I raise an eyebrow as he rolls onto his back and stretches the length of my bed like a lazy cat.

With a roll of my eyes, I throw myself into the armchair by the empty fireplace. "Pretty sure you have a room of your own, which, in fact, has a bed. I know it. I've seen it."

Lee hums in his throat and rolls on his side, shifting my

comforter between his thighs. I have to wonder if he has a death wish?

"Dude," I complain. He's only doing this to annoy me or get some reaction out of me. Without an audience, Lee is nothing.

Instead of answering, he snuggles in deeper. "How was your night? I saw you with that nerdy little library girl. How did she do? Was the change worth it? I mean since she's not really your type and all."

My gaze turns cold, and slivers of my rage fracture through my expression before I can stop them. "And what, exactly, is my type?"

"Calm down, Hulk. I'm not trying to start some shit. It's just an observation. We don't see you with many girls, but the ones we *do* see you with don't typically look like they are late for a study date or the host of the mathletes."

I keep my face blank. I don't share shit with anyone because feelings, emotions, and opinions are the exact ammunition that can and will be used against you. Everyone is your friend until the day they become your enemy. "No one needs to worry about what I'm doing or, better yet, who I'm sticking my dick in. Unless you're riding my dick, you shouldn't be worried about it."

Lee rolls onto his back and grins up at me. "If you're offering, then I'm more than willing. I'd let you fuck me."

Lee is open to anything and everything, and while I have no problem with that, it's going to be a no from me. I stare blankly at him. No reaction is still a reaction, I remind myself.

"Look, you're like a brother to me, Drew. I'm just curious. It isn't like you to restrict yourself to just one girl during The Hunt, and I'm sure the guys weren't the only ones who noticed. We had some charter members here tonight from

Blackthorn and Prescott, and they always try to model their hunt after ours. They don't have the balls to go all out like we do, but it's cute of them to try. What I'm saying is, the fact that not many saw your face last night will lead to questions."

It's a statement and warning all in one. Rage burns in my veins. I won't be questioned by the men I lead. *Fuck that.* I get enough of that shit from my father. And with my mother bedridden in the other family estate, I can only do so much. I wish I got more pushback from her. I'd take her gentle chiding over my dad's beatings any day. I clench my fists tightly and grit my teeth, my jaw aching beneath the pressure. Reacting with violence would be my first move, but it wouldn't change anything. Ultimately, everyone, even my friends, reports to my father.

The best thing I can do is bury the emotions beneath the mask and wait for the opportunity to expel them. "We both know you aren't here to discuss some girl. What can I help you with, Lee?"

My friend shifts to the edge of the bed, and I'm relieved to see he's at least wearing a pair of basketball shorts. "Nothing, really. Just wanted to let you know that others had noticed, and if others have noticed, then we both know it won't take long for word to travel."

He's asking, without asking, how long it will take to get back to my father that I'm interested in one woman, one *specific* woman. And if that woman doesn't rise to my father's ridiculous standards, she'll quickly be off-limits. As much as I do what I want around this school, my fucking father pulls more strings than I'd like to admit.

I glance away and stare at the rug near the window. Lee takes the hint and stands, edging closer to the door. "Anything I can do? Anything any of us can do to help?"

I shake my head, still staring at the ground. "No, nothing. This is something I have to deal with."

"Deal with? What's that mean?"

"The girl. She's not a problem. Just a form of amusement. I'll make sure everyone knows that."

He salutes me and walks out, shutting the door behind him. I grimace, my gaze moving back to the bed. He better not have brought anyone back here. I curl my lip, pull out my phone, and text our cleaner to change my sheets as soon as possible. The things I put up with at the mercy of friendship...

I navigate from my texts to the app I set up with the thumb drive to spy on Maybel. It's so fucking stupid to be obsessed with an ordinary girl when I could have any pick of them that I want... But Bel is different. She chose to stand up to the bully in a room full of people. She trembled with fear but still held on to her pride. She provided me with a challenge I didn't realize I needed.

I check the history in the app and browse through it. Simple. Mundane. She's gone to the library and opened her banking application about a hundred times. Based on the balance, she still hasn't deposited the check I gave her.

A part of me is enraged at her audacity, but the other part of me carries satisfaction in the fact that even with a check in hand, she still refuses to accept help. Perhaps Maybel is more of a wildflower than a wallflower.

I sit back and watch as she scrolls through tabs. She navigates between her class schedule, tutoring schedule, and an essay she's supposed to be writing. I smile to myself. *How can something so simple be so interesting?*

I'm not surprised to find that she has a full schedule on top of the tutoring appointments she does in her limited free time. I think that might be why I'm so intrigued by her. She's nothing like I'd expect. Careful, boring, normal. Even worse, she's caring. Caring enough that she's willing to give herself to a beast like me to help her mother. *Her very sick but in denial mother.* At least from what I can tell from their numerous texts. I scan through the remaining messages checking each, one by one.

My finger hovers over the next text from one of her many tutoring clients. A rush of irrational anger floods my veins, making it difficult for me to breathe and my vision blurry.

Stewart: *I was thinking maybe you might want to go out sometime?*

What the fuck? Rationally, I know I have no stake or claim over her. We fucked one time, and that's it. She isn't anyone or anything to me, just some girl with a nice pussy, but in many ways, I already know it's more than that. This makes me want to demand she drop him as a client altogether, but I doubt she would do that. I make a mental note to look into this fucker, and leave it at that for now.

I finish stalking through her recent browser history, and pause when I discover a dress she'd been looking at, that she added to her cart but never ended up buying. It takes less than a minute to copy the link, log in, and purchase it for her. If I buy the damn thing, I will feel absolutely zero guilt when I rip it off her little body before shoving my cock deep inside her pussy. Which I will be doing again and again. The image of it makes my cock harder than steel.

Father flashes across the top of the screen, and I contemplate tossing the damn phone across the room instead of answering his call but choose against it. The damn world had better be coming to an end if I'm not answering his calls. Slamming my finger against the green answer key, I bring the phone to my ear.

There are no pleasantries or kind greetings. My father

isn't exactly your typical dad. Not even close. "What the fuck did you feel the need to spend ten grand on?"

I inhale deeply through my nose and go to that dark place in my mind where I disappear too when I need to speak to my father. "Oh, you know, Pops, the usual: hookers and blow."

"Did you not hear me the first fucking time? This isn't a joking matter. Now answer me, or I'll have the nurse forget your mother's pain medication this evening."

I grit my teeth, a spiteful response sitting on the tip of my tongue. It's less violent than what he usually threatens me with, but it's still fucked up. Using my own mother and her health against me. It's insane to me that a man could use his own dying wife as a bargaining chip, but it's not surprising. It's always the thinly veiled threats of refusing to give her pain meds or treatments. It's either stay in line or risk losing the only person who's ever given a shit about me a little faster. I'll always choose to keep my mother because as long as she is still here, I know pieces of good remain inside me. "She's not just my mother, but also your wife, or have you forgotten that?"

"What did you just say to me? I think you've forgotten who you're talking to. I'm not one of your stupid fucking friends. If using your mother against you is the only way I can get through to you, then I will."

Biting back the desire to spar with him, I answer his question instead. "The money was for costs associated with The Hunt."

"I see, and how was this year's event?" It's crazy to me how quickly he can switch to business mode.

I shrug even though he can't see it. "Attendance was good. Best show out for a semi-public event in the past few years."

He hums in the back of his throat. "Good, good. Next time, clear the expenses with me first. I know you like to think you have special privileges as my son, but we run by a code. Things need to be done the right way."

No fucking thank you. I don't say that out loud, though, and choose to remain silent instead. Sometimes saying nothing is better than saying something but never being heard.

My silence encourages him to continue talking. "I'm sure you got the notification from my secretary already, but an event is coming up soon. Your attendance is expected. Black tie, of course, but do *not* bring a plus-one."

I never got notified, nor did I know about the event, but he doesn't care. All he cares about is his name and image. "I've never shown up with a date to your events. Dating isn't really my thing, and let's be honest, Dad, no one I bring will live up to your standards anyway."

It's a punch in the dark, one I'm sure I'll pay for in due time, but it still feels good to let the words fall off my tongue. He makes a noise. Some type of growl mixed with a grunt.

"Do *not* fucking test me, Drew. I have no problem hitting you where it hurts most. And speaking of pain, I better see some improvement in your grades soon. You've been playing ball too much and not studying enough. Football is another trophy on the shelf, but not your entire life. Without an education, you're nothing, and you will not tarnish our family name by refusing to study and get good grades."

I press my lips together, biting back all the responses bouncing around inside my head. Says the fucking man who just ordered me to come to one of his stupid parties. No matter what I do, I'm never good enough. We win the game, and in his eyes, we could've won by more. I attend his stupid events and smile, playing the perfect son, but away from the public eye, I'm shown it's not good enough. *Nothing* is good enough.

"You will attend, dressed appropriately. You will not bring

127

a date, and you will behave and act respectfully or else." The warning hangs between us.

"Yes. I'll be there."

The words stick tight in my throat, making me want to find the man and punch him in the face. If I didn't need him, for now, we would have gotten into it a long, *long* time ago.

When he doesn't continue, I ask the question that will surely ruin his day. "How's Mom?"

"If you want to know how your mother is, then get off your ass, go to the estate, and see her for yourself."

I'm tempted to press him and ask him when the last time *he* saw her was, but I stop myself. I don't want this conversation to last any longer than it already has.

"Fine. I'll go see her." I say it because it's what he wants me to say. I say it because I'm two seconds from unloading my shit on him, and that will only make things worse for me.

"How's school? What rank is your team currently?"

Anyone listening might think he's asking because he cares. I know better. "First, of course."

"Good. Always the best. Nothing else will do. Just remember, as I said, football is another trophy on the shelf. Your education and our family image are everything else." It's a speech I've heard a hundred times, a hundred and one times, and I don't need it again.

"Did you need anything else?" I keep my tone flat and businesslike so he doesn't chastise me further.

Thankfully, he can't see my face right now. "No, that's all. I'll make sure the secretary sends the invitation with the time. I'm sure I don't need to put into words the ramifications this could have."

He hangs up without another word, and I squeeze the phone a little too tightly, then toss it onto the desk. My hands are shaking, my muscles tense, and I'm five seconds away from destroying something. I count in my head.

One. Two. Three. Four. Five. Six. Seven. Eight. Nine. Ten. Eleven. Twelve.

My thoughts drift in and out with every number, and the anger fades further and further from my mind. After several minutes, I've calmed down enough to go downstairs to the kitchen and find something to eat. Like usual, the space is empty, and midday light slants in through the large glass doors leading out onto the large patio.

Once I reach the kitchen, I'm still pissed off and in no real mood to cook, so I throw together a peanut butter and jelly sandwich, then stare out across the grass leading down to the woods. I close my eyes and relish the memories rushing back to me.

Bel running through the leaves, the scared little whispers she made when she thought I was close to catching her. The fear in her eyes and the sounds she made when I shoved her to her knees in the dirt. The blood on her skin, the tears tracking down her smooth cheeks. *Beautiful.* A true master-piece of chaos and fear. She looked so sexy with my marks on her skin. I wish I could've had more time with her and left marks a little at a time until she was covered with them. Bruised and battered until I laid her down and showed her what a good girl she was. I wanted to praise her, tell her how beautifully she runs, how perfectly she fights me. To remind her that she'll never be able to escape me.

Next time I touch her, I want to sink my teeth into her skin, to leave marks all along her pale neck so everyone can see that she's claimed. Then no one will be stupid enough to ask her out or even *look* at what's mine. I let out a discon-tented sigh and shove the rest of my sandwich into my mouth. It's fucked up, but she's a beam of light in my dark world. I need to see her. Touch her. Smell her.

I'm not usually consumed by women. After all, when you can have any pussy you want, why be smitten with just one? But Bel is different... There's something about her, and like the rarest of jewels, I want to possess her. And I will in time, but I'll need to remain patient for now. I don't want anyone to report to my father that I'm seeing her again or make him think I'm interested in her. If he thinks I'm interested in someone, then he will find a way to use them against me. And as much as I tell myself I don't care, putting Maybel in the middle of this shitstorm with my father isn't what I want to do. I'm selfish and fucked up, but I wouldn't submit anyone to deal with that man.

As much as it pains me, I'll have to wait, even if waiting isn't my thing. However, that doesn't mean I can't stalk, tempt, or tease. After all, she did look so fucking pretty with fear painting her delicate features.

CHAPTER 12
BEL

HAVE you ever gotten that strange tingling sensation at the back of your neck? The one that makes you feel like you're being watched? All your hairs stand on end, and goose bumps pebble your flesh. Because I have. More times than I can count in the last week. And I can't decide if it's because of the events that transpired between that psychotic man and me, or if it's because he's still watching me, lurking in the shadows, waiting for the perfect moment to attack. Either way, I don't like the sensation.

I push my shopping cart down the aisle with a little more haste. It's late, and hardly any people are in the store except the stocking clerks and the cashiers. It's my favorite time to shop because it's so empty. No one looks twice at my thread-bare hoodie and slippered feet. Usually, I'd drive to the next town over and go to Walmart or Aldi's, but I'm only getting a few things.

I glance at my cart and rub my neck, my skin prickling. I ignore the sensation since it's a constant in my life now and focus on my groceries. If my math is correct, I haven't exceeded my twenty-dollar budget for food, and I can eat on this for a week. Off brand cereal, almost expired milk, and a pound of turkey I can use for salad. The lettuce is already starting to go, so they marked it down too. I'll eat it all before it's bad, and it saves me money, which is all that matters. Hell, saves the food from going to waste since they would throw it out anyway if I didn't take it.

A sudden chill skates down my spine, and I tighten my grip on the cart and move faster toward the checkout. I don't know what the hell is wrong with me, but I can't stand being here or feeling so vulnerable for a moment longer. It's not like he'd actually attack me in the grocery store, right?

I quickly step up to the empty self-checkout and scan what I have in my cart. I hit the checkout button and scan my coupon app. The screen dings, but then the total doesn't change.

"What the hell? Come on, you stupid computer."

The computer in question gives a sharp ding and an error message about bagging my groceries. I groan and hit the checkout button again, trying to make it work.

Once the screen clears with the total again, I gape at it. No. It was supposed to be twenty dollars with the coupons. Defeat washes through me. I just want a goddamn salad and some fucking cereal. Tears threaten, and I glance at the cart, trying to calculate what I can remove. Everything in there is necessary.

A deep voice from behind me cuts through the panic and shame welling up inside. "Do you need some help?"

I'm already saying no as I turn around to look at the person in question. *Oh shit.* It's the one from The Hunt. Sebastian, I think, is what Jack called him. A friend of *his.*

"No," I whisper, then clear my throat and say it again louder. "No. I'm good."

"Doesn't seem that way. Maybel, isn't that your name?"

"What do you want? Don't you have butlers or something to do your shopping for you?"

He cocks his head and ambles closer, and I can't help but look at him. *Damn.* He's pretty. Not in the rugged, masculine sort of way that Drew is; his features are slightly more delicate, but that's hard to notice when there's so much menace in his gaze. The sight of it makes it difficult for me to breathe. "I do have people who do the grocery shopping for me, but what I don't have are people to check if pretty little rabbits that get caught in a trap get above themselves. Drew isn't like you. You two aren't even in the same world, let alone the same tax bracket. Stay away from him."

I wince at Drew's name. "I don't know what you're talking about. I don't even like him. Maybe you should tell him to leave me alone. God knows I've only told him ten million times."

"Sure, Kitten. That's what they all say until they start poking holes in condoms to *accidentally* get pregnant."

I curl my lip in disgust. "That's not who I am. I don't..."

He leans in close now, and I get a cold wintergreen scent that wafts off him. "Good. Stay out of the way, and everyone will be happy."

When I open my mouth to speak again, he shakes his head oh-so gently and drops a fifty-dollar bill in front of me on the conveyor belt.

"Everyone deserves to eat," he says, and I gape as he walks past, his hands deep into his pockets. The money is just sitting there. What the hell do I do with it, and why do these rich assholes keep trying to force money on me? Do I look that desperate? Actually, don't answer that. Another glance at my cart answers that question. *Fine.* If Mr. Moneybags is paying, then I'm getting more food. It's up to Drew to explain why *he* won't stay away from *me*.

———

It's been a week since I've seen him or his creepy friends, so my first thought when he shows up at my table in the library is *oh shit, he's found me again.* But of course he did. I'm either at home or in the library. It's not like I'm trying to hide.

"What do you want?"

"To feel you strangling my cock with that tight pussy, of course."

His response startles me, and I knock over a paper cup I didn't realize he'd set there. The hot liquid spreads across my textbook. *Goddammit.* With a huff, I mop at it with some tissues.

"Has anyone ever told you you're disgusting?"

He shrugs like it's no big deal. "Sure, but I've been called worse."

I'm sure you have.

Refusing to get into an argument with him, I change the subject. I don't want to relive the memory of what happened between us.

"Obviously, you don't hang out in the library often, nor do you look like you're studying, and you can't make me believe you actually came here to do something nice... So what's up? Why are you here? What do you want from me?"

I'm pretty sure he's following me or stalking me. Maybe both. It's not a coincidence that he would show up here, especially knowing this is where he can find me. He wants something, maybe more of what happened in the woods? I hate the way my body lights up at the reminder of the way he made me feel and how savagely he took me. Shaking the memory away, I meet his eyes, and he holds my gaze. A smirk is painted on those criminally full lips like he enjoys my refusal to cower.

After a minute, I swallow hard and give in, looking away. "Just tell me what it is you want."

"Would you believe me if I said all I wanted was to see you and bring you some coffee?"

I stare down at the rapidly wrinkling textbook in front of me. So much for selling this one for the money Mom needs. There are others, though. I can make do. I'm reminded of the check he gave me. I can't bring myself to cash it. Yet if I'd made it to the cabin...despite...everything...I wouldn't have had any qualms taking that money. Then again, I'd have earned it. Unconventionally, but I'm okay with that. But this way, him just handing me a check, it makes me feel cheap like he bought my virginity or something. I slip the check I've been staring at for hours, contemplating what I'm going to do with it, out from under the stack of notebooks and hold it out to him. Maybe him showing up here is a sign. After the store incident with his little friend, I don't want to look like a charity case, not any more than I already feel.

"Here. Take it back. I don't want it." Yes, I know I need the money, but I also care about my pride. I care about integrity, and I want him to know I can't simply be bought like an item on the shelf.

He tilts his head, and his dark russet-brown hair falls across his forehead, those dark forest-green eyes piercing, narrowing to slits as he studies me like a bug beneath a microscope. "Hmm, and why is that?"

I reach farther, extending it toward him. "The reason doesn't matter. All that matters is I don't want it."

In an instant, his body goes rigid, his nostrils flare, and the tiny hairs on the back of my neck stand on end. If he possessed the will to expel daggers from his eyes, I'd be dead this very instant. "Is my money not good enough for you, *flower?*"

Strangely, I'm annoyed by the mocking way he says that stupid nickname he's given me. I shift in my chair, unease coating my insides. For some reason, I thought this would be easier. I guess I shouldn't assume anything when it comes to this Neanderthal. Slowly, I drop my hands down to my lap, the check still clutched tightly in my fingers.

"Of course you would think it has to do with you. Believe it or not, I don't care about your money. What I care about is integrity, and the fact that I didn't earn this check. Therefore I don't want it."

I watch his face intently, noting the curl of his full bottom lip and the low, simmering rage flickering in his eyes. He shifts forward like a panther ready to pounce, bracing his forearms on his knees. He looks like the evil villain in every one of my romance books. Instinct guides my movements, and I jerk away, my blood pressure rising with every shallow breath I take. I know very little about this man, but what I do know is enough to make warning bells go off in my mind. Like most red flags, I ignore the desire to run and remain seated. If that night in the woods taught me anything, it's that if I run right now, the only thing that he will do is chase me, and I don't want that to happen. This isn't a game.

"You're a smart girl, Bel. Do you really think you didn't earn that money after what happened?"

His words sting like a belt across bare skin. Who cares if he has money, power, and looks? It doesn't mean he can act like a self-righteous prick.

"I'm *not* for sale. What happened in the woods has nothing to do with this money. If you're insinuating that you bought my virginity, then we're going to have a problem."

"You can't buy something that isn't for sale, Bel, but for fun, let me play devil's advocate here, and let's say you made it to the cabin. Would you not have taken the money then? Even if you acquired it the same way."

He is definitely fucked if he thinks I'm going to let him try reverse psychology on me. I look him dead in the eyes, refusing to show him anything. I'm sure other girls would bow at his feet, but I'm not them.

"I wouldn't have acquired it the same way. Getting to that cabin would've meant I didn't get caught. It also would've meant I hadn't given my virginity to some random stranger in the cold woods, either."

It's his turn to shrug. "Not necessarily true. Making it to the cabin was all you had to do to win. I had my sights set on you and planned to claim you one way or another. You could've continued on your merry way afterward. I wouldn't have stopped you."

I turn to fidget with my books, anything to distract myself from his bigger-than-life body and presence. "I don't recall you being overly helpful afterward..."

His fingers graze my chin, and I shiver as he tilts my face up, forcing me to meet his icy gaze. "Take the money. You need it. I don't. This isn't something I'm going to continue negotiating with you."

You need it. I don't. It's difficult to remain calm when he speaks words that are so truthful, it hurts. *Is that how he sees me?* I guess I shouldn't care because who the hell is he? But I don't want to be seen as Oakmount's charity case. The girl who sold her virginity for ten thousand dollars and is willing to give blow jobs if you pay her an extra five during tutoring. God, I'm stupid. *So fucking stupid.* Next, someone will tell the administration I'm sleeping with the students for cash instead of helping them get better grades.

Shifting from his grasp, I slam the wet book shut and gather my things into a neat pile before shoving them into my bag. Our eyes collide when I look up from the bag. He's studying me, his dark brows furrowed, confusion flickering in his gaze. Despite the warning going off in my head, knowing my next move might be my last, I grab the remaining coffee he brought me, extend my hand over the trash can, and drop it inside. Usually, I'm not this ballsy or ungrateful, but I want him to understand where I stand with him, and that's not even on the same continent.

"It's been a pleasure, as always, but unlike you, I have to attend my classes."

I whirl around, ready to make a mad dash for the door. Unfortunately, I'm not fast enough, and honestly, I should know better, given my history with this man who snatches me by the wrist and pulls me back toward him.

"Oh no, you don't."

I blink, and we're moving, his unforgiving grasp keeping me hot on his heels. I peer around the library, waiting for someone to say something or even notice that I'm being dragged away, but of course no one does. Panic claws at my insides, and I know I have to do something to stop this psycho. He has money, power, and intimidation. I understand their fear of him. I'm sort of scared of him myself, but I'm more terrified of what might happen if I give in.

I dig my heels in. It's my only attempt at stopping his advancement, but all it does is earn me a snarl of disapproval, along with a tightening of his grasp. He's over six feet tall, muscular, and intimidating as hell. Stopping him would require some expertise, which I clearly don't have. The next best thing I have is my voice.

"Let go of me!" I yell and attempt to pull away again, but I might as well be talking to a wall. "Fine, then. I'll scream." The words have barely escaped my lips when he stops dead in his tracks. The movement is so sudden that I crash directly into him, almost tripping over my feet.

The firm wall of muscle shifts as he turns, looking every bit the scary monster he is. Before I can utter another word, his hand slaps over my mouth, and he shoves me backward, my lower back pressing against a dust-covered shelf. One weary glance around, and I realize we're in the stacks. The old part of the library where no one goes. This is bad. Worse than I thought.

Boxing me in with his body, he makes certain the only thing I can see and feel is him. I'm at his complete mercy. With one hand pressed against my mouth to stop me from calling out for help and his other arm snaked around my middle, holding me against him, I'm trapped. *Doomed.* Yet even with the fear trickling in my veins, this rush of excitement is building. It's sickening and wrong that I even recognize it. With my current predicament, I can't be bothered to think about how fucked up that makes me.

Not with his huge hand moving over my lower back, the searing heat of his touch burning through the fabric of my clothes. I might as well be naked at this point. Is it embarrassing that at my age, a man has never touched me like this before, with so much possession and desire? Maybe that's why I'm so excited by it. My heart clenches tightly in my chest, building the anticipation of what might happen next.

It doesn't really matter. No words will make him stop. It's clear he's not letting me go. Not until he gets whatever it is he wants. His green eyes bleed into mine, and I notice the thick lashes framing his devilish face. This close, it's hard to see the evil beast inside him and far easier to see him as the all-American boy he portrays to everyone else. Kind, charming. No one knows there's a complete psycho hiding in plain sight. Slivers of light cast an eerie shadow over us, and I shiver as if someone's dumped an entire bucket of cold water on me, but is it from fear or anticipation? I don't know. The light dances across his face, doing devastating things to his high cheek-bones and razor-sharp jawline.

I suck a ragged breath into my lungs and am greeted with the intoxicating scent of teakwood and mint. This strange calmness blankets me. His smell shouldn't calm or affect me, but somehow, it does, luring me into this odd sense of safety.

Leaning into me, he gently presses his nose into the crook of my neck. The rapid inhale of air into his lungs makes me think he's breathing my scent into his lungs, which would be weird if it also wasn't kinda attractive. I push the thought to the back of my mind because this man and his psychopathic tendencies are the last things I need in my life.

An entire cage of butterflies takes flight in my stomach as his nose skims over the sensitive flesh of my throat. His full lips glide over my thundering pulse, and there's no hiding my fear or excitement. Not with the way my heart is trying to beat out of my body. Stupidly, I do nothing to try to escape his grasp, not even when he presses his hips firmer against mine, forcing me to feel his hard cock throbbing against my jeans. I can't believe I let him fuck me with that giant-ass sword.

Goose bumps erupt across my skin, feeling his hot tongue against my cool flesh. Shit. I need to stop this, somehow. I can't let him pull me into his dark web, one that I may never escape. I need to use my brain and not let my body rule my decision-making. I garner up all the strength I have in me and place both hands on his firm chest, then I give him a hard push. Like an impassable mountain, he doesn't move. He doesn't even budge. Not an inch.

A soft, humorless laugh escapes his lips. "It would be so easy for me to take what I want from you. All I'd have to do is put a little pressure against your neck, knock you out, and then I could fuck you without complaint. I wouldn't have to worry about you running away or fighting me. I could do whatever I want, however I want, wherever I want. I could fuck your ass, mouth, and pussy. I could take whatever I want from you, and you couldn't do a single thing to stop me."

The thought is terrifying and so fucking wrong, and worst of all, there isn't anything that makes me believe he wouldn't do those things. Even I'm smart enough to know there is a time and place to be fierce and placid. It's all about human psychology.

"Don't," I demand, the sound muffled by his hand. I reach for his wrist and try to tug his hand from my mouth. He doesn't move. "Please," I mutter, and this time, he takes a tiny step back, those piercing green eyes of his flick to mine before roaming my entire face. I don't know what he sees shining back at him, but whatever it is, it's enough to melt a smidge of the ice from his harsh gaze.

"I'll save that fun for another day." The relief I feel from his confession is short-lived when he starts speaking again. "While I love your sassiness and fierce determination to piss me off, I need you to be a good girl and listen to me. Or am I going to have to shove my cock into your throat and teach you a lesson right here in the dusty stacks?"

I sag further into the shelf and ignore the notion that I'm allowing him to hold my body weight. At least he's not going to knock me out and have his way with me. I can handle a blow job and being chased through the woods, but I don't want to be taken against my will without any say at all.

All I can manage is a nod.

A smile touches his lips. "Which is that a yes to? You're going to be a good girl and listen, or you want me to shove my cock down your throat and teach you a lesson?"

I say *no* beneath his hand, my lips moving over his palm. The word comes out muffled, and he slowly pulls his hand away. "I'm trusting you, so don't make me regret it. If you start screaming like a banshee, I'll be forced to do something I'll very much enjoy, but you might not, especially after your experience in the woods. Don't make me hurt you, at least for your own sake."

"I'm not going to scream. I'm just confused. I don't understand. What happened at the event was a one-time thing. I heard you don't date or even sleep with the same girl twice, which makes all of this weird and confusing. What do you want from me? Why won't you leave me alone? I'm no one, yet you act like I'm the most interesting thing in the world."

And why can't I stop the edge of excitement this brings me? I'll never admit it, but a tiny part enjoys the attention. The nerdy book girl no one notices who garnered the attention of Oakmount's football star when no one else could. It makes me feel seen and wanted. When you've never experienced that before, it's not something you want to give up. Yet I remind myself that not all attention is the kind you want. Turns out, I garnered the attention of a crazy person.

His pink tongue darts out over his bottom lip, and I bite the inside of my cheek, refusing to acknowledge how sexy he looks.

Remember how dangerous he is, how fucked up he is. Hello, red flag, Maybel.

"Consider me curious. Are you asking around about me?"

I shake my head. "No, asking around isn't needed. I'd have to not exist not to hear about you. Everyone talks about how you never screw the same girl twice, and you don't date. I'm simply acknowledging the rumors."

I notice then just how big our height differences are. My forehead barely reaches his collarbone, so I'm forced to tilt my head back every time I speak in order to see his face. I feel tiny and insignificant beside him.

"Well, rumors are just that, rumors. The thoughts of others. Plus, plans—and people—change. I can choose to start dating or sleeping with the same girl if I want to. I don't give a fuck about what other people say about me." His voice leads me to believe him, but the look in his eyes makes me think otherwise.

"Okay, then why me? I'm no one. A book nerd who tutors for extra money, has no popularity, and is attending on a scholarship sponsored by some rich, elite family."

With a soft chuckle, he lifts me by the chin and meets my eyes. "That's where you're wrong, flower. You're the most interesting thing in my life at this very moment. Lucky for you, I don't care about your reputation or popularity. Nor do I care about the dollar signs in your bank account. You're far more unique than any of those social standards. Something about you draws me in. It makes me curious, and the more you fight against me, the more I want to grasp onto you. The more I want to know about you. Fate brought us together, and I want to test it out. See what happens next. Now, let me show you what I want from you."

His huge hands skim up my arms and then cup around my neck, coming to rest against my cheeks. Maybe it's because I remember how his hands felt on my body that night. How high I got when I finally accepted I'd been caught. I was a rabbit in a trap, and Drew was the hunter. I don't know, but I don't want to push his hands away, while at the same time, the fear thickening in my stomach makes it hard for me to just give in to this.

He's demanding and brutish. Arrogant and spoiled, and worst of all, I don't like him. Not really. My body, however, wants to explore all the things he's offering. The slightest touch of his hands on my skin has my nipples hardening and my core clenching. I'm already wet just from the barest of touches. Shivers wrack my body, and I can't stop them. He looms over me, letting me shake in his grasp, almost like he's enjoying it.

"Are you going to try to run? Make me chase you or hunt you down?" His breath fans against my ear, and I swear my shivering intensifies. "Remember how well that went last time? You thought you were going to get away, but you didn't. I caught you right between my teeth. It was only us out in those woods, at least for the most part. Here, students are everywhere. Do you want to give them a show? I could bend you over in the middle of the atrium, rip off your jeans, and sink into that hot pink cunt of yours. Is that what you want? Maybe that should be your punishment for sassing me."

My eyes bulge out of my head. The mere thought of him taking me in front of students and staff. I can feel the heat rising, embarrassment climbing up my neck.

"You're looking a little sick. Are you sure that's what you want? Do you want me to fuck you in front of everyone just to prove a point?"

I whimper and shake my head. "No. Please. I don't want that."

His gaze sharpens. "Okay, then you need to listen to me and do as I say. My patience is dwindling by the second. I've wanted to touch you since the moment I sank inside you the first time. I did what I could to stay away, but denying myself what I want isn't something I typically have to do. And well, your fire and fight turn me on. I'm closer to the edge of snapping than I care to admit, so let me touch you. Let me do what I want, and maybe I'll allow you to go for a while longer."

"A little while?" I whisper.

"If I didn't make it clear enough for you that night, I'll explain again: this isn't a one-time thing. Until I say otherwise, you're mine and belong to me. I will do whatever I want with you when I want to. Your opinion doesn't matter to me, only my wants and needs, but don't get it twisted. You're a possession, a pretty little trophy I get to set on my shelf. Be good, and I'll show you the most intense pleasure, but try to fight me, and you'll be in for a world of hurt." He bites off the last words with an almost angry click of his teeth. His even, shiny white teeth... I'm wondering how they'd feel on my skin, in my neck, my shoulder, my ass. Stupid. I can't be thinking like this.

As if he can read my mind, he gives me a small, knowing smile. "You're going to be a good girl and do what I tell you to."

Tired of his arrogance, I thrust my chin up and glare. "And if I don't?"

The darkness of his eyes seems to go deeper, and his face comes down to my level like a predator scenting his prey. "Do it. Run. We both know how it will end. Plus, it turns me the fuck on to chase you down and force my cock inside you. Maybe I'll claim your second virgin hole just to prove a point."

"You're an asshole," I growl, but any future words are cut off when he shoves three fingers past my lips and curls his palm around the rest of my mouth, securing his hand under my chin.

"I'm so much worse than an asshole, but if you behave, you'll never have to experience that side of me. Now be good, and let me touch you. I'm dying to touch you, flower."

I whimper as he shoves at the waist of my jeans, pushing them down to my knees. *Oh my god.* We can't do this here. What if someone catches us? I struggle in his grasp, ready to kick him in the junk to get away if I have to. I should've done it earlier. Why didn't I? With his body situated the way it is, I can't get my knee close enough to his junk.

"Shhh. Calm down. If I wanted someone to see you like this, we'd have just stayed at the tables."

I want to growl at him, but all I can do is stare at him with a pleading look, hoping he can see the fear painted in my features. "If it helps any, I don't share, at least not usually. I'm very possessive of my toys."

Toys? I'm not a possession. I've already told him this.

I attempt to open my mouth wider around his fingers so I can speak, but that backfires on me, and he takes the opportunity for what it is and shoves his fingers deeper. I gag on the thick digits, and pleasure zips straight through me and into my pulsing core.

I'm both furious and turned on, but at the moment, I'm more turned on than angry. *What is wrong with me?* Clearly, I have lost my damn mind because I continue to let this charade go on. My core pulses, burning with need, and all I can do is squeeze my thighs together and babble as I beg him to touch me where I need it most.

A need I hadn't ever really felt... until that night in the woods.

His hot breath fans against my ear. "I wasn't lying to you. I've been thinking about touching you since the second you ran off on me, and I've wanted to fuck you again since the moment I finished the first time. I didn't even wash your blood off my cock right away. I'm invested in you, flower..."

His lips nibble along my throat, and my every breath becomes a pant.

"It's really your own doing that you're here in this situation, about to be finger fucked against a dusty bookshelf. If only you had kept your pretty mouth shut...maybe I wouldn't have noticed you. Who knows, maybe I would have anyway."

A gurgling sound escapes my throat as he alternates between sucking on my neck and nipping at it with his teeth. The evidence of my arousal pools between my legs. I'm so turned on, it's embarrassing. Using his knee, he roughly shoves my legs apart. The fabric of his jeans is cold against my bare flesh. My nipples ache right along with the spot between my legs.

"Fuck, flower. I thought you hated me." He pulls away and directs his attention to the space between my thighs. The insides are coated and slick with arousal. "This doesn't look like hate, baby."

I'm so overcome with the need for release that I let his statement go, and instead, I try to press against him to gain more friction, anything really, so I'm not standing bare ass in the library for nothing.

"So greedy, yet you ran away from me in the woods. If I knew you were such a whore for my fingers, maybe I'd have offered you those first."

He cups my pussy, his big fingers sliding along my skin, parting me easily. Flames of desire burn deep in my gut, each touch a glowing ember setting me ablaze. "Truth is, no matter how much you try to fight it, there's no denying that you want me, that you want this, even if it feels wrong and fucked up. I don't recall you asking me to stop or saying no. Not once. But it's okay, your secret is safe with me. I won't tell anyone what you like."

Without mercy or warning, he enters me. I let out a whimper, closing my mouth over his fingers for a second. There's a slight burn as I adjust to the sudden change. He raises an eyebrow like he's daring me to bite him. I know better than that. Somehow, he can read every thought running through my head and predict my next move like a real predator.

"So tight and perfect," he growls against my throat and presses close, his erection hard against my upper belly. How did that—thing—fit inside me? "You're such a good girl when you want to be." Drew withdraws his fingers, dragging them through my wet folds and stopping once he reaches my clit. He circles the tiny bud, swirling expertly across every nerve ending, lighting my entire body on fire.

How does he know how to touch me better than I do?

My eyes bulge, and I let out little gasps at every flick of his wrists. He moves the fingers in my mouth, fucking me with them, making me gag on them, as he fucks my pussy with the other hand, and I grow wetter and hotter with every heartbeat.

"Suck. Suck my fingers like you're sucking my cock," he demands, his voice rough.

I do as he says, chasing a high I know only he can provide me. I suck and lick his fingers greedily, and he continues stroking my clit, bringing me closer and closer to bliss.

I can feel the pleasure building, and my eyes start to flutter closed, but he gives me a little shake, forcing my attention back on him. "No, I want to see your eyes when you cream all over my fingers. Look at me. Watch me. Do you feel what you do to me? How hard you make me? I'm going to explode inside my fucking jeans at any second because of you." He sounds angry, but a softness in his eyes leaves me confused.

With our gazes locked, I feel the rope tethering me to him tightening. This feels too close, too intimate, and I struggle to continue meeting his gaze, but I don't trust him, nor the repercussions I'll endure if I don't listen.

I'll be his good girl...until he releases me for good.

His fingers move faster, drawing little moans and whimpers out of me. Insanity must possess me because my hips start to buck, chasing his hand with every swipe of that magical digit. I'm a puppet, and he's pulling the strings. It feels too good to fight. I'm dizzy with lust and blinded by the promise of something sinister.

My pulse climbs higher...higher...

"Good girls get pleasure," he whispers into my ear.

Oh god, he's going to make me come.

"Bad girls get nothing."

I'm close, so close. My toes curl in my shoes, and I'm about to ignite like a firework and explode into the night sky. And then, like water tossed on a flame, my fire fizzles out. He pulls his fingers from my mouth, and his movements against my clit stop entirely.

Cold disappointment rains down on me.

"What?" I question, dazed and confused. "Why are you stopping?" I hate the desperation that fills my voice as I speak.

Drew doesn't say anything and pulls away entirely. The warmth of his body leaves me, and a shiver that's much deeper than a sudden coldness grips me. My knees threaten to buckle beneath me, and I tremble, gripping the edge of the shelf to stay upright as I tug my jeans back up my thighs. *Was it me?* I can't help but feel I've done something wrong. Shame coats my insides with a sticky sludge. I don't even like him and the way he's treated me, so I should be grateful he ended this before it went too far. Yet it feels like a slap in the face— like he rejected me instead of me rejecting him.

Anger rattles me to the core. He wants me. I can see it. Feel it.

Then why pull away?

The feelings of indifference rush back in. I'm not good

enough for him, that's what this is, and somehow, I know rationally that doesn't make sense because I don't give a shit about his opinion... But in many ways, I do.

I glance at him through a curtain of blond hair, my face burning with embarrassment. His steely eyes meet mine, and he tilts his head to the side as if inspecting me. From the little time I've known Drew, I've already worked out a couple of things about him.

The person he is with everyone else is not the real him.

It's not uncommon for people to have multiple personalities and be different people in different environments, but that's not what this is. Drew isn't the person he plays or the mask he slips on. He's unhinged, sinister, and dark. He's hiding in plain sight, afraid of what the world will think of him if they see the monster beneath the beautiful exterior.

Tears burn at the back of my eyelids, and I twist my face away.

Drew snickers. "Don't cry."

With frightening speed, he pounces on me, one of his hands coming to wrap around my throat, his meaty fingers pressing firmly into my skin, a warning of what's to come if I don't listen. "Don't cry because I really, *really* like it. My touch is a reward, and I've shown you how good it can feel. The little stunt you played back there wasn't worthy of my touch. That wasn't worth shit. Now, thankfully, I'm in a giving mood, so I'll let your attitude and behavior slide. However, you're going to listen to me very carefully when I tell you what will happen next."

"Let me go. I'm done being bullied by you. I'm not like everyone else on campus who melts into a puddle over your mere presence, and I'm not afraid to go to the campus police and tell them what you're doing." I speak the words through gritted teeth and labored breaths.

My words are nothing more than a verbal threat. I'm not dumb enough to think the campus police would do anything about him. They didn't do anything about his friend Sebastian or the others doing whatever they wanted all over campus. They don't give a fuck, not when money is involved.

His grip tightens, and I grit my teeth, bearing through the pain. My vision becomes blurry, and my lungs start to burn from the absence of oxygen. Sirens go off in my mind. The muscles in my limbs start to lose feeling, and I become weaker.

Would this guy kill me? Maybe. He's got the personality type to do it.

Blackness threatens to take over, and for half a second, I start to doubt his desire to keep me around. I had assumed he wouldn't kill me, that I wasn't worth that much trouble.

Before I can finish the thought, the pressure on my throat disappears. I sag against the shelf and half gasp, half cough while sucking precious oxygen back into my deflated lungs.

I look into the dark eyes of the man who has shown me both pleasure and pain. Menace and kindness. The look of desire, of unholy obsession that reflects back at me freezes me with fear. A smile touches his lips, and the sudden whiplash I feel over his change in emotions makes me spiral. He reaches for me, and I flinch. Of course he doesn't care, and continues doing what he wants, tracing my cheek with his finger like he didn't just try to strangle the life out of me moments before.

"I think I've figured it out, Bel. What it is that makes you so appealing. You said it best. You don't give a shit about my name, what I look like, or how much money I have. None of the superficial things matter to you. In fact, if I had to guess, I'd say you don't like me very much right now, if at all... and that's okay. I can like you enough for both of us." The boyish grin he gives me is a terrible attempt at easing the tension. "But let me warn you, there is a reason many steer clear of me. None of the superficial things have to mean shit to you, but I need you to use that brain of yours and not push me past the point of no return. Make it easy on both of us and be the good girl I know you can be."

"I'm not afraid of you," I hiss through my teeth. It's a complete lie. I'm not just afraid—I'm fucking terrified—but you can't do anything but face fear. You own it...or it owns you. What's worse, I can't tell if I'm more afraid of him or how he makes me feel.

"And that's why I want you and no one else, flower. Can't you see how perfect we are together?"

"No thanks," I mumble and attempt to make a beeline in front of him. My body crashes against his bigger stature as he steps forward, cutting me off. His huge hands come out of nowhere, cupping my cheeks, and he drags me closer. Leaning in, he presses his full lips firmly against mine. I've kissed people before, and I know what it feels like.

This isn't a kiss. It's a fucking *claiming*. A form of ownership, a show of dominance. His tongue probes against my lips, and I press my own tighter together, refusing to allow him entrance. He fixes that with a simple press of his thumbs into my soft cheeks. Pain fills my face, and I open my mouth on instinct to stop it. His tongue invades my mouth and tangles with my own. His touch, his kiss... It's a promise, a warning.

The thing is, I've been dealt a shitty hand my entire life, and I've determined the only way I can get a better hand is if I do the dealing. Choosing my next move, I lift my hands and press them against his chest flat, then I sink my teeth into his lip, hard enough that the coppery tang of blood fills my mouth. I shove him at the same time as he pulls back, his body teetering and off balance. Finally, I caught him off guard.

Those dark eyes of his clash with mine, the promise of pain reflecting back at me.

"You bit me." It's more of an astonished statement than a question. "You made me bleed."

I shrug, even as tiny warning bells go off in my mind, telling me that I should be running. The less likely of a challenge I appear to Drew, the more likely he is to walk away.

"Good. We're even then. Since you know you claimed my virginity and made me bleed."

He cocks his head to the side, clearly considering my statement. "I suppose, but there are other ways to make me bleed. Ways that don't involve pissing me the fuck off."

"It's only fair that I get to choose the circumstances in which you bleed since you got to choose mine without my consideration."

This all appears to be backfiring on me because instead of warning him off, he looks curious and interested. "Every time I think I know what you'll do next, you surprise me. I like it. I like the shock and uncertainty. You're unpredictable, the chaos to my madness."

"I don't want to be anything to you. All I want is to figure out what you want from me so I can fulfill that obligation and get the hell off your radar. Other girls might find the lengths you go to gain access to them romantic, but I am not them."

He looks me up and down, his gaze hungry and demanding. "Believe me, I know, which makes you all the more appealing. Like I said before, the more you fight, the harder I'll tighten my hold."

The reality that he isn't going to disappear into the background and leave me alone hits me like a ton of bricks. "I'm begging you, please. I won't tell anyone what happened in the woods. I'm no one. *Nothing*. I just want things to go back to normal. I want to be unnoticed and blend in with the background."

"I already told you, Maybel. The answer is no. I'm not going anywhere. I can't forget your existence. Not when I've just discovered your beauty. You're mine. Accept it, and it'll be more pleasurable for you. Don't, and it'll be better for me. The choice is yours."

His tone is crystal clear. He means every word he says, and that's as terrifying as the reality that I've garnered the attention of a man who seems intent on keeping me no matter what.

CHAPTER 13
DREW

SOME DAYS, rarely anymore, hell is on my side. And by hell, I mean I paid off one of the nurses who takes care of my mother to tell me when my father will be off the estate for an extended period. My phone pings again as my personal accountant tells me the transfer went through to Nurse Helen. She gets a bonus when I can actually sneak onto the estate to see my mother without my father knowing since he always makes a big bullshit show of things if he catches me there, especially if I'm still with her when he arrives. Yet he has no problem throwing it in my face that I don't see her enough. A complete narcissist if I ever met one.

I scrub my hands over my wet hair and walk faster to the motorcycle I barely ever use in the garage at The Mill. My father's driver usually takes me anywhere I need to go unless I choose to walk, but for this, he can't. The house was quiet when I left, and I showered at lightning speed before racing down the stairs and out the door.

It's early still, nine o'clock, the sun already peeking through the nearby forest trees.

I smile when I think about the last time I was in those woods. With Bel.

Fucking Bel.

I touch my tender lip where she'd made me bleed, and I smile all over again, the skin stretching, a lick of pain washing through the tiny cut. Oh yes, she's so much more than I thought she'd be. A beautiful, chaotic mess that I intend to dirty up. The engine roars beneath my legs, vibrating through me. The sound and feeling make me miss riding this thing. The wind in my hair, whipping all around me, the speed and agility. I hit the throttle, my speed climbing as I hurdle down the road. It's a short drive to the estate, and I hate how quickly it goes.

I slow as I approach the security gate and walk the bike to a set of nearby bushes on the off chance that someone drives by and recognizes my bike. I don't need anyone calling my father and telling him shit. My boots crunch against the pavement as I walk up to the guardhouse. Bill is standing guard as he typically does, his features tight, his eyes sweeping the front of the property. Bill is one of the nice guys, in his early forties and fairly built. He took the job here five years ago after the last guard mysteriously disappeared.

I reach into the back pocket of my jeans and pull out a hundred-dollar bill. I pass it to him through the small window, and he shakes his head, frowning at me. "I've told you half a dozen times, kid, you don't have to pay me. My job is to open and close this gate and monitor who is coming in and out. I already promised you that I wouldn't tell your father."

The thing is, I don't believe him. I don't trust anyone who works for my father. If it came down to it, they'd throw me under the bus the moment their job was threatened. The money is merely a bonus, a helpful way to remind them to keep their mouth shut.

"Don't take this the wrong way, Bill, but I don't trust anyone, including you, so take the money and consider it a form of assurance."

He knows the score, yet he says the same thing every time I show up and slip him the money. He wavers only slightly and then quickly shoves the money into his pocket. I smile and wait as he slips out of the guardhouse and quietly opens the gate manually to allow me to slip through.

It's not a perfect system, and it requires several key elements all to coincide, but the effort is always worth it to see the smile on my mother's face.

I jog up the long driveway and cut through the side yard to the back kitchen steps and the small door there. It's never locked, as it isn't today either when I turn the handle and slip inside. If any of the other staff see me, they won't think anything of it. Very few know how tightly my father regulates my visits.

My hands are tacky as I rub them on my jeans, moving quickly. It's been far too long between visits, and I feel like a piece of shit for not seeing her sooner, but with school, football practice, and my commitments to The Mill, it's been difficult to sneak away.

Guilt chews up my insides as I walk down the long hallway leading to my mother's suite. The walls are adorned with photos of our family, the three of us. The images portray us to be some big happy family, but I know better. I do my best not to look at them as I pass by. It's all a sham, a fucking lie. At the end of the hall, I turn left and enter her wing of the house. Since my mother's illness progressed, my father felt it would be best for her to move to the other side of the house, so now they occupy separate wings. Probably so he can get away with fucking whatever whore it is he brings home.

Anger simmers in my gut, and I tamp it down when I

enter her bedroom. I won't let my thoughts of him become a dark spot on this visit. The nurse glances at me as I enter and gives me a nod before going to the other door across the room to give us some privacy.

I haven't even reached my mother's bedside, and she's speaking. "Andrew Bryan Marshall, you better stop right there and explain why it's been so long since you've visited. I know school and football are important, but I can't exactly come to you. I might be sick, but I'm still your momma, or have you forgotten that?"

The sting of her words makes it difficult for me to feel anything but guilt and shame. I throw myself into the chair next to her bed and reach my hand out to her, intertwining our fingers gently. "I'm sorry, Mom. I didn't mean to wait so long. It's just been nonstop at school. I haven't forgotten you. How could I possibly do that?"

I give her a genuine smile, one that I save only for her. As always, without any further prompting, she nods like she forgives me and simply moves on. "What are you studying this year? Besides girls and parties?"

I let out a snort and rearrange my grip on her fingers so I don't hinder the IV on the back of her hand.

"It's not like that. I'm the president of The Mill this year."

Her eyebrows fly up her face, and she gives me a wan smile. Her dark brown hair, threaded with gray, spreads over the pillows in soft waves as she shifts to her side. It's grown out now at least. That's a sign we're headed in the right direction. "Oh don't tell me they're still doing that wicked hunt in the woods? I never really understood the appeal."

My face heats, and I glance down at my feet for a minute. Nope. Not talking about that shit with her. I love my mom, but I have to draw the line somewhere, and I'm not about to get into a conversation about my fucked-up deviant fantasies.

"Oh, that I'm not sure about. What about you? How do you like the new medications? Do they seem to be helping?"

Her eyes drift closed for a second, and I scan the machines on the other side of her. It's a full medical suite, gifted to her by my doting father. It makes me sick every time I see it all. He's made the perfect cage for her with no exit. He doesn't give a shit if she actually recovers. In fact, it's in his best interest if she doesn't because then he can continue with his secretaries and his mistresses without any impediment from her. It's sick and fucked up, and I hate that this is her life.

The weight of it all rests heavily on my shoulders, and if I had the means to make my father disappear and make this all end, I would, but I don't. He's far too powerful, and I can't make a single move until I have better leverage on him. Leaning over, I lay my head on the bed by her hand. There's so much at stake here, but helping my mother get better is the most important thing. She's been sick for years, since before I went to college, and no matter what we try or what my father says he tries, she doesn't ever seem to be getting better.

I've asked the doctors numerous times and always get the same answer. It's some form of aggressive cancer, but even with all the treatments and experimental drugs, there's been no change. My father refuses to allow me to attend any of the appointments, and any questions I have result in no answers and a beating from my father. Even Lee hasn't been able to find my answers, and he's damn good at hacking the systems. I'm starting to think my father asks them to do paper records instead.

I've learned quickly that asking questions gets me nowhere. Shifting, I look up into her deep brown eyes, grinning back at her when she smiles at me. With her other hand, she runs her fingers through my messy hair. The wind on the bike dried it, but it's not lying flat now. Not that I care.

"Tell me all about yourself. Do you have a girlfriend yet?"

I jerk at the question but resettle. "No, Mom. I don't have a girlfriend. I don't have time to date between The Mill and football, plus my classes."

She makes a humming noise at the back of her throat that sounds a little like she's calling me out on my bullshit. *Fine.* I'll take the bait.

"There is one girl I think I'm interested in."

I don't share what I'm interested in her for because that aspect doesn't really matter. A mere mention of interest is all my mother needs to glow. She has always been a romantic at heart. It makes me wonder how she ever ended up with a man like my father. The bubble of joy from the moment bursts in an instant when the hall door creaks open, and my father walks in. I guess I didn't realize it was this late in the afternoon. I thought for sure we'd have more time together before he arrived home. His fingers work to loosen his tie, and I watch as the light on my mom's face dims. She still turns her smile to him. A fucking smile that bastard doesn't deserve.

"Andrew, we weren't expecting you today." His tone is curious like he expects me to explain why I'm here. *Obviously to see my mother, idiot.*

I stand and pat my mom's hand tenderly. "It was a last-minute drop-in."

My father crosses the space, clamping my shoulder in his hand, his grip hard and heavy. "Do let us know next time, so we can make sure we're prepared to have you stop by."

Not fucking likely, asshole.

I lean in and press a kiss on my mom's cheek. "I'll see you later, Mom. Get some rest."

She lifts her head and shakes it. "No, don't go yet. You only just got here. We have so much to catch up on."

Instead of trying to speak around the lump in my throat, I give her another smile and head to the door. My father says nothing as I exit. *Asshole.* I stand on the other side of the cracked door and watch them for a moment. I wouldn't ever put it past my father to hurt my mother, not when he hurts me as he does.

My father leans down and gently kisses her forehead. She cups his cheek and whispers, "Leon, you haven't been coming to see me either."

"I'm sorry, sweetheart. Things at the office have been hectic, and we've taken on a few more clients." His soft tone is gentle, but it's empty and vacant. He doesn't care any more about her than his fancy watch or his designer suits. Especially when he threatens me with withholding her pain meds or her nurses.

I stare at my father's joke of a mask, of the way he plays the doting husband, and it's enough to make my stomach turn. He doesn't give a shit about her or me. I can only hope for the day when the truth about the man he is and all the things he's done come to light.

I take a step away from the door when I hear my mom's soft voice. "I think Andrew's found himself a girl..."

My father responds softly, "Oh, how interesting. I'll have to ask him about that the next time I see him. He never mentioned anything to me."

All I can do is shake my head angrily. My hate for him grows every single day. Not wanting to risk running into him, I quickly head out of the house, exiting the same way I entered. One day soon, I'll have the dirt I need on him and make him pay for everything he's ever done. He thinks he's the most powerful person in Oakmount County, but he doesn't have a fucking clue about the lengths I'll go to destroy him.

CHAPTER 14
BEL

CAN ONLY STARE at this check for so long before ripping it up or cashing it. The corners are already creased from how many times I've taken it out of my bag to stare at it. It taunts me, and I don't like it. The suite door opens, and Jack walks in, her hair a mess. I'd call it a walk of shame if she didn't look so damn satisfied.

She stops short when she sees me sitting at the table. "What are you doing, Bel? It's like eleven in the morning? I thought you'd be at a tutoring session or something?"

All I do is shrug. *What the hell am I doing?*

Her eyes dart to the scrap of paper in my hand, her forehead crinkling with confusion. "What're you looking at?"

I let out a defeated sigh. "Nothing."

She gives me a disbelieving look, deposits her stuff on the counter, and marches over to the table to get a better look. I don't even bother trying to hide the check. "Nothing?! That's not nothing. That's a ten thousand dollar check, Maybel!!"

I mean, I guess when she puts it that way. I clear my throat and drop the check to the worn scarred wood of our shared dining table. "It's nothing, really. I don't even think I'm going to cash it."

She picks up the check off the table to inspect it, and her eyes meet mine over the top of it a second later. "Hmm...Mr. Marshall, huh? I suppose the one and only Drew? Unless you're seeing his dad, which I mean, to each their own."

I wrinkle my nose at her and shake my head. "Yeah, no."

"Okay, so this came from Drew. What's it for?"

I consider my response because I'm not really sure what to say. How do I explain the check without it seeming like he paid me for sex?

"I don't know. Maybe it's his way of apologizing."

"That's quite an apology. I wish someone would pay me ten grand as an apology... What did he do?"

My skin crawls, and I try to hide my cringe. I don't want to go into the details about what happened that night in the woods, even with Jack. I'm still embarrassed about it myself and my body's reaction to the things I allowed to happen.

"He didn't say, just told me to take the money. I think it's his way of saying sorry for how things went during The Hunt."

Her eyes take on a gleam, and her hand clenches as she places the check gently on the table. "Just tell me, do I need to castrate that bastard?"

With a laugh, I shake my head and stand to get some coffee. "No, it's not like that. I don't need you getting yourself put in jail because you tried to defend me against some rich prick. I've got it taken care of."

She places her hands on her hips and looks at me like she doesn't believe me. "Are you sure?"

I nod and decide to change the subject. I'm not used to having so much attention put on me. "Where are you coming from anyway?"

She shakes her head. "Ha, not falling for that. Let me shower really fast, and then you and I are going out."

I freeze, coffee cup on the way to my lips. "Going out where? I'm only in my leggings, and I don't even have a bra on. I haven't even brushed my hair or teeth."

All she offers is a shrug before disappearing into her room. A moment later, she reappears and slips into the bathroom with her bath basket in hand. "You better be ready to go when I get out." There's no questioning her, not when she's demanding I be ready. The bathroom door closes, and the creaking of the pipes fills the space as she turns on the water.

I roll my eyes and take a sip of coffee and head into my room to put a bra on. I make myself look half presentable, tossing my long blond hair up into a messy bun. Then I walk back out into the kitchen and stare down at the check sitting on the table. I hate how much I need that money, but I hate even more how I obtained it.

I'm not sure how long I stand there, war raging inside my mind, but it's long enough for Jack to finish her shower. She's fully dressed when she exits the bathroom, and her long, silky, wet hair is piled on top of her head.

"Are you ready? Because you're standing in the same spot I left you, minus your hair being on top of your head."

I grin. "Yes, I'm ready."

She beams and motions to the table. "Good. Let's go. I'm driving. Grab your wallet and that guilt check." I do as she instructs while she grabs her car keys and wallet off the counter. We make the short trek down to the parking lot, and she unlocks her car with the key fob. She drives a silver crossover made in the last five years at least, unlike my own beat-up vehicle. I sigh when we climb in as the scent of vanilla from her air freshener reaches me. My car always smells like one-hundred-year-old chicken nuggets, no matter how many times I clean it or the type of air freshener I purchase.

Jack's driving scares me a little. Okay, a lot. A couple of months ago, she hit a person in the crosswalk, and her excuse was they were moving too slow. Luckily, she ended up with only a ticket, but I'm not sure how. Since then, I've been overly cautious when she drives. Except for today. I'm too tired to really care. I don't even question where we're going or how long we're going to be gone. Since school started, we've both been incredibly busy, only having enough time to see each other in passing. She's always out, and I'm always at the library. We need this time together.

"So what's going on with you and Drew? And don't say nothing."

I flinch at the mention of his name. "He's...nothing. We don't even live on the same planet. He's a rich spoiled jock, and I'm well...me. I'm not lying, Jack. Nothing is going on between us."

She turns her head to glance at me. "Stop talking about my friend that way. I happen to find her awesome. She's smart, sexy as hell, and honestly, a complete catch."

"Stop it." I shake my head. "I'm glad you think so highly of me. If only I could see all those things as well."

"You can, silly. You just choose not to."

Jack turns right at the stoplight into the parking lot of a mini mall with numerous shops. There's a cookie place, a cell phone store, and a bank. I turn in my seat and stare at her for a moment. If she thinks I'm going to cash this check...

"What are we doing here?"

She grins. "Do what you do at banks, duh."

I let out a defeated sigh and stare out the windshield. "I can't, Jack. If I deposit it, then that will make me a whore.

Since technically he paid me for..." I can't even finish the sentence.

She grabs me by the arm and pulls me toward her, forcing me to look at her. "No. Hell, even women who sell their bodies aren't whores. Whore is a word men use to make us feel guilty about what we do with our bodies so they can control us. When men sleep with countless women, they're called playboys and clapped on the back and congratulated. Society is fucked up. Don't discount yourself or let anyone make you feel like you don't deserve that money or that accepting that check is wrong when if a man was in the same situation, his friends would brag him up."

Well, shit. That got deep.

"Now get your ass moving, or I'll personally pull you out of the seat and drag you inside. Once we're done here, I have an idea, something to cheer you up."

"Fine," I grumble and grab my stuff before climbing out of the car. We enter the bank together, Jackie following me up to the teller. I hand her the check and ask to deposit it into my account. The entire transaction takes less than ten minutes, and thankfully, the teller doesn't ask me any questions or give me any strange looks. At the end, she hands me my receipt and smiles. I take it happily, and we head back outside.

Back in the car, Jack swings through my favorite fast food place. I haven't eaten here in a month because I can never afford it. Especially with Mom...

I pause mid-thought and stare at the bright red exterior of the restaurant. We get through the drive-through line, and I can't even be mad she made me pay for it. Especially when I tip the fry carton back and let the hot salty fries scatter into my open mouth. The perfect way to cheer yourself up is with some greasy food.

After I chew, I set the box on my lap and look in the bag. "Why did we get three meals?"

She shrugs and smiles, but it doesn't take long for me to realize where we're going. My childhood home is on this side of town. We're pulling into Mom's neighborhood and then the driveway a few minutes later. Outside the house, she parks, slips off her seat belt, and grabs the food.

"Come on. You're feeling some sort of way, and I know seeing your mom always makes you feel better."

My heart swells. Jackie is the best. I don't even have a response to give her, so I climb out of the car and walk with her up to the house. At the door, my mom answers with huge bags under her eyes. She visibly straightens, a smile gracing her lips when she realizes who stands on her doorstep.

Jack holds up the bags. "We brought all the deep-fried deliciousness."

Mom chuckles, clutching her oversized black cardigan around her waist and opening the screen door. "I knew I smelled something delicious. Come in, girls."

As I pass her, she gives me a quick peck on the cheek. "What has earned me an early morning visit from two of my favorite people?"

We lay the food out on the coffee table. Mom takes up her blanket nest on the couch again with a cough. Jack and I sit cross-legged on the floor, leaning over the table with our own meals. "Jack dragged me out to see you and even made me stop in the drive-through of our favorite place."

My mother laughs. "Sounds like she really had to force you."

We all chuckle and eat in silence for a moment. A soap opera plays on the TV on low volume. Someone's brother has gotten someone's mistress pregnant from the sight of it. It's mindless, which is why she loves it, I think.

She smooths my flyaway hairs off my face back into my messy bun. "Are you okay, sweetheart? You look stressed?"

I nod around a bite of burger. "Yeah, I'm fine. I've just been super busy with clients."

It feels good to be doing something normal for once. To be spending time with her without fighting about her illness, medications, or money. I watch as she picks at her food, but she eventually takes a few healthy bites of the burger, so I don't complain, not wanting to ruin the moment. Despite everything, despite Drew being a complete asshole, he has no idea what a gift he's given me. That money will pay for some of my mom's treatment, but more so, it's given us a normal, pain-free moment to spend together.

Not discrediting that he was a complete asshole, I decide to hate him a little less. Yes, he was rough with me, but he gave me pleasure. It seems like it's always a give and take with him, and I've had so much more take than give in my life.

It's always been this way, so I'm not sure how to handle when things are more equal.

Not exactly fair since he insists I belong to him, but I can't do anything about that. Not when secretly, in the deepest, darkest parts of my being, I crave him. The deep, dark, depraved part of him speaks to that same darkness hidden inside me. I don't know how to wrap my head around it or make it make sense, but like everything else in my life, I'll learn with more practice.

We turn up the terrible soap opera and sit back to watch. My mom runs her chilly fingers through my messy bun, and I lean in, enjoying her touch. It's been so long since we shared a moment like this together. If we stayed like this forever, I'd be happy.

Like a death knell, my phone pings the moment I let my stress drift away for the first time in weeks. I don't even want to look at it, knowing that it can only be a few people, one of whom I dread hearing from. I grab my phone from the table and stare down at the screen.

It's a text from Drew, and despite my desire to delete it without looking at it, I open the message.

Unknown: So proud of you for finally depositing that check, wallflower. Wasn't that hard, was it?

An icy chill blankets my skin. First because how the hell did he get my number, and second because I knew I shouldn't have cashed the check. There's no going back now, but that doesn't matter. All Drew sees is ownership. Cashing that check was the equivalent to signing over the ownership of my body to him. He knows how much I need the money, and because of that, he's put me between a rock and a hard spot. I close out the message, choosing not to respond.

Responding wouldn't change a thing. Nothing I say matters to him. I glance over at Jackie and find she's laughing at the dumb show, right along with Mom. All I can do is smile because I can't bring myself to ruin this moment. Nor will I allow him to. Drew might think he owns me, but I'll show him real quick that I'm not the girl he wants.

CHAPTER 15
DREW

IT'S ONLY BEEN a couple of days since I've seen her, and I'm already yearning to touch her again. I keep a close eye on her activities to make sure she's not getting herself into trouble. I've been staying away so I don't draw attention to her. It's been a pain, but at least I won't have to endure this much longer with the event taking place tonight.

Tonight, I have to put on a tux and smile. Shake hands. Be the perfect son my father expects in public. It makes me sick to perform like a circus monkey, but right now, I don't have a choice. During the day, I attend classes, go to practice, play ball, rinse, and repeat.

In the evening, I head over to the family estate. Huge oaks tower over the sprawling property, and it has a fountain with an angel spitting water out of its mouth. My mother wanted that water fountain so bad, and now every time I come here, it's a reminder of her. Land on lands to show our wealth in a place of towering skyscrapers and high-rises.

Inside the house, I brush past the staff, heading to my room to find my clothes. They are already pressed and laid out neatly in a line on my bed. I take a quick shower, washing away the day's remains from my body. Like most days lately, my thoughts drift to Maybel. The puzzle I cannot seem to solve.

I'd feel guilty over my behavior from the other day, but it was merely a warning as to what's to come if she doesn't learn to stay in line. She might be different, and that appeal holds my attention most, but the fire inside her threatens to break my resolve.

It isn't long before I'm showered, dried, and dressed. I don't want to attend these events, but I have no choice, and I still have one more stop to make before the party.

Once I'm dressed with every hair in place, I pull out my phone and snap a photo. I send the picture to my little wall-flower and close my phone. Someone should appreciate this tux because I certainly don't.

Dots appear after she reads the text, but then nothing. I don't know why she keeps fighting so hard against what we have. She wants me. I know it. She knows it. Soon, I won't allow her the luxury of doubting us.

When I can't stall any longer, I make the trek across the estate to my mother's suite. All backed up to the edge of the gardens, but not close enough that people might look in and see her.

I enter to find a nurse on a chair near the window, my mother in the bed, eyes glassy, as she watches the door.

Her eyes go wide, and excitement fills her tired features as she tries to sit up. I rush over and gently help her lie back again. "No, Mom, stay put. You can admire me from there. I don't want you hurting yourself trying to sit up."

She chuckles, and her laughter soon becomes a cough. "You look so handsome, sweetie."

I can't help but grin at her old nickname for me. "Thanks. One of Dad's parties, you know how it is?" I make my voice deeper and sit in the chair by the large hospital-like bed. "It's be there or else."

Her lips thin, and she shakes her head. "I know you don't like the events, but it comes with being a Marshall, Son. As difficult as your father can be, he's still your father and wants the best for you. Someday, these events will get you a job or a connection."

My mother is lost in space. She has no idea how heinous and terrible the man she married is. I'd like to say it hasn't always been this way, but it's always been there. A monster lurking in the dark. Either my mom never saw it, or she didn't care to try. Nevertheless, I don't want to spend the few minutes I have with her arguing, so I just nod and ease back in my seat. "So what have you been up to, Mom? Prepping for a marathon? Wrestling bears?"

This makes her smile, and it's worth it to endure her unending devotion to a man who has never cared for anything but himself.

"Sure, something like that. In fact, I just reached a personal record on my sudoku app, and I'm pretty sure I've seen every episode of *Jeopardy* ever recorded."

"Whoa, watch out, world."

Another small smile that turns into a wince. I love seeing my mother, spending time with her, and talking to her, but every day that her health declines is a reminder that she might not pull through, and that opens the never healing wound in my chest. If my mother dies, then I'll have lost the last person who truly ever cared about me.

The thought stirs unspeakable emotions to life, and I push it away before I allow myself to react to them. I wish I could see my mother more often, but the truth is, seeing her like this kills me, and it's even worse that in order to see her, I have to return home and risk running into my father. I wish I had more time.

"Maybe one of these days, you can come over, and we can spend the day watching movies like we used to when you were a little boy and came home from school sick."

I smile and grab her hand. It's cold in mine, and I flinch at the temperature of it. I miss her so damn much.

"I'd love to do that, Mom."

"Good, I miss my boy." She squeezes my hand as tightly as she can.

My phone dings in my pocket with an incoming text. *Fuck.* I can't risk being late. Abruptly, I drop my mother's hand and stand to button my jacket. "Okay, Mom. I've gotta go, or I'll be late, and then I'll never hear the end of it. If I have time, I'll drop by before I head back to school tomorrow."

She gives me a frail smile, and I swear the light in her eyes dims a little more every time I see her. I remember her as the bright, vibrant woman who chased me through the gardens and held me close when I fell. Sometimes, you can have all the money in the world, but money means nothing when it comes to your health. Poor or rich, we all die the same. No matter what, I love her regardless. Until the end.

I swallow a lump in my throat, kiss my mom on the cheek, and head out of the suite toward the ballroom downstairs. Music from the band echoes down the halls. If I can hear it where I'm standing, I wouldn't be surprised if Mom could as well. The thought enrages me. How can he act as if she's already gone, buried six feet in the ground?

My jaw aches as I clench it. If I ever get married, there won't be a single person or thing that stops me from being with my dying wife.

His absence makes me wonder if he even loves her? Thinking about it depresses me further, and I force myself to think about something else, anything else. I follow the sound of music. The party is already in full swing when I enter the ballroom. Rich assholes mill around, drinking overpriced liquor, talking boardrooms and stock profiles. A ragged breath leaves my lungs.

Why the fuck am I here? This isn't my future. *But it is... This is all you have.*

I spot my father on the far side of the room. At first, I head that way, but then I freeze when he places his hand low, *very* low, on the back of a woman standing beside him.

She's wearing a backless dress, black like Dad's tux, and leaning into his side. Their bodies are nearly touching. *What the actual fuck?* I don't know why I'm surprised. It's not like my father has stayed faithful to my mother. I'm sure she knows he sleeps with other women, and knowing how soft my mother is, she probably convinces herself that it's okay since she can't fulfill her own wifely duties, but it's not. It's not fucking okay. It's disgraceful. I'm not sure why I expected him to have the decency to wait, not when he doesn't appear to have a decent bone in his body.

I march across the room and skirt the small group he's with to get in front of them, pointedly staring at his hand on this woman's ass. This plastic Barbie who will never be the woman my mother is.

My father doesn't seem to notice my mood or more likely doesn't give a fuck. The woman, however, can tell immediately, her eyes going wide the moment they meet mine.

I extend my hand out and give her the grin that's been charming the panties off the ladies for years now. "And you must be..."

She rushes to tell me. "Maddie Benson."

I lean over and kiss the back of her hand. By the looks of it, she can't be more than a few years older than me, and definitely a lot less than the twenty-five years older my father is. After the introduction, I slip my hands into my pockets and stare pointedly at my father.

"I'm here. In the flesh. Please explain what you needed my attendance for again?"

"You're here because you're a part of this family, and I told you to be here. In the future, the business will belong to you. It's important that the clients see your face and learn to trust you."

My gaze swings around the room. "Most of these assholes will be dead, in assisted living, or in jail before it's my time to take over."

My father's jaw tightens, and he straightens to his full height. Some say I take after my mother; fewer say I look like my father. Staring at him now, the hard line of his jaw and similar dark hair peppered with gray, I can't say I see it.

His eye twitches, and it's the only sign I ever get that he's truly pissed. "Excuse us for a moment. I need to have a word with my son."

The way he grits out the words... He's furious, and that's fine 'cause I'm angry too.

My father grips me by the back of the neck, his fingers digging into my pressure points. I welcome the pain and bite back an asshole retort. The woman skitters away from us and toward the bar.

Good fucking riddance.

My father leads me through the double doors that exit to an empty room. As soon as we're alone, he releases me with a shove. I've barely turned around, and he's on me. He attacks like a provoked dog, giving me no time to prepare for his assault. His fist lands against my cheek, pain radiating through my face. I remain standing, my muscles burning with rage that needs to be unleashed. I can't tell you the number of times I've thought about killing my father before, about watching every last drop of blood drip out of his body.

One day, it's going to happen. I swear it. I'll snap, and there won't be any coming back. I grit my teeth as he lands another blow, this one on the opposite side. It's easy enough to tell people the injuries are from practice or a game, so it gets swept under the rug like it's no big deal. Not that I could report my father for abuse anyway. Corruption is at its finest in this town. We own the police, doctors, and nurses.

I sigh as my father stands, straightening his suit jacket. "Are you done, or do you need more?"

I keep my face blank, not reacting either way. The spots where he hit me throb, and I know it won't take long for a bruise to form. "What do you want me to do? Just tell me so I can do it and get the fuck out of here."

"In a rush to be somewhere? Did you stop and see your mother?"

I'm not about to play games with him. "Yes," I bite out. "I always see her when I come home. I'm just glad she couldn't come tonight."

"What's that supposed to mean?"

I don't want to fight here, not here, not right now. I sigh loudly and blow air out through my nose. "Nothing. It means nothing."

His dark eyes narrow, but he doesn't pursue it. "I want you to meet my investor's daughter. Dance with her, get her a drink, charm her. Do *not* fuck her, even if she tries to climb you like a goddamn tree. Do you understand me?"

"Flirt with the investor's daughter. Got it."

He blinks and opens his mouth like he might say more, but then stops. "Yes, *flirt*. Nothing more. Get in there and charm her. Get her phone number. Make her feel wanted. *Special.*" He sneers the word special, then turns on his heels and heads back into the party.

I follow a minute later, letting him get some distance, and make a beeline straight for the bar. In minutes, I've thrown back two shots and a bourbon. Enough to take the edge off so I don't get myself beat in front of the city's elite. I think the worst part is that these assholes would watch, toast, and then walk away while my blood sprays the parquet floor.

I won't be a source of entertainment for them. It's even worse on nights like tonight, when my friend's parents are here. Lee, Sebastian, and Aries have their own parental issues to deal with, but it doesn't make them witnessing my humiliation at the hands of my father any less.

Sometimes, my friends show up, too. Those nights are a little easier to bear, as my father always tries to be on his best behavior, like he's somehow going to win them away from me.

When I've fortified myself, I approach my father who's talking to a young woman and an older man. The girl is the one, I assume, he wants me to charm. Maybe I should take her to the other room and flip up her skirt just to spite him. I'm sure it wouldn't take much effort.

I turn on the smile and ask her to dance. She watches me with enough hunger in her eyes. Just like all the bitches at school do. She wants me, and I could have her just as simply if I wanted. I lead her onto the dance floor and wait until she speaks.

"So your father says you play football."

I make a noncommittal hum as I lead us around in a slow waltz.

"And you are the current president of The Mill."

This time, I grin at her. "That's not supposed to be common knowledge. Did he tell you that too?"

She shakes her head frantically. "Oh no, it's just something I heard. I go to school in the city. They talk about you there, sometimes."

"Glad I'm a celebrity elsewhere too." I mock, but she's too dense to see it, rushing ahead.

"Oh yes, a lot of people talk about you. About how good you are at football, and well, other things too."

"What other things?" I press, curious to hear any new information about myself that I might not know.

This time she smashes her tits against me and lowers her voice. "Well, specifically The Hunt in the woods. It's a big thing since it's by invite only. The rumor is you like to chase girls down and get dirty in the mud."

I lick my lips and lean in, whispering into the shell of her ear, "What you heard is true. Unfortunately, you just missed our annual event, or I'd have extended an invitation for a beautiful creature such as yourself."

It's a flat lie. I can't stand touching this girl. She's not mine. I don't want anything to do with her when my little wallflower waits for me.

We go silent for a while, and when the song ends, I escort her to the bar for a glass of champagne. It's dry as fuck, but it's keeping me from losing my shit at the moment, so I order another round.

It's still not fucking enough.

She grabs my hand, interlacing our fingers, and pulls me to the edge of the ballroom. I allow her to drag me away, just to see what the little heiress will do.

That's all she can be, or else my father wouldn't ask me to spend time with her.

In my father's world, there is never enough money, and marrying me off to a rich brat will secure the family plenty more money. Security is the most important thing to him.

179

I'm actually surprised when she leans in, unbuckles my belt, then goes for the button of my pants. I place a gentle hand against hers when she reaches for my zipper. "I'm sorry, I'm flattered, but there are things I want to do with you that can't be accomplished here."

Her eyes go round, and she nods, oblivious to the threat lacing my tone at the statement. What a fucking idiot. I lean down and place a chaste kiss on her cheek. "I have to go. I'm sure I'll see you soon."

I feel dirty as I leave the party. Like I did something wrong when, in reality, I didn't... right?

I don't belong to anyone. Not even Bel, even if that's the only person I want to see. The only person I can be myself around. I fix my pants, fish out my cell phone, and send Bel another text. Again, she reads it but doesn't reply.

With what I've endured tonight, I'm not taking shit from her too. If she wants to push me, then she'll endure the consequences.

I slip out the back unnoticed and hop in the car, I direct the driver to take me to the dorms, and then I text Bel again.

Me: This is a warning. Answer me or suffer the consequences.

Her response is almost immediate.

Bel: Fuck off and leave me alone.

I grin at my phone before typing back a response.

Me: Did you just tell me to fuck off? Because you weren't saying that when you were practically begging me to fuck you in the library. Try again. Be nice this time.

This time, there is no response. I direct the driver to her set of dorms and hop out of the car. I strip out of my jacket and carry it over my shoulder as I stride down the sidewalk. That five hundred I paid the maintenance man to make a copy of her building key card and room key is showing its value. Playing the doting boyfriend always works, especially when a few hundred bucks sweeten the pot.

I slip inside unnoticed and down the hall, stopping once I reach her room number. Taking the doorknob into my hand, I twist it and test to see if it's locked.

All I can do is smile when I find the door locked. At least Bel's smart enough to try to keep me out.

I pull out the copied key I had made from my pocket and insert it into the door and turn it. The lock disengages, and I twist the knob, pushing the door open gently. I'm greeted by darkness and silence. I peer around the living room. There's a soft light under Bel's closed door. Her roommate's doorway is dark. She's either sleeping or gone. My bet is she's out being a normal college student. And that means my little flower is all mine for the taking.

I toss my jacket and bow tie on her table and approach her bedroom door. I throw it open; the door hits the wall with a harsh thud, and I brace my hands on either side of the frame, blocking the only exit from the room.

Frozen like a deer caught in the headlights of an oncoming vehicle, she stares at me. It only takes a moment for reality to come crashing back down, and then her gaze widens tenfold.

"What the fuck?"

"The better question is, did you really just tell me to fuck off?"

Just try to run, flower.

CHAPTER 16
BEL

IT TAKES a moment for my brain to catch up with my eyes. Is that really him standing in my doorway, looking like a snack in a fucking tuxedo, or am I imagining it? I force another breath into my lungs, hoping maybe more air will make my brain realize this isn't real and move to sit up, but the second I flinch, Drew saunters into my room like he owns it.

Nope, he is very much real. His tall frame is tense, his shoulders are tight, and his back is like a panther ready to spring.

His words hang heavy in the air. "I'll repeat myself only once, Bel. Did you tell me to fuck off?"

A boulder sits heavy in my throat, making it difficult for me to speak. I'm not feeling as brave when faced with all of him. His size, his anger, and all the things that lie between us. Big, bulky things I don't know where to stash away or hide.

I try for honesty instead. "I was busy, and I didn't want to see you."

"You don't think a simple, can't talk, I'm busy right now, would suffice? You had to push me? Today of all days. I'm pretty sure I already warned you what happens when I'm pushed too far?"

I glance around the room like I missed something. Who the fuck does he think he is? "What's today? Did I miss your birthday or something? If so, I apologize for not getting you a gift." The snark of my voice is unmissable.

"No, sassy little wallflower, it's not my birthday. But that doesn't matter. I'm not in the mood to deal with your attitude right now."

A loud, rumbling noise fills my ears. *Oh god.*

Drew's dark gaze narrows in on me. "When was the last time you ate?"

I clear my throat, gripping the blankets tightly, like they have the power to save me from this brutish man. It's like he only just noticed how much I'm using them as a form of security and reaches out, tugging the blanket from my fingers. I'm not prepared for the hard jerk he gives and nearly tumble out of bed in the process.

"Hey! That wasn't very nice!" I grumble angrily.

His eyes rake over my suddenly chilly body. An eruption of goose bumps develops when his eyes lock on my ever-rising chest and my tight nipples that press against my thin white tank. I notice the way his nostrils flare, and the hard clench of his jaw, and the tightening of the muscles in his body almost like he's trying to control himself. Like he's a prowling animal waiting to eat me alive at any moment.

Regardless of my thoughts, and with the reminder of what happened in the library between us, and how heartless and temperamental he can be, my body's reaction to him is the same. My muscles tighten, and my core becomes damp. I *swear* the temperature inside the room rises ten degrees. My physical attraction to him makes it harder for me to deny that I actually hate him, especially when my body tells me otherwise. Part of me even likes him, at least the glimpses of him he shows me that aren't hateful and cruel.

Why am I like this? Why does he have this control over me? I should despise him, but somehow, I...can't.

"I never claimed to be a nice guy, now did I? Get up!" he orders, shaking the blanket and tossing it on the folding chair braced against the end of my bed.

I swallow hard, hoping to keep my voice steady. Men like him prey on any type of weakness. "No, I don't feel good."

"Maybe because your body is trying to eat itself because it's starving. You need *food*, Bel. Get up."

It's on the tip of my tongue to scream at him, but the words come out in a rush of a whisper instead. "Why do you care if I haven't eaten?"

All I can think is that maybe I should've thought that response through better since immediately he advances, bracing himself over me, one hand on either side of my torso, his long body stretched tall over the side of the bed.

"I really hate repeating myself, flower, yet you make me repeat myself often. Don't make me have to teach you a lesson. Get the fuck up so I can make you something to eat."

I listen only because I hope that if I do it, he'll make me food and leave. Plus, I *really* don't remember the last time I ate something. When I'm busy or stuck studying, I tend to forget about normal life functions. That or I skip meals to try to save the money for Mom. Not that I'd ever tell Mom that. *Or* Drew.

He stalks out to the kitchen, all coiled tension and rage, and I follow, still in my underwear. Why bother when he's seen me completely naked, anyway? I throw myself into a chair at the table, my knees shaky and weak, my head spinning. Okay, maybe I waited too long to eat. Like the caveman he is, he opens the cabinets, rummaging through them before going back to the beginning to tug out a loaf of bread, peanut butter, and strawberry jelly.

It's on the tip of my tongue to warn him that those belong to my roommate, but she dragged him into my life, so the least she can do is sacrifice a sandwich or two. I cautiously watch him as he lays the bread out in a row and spreads peanut butter and jelly on alternating pieces. Then he carefully folds each sandwich together.

It's only now that I really take in his attire, the dress pants, dress shirt, the way his hair is styled so that little bit in the front won't fall down into his face like it usually does. Curiosity blooms in my mind, and I can't stop myself from asking.

"Where did you come from?"

He doesn't answer for so long that I wonder if he even heard me. But he finally speaks when he places a plate with a sandwich, cut diagonal so it makes two triangles, in front of me and joins me at the table.

"I had to attend one of my father's parties tonight. I was texting you on the way back when you decided to get sassy."

His own sandwich isn't cut, and it's slapped together in a messy mash, two stacked up together. Even looking at the way he makes a sandwich tells me that he cares more about others than he does about himself. Maybe Drew isn't as heartless as I thought. Maybe he just needs someone to make him care, to show him what compassion and love is?

"Your father? You've never mentioned him before."

He shakes his head. "And I'm not mentioning him now either."

I stare down at the sandwich, and he lets out a loud sigh, then slides his chair next to me. As if I'm a child who can't feed themselves, he proceeds to hold one side of the sandwich up to my mouth. "Eat."

I can feel the heat from his body radiating into mine. The

hefty smell of his peppermint and teakwood cologne makes it hard for me to focus.

"Maybel, eat the damn sandwich," he growls, and the vibration of his voice echoes through me. Every fiber inside me wants to fight him, to push his hand away or tell him I can fucking feed myself, but I know the power of those hands, and with the tense mood he's in, I wouldn't put it past him to hold me down and force-feed me.

Leaning forward, I wrap my lips around the bread and sink my teeth into it, taking a big bite. He nods in approval, his eyes darkening as he watches me chew.

"I can feed myself," I remind him.

He shrugs one broad shoulder up. "Are you sure? If I left it up to you, you'd still be sitting in your bedroom, listening to your stomach growling. So now I'm feeding you. More." I take another bite, and he continues to feed me, a little at a time, until the entire sandwich is gone and my belly is full.

Definitely haven't been eating enough.

He snags his own sandwich off the plate and eats almost half of it in one bite. I don't know why, but I stupidly smile at him. Maybe because, for the first time ever, our interaction isn't sexual or violent. It's just simple and normal. Either way, he returns the smile, and there isn't any denying how handsome of a man he is. If only he smiled all the time.

"No need to rush through eating. The other football players aren't going to steal your food," I joke.

He gives me a puzzled look. "And here I thought you'd send me out the door the moment I arrived, but you haven't even thrown something at me yet."

"On second thought, hurry the hell up." A bubble of laughter escapes me, and Drew gives me another megawatt smile that somehow makes me feel like I'm seeing the real him. The tension between us seems to ease, and the heavy feeling on my chest lifts. If only every interaction between us went like this.

Maybe then I could picture us being...

My phone buzzes in the next room, and then there's a thud, the sound of it hitting the floor after it falls off the nightstand. That damn thing is always going off. Between clients texting me and conversations with my mom, it's not surprising.

I look at Drew, and something close to suspicion flickers in his eyes as he glances toward my bedroom. "Who is texting you this late?"

"Well, I mean, you were texting me before. It's not abnormal to receive texts from clients or even my mother at this time of night."

He jerks his chin up, shoves the rest of his sandwich into his mouth, then turns toward my room. I already know what he's going to do. Call it instinct or just the knowledge of starting to understand his mannerisms, but I race after him, trying to get to the phone before he does. He makes it into the room first and snatches it off the floor in his big bear paw.

By the time I reach him, he's thumbing through the messages and using his other hand to fend me off. Despite his six-three height and broad shoulders, the guy is fast as hell. I make a mental note to put a damn passcode on my phone.

"Look. I know you think you *own* me and everything, but my phone is *not* your property." I huff.

Ignoring my statement altogether as he continues thumbing through the messages, he growls, "Who the fuck is Stewart?" His dark gaze penetrates, daring me to lie to him. "Don't tell me this is one of your tutoring clients."

I sputter. "Of course it is. Who else would it be?"

"I mean, you tell me? What do you call a text this late and

him using a nickname to address you? I know you're smart, Bel. Surely, you can see what I'm seeing."

I roll my eyes because this entire conversation is draining and stupid. "Apparently, I can't. We're just friends. He's probably up late studying, same as I usually am." I grab for my phone again, but his hand moves, resting gently against my collarbone, almost cupping my neck.

"Just friends? Huh? Did you fuck him?"

The words are a literal slap to my face. I sputter and try to step away, but he closes his hand, his fingers coming up around my neck, encasing my throat in a collar of warmth.

"Did. You. Fuck. Him?" he asks again, each word a jab at my heavy beating heart.

I gulp, feeling his hand press tighter as I do. How could he even question that?

"No. Of course I didn't. That night with you... It was my first time." The one I still can't talk about, hell, even think about. "You know I didn't...I hadn't... been with anyone else."

The feral, animalistic rage in his eyes drains away as reality rushes back to the surface. His grip loosens only slightly as he remembers, weighing my words.

"You're right." I wait for something more: *an I'm sorry for being an asshole, Bel. I'm sorry for jumping to conclusions, Bel.* Even an...*I don't know what I'm talking about, Bel.* But I get none of those things. He only stares at me, his eyes skimming down to my breasts where my nipples are peaked from the cold and his touch.

The electrifying current rages between us, making the air tight and hot, crushing around us. What is this, and why do I only feel it with him here when he touches me?

"Why are you like this?" I whisper, afraid that raising my voice will spark some raging fire into existence.

His fingers roll against my skin like he's testing how each one feels wrapped around my neck. "What do you mean?"

"Why are you so..." Words fail me because I don't have any idea of what I'm trying to say. I've never met anyone like him. Like this. The things he makes me feel...

He lowers his head and presses his forehead against mine. A shadow of what appears to be understanding casts upon his face. "I don't know. I don't fucking know."

The answer feels too honest and open for the man I've slowly been getting to know.

Since he's in an honest mood, I try my usual question. "What do you want from me Drew? Please just tell me."

"Bel...wallflower...come here."

He loosens his grasp on my neck, sliding his hand down my spine, tucking me tight against his chest. I lay my cheek against him, letting his warmth fill me. This shouldn't feel so damn *good*. I should put distance between us and stay away, but right now, I don't have the energy, mentally or physically. And there's no denying that he makes me feel wanted and desired.

When he pulls away, I almost stagger, and he lowers me back to sit on the bed. Then he crouches in front of me, his tailored pants tight over his thick thighs. My face heats because I'm turned on right now, staring at his fucking thighs.

"What's that look, Bel?"

I swallow. "Nothing." Knowing he won't buy it, I scan his face, now that I can see it, so close to mine. I spot the newly forming bruise on his cheek, the swollen skin. Did someone hit him? Or did he get that at football practice?

Gently, I reach for him and brush my finger across the tender flesh. "What's this?"

There's an instant change in him. His body goes rigid, and he shoots to stand, towering over me, his eyes downcast on his lowly subject. The behavior change gives me whiplash, and I don't know if I should cuss him out or beg him to tell me the truth.

"It's none of your fucking business, that's what it is. Go to bed. I'll see you soon." I stand, but he grabs my wrist, his fingers pressing into the sensitive flesh there. Then as if to bring his point home, he squeezes as if warning me. "Remember what happened the last time you put your nose where it wasn't needed?"

Yeah, I came face-to-face with a new kind of crazy.

Still, regardless of how he treats me or how hot and cold he gets, a tiny piece of my heart aches for him. It wouldn't surprise me if someone is hurting him because his attitude and behaviors coincide with that possibility. Still, a part of me thinks I can reach the darkness inside him and shed light on it. It's a mistake, but one I willingly make. With my other hand, I grab his hand, ignoring the pain radiating up my arm.

"I'm not the enemy, Drew, no matter how many times you try to make me or tell yourself that I am. I was asking because that's what good people do. They step in and try to help if they see something bad happening."

Drew's features harden to stone. "I don't want your pity, nor do I need it. I won't bore you with my problems, and even if I did tell you what's going on, there would be nothing you could do. Believe it or not, you can't save everyone."

"I'm not trying to save you. I'm just trying to help in whatever way I can."

"And you are, by letting me fuck you every single way I want without complaint."

My heart sinks into my stomach, and I drop my hand, the connection between us fading. He releases my wrist, and I hold it to my chest, rubbing the spot he just held. Those smoldering eyes of his follow my movements, and I swear I see a twinge of guilt there.

Is he sorry for hurting me? Maybe, but he doesn't seem like he wants to apologize.

I think back to that saying my mother once told me when I was being bullied at school because of my glasses. *Hurt people hurt people?* That seems closer to the truth here.

"Well, I guess I'm of no service today then." I take a step back. "There will be no use of my body without complaint."

"It wouldn't take much to get you ready and willing. Plus, your mouth would be too occupied to air your complaints." The way he drags his gaze over my body's length is calculating and sinister.

My heart hammers against my rib cage, and I can feel us heading toward an impasse. I won't be a doormat for him to step on. If he doesn't want to talk, fine, but that doesn't mean I have to put out either.

"I think you should leave," I demand.

"Oh really? I could always make you... a little manipulation... It's done the trick before."

"Keep telling yourself that, but I know more than anything, my fear of you is the driving force of your pleasure. Except you don't want me to be so afraid of you that you have to force me to do anything. You want real fear, but you don't want to break me, and forcing me to have sex with you would break me, so the choice is yours."

His full lip curls with disgust, and I watch his meaty paw clench and unclench. Anger simmers just beneath the surface. He knows I'm right yet doesn't want to admit it.

"Until next time, then," he snarls and turns on the heels of his shiny dress shoes, walking to the door. He opens it and slams it shut behind him. I rush forward and click the lock into place. *How did he get in?* It never occurred to me until this very moment to question how he got in. I was sure I had locked the door, but I don't know now. I slowly walk back-ward until my legs meet the table's edge, and I sink my hips against it.

All over again, I'm left spinning in the wake of his turbu-lence and have to ask myself what the hell am I doing trying to defeat a man like him? He's a monster, a playboy bent on using and abusing. I can't be the person to fix him, yet I can't be the person to watch him drown either. I don't know what to fucking do.

CHAPTER 17
DREW

T'S OFFICIAL. I've found a new hobby. Though it might not come as a surprise. Watching Maybel. She is stunning. I could sit here in the library and stare at her all day. I've been here for an hour, alone, but any minute now, she'll spot me, glare, and then pretend to ignore me until I leave or talk to her. She's a creature of habit, after all.

Guilt eats away at me slowly. I'm an asshole for treating her like I did the other day. It's a habit that's impossible to break with my father breathing down my back. I shouldn't have snapped at her, but she needs to learn quickly that I won't discuss my family with her. If being cruel is the only way to impart that lesson, so be it. I can't have her getting too close or seeing beneath the surface. Everyone prefers the person you portray. They never really care to get to know the person beneath. No one wants to see the broken, dark pieces of your soul. They only want to see the good, the image you portray to the world. The moment you show them the real you, they become scared or disgusted.

I watch the basketball player dickhead sitting beside her

the one she's tutored *twice* this week already, and I note his every twitch. If he makes even one inappropriate move toward Bel, I'll be ripping him apart with my bare hands. I choose to ignore the territorial possessiveness I feel for her.

She's tutored several basketball team members, but I haven't seen a single member of the football team with her since I started watching her. Either we are just smarter or the team is steering clear for my sake. Probably the latter. The basketball player's arm goes to the back of her chair. I clench my hand into a tight fist. I'm about two seconds away from jumping out of my chair when a tiny little brunette cuts into my line of sight. Immediately, I'm pissed. She's blocking my view of Bel.

She leans down, pressing her tits together so it's all I see on the way to her face. "Can I help you?"

Her grin is lecherous, and I know exactly what she wants. She's wearing so much makeup I can't even tell the true shade of her skin, unlike Bel, who doesn't seem to wear much makeup at all, letting me see my marks all over her creamy flesh.

I sit forward, a hard-on hitting me fast at the thought of Bel's bare hips in my hands. The girl still standing here strangling me with her perfume glances at my twitch and grins like she's the cause for it.

"Did you need something?" I prompt again.

I lean to the side to look past this girl and keep my eyes on Bel. Shockingly, I find hers locked on my little tableau with her gaze narrowed. Even if it finally gets a reaction out of my little wallflower, I don't want to encourage the little groupies. As strange as it is for me to say it, I only want one woman right now.

Thankfully, as I'm about to tell her to fuck off, a shadow cuts across the table, and I glance up to find Sebastian. He presses his knuckle to the wood, and the little girl takes an instinctive step back. Clearly, she doesn't need to be told to leave. I'm sure it has nothing to do with the dark halo of energy surrounding us. The girl flees without another word, and he takes the seat across from me, focusing his dark eyes on something over my shoulder, staring down anyone who might be watching us now.

"What's up?"

He lets out a long sigh. "I'm sure I don't have to tell you, but it pisses me off when I have to chase you down. I text you, no response. Check your room, empty. It's like you've vanished, but for some reason, I thought to check the library since your latest obsession basically lives here, and would you look at that, found ya."

"Okay, so that doesn't explain why you're here?" I stare at him blankly.

He rolls his eyes and grits his teeth, impatience dripping off him. "I'm here because you haven't signed up for one of the fucking volunteer slots for the carnival. The charity carnival we are obligated to put on by the school. The one you fucking asked me to run this year. Ringing any bells?"

We stare at each other a moment, and I lean in enough so I can see Bel over his shoulder. Basketball boy still has his arm on the back of her chair, but his hand isn't touching her, so I guess I'll let it slide for now. As I anticipated, he notices my movement and glances back over his shoulder. There's no way he doesn't notice her, and it makes me want to rip his eyes out of his head and remove the memory of her from his mind.

It's completely unhinged and wrong, but I don't want anyone else to look at or touch her. *Only me.* Turning back around, he gives me a scowl.

"Don't start," I say. "I already got a lecture from Lee, so I don't want to hear it from you too. Who I'm fucking has nothing to do with any of you."

"Your fath—"

I cut him off before he can finish. "No. Don't ever fucking start a sentence with *your father* to me again. What he does has nothing to do with me. I make sure he has what he wants, and that's all I need to worry about. None of you assholes need to have anything to say about it."

He leans in, his voice an urgent whisper. "No, you're right. Your father is your business, but as your friends, we have a right to worry about you. We don't want him to pull you out of school, and we sure as hell don't want you to show up with a busted lip and a fucked-up eye again. Your actions have a direct impact on all of us."

I pull back, swallow hard, but keep my face neutral. "That wasn't..."

"Bullshit!" His voice rings out across the nearly silent room, and everyone in the area turns to look at us. I can lie to myself and everyone else at this school, but I can't lie to my three best friends. They've been with me through it all. That doesn't mean I have to be okay with the way he's calling me out, though. We continue glaring at each other, the tension strung tight enough to choke, until everyone returns to their business, talking and whispering loud enough we can resume... no, *finish* our conversation.

"The carnival," I prompt, making it clear we aren't fucking talking about this anymore.

My friends have earned the right to be a part of my life, but that doesn't give them the right to question my need to have a life outside what my father requires of me. Yes, everyone wants to keep Dad fucking happy, but I'm not willing to sacrifice my own life to make that happen. At least not anymore.

Sebastian's jaw tightens, and he stares at me, his eyes blazing. I can see from the slight twitch in his arm and the curling of his hand into a fist that he wants to swing on me. It wouldn't be the first or last time. Now that I think about it, we're overdue for a fight.

"You're a real asshole, you know that? I don't have time to sit here and have a staring contest with you all day, not when I have to finish this fundraiser you saddled me with. Don't you have your own shit to do? And what the fuck is with the girl? She was a chase in the woods, a good lay is what you told us, so why are you so far up her ass all of a sudden?"

Feeling a bit like we're on safer ground, I sink in the chair and let out a long, breathy sigh of my own. "Yes, she was a chase through the fucking woods, but there's something about her. Something that draws me in, something I'm keeping."

"Keeping...like exclusively?" His face twists up in a scowl, incomprehension etched into his high cheekbones.

I don't answer the question. I don't want him to know how much interest I really have in Bel because like me, he gets his own fixation from time to time. "I haven't decided yet. Now, the carnival? Just sign me up for something, and let me know where to be and at what time. We have practice before, so make sure I have enough time to get cleaned up."

I shift enough to catch a glimpse of Bel over his shoulder again, and I notice that her eyes keep tracking over to us every couple of minutes. Like Sebastian's outburst has her more on edge than the girl who came over to flirt with me. Not sure how I feel about that.

Sebastian makes a frustrated noise deep in his throat and shoves out of the chair to stand. "Watch for a text from me, asshole. If I have to hunt you down like a kid again, it won't be to give you a date and time. It'll be to kick your ass." I give him a cheeky grin and flip him the bird.

He shakes his head and turns, walking away. I keep my eyes trained on his back as he crosses the library. My heart clenches in my chest, sinking low into my stomach when he stops at Bel's table. I shove out of my seat and pretend to stand nonchalantly. The basketball player and Bel glance up at him for a moment. I see Sebastian speaking, and what he says makes Bel's nose wrinkle in disapproval.

What the hell is he up to?

Curiosity wins out, and I stalk over to them and shoulder up to Sebastian. He's a few inches shorter than me, but his shoulders are wider and broader. Still, he doesn't move an inch as I bump into him, subtly telling him to get the fuck out of here. In all the times we've fought, it's never been over a girl. Not that there's a fight to be had. *Maybel is mine.* Still, his interest in what I'm doing with her, and if we're exclusive makes me question his loyalty and our friendship.

Turning my back to Bel, I grab him by the arm and lean in. "What the fuck are you doing?"

He doesn't even glance at me. "Oh, I was just telling Bel what a cute couple they would make. What do you think, Drew? I suggested that Parker here buy some tickets for the carnival and take his little tutor on a date. She's been working so hard on his behalf, after all." He bats his long lashes in a mockery of innocence. "Or I guess, if I get planning wrapped up, I could take her."

Every cell in my body vibrates. No one is taking her anywhere, and fuck Sebastian for even suggesting it. My teeth gnash together as I hiss at him. "Back the fuck off."

"No can do. I think I like this look on you," Sebastian says, finally looking at me, and the challenge in his eyes ignites a raging inferno in my gut. Again, he doesn't budge.

"Excuse us," I growl.

Of all my friends, Sebastian might be the most like me. The most stubborn, the most hardheaded. A hard fucking head I'm about to slam into a table. I cast a warning look at Bel over my shoulder that she better read as *don't you fucking dare* and haul Sebastian back by the arm. He doesn't even try to stop me. If anything, I'd bet there is a grin on his stupid-ass face. I walk through the double doors ahead, and once we're outside greeted by the cool fall air, I shove him hard enough that he stumbles back a step. He easily catches himself and comes to stand face-to-face with me.

"What the fuck?"

He shrugs, all nonchalant, but I can see a war waging in his eyes. He wants blood, he wants to hurt me, but all he's going to get is my foot up his ass. "I don't get into your business...you don't get into mine, remember."

"Fuck off, Sebastian." I shake my head, and just as I expect, he rushes forward and shoves me back, his usual blank face twisting into a mask of fury.

"Oh, is that right? You don't get into my business, huh? What about when my grandpa tried to sell me off to the highest bidder among his rich friends for connections? You didn't get in the middle of that?"

Suddenly, what Bel said the other day sinks in and makes more sense than I want to admit. *"I'm not trying to save you. I'm just trying to help in whatever way I can."* I failed to ask her if she understood what helping me meant because I knew more than anyone she wasn't capable of hearing about my life problems.

"There's a difference. I try to help you, you dick! I stepped in to make sure he wouldn't try that shit again. I wasn't sabotaging you."

It's like my words have no effect on him. "Okay, and what

about Lee...when his dad beat the shit out of him for flirting with a man at the last alumni party, you didn't step into the middle of that either, did you?"

The rage is still burning in my gut, and I clench a fist full of his shirt, hauling him close. "Again, I was *fucking* helping."

"Helping. Hmm, and you think any of us want to see what your father will do to you if he sees you getting attached to some poor little fucking scholarship girl? Maybe you have memory loss from all the football hits to the head, but need I remind you how much hell he's made your life? We all know what he will do. It's not my fault that I'm the only one brave enough to face you about it. Don't let her become a casualty in a war she didn't sign up for."

If I didn't know better, I'd think Sebastian is growing a heart because that's the nicest thing he's ever said about anyone. We stare at each other, so close I can smell the toothpaste on his breath. With a growl, I shove him back and turn around, taking a couple of steps back so I don't look at him. So I don't hit him because I really want to fucking hit him.

"You know I'm right, and I'm sorry if it pisses you off, but she doesn't deserve that. No one deserves that."

"She's none of your concern. You've never shown interest in what happens to any of the other girls I fuck, so don't pretend to care now." I toss the response over my shoulder. Maybel is my problem. Mine. All. Fucking. Mine. I start my walk back into the library, ignoring his mere existence.

"She's different," he yells once I reach the doors, and I pause for a millisecond before tugging them open and stomping inside.

Stalking back to where I was sitting earlier, I collapse into one of the chairs, directing my attention to Bel. The territorial rage and desire refuse to go away. I want to claim her right here, mark her skin, and tell everyone she belongs to me, but

I can't. *I won't.* Her client is gone now, but I narrow my eyes since a new guy sits beside her, and worse yet, he's wearing my fucking team colors.

I stand and march over, bracing my hands on the desk and leaning forward. His hand is on the back of her chair, his thumb brushing the collar of her shirt like he's waiting to touch her bare skin. I don't think. I simply react.

"Reb, I suggest, if you want to keep all your limbs for the next game, you take your hands off my girlfriend."

A moment of stunned silence passes between the three of us. Then Reb, one of my defensemen, stands, his hands up in a form of surrender. "This is your girlfriend, man? I thought...well... We all know you don't date. You barely ever even see the same girl twice. I didn't know, I promise." He's panicking. I can tell by the way his eyes dart between Bel and me. The way beads of sweat form against his hairline. That's the only thing keeping me from ripping his damn idiot head off.

"Get the fuck out of here."

He skitters between the chairs, and I shift my gaze to Bel, who sits with her mouth hanging open. She looks as shocked as I feel.

"Did you just call me your girlfriend?" There's something in her blue eyes, something softer than before. I don't like it. It makes me think she's starting to like me, fall for me, and if she does, I'll have a bigger problem on my hands.

I give her a sneer. "Don't read too much into it. I just want to make sure he knows not to touch what's mine. Apparently, people are hard of hearing and dumber than I thought. I guess a label is needed, even if it's fake."

"Drew, are you okay? What's going on?" Her concerned expression and whispering voice annoy me. I shake my head; anger and jealousy fuel me at the moment, and it's not a good combination. In fact, it's dangerous as hell, and if I take it out on Bel, it will only make it harder for me to get her to do what I want.

"Don't worry about me. Worry about yourself and the repercussions if you choose to let another man touch you. I'm not lying when I say I'll kill someone. I'm past rational thinking. Don't make me do it. You're a good person, and I'd hate to put that on your conscience." She opens her mouth to speak, but I don't give her the chance. I give her one last long look and leave the library, heading back out into the cold. I need to put some distance between us.

Thankfully, Sebastian is gone, and I stalk in the direction of The Mill. As I'm walking, pushing my pace faster, feeling the burn in my muscles and using it to calm down, my phone buzzes to life in my pocket.

I jerk it out and squeeze my hand tight around the device, willing my strength to crush it into a million tiny pieces. It rings again, and I answer regretfully. "Hello?"

My father's deep voice fills my ears. "The carnival is coming up. Is everything planned?"

I keep walking, letting my breath puff out into the air. "Yes, everything is ready. Including the office in the basement of The Mill where you can conduct your meeting. It's stocked as requested. Everything is in order."

"Good." My father hums in approval. I hear some papers shuffling, and then he speaks again, "Tell me your thoughts about the young woman you met at the last party?"

Anxious knots tighten in my belly. I know what he wants to hear, but I can't give it to him right now, not with so much anger simmering in my blood. "She's just a girl."

"Sure, yes, but an important connection, possibly."

My patience and will to play nice snaps. "What do you want me to say, Dad? Is she my type? No. She's some rich man's daughter looking for a knight in shining armor, and I'm not that guy. You know it, and I know it too. So please tell me what you want me to say to end this conversation, and I'll say it. Better yet, fill in the blanks and pretend I said what you want me to say and go with that."

"I'm very close to ending you and taking it all away. Is that what you want? Do you want your mom to suffer? Do you want to be out on the streets? I'll take it all, football, your friends, the money. Don't think otherwise, because I will. I don't make idle threats, Drew. I just do it. Oh, and by the way, if I hear you're seeing that little white trash whore again, I'll make sure there's nothing left of her for you to see."

I grit my teeth, squeezing the phone as I rush up the front steps of the Mill. No matter how many times I walk through that old wooden door under the stained glass, it always makes me look. Once inside, the heat hits me quickly, and I walk straight into the kitchen to get some water or maybe something stronger. "I'm trying to give you what you want. She was a girl, *Father*, I don't know her. I don't care about her. I danced with her because you told me to. That's it. Besides, she seems like she'd be a lousy lay anyway."

My father makes a noise like a snort. "Well, that's what mistresses are for, Son."

I tense and gulp, forcing myself not to erupt at the mention of a mistress, not to confront him or call him out on how he treats my mother.

"Sure," I reply vaguely. "Anything else you need from me? All arrangements are in order, and the house will be empty that night."

He sighs. "No. I'll see you for the next event, and you better be far more fucking excited about the prospect of that girl. She's the future of our legacy. I expect you to pay attention to her."

I swallow thickly. "Fine. I'll see you then."

He hangs up without another word, and I brace my hands on the kitchen counter. I don't know what's happening. I'm playing a game of blind chess, and every piece I move, costs me another. All I can think now is what the fuck will be his next move, and can I make my own before he does?

'M STARING out the foggy glass of my windshield at a crack that runs up the middle from the hood to the top. It cracked this morning when I turned the heat on in the car. It doesn't matter. Nothing really matters at the moment. The world could implode around me, and all I'd do is shrug my shoulders. Not when I'm staring down at the text from my mom showing the test results the doctor sent her.

She's really sick. *Dying.*

It shouldn't exactly be a surprise, not by how hard things have been for her lately, but it's the confirmation from the doctor that's brought things so into focus I can't see beyond it. My mother is dying. She's fucking dying. I'm angry, so angry with God, my own mother for taking so long to go to the doctor, precious time we could've had to catch this earlier, and my father for abandoning us.

A large red cart rolls by, a hunky football player pushing it easily toward the football field they've turned into a makeshift carnival. Everyone is stupidly excited about it when it's just another fundraiser for the rich. I'm not really angry about the carnival, more the things taking place in my life.

My biggest priority is helping my mom and getting her the treatments she needs. I watch the cart wheel by, my gaze falling on the library ahead. The library is across the parking lot, a new tutoring student probably already waiting inside. I need to focus on that, put together a plan, and get the money going steady from my clients so I can help take care of my mother.

My phone buzzes in the cup holder near my thigh. I stare down at my mom's picture flashing on the screen. *Shit.* She likely wants to know what I think. I sniff hard to clear my sinuses and then swipe my fingers across my cheeks. If she thinks I've been crying, this will turn into her focusing on me when it needs to be the other way around.

I force out a long exhale and hit the green button. "Hey, Mom. I was just going to call you. I have a new tutor client I have to meet soon, but I wanted to talk about your test results."

There's some static, and then my mom's voice cuts through, reedy and thin. "Oh baby, I won't keep you. I just wanted to check on you, make sure you were okay."

There's a long pause where I guess neither of us knows what to say. The results are...the results. It feels like there's nothing I can do, and my mother just won't accept we need to be doing everything we can to treat her. It's like she's made up her mind. Every time I bring it up, she tells me the money should go toward my education, not her medical bills. Medical bills that keep growing with every test and every prescription to keep things at bay.

It's why I give her the answer she wants, so I can get off the phone faster. If only so she doesn't have to listen to me break down again. "I'm fine, really. I'm more concerned about you. How are you handling the results?"

What I don't say is how much I don't want to think

about it for five minutes. I want things to be normal, and every second that ticks closer to her death feels further and further from normal. In a world where everything is at your fingertips and you can have whatever you want when you want it, the only thing that I want or need is for my mother to survive this. She's all I have, the only thing that matters. Yet the diagnosis on that paper is final. The chances of beating this are slim to none. We can elongate her length of time on earth, but she will succumb to the cancer eventually.

"I'm fine, honey. It's not like we didn't know this is where it was headed, right?"

I bite my lip to keep from spilling out my true thoughts. I'm not in any mental position for a fight right now. "No, but I didn't anticipate this. Do you have a timeframe on when you want to start the recommended treatments?" I've thought about it for a couple of days now, and I have an idea. Getting my mother to agree to it will take some convincing. "I can postpone school for a year and get a full-time job. They'll allow me to come back."

"No!" Her sharp tone is more full of life than I've heard in months. "I won't have you giving up on your education for me. Promise me that you will stay in school and not make any irrational decisions because of this."

"That's not a promise I can make to you. You're all I have. If I lose you..." I can't stop my voice from cracking. Tears fill my eyes, and I blink them back as much as I can. I really do not want to start crying again.

"Oh sweetheart, we will get through this together. I promise you will never be alone."

It's a promise she can't keep and one I ignore altogether. Eventually, I will be alone, and if I can't get her the medication and treatment she needs, that time will be sooner. She lapses into a coughing fit that makes me squeeze my phone. I want to take her pain away, take her illness from her.

"We can finish discussing this when I come see you tonight. I have to get into the library and get ready for my next client, but I love you. If you need anything, please text me."

"Just a minute... I...there's something else I need to talk to you about. Something very important, honey."

Immediately, I panic, afraid there is more news she hasn't shared with me. What if she needs my help? Or she can't make it to the bathroom again. The possible what-ifs are endless. "Okay, what's up? Do you need me now? I can cancel if you do. It's really okay."

She sniffles into the phone and whispers my name. "Maybel. Just...get to your appointment, and we can discuss it later. I need to go lie down for a bit."

I nod, then shake my head. "It's really not a big deal. I can be there in ten minutes or less."

"No! Stay there and do your work. Even if I'm sick, I'm still your mother, and that means you have to listen to me."

I don't bother continuing the argument, not when I know I've already lost. "Okay. Get some rest. Text if you need anything. I love you, Mom."

"Love you too, sweetie."

I hang up and drop my head back against the headrest. The bulk of my bun bounces off, and I groan loudly, scrubbing my hands down my face. "FFFFUUUUCCCCKKKK!"

The outburst doesn't make me feel any better, and I'm not the type to dwell on something I can't change. I'd rather put my frustrations into my work where I can see progress, so I grab my bag from the passenger seat and climb out of the car and into the chilly morning air.

A short jog later and I'm inside the library. The smell of

books and coffee fills my nostrils. *Home.* This place is the equivalent of that. The large study area is mostly vacant, but I still scan the expansive space to see if my client is here—or worse, Drew.

No Drew, but also no client yet either. I'm relieved as I lug my bulking bag up onto a chair and sit at my usual study cubicle. The basketball player I'm meeting with will find me when he arrives. He paid in advance so if he sleeps through the session, I can't say I'll care too much. I dig through my bag and rip out a math textbook. Once I have my notebook, the text, and my water bottle arranged on the desk in front of me, I scan the room again.

Nothing crazy, a few people are studying early; there is no reason to feel like my nerves will slither out of my body. My last encounter in the library was strange and a bit disconcerting. Drew's friends creep me out. Not as badly as he messes with my head, but all of them are intense, and Sebastian looks at me like he wants to bite my head off and see what's inside. To him, I'm simply prey, even if he's not the one who hunted me down.

Out of nowhere, a hand lands on my shoulder. I jolt and spin around, ready for a fight, but talk myself off the ledge when I realize it's just my client.

"Ah, Stewart, sorry, I was distracted."

He throws his super-tall body down in the chair beside me. I break out into conversation immediately. "How are you feeling after that last test? I know we reviewed, so I want to see how you think you did? Did you get the results you wanted?"

He shrugs. "I passed. That's good enough for me."

"Nothing you want to review again or go over?"

With another shrug, he scoots closer, his knee bumping against mine. It could be by pure accident, or it could be something else. I do my best not to look too deeply into it. I can feel my cheeks heat, and I slam my legs to the other side of the chair under the desk. "Okay well, you have another essay coming up. Have you decided what you want to write about?"

I'm about to grab another textbook when he pulls out a large bottle with some type of green liquid in it. Looks like a smoothie or protein shake.

"I was thinking something about the Civil War."

Well. I blink. "I mean...if you were in an American history class, that might work, but not so much for European history." I smile to try to soften the critique.

He shrugs, then flashes me a smile. His teeth are straight and white in his perfectly tanned face. "I have a question, and it's a bit off subject, so I apologize, but why do you do this, Bel? You're like at the top of the class, right? Tutoring people can't be fun. What do you get out of this?"

"Learning is always fun, and I enjoy it. Plus, it helps me pay for school, and I consider that a win. If you have any friends who need help, send them my way. I still have some openings."

He nods, accepting my response. "What about Napoleon?"

I latch onto that. "Perfect, a central figure in European history. Let's do it."

We settle into a discussion about the Napoleonic Wars, and I'm surprised he's at least showing an interest. The last time we reviewed material, it was like pulling teeth to get him to talk. I set him up to outline, and I read over some of the textbook while he works. The silence buffers the world all around me, making it easier to think. To some, silence is terrifying, but that's because they fail to enjoy the peace and tranquility that comes with it. To be comfortable in complete silence would mean you would be comfortable facing all your demons, and acknowledging yourself and the choices you make. In silence, you're incapable of hiding from your own true self. Which is why some of the grief and despair over my mother shifts away. I know it'll return eventually as it always does, but for now, I allow myself to sink deep into the quiet.

Stewart reads quietly, and I zone out after I finish reading the sections on Napoleon twice over. Once he finishes the short outline, he slides the paper over to me for review. I smile, accepting the paper. His handwriting is little more than a scribble, but I'm pretty adept at reading chicken scratch by now. A lot of the jocks don't really focus their attention on penmanship.

I skim the page and nod in approval. "This is a great start."

Leaning in, he subtly slides his arm over the back of my chair. "What about this part?" He points at the bottom section. I nod again, moving my shoulder to put a little distance between us. He smells clean like soap, but I don't want him touching me. Not only because at any moment I know Drew will pop up and bare his claws but also because I'm not really attracted to him.

"It's good. This should give you a well-reasoned essay. Once you finish, you can send it to me for review."

"I'll wait until tomorrow to work on this since I have a shift at the carnival when it opens this evening. Are you going, Bel?"

It takes a moment for me to process his question. "Oh yeah, the carnival. I think I'm going to skip it this year. I want to stay home and spend some time on booking some more clients, prep for next week, and of course I have my own homework that needs to get done."

I grab a pen out of my bun and scribble across the notebook. "Did you want to schedule another time to meet?"

"Yeah, actually, I was thinking we could discuss tonight when you come to the carnival as my date." He winks at me.

I start writing before I think about what he's said, then I pause and nearly choke on my tongue. "Your what?"

"My date. You can meet me there if it would make you feel more comfortable. We can hang out, ride a few rides, play some games. I dominate at Skee Ball by the way."

His matter-of-fact statement causes a laugh to slip out of me. It's been so long since I laughed that I don't recognize the sound. "I have to admit, I'm not great at carnival games."

He grins at me. "Can't get good at something if you never try it. Plus, it would be a nice change since you're the one usually teaching me."

I stare at him, only a little shocked by his straightforwardness. He did ask me on a date previously, so it's not really surprising. Then I realize he's waiting for an answer. *Shit.* Responsibly, I know I should go home after I get done for the day because my mom will need me, but at the same time, the thought of returning home makes me depressed. I'm either tutoring, sleeping, or helping my mom. I can't recall the last time I did something for myself.

"Come on, Bel. Don't overthink it. When was the last time you did something for you? I see you tutoring all the time, but I never see you anywhere else?"

Is it that painfully obvious that I'm a hermit crab? Indecision weighs on me. Drew could be there, but we aren't together. We're barely friends. Without a label, I'm technically allowed to go on a date if I want to.

"Yeah, you're right. What time should I meet you?"

"How does five sound?"

I nod, tucking my chin so he can't see me blushing. He's

cute, and he's always been nice to me. There's really no reason I shouldn't go with him. He doesn't loom over my shoulder, grab me, or hunt me down. Maybe I'm ready for a normal relationship.

Or maybe a little piece of you wants to make Drew jealous?

As soon as the thought pops into my head, I can't forget it. Messing with Drew is dangerous, but he's already told me how he felt and where we stand. Maybe this is the push he needs, or maybe this is what I need to prove to him that he's not in control of me. At least not completely. Or hell, in a last-ditch effort, Stewart is captain of the basketball team. Maybe Drew will leave me alone if he sees I'm interested in someone else.

The idea is sound, but the thought of never talking to Drew again makes me feel a bit queasy. *Why? I hate him...right?* Stewart packs away his belongings, and I wave him off. The room is still quiet, and I relax into the chair with a deep breath.

I have several more clients lined up for the morning, but nothing for the afternoon. The carnival is cutting into my afternoon client base. It's fine, though. I use this small lull to head over to the vending machine. I found some change in my car and use it to buy a packet of S'more Pop-Tarts to eat while I wait for my next appointment.

My next appointment is with Gracie, a girl from my geometry class. She has her dark brown hair pulled tight into a high ponytail. She's wearing leggings and an Oakmount Elite sweatshirt. She looks like your average college student, minus a face full of makeup.

She greets me with a smile and sets down two plastic to-go cups. I've known her for a couple of months, but we never really talked before until the other day when she mentioned how much she was struggling with the last test. I told her I do tutoring, and she asked if I had any time to help her. Now here we are.

"Hi! Sorry if I'm late. I stopped by Beans to get some hot chocolate and grabbed you one too. If you don't like hot chocolate, that's cool too." She gestures to the cups. It's very thoughtful of her, and I happily grab one, a smile tugging at my lips.

"Thank you. That's very kind of you."

"No, what's kind is you taking the time out of your day to help me learn this shit. I swear I wasn't there the day we picked classes."

A bubble of laughter slips out of me, and I feel ten times better now. Gracie takes a seat beside me, and I open the textbook to the parts we're working on in class. She explains her difficulties, then I put together some sample problems for her to work on.

I munch on my Pop-Tarts and feel a tingle down my spine while she works.

Expecting Drew, I snap my head around to look for him, but nothing. Instead, I lock eyes with one of his equally strange but intense friends, Sebastian. He's sitting across the library, staring at me openly. I bite my Pop-Tarts a little too deliberately, which earns me a slightly unhinged smile from my gawker.

Shit. I don't want to attract more attention from these assholes.

I nibble on the Pop-Tarts some more and watch him watch me. Part of me is tempted to walk over to him and ask him what he wants, but again, I'm reminded: *don't poke the fucking bear.* Not when he's staring you down in the woods.

Feeling unsettled but still better than when I arrived, I finish up with Gracie, gather my books, and turn my back so I don't have to see him anymore. I'm conflicted and unsure of how I feel about Drew, so I don't know if going on this date with Stewart is really a good idea.

Did Drew send his friend to watch me in his place, or is this another mind game? I don't even want to touch the disappointment I feel over another day of not seeing him. I won't lie. I half expected him to be here today, and now that he's not, I'm not sure if I should be relieved or sad. One thing I do know is that I need to stand my ground. If Drew wants anything from me, he'll have to work for it.

CHAPTER 19
DREW

THE FUCKING FALL CARNIVAL. That's all anyone is talking about, and I'm already over it. Even my father texted to make sure I'm playing my part for the family name, for The Mill. I shove an elbow into Hoover's chest pads and use his prone form to push off into a stand.

He lets out a groan. Everyone around me groans, wanting practice to be over, but I'm not done yet. "Let's go, you assholes. We aren't done with practice yet. Get up. One more play."

There's more groaning as everyone resettles into the line, and I call the play.

We snap, and it only takes a minute to get the ball down the line. The defense does nothing to get near me.

Maybe they can sense I have no mercy in me today.

I want to run, shove, punch, kick, fight, all of it. Do anything I can to get this negative energy out of me, but as I promised, I call the end of practice after that play and head toward the locker rooms. *Wouldn't want to miss the goddamn carnival.*

In the locker room, everyone can sense my foul mood. I

ignore them all and throw back an almost full bottle of water as I strip off my pads. They hit the floor with a clatter.

Stripping off my sweaty clothes takes seconds, and I march into the showers to spin under a hot showerhead. I quickly wash myself and rinse. When I exit in a towel a few minutes later, I stalk back to my locker and take a seat on the bench. It takes moments for Lee to join me, mud still streaked across his cheek.

He grabs me by the shoulders and gives me a shake. "Fuck man, why do you look like you shut your dick in your locker?"

I scowl and shoulder him off me. "Fuck off, Lee. I'm not in the mood."

He only smiles, accustomed to when I get into one of my brooding sessions. "You should be excited. The carnival is tonight. All the single riders will need a buddy to ride the Ferris wheel. It's the perfect opportunity to snag pussy."

I don't answer. Instead, I stand and strip off my towel to get dressed.

Lee continues like I've joined him for the conversation. "You know Sebastian saw that girl at the library the other day. The one you keep talking to."

"So? What do I care?"

I can feel his eyes on me, weighing my words. "What do you care, indeed? You know your father contacted all three of us and instructed us to keep you away from Bel, or Bel away from you, by any means necessary. In fact, he's offered a reward."

I freeze. He wouldn't? My mind instantly flashes to Sebastian every time he's gotten close to her recently. *He* fucking wouldn't, either. Would he?

He continues to chatter about the carnival, and I don't even bother listening. It's nothing more than musing about how much pussy or cock he's going to get by the time the night is over.

A few of the guys on the other side of the room complain about using the backup field today. Some wish they were called out of practice since they are already sore. Yeah. These fuckers don't know how lucky they are. I could have run us all into the ground.

Once I'm dressed, I slip on my sneakers and a hoodie. It was warm today, but being in the dunk tank tonight, I'll need a hoodie afterward. The water in the tank better be heated, or I'll be murdering Sebastian after I finish my shift.

Lee stares at me, his head cocked. "Dude, what's up? Really." When I don't reply, he moves closer, his voice low. "You seem a little tense."

It's on the tip of my tongue to lay it all out there, but I don't. It won't change anything. Talking about the problems doesn't fix them. It just makes you more aware of them, and believe me, I'm aware of all my problems. "Don't worry about it."

I'm even more tense as I cross the field toward the music blasting in the area. It's annoying, but I better fucking get used to it.

I scan the crowd, hoping to glimpse her, my wallflower, but I don't see any messy buns or oversized clothing. It's all cheerleaders and basketball players. I shouldn't be surprised. I wouldn't take the carnival as her scene. I strip down to my boxers. Fuck, it's cold. I swear to god, if I get pneumonia from this event, I'm killing someone. A few passersby catcall me, but I ignore them.

Sebastian greets me, a clipboard in his hand. "You're one minute late."

"Ask me if I care?" I flip him my middle finger and climb the short set of stairs, plopping my ass down on the small metal bench hovering over the tank of water. "This better be fucking warm."

"Nope. I made sure it's ice cold. All for you, princess." Sebastian laughs like the asshole he is, and I grit my teeth, preparing for the worst when my feet hit the water. Instead of ice-cold pricks of pain, I'm greeted with warmth. *He's fucking lucky.*

As soon as people spot me in the dunk tank, they start to meander over. Sebastian takes their cash and hands them a ball. *Miss. Miss. Miss.* I sit there peacefully without having to speak a word while Sebastian does all the work. People funnel in and out. A few of the football players take a chance on dunking me. No doubt for the brutal practice, but no one sends me into the water. I do my best not to scan the crowd, looking for her, but it's impossible. She's taken over my thoughts in more than one way, and I don't like how weak that makes me. Time trickles by slowly. There's more catcalling, and some cheerleaders try to hit the marker with one of the bigger softballs.

Sebastian graciously allows them to move forward a bit, but none of them still send me into the water.

"How long do I have to do this?" I question, knowing I've been here for at least an hour already. His response is to step up and toss a ball at the target, hitting the mark hard enough to collapse the bench beneath my ass. I fall into the warm water below and pop back up a second later, spitting water and sweeping my hair back against my scalp.

Now that someone has finally dunked me, a crowd forms. People cheer him on, and Sebastian directs everyone to form a single file line and collects their payment as they wait. There's laughter and joy all around me, but I can't bring myself to smile. A couple more people dunk me. A girl and one of the baseball players. The water's warm, and I don't mind now since each dunk heats me, cutting through the chill on my skin.

There are other games, the sound of music, and ringing bells press in on me. The smell of caramel apples and popcorn fill my nostrils. Every year we would come to the fall carnival as a family. Mom and I would share a bucket of popcorn and drink hot cocoa together while playing every carnival game. Dad even tagged along. That feels like forever ago. I can barely recall who that little boy was. Now all I have are the memories of abuse and the rage I have for my father. In some ways, it's like my mother is already dead. I shove the terrible thoughts to the darkest part of my mind.

Only an hour left and then I can go find her and make sure she's not gotten into trouble. I start to count back to myself in my head.

One. Two. Three. Four. Five. Six. Seven. Eight. Nine. Ten. Eleven. Twelve.

That's as far as I make it when my gaze lands on a familiar face in the crowd.

"Hey! Jackie, come here for a minute!"

Her eyes dart to me, and she freezes mid-step. There seems to be an internal battle taking place, but eventually, she turns and ambles over to the side of the booth.

I splash her with a little water, and she scowls at me. "Where's your roommate?"

She looks visibly anxious as she leans against the side of the tank. "Around. She's been at the library doing her tutoring thing, you know?"

I *did* know, but I don't like how anxious she's acting. "What are you hiding, Jackie?" I make it a request, soft and low.

"Nothing, of course. I have nothing to hide."

"You can't lie for shit, you know that?"

She huffs and then sighs. "Yeah, I know. I'm not good at it."

I raise an eyebrow, waiting for her to continue. Her shoulders droop. "For what it's worth, I told her it was a bad idea. I mean...you're you...why would she want to go out with someone else?" Her hand slaps over her mouth, horror filling her eyes.

I blink, and a slow rolling wave of rage crashes against me. "Excuse me? I think I have water in my ear because there's no fucking way I just heard you correctly. Did you say go out with someone else?"

Who the fuck would have the balls, or better yet, who would be stupid enough to go on a date with her? *Only someone who wants to be buried six feet in the ground.*

Jackie shakes her head and keeps her hand clamped over her mouth like she's afraid she'll say something else that she shouldn't. "I didn't say anything," she mumbles through her fingers. I'm about to slip off the bench and into the water to grab her, but she skitters back and then rushes away.

I watch her run away, unable to do a damn thing. "Fuck," I mutter.

The tension in my shoulders tightens, and the buzzing under my skin increases. I need to get the fuck out of here. Jackie better be joking, or Maybel better have miscommunicated because... I can't even think about losing my temper at this moment. A new group of people steps up to the booth, and I force a breath out of my nose before sucking it back in. It's the poorest example of how to calm down ever, but it's that or lose my shit and turn into a feral animal. I'd rather not make a giant ass out of myself...not yet. I'll find Maybel shortly. This shit show is almost over.

I count back in my head: *ten, nine, eight, seven, six, five, four, three, two, one...* I'm about to start over again when one of the basketball dickheads jokes with some friends as he puts his feet on the line. I recognize the fuckface as one of the guys who Maybel tutors. Stewart, I think. I did a complete dissection of his life the moment I saw his number in her phone.

Seb passes him three balls. The guy's tall, with big hands, and easily holds all three balls in one hand. I glare at him, wishing he would hurry the fuck up so I can get on with this shit. He tosses the first ball and of course misses. It's with that movement that I notice the small shadow standing beside him. My heartbeat skyrockets. The blood in my veins reaches boiling.

All I can think is how she told me it wasn't anything, that he's a friend. Ha, a friend that wants to fuck you five different ways. I'm seconds away from coming unglued. I should look away. She doesn't deserve my attention or desire, but I can't bring myself to do it.

I grit my teeth and stare her down. She's wearing her hair down, the blond waves end just above her tits. As my gaze lingers, I notice she's wearing a dress. A goddamn *dress* when it's cold outside. I would *never* let her leave her room in a fucking dress in the cold. She gently touches the basketball player's arm, and the rage unfurls in my gut.

I call out. "Yo, Dick. You going to hit the target or not? I don't have all day to sit here."

A few people in the crowd chuckle. He throws another ball. Misses again.

Bel moves her hand off his arm, and I relax my shoulders a bit at the distance. It doesn't matter. This little fucker is going down anyway, but...her not touching him keeps me from launching myself at him right this second.

She is mine. MINE.

I grit my teeth and stare him down. "You having a little

trouble performing there, Dick? Do you need me to take care of your girl for you?"

She jolts, and her eyes fly wide to meet mine. I give her a smile, all teeth, making sure she knows how much fucking trouble she's in. She knows better than this, yet here she stands with another man, acting like she doesn't belong to me. *Did she let him kiss her, touch her?* If so, his fucking hands will be broken too.

Stewart throws the last ball and, once again, misses.

I laugh. "It's okay, honey. Come over here. I'll make sure you're taken care of until Dick can actually perform."

She frowns at me and crosses her arms over her chest, her hair looking more like a halo now. I want my fingers in it, to tug it tight and watch her mouth part. She belongs to me, and I won't be leaving this carnival without her. Stewart laughs between sending glares my way. Sebastian hands him another three balls, and I yawn and bounce my foot, waiting.

He tries two more times and misses both times. Pathetic, and he calls himself a basketball player? Bel steps up beside him and takes his last ball. He bows like he's conceding a prize and steps out of her way.

What are you up to, flower...

I keep my eyes locked on hers while she raises her arms and lines up the shot. I exhale and count back from ten, watching her. *Ten. Nine. Eight. Seven. Six. Five. Four.* The ball leaves her hand and smashes against the target, sending me ass first into the water. I almost inhale a gallon of water from the smile that pulls at my lips and rise to the surface, coughing. Laughter cuts through the sloshing of the tank when I reach the surface, but I discover everyone except Bel is laughing. Instead, she casts a guilty glance my way and follows Stewart the fucking dick, away from the booth to another one. Not fucking happening.

"I'm done for the night," I announce while climbing out of the tank. I grab the duffel bag of dry clothes I had Sebastian stash for me earlier.

"I have you on for four hours," Sebastian replies.

"Sounds like a you problem."

My only priority at the moment is making sure Maybel learns her place. If she thinks I'm going to sit here and let her be paraded around this place by another man, she's out of her fucking mind. I keep my eyes trained on her back as I dry off and pull on a clean T-shirt.

"That girl's got an arm on her." Aries walks up, crossing his thick arms over his chest. He's wearing his usual perma-scowl, though his tone is curious.

Before I can say anything to him, Sebastian interjects in a menacing whisper, "Didn't our conversation at the library mean anything to you?"

I slip into the self-made changing booth, swap out my boxers for dry ones, pull on a shirt and tug on a pair of jeans. I shove my feet into my boots and exit the changing room, coming face-to-face with Sebastian. His expression is unreadable, but I don't give a fuck about what he thinks. Not right now at least. "Your opinion doesn't mean shit to me, Seb. She's mine, and I will do whatever the fuck I want with her. Get off my back about it, or we'll have problems. You're one of my best friends, but you don't get to tell me what to do." I lean in so my mouth is near his ear. "Not even if my father is paying you to make sure it stays otherwise."

I don't give him the opportunity to respond. Time is being wasted as it is. Back at the front of the booth, Lee mocks the gawkers with lewd comments while handing out tickets in Sebastian's place. They love it, and he is so much better at this than I am. Unease coats my insides. I scan the crowd, looking for Bel and her...*date*.

If Bel wants to play games, then we can play games, but she should know better than anyone else that I don't play fair, and when I get my hands on her, there will be hell to pay. I thought I'd made it clear that she belongs to me, but I guess I'll have to do something drastic to show her otherwise.

"Aries! Lee! Follow me."

KNOW I shouldn't feel so pleased with myself about dunking him, but the smirk on his face when I grabbed that ball just pissed me off. As usual, he underestimated me.

He'll make me pay for it when he gets out of the tank and off volunteer duty, but for now, I feel a little like I've won. And I *really* need a win, both in life and against Drew.

Part of me thinks he sees me as a scared little rabbit, and that's the only reason he continues to mess with me. Maybe that's true. He certainly hasn't said anything besides *you belong to me* a whole damn lot, so I don't know what's going on in his head.

Maybe that's it. He has a concussion, and this obsession he seems to have will pass once his head is straight again. Either way, he won't appreciate me dunking him, so I want to put as much distance as I can get between us.

I turn to Stewart and point toward a water gun game. "Do you want to try this one?"

He scowls, looks me up and down, then tips his head in a smile. "Sure, yeah, let's try it."

He hands the game operator some cash, and we settle on

the stools in front of the guns. The bell rings, and I pull the trigger, watching as the water gradually comes out. *Hurry, hurry.* I speak internally, excitement building in my belly.

"Nooooo!!!!" I squeak when Stewart's bowling pin tips over first. He turns to me grinning, and for the first time in a long time, I return a smile.

How can you feel better and worse all in the same day?

"Want to do another round?" he asks.

I shake my head. "Nah, let's walk around and see what else is happening."

"Yeah, sure. Let's go." He offers me his hand, and I take it, letting him pull me up from the stool. It's soft and warm, and holding his hand even briefly makes me feel like I'm doing something wrong. Like I'm cheating on Drew, which is impossible since we aren't anything.

It doesn't matter, though. My body refuses to acknowledge what my brain says, and I release his hand immediately. We walk around for a little bit, taking in the small shops and food stands. After a little while, his body inches closer to mine, and soon, he's got an arm wrapped around my waist, keeping me close to him. He guides us through the crowd easily, and I tell myself he's just protecting me, but I feel weird about it as his hand oh-so slowly begins to drift lower. I don't think I like where this is going.

Needing to put some space between us, I jump from his grasp. "Did you want to get something to drink?"

He gives me an easy smile. "Sure, doll."

How is it that I hate him calling me *doll* way more than I hate Drew calling me *wallflower?*

We cut through the building crowd toward a beer tent. I remember Jackie complaining about the university limiting the number of products being sold for liability reasons, but from the homemade flyer stapled to the wood, it looks like they have beer, soda, and water.

"What can I get ya?" A leggy blonde in a cheerleading uniform greets us. Her eyes glitter as they dart back and forth between the two of us.

"Two beers, please," Stewart says, his tone gentleman-like.

We don't even have to show our IDs since we had to do that to enter. Anyone over twenty-one was given this bright green wristband. It's another way the university is trying to limit underage drinking. Although I admire the effort, the carnival is the least of their problems. The cheerleader pours from a tapped keg, filling two red Solo cups before bringing them over to us. Stewart pays her and slips his wallet back into his pocket. He moves to the side to get out of the way of other paying patrons. For a moment, we get separated, and someone grabs me by the arms, spinning me around. Panic bubbles to the surface and then evaporates when I see a familiar face before me.

Jack's face is bright and smiley as she glances over my shoulder meaningfully. "My oh my, look at you being all social. I'm so proud of you."

I laugh. "Don't worry. I definitely plan to be in bed by nine."

She waggles her eyebrows at me, and I laugh again and bat her hands away. "Alone." I lower my voice. "I plan to be in bed by nine, alone."

She leans closer like we are conspiring. "Who says you have to be alone? Just put a sock on the door."

"Do people still need to do that when they can just write 'brb having sex' on their whiteboard and people will leave them alone? Better yet, next time I want to have sex in our suite, I'll just text you a play-by-play update."

I notice Stewart out of the corner of my eye. He saunters forward, his long legs eating up the short distance between us.

Jackie laughs. "Well, if you want to send visual aids as well so I can see where you are in the process, I won't say no to that."

I roll my eyes and decide we need a subject change. "Stewart, this is my friend and suite-mate Jackie, or Jack, as I like to call her."

He gives her a smile and a shrug with the beer in his hand. "What's up, Jack?"

"Nothing much. Going to go get some popcorn and have my next conquest eat it off me," Jackie jokes, or at least I hope she's joking. She's different in many ways.

Stewart laughs, but I can tell it's forced. She smiles in return, but his doesn't quite reach his eyes. "Anyway, I'll leave you two alone to enjoy the evening. I see a football player scowling at me, which basically means he wants me."

"Okay, well, have fun and be safe," I yell after her like I'm her mom.

As soon as she's out of earshot, he leans into my side. "She's...interesting."

"She's a little different, yes, but she's a great friend. One of the best, honestly."

He nods and passes me the beer I've just left him holding. I grab the cold Solo cup and clutch it to my chest like it's a barrier between us. "Let's get out of the way and go sit on those benches over there."

It's a beautiful fall evening, the sun slowly setting, painting the sky in an array of oranges and reds. A cold chill ripples down my spine. Maybe I should've gotten hot chocolate instead. We head toward the edge of the carnival, and once we reach a bench, an awkward silence settles on us.

What the hell do we talk about? The only thing we really

have in common is tutoring. I don't even know why he asked me out. I know why I agreed, though. I wanted to make Drew take the hint that I don't belong to him. Okay, and maybe make him a little jealous, and gain some new tutoring clients in the process. Now, though, I'm a little lost. Dates and relationships, in general, are out of my wheelhouse. The excitement I felt earlier gives way to anxiety. I guess if I have nothing to say, I should take a drink. Maybe after this, he will introduce me so I can start setting up tutoring times. My calendar is already loaded into my phone and ready to go.

I raise the cup to my lips, intending to take a large gulp, hoping it gives me the courage to talk about something, anything. Except that never happens because the second my mouth touches the iced-over plastic, someone snatches the cup from my hand. Cold beer sloshes out of the cup and over the rim, soaking my hand and wrist.

What the hell? I shake my hand off to get rid of the excess liquid before wiping it against the side of my dress. When I look up to see who it was that took my drink, my stomach drops to my feet. *Drew.*

"What the fuck, man?" Stewart growls, stepping between us and shielding me from him.

Well, he's either incredibly brave or stupid...I know where my money is in this situation. Drew looks furious, his dark hair still damp from the dunk tank and slicked back to keep the strands out of his face. I drink him in for one moment: he's a nightmare, a painting of destruction and rage. Those dark emerald eyes of his are manic, his pupils dilated, his chiseled jaw is clenched so tight, I'd be surprised if he still had teeth. I'm momentarily blinded by his beauty, and then reality comes crashing back down on me.

"Can I have my drink back, please?" I try to be nice since

I know he's pissed off, and meeting his anger with anger will only ignite the fire.

The sharp cut of his words from the other day floats through my head, and I use them to bolster my confidence. He claims he doesn't even like me, that I'm nothing more than a game to him. The main reason I came here was to prove to him I'm not *his*. I don't belong to *him*, no matter how many times he demands and claims otherwise.

He cocks his head as two of his oversized friends surround us. One, whose rage-fueled energy matches Drew's right now, circles right, and the other, who I haven't really seen around much, heck, I don't even know his name, circles left.

Drew points at Stewart. "Aries, step over here, please." *Aries it is, then.*

The man I don't recognize sweeps around behind us, and Stewart shifts to keep Aries from being directly behind him. "What the fuck do you want?"

"Drew, please can we talk about this somewhere private?" I try.

His eyes remain trained on Stewart, and every time he breathes, his nostrils flare. I bet he doesn't even see me. I move to step forward, but an arm circles my waist, pulling me backward. I crash against a hard chest and immediately start to struggle. It's no use, not when the man holding me is twice my size. Lee, I think his name is.

"Calm down. You don't want to miss the best part."

"What are you talking about?" I ask but keep my eyes on Drew and Stewart.

Drew steps forward like he might punch him and slaps the beer out of his hands, then shoves mine into his grasp. "Thirsty, Dickface? Here, have a drink."

Nothing but menace laces his words, and I gulp, which earns me a chuckle from Lee, who I feel against my back. I guess I should be relieved he's just holding me in place. No wandering hands from him... He's clearly met Drew.

"Let's be rational here. Can we talk? He didn't do anything, and I don't want you to do something that could get you in trouble."

Who am I kidding? No one can touch these elite assholes.

Drew doesn't even glance my way but narrows his eyes at Stewart. "Rational? If you think this is irrational, you haven't seen shit. And trouble? I'm not worried. Not even a little bit. If this idiot uses at least one of his last remaining brain cells, he won't tell anyone about this."

A red flush sweeps up Stewart's neck to his face. "What the fuck is your problem, man? She's not your girlfriend."

"Who said that? Not that it matters. She's been claimed by me, and it certainly doesn't excuse the fact that you're a useless piece of shit who should be put down, especially after what I just witnessed you do."

"What are you talking about? What did he do?" I struggle in Lee's grasp.

"Easy, Bel. He's getting to it. Just wait," Lee whispers into my ear.

Carefully, I lean my head away so his warm breath isn't fanning across the sensitive skin of my ear. Something tells me I'm about to lose a client. I let out a long sigh, my shoulders slumping.

The men stand chest to chest until Drew practically growls, "Drink it. Now."

Stewart moves his hand like he's about to throw the drink in Drew's face, but Drew grabs him by the wrist, holding him there with what seems like minimal effort. Being this far away from the crowded carnival and with darkness approaching fast, no one can really see or hear us, so getting the attention of someone to help isn't going to happen.

"Drink it," Aries orders from behind Stewart. "Or we'll make you drink it."

His tone has an equal amount of menace as Drew's. I don't like this, not at all.

"What's the big deal with the beer? If he doesn't want to drink, he doesn't have to," I chime in.

Stewart's eyes fill with panic, and he tries to wrench away, but Aries grabs him around the shoulders and holds him back against his chest. Drew snatches the beer, grabs Stewart's nose, pinches it closed, and dumps the drink into his mouth.

My entire body trembles. "What the fuck? Why would you do that?"

Stewart makes a gurgling sound as if he's choking, and all I can do is yell. "Help him! He's choking." Neither Drew nor Aries makes any attempt to help him. Instead, they release him and watch as he falls to his knees, his shirt soaked with beer.

Rolling to his side, he starts coughing, and I hear him suck a ragged breath into his lungs. Relief washes over me, but it is short-lived when Drew crouches in front of him. I can't stand here and watch him bully someone who had no idea what he was getting into. Who cares if he touched me or asked me out? It's not like anything happened anyway.

I try to jerk free of Lee's hold, but there's no give. He tightens his grasp, which is now almost bruising. "Let go of me!"

"Wait for it," he insists, his tone softer, gentler, like he's coaxing a small animal.

I'm two seconds away from kicking him in the balls when Aries stands, holding up a baggie between his index finger and thumb. "Wonder how long it takes to kick in? I sure as shit have never had to use it. What do you say, Stew? How long until you can't even remember your own name?"

I glance back and forth between Aries and Stewart, looking at the bag, confused as to what I'm seeing. There's some cursing as Stewart pushes himself to his feet. Drew doesn't let him move an inch without towering over him.

"Not only do you take out my girl but you try to drug her, too. *No.* Don't look at her, don't talk to her, and you sure as shit will keep paying for the tutoring you won't be getting, or I'll find you, and I promise you, I won't call the cops. I won't talk to the school. I'll deal with you as you should be dealt with. Dead. Six feet in the fucking ground."

There's no reprieve. No give. Nothing but cold hard steel in every word he says. The reality of what could've happened presses against me. Was it too much for me to think he might actually want to go on a date with me? Not drug me and have sex with me? I blink back the rapidly forming tears from my eyes. I get it. It wasn't like I was honest in accepting his invitation, but his intentions were to hurt me.

Drew motions to his friend, not even looking at me. Shame coats my insides as Lee releases his hold on me. My skin feels tender, and I try not to rub at my arms and give away my discomfort. It's the equivalent of blood to sharks with these men. Instead, I wrap my arms around myself and ignore the cold settling into my bones.

How stupid could I be? I should've known this was a setup.

"I should kill you right now," Drew taunts, his body a wall of pure fury. "What do you have to say for yourself? Can't get a date any other way?"

"Nah, I could. Just wanted to see what all the fuss was about." His eyes drift over my body, and he licks his lips like he's getting ready to take a bite out of me. Gone is the easygoing, kind gentleman he showed me in the library for the past month. It was all a lie. A mask he wore to get me to do what he wanted. Rage burns through me, white hot, and I clench my fist tightly and take a step toward him.

"I can't believe I thought you were a nice guy," I growl and haul my fist back before slamming it against his cheek.

Pain lances up my arm, and my knuckles burn at the impact, but I ignore it. Landing a hit on him is worth it. He teeters to the side, his body off balance from the blow, but also the drugs which are now probably active in his system.

Lee and Aries move forward and scoop him up under his arms. Drew steps between us like he's shielding me, and he looks at me for the first time during this whole thing. His eyes shine with what I can only describe as disappointment and surprise.

"Take him to the dungeon. We'll deal with him later."

"On it," Lee and Aries say in unison.

Once they drag Stewart away, I'm left alone with Drew, his gray long-sleeved Henley stuck in wet spots across his broad shoulders almost like he didn't bother drying off completely before he came to find me. We stare at each other, a long moment loaded with unsaid things between us.

I should say thank you, but the words are stuck in my throat.

"You got anything to say?" he prompts, his voice fury and fire now compared to the cold burn it was when he spoke to Stewart.

I swallow hard and stare at my scuffed-up boots. "Not really." Even I hear the sullen note there. *Fuck*. I sigh. "I didn't realize that's what he would do. He seemed nice."

Drew grabs me by the arm and hauls me closer to his body, then he reaches out and wraps the other hand around my throat tightly enough to get my attention but not enough to scare me. "You shouldn't even have been with him. You belong to me."

"So you keep saying," I croak. "You're also confusing me. You made it seem like I was your girlfriend when you were talking to him. And you called me that the other day in front of your football friend. But you treat me like shit on the regular. What the hell am I supposed to think?"

His fingers pulse like he's tempted to tighten his grip. "We can discuss that later. Right now, we have more pressing matters. And don't think I'll just let that little dunking booth incident go either. Before the night is over, you'll be sore in a couple of holes as punishment."

He leans in. He's so close now, his mouth nearly hovers over mine. The scent of damp skin and peppermint washes through my sinuses. "And maybe, *maybe*, if you're a good little wallflower, I'll let you come while I use you."

CHAPTER 21
DREW

SHE TUGS on her arm like she has any chance of pulling herself from my grasp, from the red-hot rage burning through me. How *dare* she put herself in this type of danger. I almost snort at her excuse of him being a nice guy. Everyone looks nice until you peel back a couple of layers. It's all an illusion.

I clutch her bicep tighter and drag her along behind me through the mass of fellow students. The sun set an hour or so ago, and the darkness has lured more people out.

When she wrenches away, I stop short, spin, grip the back of her neck, and pull her in close. "Stop fucking resisting and fighting me, or I'll make this miserable for you."

Her eyes are wide... *Is it my tone or something else?*

She stutters. "I-I just...want to know where we're going."

I grit my teeth to keep from screaming in her face, or worse, shoving her to her knees right here in front of everyone. My patience with her is running so thin, it might as well be nonexistent. A war rages inside me. The instinct to claim her truly and let every dumbass at this school know she is mine officially threatens to consume me. Along with the desire to murder that fucker for slipping the date-rape drugs in her drink. What if I didn't get there? I could only imagine finding her limp on the ground. The image in my mind festers, dousing gasoline on the raging fire consuming me. "Does it fucking matter where we're going?"

"No, but I...I'm sorry." Her apology, if you could call it one, grates on every cell in my body. I tighten my grip on her arm and tug her forward roughly. She stumbles beside me, but I don't slow. I can't, not with the edge of my anger still digging deep. We stop in the line near the Ferris wheel. It's the first thing I thought of when I considered a place where I can get the fuck away from everyone for a minute. A place I can sit and breathe for a moment to calm the rage. Thankfully, one of the football players is running the thing. I recognize him as Nash Winthrope. I wave to him, and he gives me a nod. I'd skip the line altogether, but he's got a wheel full of riders already.

Maybe this is a bad idea.

I want to break things, throw things, strip, and scream. Seeing that piece of shit with his hands on her, smiling. Touching what is mine. The possessive need grew with each second I saw them together. The thought pushes me deeper into my anger until I reach out and instinct takes over. I grab her by the back of the neck. Her tiny body crashes against me, and I tighten my hold. She even smells like him and the cheap beer he bought her. Fuck, I want to rip this dress from her body and give her my shirt just to replace the scent. I know it's irrational and fucked up to want to punish her, but there is a huge difference between guys like Stewart and guys like me. I've never hurt Bel. I've never done anything with the intent of raping her. It might have hindered on dubious consent, but I didn't drug her, and she always had the option to say no.

"Drew, stop. You're hurting me," she whines, struggling to get away.

As badly as I'm tempted to wring her pretty neck, I can't. The thought of breaking her, of watching the warmth leave her skin, makes the cold organ in my chest ache. That doesn't mean I'll let her get away with this, though. There are other ways of hurting someone.

"I'm feeling really fucking murderous, flower. Is that what you want? Is that why you came here with him tonight? To see how far you could push me? Do you want me to kill him? Don't tempt me because I'll do it just to prove a fucking point." I speak through gritted teeth, peering down into her heart-shaped face. The reality is that might very well be his fate. I haven't decided whether I'm going to do it or not.

"Don't make choices you'll regret, and don't spill someone else's blood for me. I'm not worth another person's life." How can't she see that she's worth that and so much more? This may have started with The Hunt, but from the moment I claimed her as my prey, she was mine. It doesn't matter if he didn't know because *she* did. What I did to that fucker is a direct consequence of her actions.

The wheel circles around a couple more times, and then Nash slows it down, letting the patrons off cart by cart. It takes forever, but once it's time for us to load, a little of my steam has dissipated. I practically drag Bel up the steps and push her into the cart.

As soon as she's out of my grasp, she scurries away, putting as much distance as she can between us, which isn't much given the size of the small pod. It's round and large enough to seat at least four people. I plop down onto the bench seat and grab onto her bare thigh, pulling her across the space. She looks up at me and I see a small amount of fear, but there's something else beneath the surface. Something depraved and dark, something that speaks to me.

"Is that only fear I see in your pretty green eyes, or is there something else there? Does what I did turn you on?"

"Not everything is about sex."

The wheel moves again. "No, you're right. Not everything is about sex, but it happens to be my weapon of choice with you. So tell me, flower, are you as depraved as me? Because even as afraid as you appear, something tells me you're a little bit curious and a whole lot turned on by violence."

"Violence doesn't turn me on. You're psychotic, Drew."

I laugh. "Thanks, Doc," I mock, "but you aren't telling me anything I don't know, and maybe the violence doesn't turn you on, but the thought of being taken does, the helplessness of being at my mercy. The thought of me doing whatever the hell I want to you while you beg me to stop, all while knowing that I won't." I dig my fingers between her thighs, and the smallest moan slips free of her lips. She doesn't have to say anything. I already know the truth. "It's okay if you're too embarrassed to admit it. I won't judge you. It can even be our little secret." I push her thighs apart. "It's time to discuss that bullshit version of a date you went on, and I'll need you to be honest with me. Otherwise, this could get bad for you."

She swallows hard, her throat working. "It's not what you think..."

"Oh really? What do I think? Can you read my mind now? Going out with another man when you know you belong to me? Humiliating me in front of my friends and teammates? Tell me, *Maybel*, what the fuck am I supposed to think?"

Her lips part, and she speaks, but I shake my head. If I have to hear another pitiful excuse fall from her lips, I'll find another use for it besides talking.

"No, I won't be quiet." She sneers and then frowns. "I

went with him because I was mad at you. All you do is take and never give anything back. And yes, I guess I wanted to make you a little jealous. You expect me to sit around waiting for you, legs spread. I'm not that girl." Her eyes dart down to her hands, which now rest in her lap.

I narrow my eyes. "Wow. That's some agenda, with one fucking hour of wandering this stupid carnival. Ambitious, flower. You thought I'd be jealous?"

"Yes." She sighs.

Did she make me jealous? Fuck yes. She accomplished her goal there, but she also taught herself a valuable lesson as well.

"Did you let him touch you?"

She shakes her head. "I didn't let him. He was just doing what any guy does on a date."

The statement makes me see red, and I grit my teeth to keep from launching myself at her. "It doesn't matter. He shouldn't have asked you to begin with, and even if he did, you shouldn't have agreed. By the time I'm through with him, he won't even be a ghost on campus."

She tangles her hand in the fabric of her dress almost nervously.

"Nothing to say to that?" I prompt.

She sighs loud enough I can hear her across from the carriage. "What do you want from me?"

That's the question, isn't it?

Am I using her as an outlet? Probably. Is she a challenge unlike any I've ever come across? Also yes. But I think it goes deeper than either of those things. I'm finally taking some-thing for myself after years of doing what everyone else wants and expects. Maybe that's why I'm so damn hard on Maybel. She needs to be perfect for me, and by god, she will be when I'm through with her.

"Looks like you got what you wanted, or more than that,

if I'm correct, because now I'm a twister of emotions, both jealous and pissed off. The only person you have to blame is yourself. So tell me, how do you plan to fix this?"

Her eyes go wide at my calm tone. I'm anything but calm inside, more like the calm before the storm. When a moment passes, and she doesn't respond or move, I take that as my answer.

"Come here." I gesture toward the floor of the carriage.

"Please, Drew," she pleads, but she doesn't realize her begging only turns me on more, as tears well at the corners of her eyes.

I shake my head, and when she doesn't move, I repeat myself and give her a second chance. "Come here, now!" There's a long moment when the scent of popcorn and the music that just started on the speakers cuts between us. Her entire body trembles, and goose bumps pebble across her skin. "I won't tell you again. My next move will be to put you on your knees myself, and when it comes to you, I can't be responsible for what I might do when I'm as angry as I am right now."

I watch, impatiently awaiting her choice. She looks out over the edge of the wheel. We've stopped at the top, and she knows there's nowhere for her to go. Nowhere for her to escape. She's as trapped as she was the first time I caught her. I give her only a second more. I'm about to lurch forward when she slithers off the bench and folds her dress under her knees before dropping to the floor in front of me. I spread my legs and sink a hand into her hair, dragging her forward.

"What do you want me to do?" She looks like a fucking angel, with her pleading eyes and blond halo of hair. I almost feel bad for what I'm about to do. *Almost.* I slowly drag my thumb across her plump pink bottom lip, then press down hard, forcing her mouth open.

"Prepare yourself, flower. I'm going to fuck your face, and I'm not going to be gentle."

Fear and excitement sparkle in her eyes. "What if I say no? I could just sit here and wait until we go back around, then get off and go."

I shrug like I don't give a shit. Like I'd actually let her do that. "You could...sure, but you won't make it off this ride before I'm inside you. And it'll only make for a better show when everyone sees you bent over, my cock pumping inside your tight pussy."

Her eyes narrow, and she looks at me with disbelief. "You wouldn't..."

"Oh, I definitely fucking would, and you know it. Or maybe you want to test me and see if I'd really do it." I snap my teeth at her, anticipating her next move before she makes it.

She has too much dignity and self-respect to push me and see if I'd actually do it. The better question is, would she let me, or would she fight me? The thought makes my cock harder than steel. Slowly, she reaches for the button on my jeans, flicking it open. I lift my hips for her and allow her to pull the fabric to my knees.

"Hurry, Bel, or do you want everyone to watch me take your pussy raw?" I taunt.

My cock springs free, and I watch her throat moving as she visibly gulps. Watching her face every time she sees my cock is a sight I'll never get tired of. She's so innocent and fragile. I can't wait to dirty her up and bend her to my will.

"Ticktock."

She wrinkles her nose at me and scoots closer. Leaning forward, she licks her lips and parts them as she closes them over the thick mushroom-shaped head. A pleasurable sigh escapes me, and her warm, wet mouth is the perfect distraction. Through hooded eyes, I watch as she circles the base of my cock with her hand and jerks me off, all while doing her best to take as much of me into her mouth as she can.

She struggles, but it's a magnificent sight, and I'm tempted to lift my hips and touch the back of her throat just so I can see her pretty green eyes fill with tears.

No, not tempted.

Going to.

With a single finger, I tilt her chin up so I can see her eyes while she sucks me deep. I choose then to thrust forward and let out a throaty moan when my cock brushes against the back of her throat. Tears immediately fill her eyes, and when she blinks, they trail down her cheeks.

"Fuck." I growl and do it again. She tries to look away, but I stop her, my fingers sinking into her hair, holding her in place. I need to see her, but more than anything, I need her to see me. "No, keep looking at me. I want to see how beautiful you look with tears staining your cheeks while I fuck your throat."

Those big green eyes of hers shine so brightly and only encourage my fucked-up behavior. She makes a gagging sound as she chokes on me, and I'm so gratified by it that I hold myself there at the back of her throat until she struggles for air, her hands pushing against my thighs. The fearful haze that fills her features makes my blood sing. I crave her fear like an addict craves his next hit. After a few seconds, I pull back, and that's when she pulls away altogether. I let her go only because I want to see what she plans to do next.

Saliva dribbles out the side of her mouth, her lips are swollen, and her eyes are blurry with fresh tears. She's so fucking beautiful, and she doesn't even know it. Swiping at the side of her mouth with the back of her hand, she peers up at me remorsefully. "I don't want to do that again. I thought you were going to choke me to death. You know I have no experience with any of this."

"Okay, well if you don't want to choke on my cock, then stand, lift your dress, and bend over. I'll take your ass instead."

She shakes her head frantically, blond pieces of hair flying. The fear reflecting back at me isn't fake. *It's real.* She knows that I'll do whatever I want to her, but she also knows that I don't really want to hurt her. Not truly. Which is why beneath that fear, I see desire, red-hot desire. "No."

"A hole is a hole, flower. Choose before I choose for you."

She releases a ragged breath and appears to be talking herself up because a second later, she takes me into her mouth again. I smile and sink my fingers into her hair, gently stroking her while also holding her in place as I lift my hips, fucking her face slowly.

Little gag sounds escape her, and saliva dribbles from the corner of her mouth and onto my jeans, but she doesn't try to fight me. I swipe at the tears as they trail down her cheeks and thrust faster and harder.

"You're such a good girl, taking my cock into your mouth and letting me fuck your throat. But you better work faster. I can feel the wheel starting to move."

That frantic look appears again, and she ups her pace, her cheeks hollowing out as she sucks harder. My abs contract as the pleasure builds in my gut. *Fuck me.* Little by little, the anger she stirred to life fizzles out, and all I can feel is her and the pleasure she gives me.

I lean a little forward, using my abs to keep myself up. "Faster, Bel. If I don't feel my cum hit the back of your throat, we'll do it again until I do. I don't care if we have an audience or not."

The wheel lurches once, and I smile as her hot, wet mouth

moves frantically over my length. If we make it to the bottom with her still sucking me off, then we do. I know she doesn't want anyone else to see what I reduce her to. How she becomes workable clay in my hands at the mere mention of being owned, especially now that I know this is what she wants, that even as afraid as she acts, parts of her crave this. Crave me.

Her tongue swipes over the head of my cock while her mouth suctions against me, squeezing the fuck out of me. So tight and warm. *Yes. Fuck yes. This is what I needed.*

I sink farther down on the bench. "Are you wet for me, Bel? Does sucking my thick cock make your pretty pussy weep?" She rewards me with a tiny moan, and more tears track down the apples of her cheeks, carrying with it a line of black mascara. I'd love to go all night with her, but I can feel the tension building. I'm close now, lucky for her.

I piston my hips, forcing myself deeper into her mouth. Each thrust is hard enough that she makes little mewling noises as I curve down the hot channel of her throat. Her nails dig into my skin, hard enough to puncture, and the rush of pain that sears across my flesh only turns me on more.

Fuck yes. Faster. Harder.

The wheel moves again, our bodies swaying slowly, but I don't stop. I'm so close to the edge. I can feel her struggling to pull away, and I grab onto the back of her head and press her face against my base, holding her in place.

"Not so fast. I don't care who sees us. We aren't stopping till I fill this pretty throat with my cum, so you better keep going."

Her loud gag resonates through me, and the tightness in my balls threatens to make me explode. "Your mouth is perfect, even if I wish I was fucking your cunt right now."

She lets out what sounds like a growl, but continues her

quick pace, and I let it carry me higher and higher until I explode. Fisting her soft strands, I go off like a rocket and come hard with a groan, shooting my release down her throat. Her movements slow, and I hold her in place, making certain she gets every drop.

The look of disgust on her face is enough to make me smile, and I cup her by the cheek gently. "Don't make me take you over my knee and spank your ass, Bel. Swallow my cum like the good girl you are." She wrinkles her nose, struggling to swallow, but eventually does.

When I've finished, I pull out of her mouth completely. I notice a little cum leaking out over the tip, and I nod to her. "You better lick it off."

All she does is glare at me and swipe her tongue over my sensitive crown. A shiver ripples through me. She's so obedient when she wants to be, and other times, she's like a kitten ready to attack.

"Good girl. Pull up my pants, then sit back down beside me. I'm not done with you yet, my wicked wallflower."

Her eyes are hazy, and there's a flush to her cheeks as she stumbles on her knees, her fingers slipping over the button. She wobbles as she stands and then all but sags into the spot beside me. I peer over at her. Her dress is wrinkled around her thighs, and her hair is a mass of tangles and curls. I love the way she looks right now, used and abused. *Mine.*

A tiny drop of my seed sits at the corner of her mouth, and I grow hard, wanting to take her again. She sits quietly, almost too quietly, beside me, and this moment gives me time to think about what she said, of how she went on that date to make me jealous, make me see her. Truly see her. I guess she got her wish. Because now I do. Every depraved thing in her mind. Everything she keeps hidden so well. She's told me she hated me so many times, but it's apparent now that she's growing to like me, and I don't know if I should be angry or proud. Worse yet, I don't know how her liking me makes me feel.

Of course, there's some type of emotion there for her, but I can't pinpoint it. I don't want anyone else to have her, but I wouldn't call myself *hers* either. I don't have girlfriends. I don't even have fuck buddies.

The wheel finishes its round, and we stop at the platform. I stand and adjust myself before we step out, Bel first, then me. I nod at Nash, who gives me a smile as we pass by. As expected, Bel takes off on a dead run, disappearing into the masses.

Now that I'm calmer, and my thoughts are less red and murderous, I can make better choices. As the hunter, I prepare myself to capture my prey. Clearly, there is still a lesson to be taught. I head after Bel at my own pace. There's nowhere else for her to go but back to her dorm. She's trapping herself, and if she thinks she can escape me, then she doesn't know me at all.

I'm not even winded as I shoulder my way through the rest of Oakmount's student body. It doesn't take long for me to catch up with her. I let her stay ahead, but smile every time she glances over her shoulder and catches sight of me. If I didn't know better, I'd say she looks scared, *truly* scared, like that first night, and it suits my mood just fine. This is how I prefer her, my little flower.

CHAPTER 22
BEL

I HAVE to be in shock since I barely feel the cold night air as I rush through the crowded carnival and out the other side. My car is here, but I'm in no condition to drive, not when my hands shake and my stomach is an anxious knot. I'm so turned on right now I nearly moan as my thighs rub together with every step I take. The friction is enough to make me go off.

What is so wrong with me that I found that so erotic, *so* exciting? Drew calling me out on the fantasy makes it even worse. *How does he know?* And if he knows, do other people too? I was scared through it all, scared that someone would see us, that he'd do more at any second, but not scared of *him, not* when I should be.

With a stumble, I refocus my attention on walking. *Fuck.* I can't even think straight with his taste on my tongue and my body clenching around nothing, yearning for something I know I shouldn't want. People stroll past on the way to the carnival, and all I can think about is getting away from the scent of cotton candy and popcorn, and the sound of laughter and happiness. I just need to get away. Run home. Put some distance between us and everything else.

After tonight, I won't be able to look at myself or him the same. I can't believe I allowed this to happen. Why did I go through with it? I could have walked away, screamed, *anything*. He can try to force me in this world where he is king, but he won't actually succeed surrounded by people, not in today's world. I'm mortified that I let him degrade me like that and even more ashamed that I liked it.

I slow to get a better grasp on my breathing and body. He's just a man who pushes every single button I have, in both animosity and arousal. It's getting hard to tell myself there isn't something else here, something dark and sinister growing between us. He brings out the worst and best in me, and I want to revel in it. I want to let him own me. The person I was before him never would've gone out of her way to make a guy jealous. She never would've worn a dress like this. The old me is slowly being chipped away, revealing something I didn't know even existed.

While I walk, I risk glancing behind me, even if I know I shouldn't. It would appear I've gotten away scot-free since I don't catch sight of his towering silhouette in the dark, but just because I don't see him doesn't mean he isn't there.

God, I'm such an idiot.

Some of the heat in my body finally begins to fizzle out. It's not like he's said anything. It's not like he cares, not past the point of me being an object he physically owns. He didn't even say anything about me trying to make him jealous other than confessing that it worked. I bet he was only jealous because someone else was touching what's his, not because he actually cares—which was the whole fucking point of the night. I want him to see me as a person. Instead, he saw the darkest parts of me. I huddle into myself and walk a little faster, the cold air sinking through my thin dress. The side-walks are mostly empty. Everyone is either staying in for the night or already at the carnival. A couple passes by me, and I avert my gaze to the ground.

If only I could get my brain to stop thinking about him. I'm so done with this bullshit hot-and-cold routine with him. I don't ever know which side of him I'm going to get, and that's just as frustrating. The dorms come into view after a short while, and I'm more than relieved. I march up the steps into the building and use my key card to get in. Once inside, I feel a little safer. At least he can't get inside the building unless someone lets him in.

It only takes a few minutes to get up to the suite. Jack was at the carnival earlier and talked about shacking up with some football player, but I know she has an early lab class tomorrow morning, so she might be sleeping already. Possible but unlikely. Jack isn't the type to pass up a party or moment to socialize.

By the time I make it to my room, my mind is still reeling. It feels like hours ago since I threw that baseball, and he pushed me to my knees on the Ferris wheel.

Quickly, I strip off my cross-body bag and toss it on the table. Then I brace my hands on the worn cheap wood. This isn't me. I need to get myself together and just stop thinking about it, about him.

I sit at the table and spread my fingers, digging in, focus-ing. Breathing. This is just a fling. It'll go away once he's done with me, tired of me. It'll be just like what my dad did to my mother. Pretty little rich boys get tired of white trash, eventu-ally. I grit my teeth and stand, unzipping the side of my dress before marching into my bedroom to grab my toiletry bag. A cold shower still sounds like the best idea.

Once I have my bag in hand, I exit back into the suite and

connect my phone to the Bluetooth to turn on some music, hoping it will help me relax.

It takes me a moment to find a song before I hit play and slip in my earbuds. The noise canceling cuts out more often than not, but right now, it's working, and I can't hear anything but the sweet tones of one of my favorite singers. Worth the weeks it took me to pay for these on the school marketplace.

I can already feel the tension easing, my muscles growing soft, my heart rate slowing. Music does that to me sometimes, that or a long session at the library. But now, every time I go to the library, all I think about is Drew.

Shit, I need a towel. I walk back out into the suite, making a beeline for my room, when a hand clamps over my mouth and pulls me backward into a solid chest. I'm lifted off my feet a second later, and I kick back at my assailant's legs, but every hit I make is dismal.

A scream clogs my throat, and my ears ring between the music and the erratic beat of my heart. The headphones tumble from my ears and hit the floor with sharp clicks. Teeth sink into the soft spot beneath my ear, and my body, still primed from earlier, grows hotter.

It takes a moment for my mind to catch up with what my body tells me. It's him. *He's here.* He broke in, and now he's going to take me. I don't know if I should scream and run, or beg him for it, beg him to stop this terrible ache he created. To ease me in a way I know only he can.

The more I struggle, the deeper his teeth cut into my skin. Pain sears my shoulder, and the sound of my scream filters into his big hand that's still clamped tight across the bottom of my face. He releases me from his teeth but not from his grasp.

"Good girl," he grates into my ear. "Scream for me just like that."

I can feel him hard against my back as he hauls me toward the table in the middle of the room. My reprieve comes when I land against the wood flat on my belly. Before I can mutter a single word, he loops something into my mouth and ties it tight enough that it digs in at the corners. Oh my *god*. The chase in the woods felt absolutely insane, but this...it's something else entirely.

The need to draw blood and make him feel the same pain encompasses me. With my arms still free, I flail, reaching for him, and when my nails sink into his bare flesh, I sink them deeper before I drag them across his skin.

He lets out a hiss, the only sound of discomfort as he presses his body over mine, securing my hands under his, pinning me hard, his hips flush against mine.

"You'll pay for that, flower." He chuckles, his voice dark and smoky.

My legs tremble, and I can feel the evidence of my arousal dripping down my legs.

"Done screaming already? This doesn't do it for you, does it?"

My dress is shoved up to my back, my panties torn off in a rough jerk that I know will leave marks. He presses his hands against mine over the edge of the table. "Leave them there, or I'll tie you up and leave you this way, so wet and needy you can barely think straight."

I clutch onto the table and squeeze my eyes shut to focus on the sensations. His calloused hand smooths over my bare ass, then his thumb dips into my crack, drifting lower and lower until he reaches that tight ring of muscles. Gentler than I anticipated, he prods against the hole until his thumb slips inside. The sensation is strange and a little uncomfortable.

I squeak, and he pushes in a little more. "Your ass is even

tighter. Soon, I'll fuck you here, but not tonight. For this, I want your pussy."

He leans over me again. There's the soft whish of fabric being moved then the thick head of his length brushes against my swollen, aching flesh. Goose bumps pebble my flesh, and when he presses against me, I reach back to try to slow him.

The air leaves my lungs when he presses all the way in, hard and fast, so brutal my hip bones dig into the table. His hands clamp onto mine. "What the fuck did I say? Don't move."

I try to speak, but the words are all muffled with the stupid gag in my mouth. When I squirm, he takes one of his hands and presses my cheek into the wood. I reach up again, red-hot rage simmering in my veins, and scratch at him, trying to make him let go.

"Is that how you want it? *Fine*."

He pulls out and slams back into me. The tight muscles clamp around him, and the sensation vibrates through me. Why does this feel so good when I hate him for every second, for all the shame already building inside my chest for wanting it, and needing it? His other hand tangles in my hair, and he pulls me up, one arm slipping around my waist. Keeping his fingers wrapped in my loose hair, he curves me backward, keeping control, steering me. It hurts and feels so good at the same time.

"Go on, then, little wallflower. You want to fight me? Then fight me."

I squirm, but it only causes him to go deeper, so deep, it feels like he's in my stomach. I scratch at his arms and try to kick out my legs, but he has me pulled up tight against him, and my legs only manage to tangle with his. The world starts to spin, and I realize that we're moving, each step making me take him deeper. I barely have time to try again when we are in my room, and I'm slammed against the window. My face smears on the glass, my breath fanning out in a steaming arc to fog it.

"Open your eyes. Take a look out there."

I blink, his words sinking in. Outside the dark window is a bench, and a man, one of his creepy friends probably. Before I can comprehend what is happening, Drew pulls out and shoves back in hard. The sill digs into my skin, and I grab it to put distance between the wood and me.

"You tried. Now it's my turn."

Then he shows me he's been holding out all along when his grip tightens all around me. He bends my spine almost painfully and pounds into me harshly. His pace is brutal, and it feels like he's trying to fuck himself through me. Beneath the pain is intense pleasure, bringing me higher and higher. Soon, I'm pressing back against him, wanting more, needing it harder and faster. *What is wrong with me?* I shouldn't want this, shouldn't want him, but I do. I want it so badly it's all I think about, all I can feel. I'm consumed by Drew, and I don't know how to save myself from drowning in his need.

"That's a good girl. Show them who you belong to, let the world know you liked to be fucked like a dirty little slut." *Fuck.* I let out a little whimper, and he leans down to whisper in my ear. "You want more? Tell me what you need. Does my little flower want more of my cock? Or do you want me to stretch out that tight ass of yours? Will you still beg me with your weeping pussy if I do?"

"No." I gasp behind the gag. The fear of him fucking my ass without proper foreplay is terrifying.

"Are you sure? I think your tight little ass would look glorious with my big fat cock pounding inside of it until I explode. I'd pump your last virgin hole with every drop of seed in my balls, and then I'd watch it leak out."

Fuck, his words are filthy, but I want them. Every single one of them. I can't explain how much it turns me on or how much further it pushes me toward an orgasm. At this moment, with him, I want him to fuck me hard. I want him to break me into a million pieces and put me back together.

His thrusts are forceful, and the pleasure in my belly unfurls with every slap of his balls against my clit. A whimper escapes me, and I feel something cold against my cheeks, sliding down slowly. *Am I crying?*

"After that little stunt you pulled, I should deny you the opportunity to come, but you're lucky I enjoy feeling your cunt clenching all around me and sucking me deeper inside." He grunts, his movements becoming faster. "Now I'm about to explode, so you better hurry up. Make that pussy clench. Come on my cock. I need to feel you spasm all around me. Need to know who it is that owns this pussy."

Oh god. I tighten my grip on the wooden frame holding myself in place. Every muscle in my body tightens. I'm so close. I try to press back or wiggle forward, anything to get more friction. I need it. Need him...to finish it. His long fingers weave through my hair, and he tugs my neck backward, his lips pressed against the shell of my ear.

"Come on, flower. Be a good girl, and come on my cock."

I'm panting like a dog in heat, grinding my ass against him. His hips go erratic as his thighs shake against mine. "That's it. Fuck, yes. I'm about to come. I'm about to fill your cunt with my cum."

Oh god, he's going to come. He's going to come inside me without a condom on again, and nothing pushes me over the edge like that thought. Light flashes before my eyes, and I explode into a million pieces, my entire body shaking as I scream against the gag.

"So good, so fucking good." He grunts into my hair and slams into me one more time. He holds himself there, his body flush with mine, one hand in my hair, the other pressing me hard against the glass. It hurts and feels so good at the same time, and I swear I black out for a second from the sensations.

Slowly, like a feather, I drift back down to reality. Fresh tears trail down my cheeks, and drool dribbles out the side of my mouth and down my chin. I feel thoroughly used.

Drew loosens his hold and unties the gag, and I barely keep myself upright. His arms wrap around me, and he gently lifts me, carrying me over to the bed. I'm only half coherent now, my brain unable to put together what is happening around me. I watch through an orgasm high as he slowly undresses me, his touch gentle, caring, and I can see his eyes moving over the length of my body, assessing my bruises and whatever other marks he's left. My shoulder hurts like hell, but I don't say anything about it.

"Stay like that," he orders and disappears out the doorway. Without thinking, I find myself reaching for him. I don't want him to leave yet. I'm relieved when he reappears a few seconds later with a washcloth in his hands. Easing my legs apart, he says nothing while cleaning me up. The warmth of the rag on my sensitive folds makes me shiver.

"I advise you to take some ibuprofen and a bath in the morning. You're going to be sore as hell tomorrow." There isn't an ounce of regret or remorse in his voice. He's not sorry for marking me or making me come so hard I saw stars. He's unapologetic, and there's something raw and deep about that.

I'd call myself crazy, but I blame my next move on the pleasure endorphins pumping through my veins at this moment. I've never really touched Drew, not in a simple, nonsexual way, so when I reach for him and place my own hand over the top of his, it feels strange, different.

"Will you stay with me? Just until I fall asleep? Please?"

Drew seems taken aback by the question, and I half expect him to turn around and leave because that's what he does. He runs and hides from anything that makes him feel something he isn't ready to face, but he surprises me by doing the opposite.

"Fine, but only because you asked so nicely."

Still in his clothing, which is perfectly in place like he didn't just fuck the daylights out of me, he climbs over my limp body and slides between me and the wall. My muscles protest as I inch over to make room for his massive frame. Once he's in place, he snakes an arm beneath the pillow and the other around me, pulling me into his chest. I grab the comforter and tug it over us. Warm and secure in his embrace, I press my ear to his chest, listening to the heavy thump of his heartbeat. The smell of sex lingers in the air but has a calming effect on me when mixed with his heady cologne.

"Why can't you always be like this? Warm. Kind. Sweet. It kinda makes me want to like you, but only like a little tiny bit," I say, my eyes getting heavier by the second. Sleep threatens to pull me under, but I fight against it, refusing to let this moment between us end.

"I wouldn't do that. It'll be easier if you hate me when this is all over. I'm not cut out as boyfriend material."

I won't lie, my heart aches a little at his statement, but it's not shocking. I've known what Drew's intentions were this whole time, but now things are changing because my feelings are getting involved.

I decide to change the subject and say instead, "Who was that watching us?"

"I don't know, and I don't care. Probably someone wanting to gather intel to share with my father."

"What does that mean? Why would anyone want to tell your father what you're doing?" I'm confused by his comment but too exhausted to piece it all together right now.

"It doesn't matter. Go to sleep, Bel." He huffs like he's frustrated with my pestering.

"I'm sorry." I yawn. "I keep telling myself not to care about you, but I can't. Somehow, I always end up back where I was before." I let my eyes drift closed, and just as I'm about to sink into the darkness, I swear I hear him whisper, "Me too."

CHAPTER 23
DREW

AFTER SPENDING the majority of the night with Maybel, holding her while she slept, watching every twitch of her face, I forced myself to leave and headed home at around five o'clock. It was the first time I ever spent the night with a woman, the first time I held one in my arms while they slept. It felt good but foreign. Maybe that's what I needed because today, I feel calmer than I have in a long time. Like this heavy weight on my shoulders has finally lifted.

I recall assessing her body when I removed her clothing and tucked her into bed. The bruises on her hips and the bite marks on her shoulder. I was rougher than I intended to be, but she fought me *so fucking* good. I'm so fucking proud of her.

There's just something that happens when I'm around her... like she's looking at me, not through me, not for me, but at me. Not seeing what she wants from me but me the man. The feeling is heady, dragging me into her orbit in ways I don't understand yet. I'm not sure I want to try to understand it.

I smile and roll on the bed, already hard thinking back on the memory. When I'm about to grip myself and relieve this ache already growing in my balls, my phone rings. I glance at the screen and consider throwing it at the wall.

"Fuck."

My father. My dick deflates instantly, not surprising. My father has that effect on people. I dread answering the phone. It's always one thing or another with him. I'll never be what he wants. Never be perfect enough.

I sigh and regretfully answer. He's always more pissed if he has to call me back. It takes me a second of breathing to speak, but before I get the chance, his voice cuts across the line, sharp as a whip and twice as painful.

"What the fuck do you think you're doing, Andrew?" I hate when he calls me *Andrew,* and he fucking knows it.

I flop over onto my back and stifle a yawn. "Should I know what you're referring to this time?"

There's a huff through the line. "Fucking watch the tone. Yes, you fucking should. Last night, at the carnival, where were you?"

I sit up and glare at the wall. "How do you know I wasn't there all night?" I already know the answer. It had to be the mysterious person standing outside Bel's window while I fucked her. Or it could be Sebastian.

"Because the fucking profit margin from the carnival, the one that is supposed to raise half of The Mill's annual charity donation, was exceedingly short, and you know who the alumni board will expect to make up the difference? *Me.*"

Of course it boils down to money. It's always about money with him. "What do you want me to say, Dad? I was there for my time at the dunking booth, then I rode the Ferris wheel. It was dark when I left and went home."

A long moment of silence passes, and I wait, holding my

breath. He doesn't want to hear me talk or defend myself anyway, and I'm getting so fucking sick and tired of these little phone conversations we seem to keep having after every event.

I think back to him calling the first time too. Who the fuck is talking to him? Funneling information into his ear?

"I see. Looks like you have fucking answers for everything, don't you? How about you explain to me what's going on with your grades? Do you have an answer for that?"

"Nothing is wrong with my grades," I snap.

"You think scraping by with the bare minimum is okay? Because it's fucking not. You're representing the Marshall name, or have you forgotten who foots your bills? You graduate at the top of your class, or you come here and work for me. I don't need you to have a degree to do the kind of work we do here. I can teach you everything you need to know."

Yeah, who needs a degree to knock heads around and threaten rich asshole's mistresses to keep them from talking.

His tone turns sharper. "But what I really want to know is why the fuck you saw that girl again? The white trash bitch I told you to stay away from? That is not protecting the family name.

"Maybe you want me to pull you out. Maybe that's what you want? Do you want me to pull you out of school and put you to work in the basement here? I can lock you up in the dungeons and let you rot. You're my heir, and you will fucking act like it, or I will make you!"

The last part is shouted, and I hold the phone away from my ear and focus on my breathing so I don't snap back at him. It will only make him yell and argue more, making this conversation even longer than either of us wants it to be.

"I'm not doing anything wrong. Is there something you need me to do? Can we just get to that part?"

This time, he doesn't warn me about my tone. Instead, he explodes, his voice becoming a scream on the other end. While he's ranting and cursing, I climb out of bed and grab a T-shirt off the floor. It's the one I wore last night while I lay in bed with Maybel. I take a second to smell the scent of her sweet perfume, still clinging to the fabric. I put it on my desk and then find a clean T-shirt to pull on while I waffle the phone between my ears, still not even listening.

There's no point when he goes off like this anyway, not until he finishes cursing and finally explains what the fuck he wants from me. I hold the phone between my shoulder and my ear while I pull on a pair of black sweatpants. It would be easier to put it on speaker, but somehow, he always knows when I do that to tune him out.

When he finally finishes ranting, I wait for the inevitable curt hang-up. It happens with a soft click, and I shove the phone into my pocket. Another great morning with dear old dad.

The house is quiet as I leave my bedroom. The boys are all probably still sleeping. I stop short in the kitchen when I spot Sebastian standing shirtless against the far countertop, a mug in his hands.

I spot the freshly brewed coffee in the pot and walk around the island, grabbing my own cup from the cabinet.

"That was an interesting show you put on last night? Feeling a little...possessive?"

I shrug and make sure to keep my voice level and calm. There's a snake among us, and I'm going to figure out who it fucking is. "No, that was a punishment, earned and delivered. You know more than anyone how important it is to keep someone in line."

He smiles wistfully. "That's the best part."

I roll my eyes and sip my coffee, but he doesn't drop it.

"You're done with your punishment now, your infatuation. I don't want..." He pauses as if he knows what he was about to say will piss me off. "I want you whole and healthy."

Yeah, definitely *not* what he was going to say.

So I'll be the one with the balls in this conversation, then. "Are you spying on me for my father?"

His eyes go wide, and he blinks like he's shocked that I would ever consider such a thing. "What? No. You know I would never do that."

"You seem super interested in my relationship with Bel, so what else am I to assume? Because I know you aren't stupid enough to try to take her away from me."

There's a tense moment as we stare at each other over our coffee cups.

"I'm not spying on you. And *no*, I don't have any intention with your little bookworm. But do you hear yourself? You just said relationship. Is that really what you're calling it now? You know if your father finds out it's more than just a quick fuck, he'll make you regret it. I don't want anything to happen to you, and especially not because of some fucking girl."

I consider his words. Of all my friends, Sebastian and Aries have been with me the longest. All of them belong to the same world I do, the same world my father does, but Sebastian and Aries are the only ones who truly know what my father is capable of. They've seen me in some of my darkest moments with him. They picked me up and wiped away my tears after he beat me the first time. I take my mug and cut across the kitchen to grab a jacket off the hook by the door.

"You don't need to worry about it. She means nothing to me."

He glares after me, and I hear him as I walk out the back

door of the house. "If she means nothing, why the fuck did you feel the need to punish her, then?"

———

It takes a few minutes to walk down the long drive to the main campus, then cut across the courtyards to the library. It's the only place I know I'll always find her.

Sebastian's words continue to ring in my ears. He's right. If she meant nothing to me, I'd just drop her, not punish her. I'd have no need to mark her, and ensure everyone knows who she belongs to. I sip my coffee as I walk. Usually, I bring a travel mug with me, but I feared what I'd do if I stayed in the kitchen with Sebastian. No doubt we'd have progressed to an argument or worse. The inside of the library is quiet. It's still early. I'm honestly surprised to find her here, especially after last night's events, but she's determined when it comes to her studies. She's in her usual spot; a freshman from the baseball team, I think maybe, sits beside her studying his math textbook.

I stop by her cubicle, and they both look up at me. I point at the kid. "You...go."

To his credit, he doesn't ask questions. He simply gathers his belongings and leaves, just like that.

It pays to be king.

I sit and slouch into the chair he vacates, and she gapes at me with her mouth open. "What the hell, Drew? I'm working here."

"You were working, sure, but now you're not. Plus, I want to talk to you, and I can't do that with your clients standing next to us."

She removes her glasses and sets them carefully on the book in front of her. "You have no right to come in here and order him around. I highly doubt he's going to pay me now."

Carefully, I scan her features. There's a faint red mark on her cheek where I pinned her against the window and a smudge of a bruise on her neck where I bit her. All my other marks are covered by her clothing.

When the memories surge back, I set my coffee on the desk and lean toward her. "Are you okay?" I didn't ask last night, mainly because I wasn't sure how I felt after it all happened. When I held her in my arms, it felt perfect and right, and as much as I didn't want the moment to end, it needed to. In the world I live, there is no chance between her and I.

She glares at me, but there's a strange softness that lingers beneath. "After your caveman routine last night? Yes, I'm fine. You must've got up early and left?"

I lower my voice and take her hand. When she doesn't pull away, I squeeze it between both of mine. It's warm, soft, and so delicate. "Yes. I left at five o'clock. I usually get up and work out during football season. Now don't evade the question. Are you really okay?"

"What's it matter? You can't take back what happened. The better question is, are you going soft on me? Is that icy heart of yours slowly unthawing? Because you've never asked me if I was okay before."

It's my turn to glare, and I release her hand. "Call me soft again, and I'll make you try to say it while you choke on my cock. How about that?"

She rolls her eyes and turns her attention back to her notebook. "I don't have time for this. I'm fine. You could've texted me to ask me that, not sent my client away and cost me one hour's worth of work."

I grab the back of her neck and steer her head back to

look at me. "No, I'm not going anywhere. And I'm not checking on you because I'm fucking *soft*. It was a question. I meant more so after what happened with fuckface."

In my murderous haste to punish her, I never thought to discuss with her if she was okay after everything that happened. I sent Lee a text before I went into Bel's dorm to break both of the fucker's hands and leave him in a ditch somewhere. It'll teach him not to fuck with me and what's mine. I wanted to kill him, but I didn't want to hurt Bel, and if someone came sniffing around asking questions, she'd be the first person they go to.

Bel frowns. "I'm okay. The whole thing made me feel stupid, and now I need to cancel his tutoring appointments. As much as I need the money, I can't trust him."

Sitting back in the chair again, I sip on the mug of coffee. She glares, reaches for the mug, and snatches it from my grasp. I watch as she slowly brings it to her lips and takes a sip.

"Ugh, it's cold."

"I walked from the mill to here. Of course it's cold."

With a roll of her eyes, she reaches under the desk and grabs an old battered thermos that looks like it belongs in a 1901 mining biopic. I extend my cup toward her, and she refills it with steamy coffee. When I let out a long sigh and sip again, it earns me a smile. A smile that does something in my chest, twisting things around, and burrowing a thorn deep enough to leave a gash. Fresh blood fills that small crevice, the warmth of it a small dot in my normally icy, barren chest.

Since it's not something I want to touch at the moment, I push the thought to the back of my mind and focus my sole attention on her. "Well, I have good news, and since you're down a client, this should help. I need a tutor."

She stares at me dumbfounded for a few moments and

then whispers the question as if it's a secret. "A tutor for what?"

"For myself, obviously." I grin.

A smile tips at the corner of her lips, and then it grows until she bursts into full on laughter. Her slim arms wrap around her middle, and she chuckles like I've told her the most hilarious joke of all time. It's honestly kind of cute how she tips her head back, and how she appears to let go and be herself for one moment. It's like looking through a telescope into space at a star, knowing you'll only see it implode on itself once. It's also something I have little patience for...

"Laugh it up, flower, but what if I pay you five hundred dollars a session?"

She goes from smiling to neutral in two seconds flat. *Not a joke anymore, huh?*

Suddenly, I'm the one smiling. "You can't...that would be...too much," she finishes softly as if she can't really believe the words she's saying. "Besides, I'd kill you."

My smile becomes a full-on grin, turning up the charm, something she hasn't seen a lot of from me yet. I say, "I can, and I will, but I'd have a few conditions."

"Of course you would. You wouldn't be you without conditions." Her delicate eyebrow arches in question, almost as if she's waiting for me to reveal said conditions, and I bite, continuing to speak.

"This arrangement would secure your services for me exclusively."

She shakes her head, gold strands of hair start to fly, and her pretty pink lips part. I know she's about to start sputtering some nonsense, so I grab the pencil in front of her and place it between her lips. "Be quiet and let me finish, or I'll put something else in your mouth that I know will keep you quiet."

She takes the pencil out, and I give her a warning glare. "Exclusive services, tutoring sessions whenever I need them. You help me get to the top of the class."

She jerks the pencil from her mouth and throws it at my chest. It's easy enough to catch, and I tuck it behind my ear, still damp from her pretty lips.

"What's the catch, *Andrew?*" The way she says my full name grinds over every last nerve ending in my body.

"No catch. I admit I've let things slip a little. Football is important, and they'll bench me if my grades fall too far. Anything but stellar performance is a failure to my father." The mere mention of him makes my blood boil. The rage and anger are always lurking beneath the mask, threatening to bubble up and over and reveal the real man beneath. I remember her question from last night. She wanted to know why my friends would speak to my father and tell him things, and I don't have an answer. I'm trying to figure that out myself.

"Oh yes, I forgot. You rich boys and your overbearing need to please your fathers." She shakes her head, and the tension snaps, crackling and popping like fire. I lurch forward and grip her by the back of the neck, giving her no escape. A kitten-like whimper escapes her lips, and I squeeze a little tighter. I want to hear her make that sound again, for me. Only ever for me.

"Let go of me," she hisses.

"No, because what you said pissed me off, and you don't seem to understand what I'm saying unless I'm inside you or physically touching you." I peer down at her, noticing the slight dilation in her pupils and the rapid rise and fall of her chest. I'd bet her nipples are tight little peaks, and that pretty pussy of hers probably weeps in despair for my cock at this very moment. Perhaps I've made a slut out of the sweet and innocent wallflower.

"This has nothing to do with pleasing my father. I don't give a fuck about what my father wants. This is what I want. Football... It means something to me. It's one of the few things that actually fucking matter in my life, and if I don't have it as an outlet..." I'm unable to finish speaking because confessing out loud what I might become terrifies me.

I banish the thoughts away. "Plus, you could use the money, and I'm nothing but a helpful guy."

She pulls back, and I release her from my grasp, her pretty eyes narrowed to slits. "I need the money, but I don't need your money, and before you say anything else, yes, there's a difference."

Sometimes I think she wants to push me to my limits just to see how far I'm willing to go. "So I've been told by you once before, but I'm afraid you forget who I am and what I'm willing to do to get what I want."

"How could I possibly forget? If my memory serves me correctly, any time you can't get what you want from me, you take it."

All I can do is smirk because if she's trying to make me believe that she didn't want what happened to happen between us last night, then she'll need to try way fucking harder. "If you want me to believe you don't want it next time, maybe don't come so hard you strangle the life out of my cock while you're milking it with your cunt, and I might believe you."

"I don't think this is a good idea. We barely get along. I'm pretty sure you're going to kill me soon, and if you don't kill me, I know I'm *definitely* going to kill you."

"I'm harder to kill than I look, baby." I wink.

Her expression turns serious, and her little button nose wrinkles, "I don't know..."

Frustration stacks like concrete blocks deep in my gut. Why is she showing so much resistance to tutoring me, yet she has no problem saying yes to jackasses like Stewart? I know it's going to make me an asshole to threaten her like this, but I do it anyway because I want her to understand that there isn't any other way around this. She'll do what I want her to do by choice or by force. It's up to her which road we take.

"I mean, if it's really an issue, I can go to the dean and share with him that you're refusing to offer me services and discriminating against me, claiming that I'm a rich jock who shouldn't need services."

I watch as her face morphs into anger. "Prime example of why we should not do this and why I will, in fact, kill you."

"You wish you could kill me, but then if you killed me, who would make you come so hard you nearly pass out?" The question makes the centers of her cheeks turn a soft pink color, and I gently run the pad of my finger over her flesh. "The answer is no one, by the way, because just in case you get any other stupid ideas about going out with other men next time, I won't be so nice. Next time, I'll kill the fucker right in front of you, and then I'll fuck you and use his blood as lube."

"You're absolutely insane," she whispers. My phone dings with an incoming text that I ignore. I'm not done with this conversation yet, and I don't want my attention to deviate elsewhere.

"Believe me, I know... But for five hundred dollars a week, you're putting up with me."

"I didn't agree to that," she growls angrily. "And blackmail is pretty low, even for you. You know I need the money from these sessions."

"Then I guess you better make the right choice, flower."

I leave the choice in her hands and push up and out of my seat. Before I leave, I press my lips to the crown of her head, letting them linger there for a moment longer than necessary. Her intoxicating strawberry scent fills my lungs, and I breathe as much of it into my lungs as I can. Where she's concerned, I'm more out of control than I ever expected to be, but I don't care. Before her, I never had a choice. I never had a voice. Now it's like the pieces of the mask I'm forced to wear are slowly chipping away, revealing my real identity beneath.

CHAPTER 24
BEL

NERVOUS ENERGY RIPPLES through me as I stare at the cell phone screen. It's only been three days since Drew announced I would be tutoring him and only him. I hate the idea of being alone with him again, but I don't have much choice.

I'm not sure what he would do if I chose to tutor the other students still... but I don't want to find out. Something deep in my gut leads me to believe this man is far more deviant and dangerous than even I know, and pushing him would be a dumb idea. He has money, a family, a future—everything I don't—so his strange obsession with me makes no sense. I'm no one, nothing, yet he won't leave me alone.

What would I even do if he left me alone?

Goose bumps erupt across my skin, and my thoughts swirl. With Drew, I'm out of my comfort zone. He pushes me to my limits, and when I think I can't go any further, he shows me a new limit. He makes me feel, and I hate it. I hate how much my body craves him when he's not here, and how my thoughts always trail back to him. Even with all the hate that seems to pulse for him in my veins, a small part of me craves his darkness and danger. That craves the jagged pieces of his heart.

All over again, I'm reminded of him overtaking my thoughts. I decide then that I need a distraction. I grab my phone and type out a quick message, sending the mass text to all my clients, letting them know I'll be canceling all future sessions. It's not worth the risk of losing the money he's offered me, not when money is the one thing I need the most.

Doing this means inviting that man into my life. It means no longer pretending I didn't have a choice when things happen between us. I've been telling myself it's been all him this whole time, but it hasn't. He's never done anything that I didn't want him to do. A tiny voice in the back of my head reminds me that I'm the one who joined The Hunt, and I'm the one who went into those woods. How could I have expected someone like Drew, though? How could I have known what would happen? That I would be noticed by the ruthless, vindictive man who always gets what he wants? I never could've anticipated him, but that's the thing. You don't predict the bad happening.

Once I pack my bag, intending to get some study time in, I stop in the kitchen to grab something to eat. As I pour a bowl of cereal, Jackie comes out, smiling. "I saw you leaving the carnival the other night. What happened? You ran out of there like someone was chasing you."

Shit. I forgot I'd seen her there. "No, I was just cold and tired. I shouldn't have gone in the first place. I was just trying to get back here as fast as possible."

It sounds like a stupid excuse, even to me. Her eyebrow twitches up as her lips turn down. "You left your car there, though, didn't you?"

I turn my back to pour some milk and to get my face

under control. "Yeah, I had a beer or two, so I decided to walk back. Better to be safe than sorry."

It's not like she'll care what's happening with Drew and me, so why am I keeping things to myself? I don't know... Something happens when I'm with him, some part of me feels set free, and I'm not quite ready to talk about that yet. Confiding in her would make all of this that much more real, and I don't know if I'm ready.

I hear her shift and glance back to find her leaning against the doorframe, her arms crossed, staring at me. "What?"

She huffs. "Whatever, it's your business."

I turn to face her, bowl in hand. "No, what is it?"

"I saw Drew, that football player, chasing you. Why were you running?"

I shovel food into my mouth and mumble around the Cocoa Puffs. "I wasn't running from anything." It's a blatant lie, one that she must see through since she makes a sure sort of noise, and my annoyance catches up with me. "What do you want me to say, Jackie? I'm an adult. I don't have to justify my whereabouts with you or why I was doing something."

She holds her hands up in surrender, but her eyes flash with anger. "I'm not interrogating you. I just want to make sure you're okay. Drew is...*fun*...but he's a one-and-done kind of guy who throws girls away after he's had his fill. And you definitely aren't a one-and-done kind of girl. I don't want to see you get hurt by him. That's all."

She's offering me a lifeline, a chance to talk to her, yet I can't make myself do it. There's no way in hell I'm going to explain what happened the other night, not when I'm not even entirely sure myself.

I slump into the chair at the table, and my mind immediately flashes to him holding me down there, a rush of heat zinging straight to my core at the simple memory. "It's noth-ing. I'm nothing to him. He only wants me because I said no."

She shifts against the table, making it creak in protest. "Just be careful. Guys like Drew don't know where the line is, and the game he's playing this time isn't one he's ever played. No one has seen him with the same girl more than once. I just... If you ever want to talk about it, need advice, or even need help hiding a body, I'm here."

I smile. It's a jagged dim thing, but she smiles back. Maybe telling her would make me feel better? Help me under-stand my own feelings better. I'm about to open my mouth, and spill my guts to her, when my phone vibrates on the table, scaring the shit out of us both. We share a chuckle, and I look down. It's a number I don't recognize, but in my mom's area code. I hit the green answer button and press it to my ear.

"Hello?"

"Hello, is this Maybel Jacobs?"

"Yes?"

"I'm Angela Black, calling from Saint Michael's Hospital. We have your mother here..."

Static immediately fills my head, and I jerk to standing, jostling the bowl and spilling milk across the table. "*What?* Is she okay?"

"Don't be alarmed, but we got a call to pick her up earlier this morning from a neighbor. They found her passed out in her home."

Oh my god. Why didn't she call me? I knew I should've stayed at her house last night. Tears track down my cheeks, hot and heavy as I rush into my room, holding my phone between my face and my shoulder while I tug on a pair of boots. "I'm coming. I'll be right there."

"Very good, Ms. Jacobs. We'll see you soon."

Jackie hands me my bag that I'd left on the floor and my

car keys, and I rush out of my room heading for the door. "Call me if you need anything."

I nod, and pull the door open, escaping into the hall. My feet pound against the floor as I race down the hall and outside to my car. *Dammit.* Drew pops into my head. I won't be able to meet with him this morning like I promised. Surely, he'll understand. I send him a quick text, only a few words, and race out of the dorm parking toward the hospital.

It feels like it takes me hours to drive there after hitting every light and getting behind every single slow driver in the city. I beep my horn impatiently and do my best to keep my emotions in check. When I arrive at the hospital, I slam the car into a parking spot and put it in park. Grabbing my phone from the cupholder, I notice Drew's name on the screen and a text alert. I'm too frazzled about what's going on with my mother. I don't have time for this right now. I shove my phone into my bag as I run into the hospital. My mother is the only family I have left. I can't lose her.

I can't.

It seems to take an eternity before I can get to her, but soon enough, one of the nurses comes to get me and directs me to a small room down a corridor. My mom looks up wearily from the bed. "Hey, Little One, you're here."

I smile. "You must be on some good drugs. You haven't called me that since I was a kid."

She laughs, and then it turns into a cough as I sit beside the bed. "Mom...what happened?"

She reaches for me, and I immediately clutch her hand tight in mine. It's cold and dry. "I'm okay, baby. I just got dizzy and passed out. It's a side effect of some of the medications. Low heart rate. You know the drill."

I try to give her a smile, but I know it's more of a grimace. She pretends anyway and give me a brittle smile.

There's a drumbeat in my head, chanting I can't lose her over and over, and it's all I'm thinking about now. "When are they going to let you out of here?"

"I'm not sure—"

Someone knocks on the door, cutting her off, and our attention is directed to them as a doctor walks in. "Hello! I'm sorry to see you again under these circumstances."

"Do you know when she'll be released?" I ask the doctor since my mother said she didn't know anyway.

"I'm afraid we don't know yet."

I try to rein in my panic. "What does that mean?"

He smiles back and forth between us. "Your mother and I have already spoken, but I'm afraid things have progressed more quickly than we anticipated. She's going to need extensive care, and then I think we should talk about hospice options so her last days are as pain-free as possible."

Hospice? Last days? This doctor is talking gibberish. My mother is sick, yes, but there is still hope.

"No!" The word shoots out of my mouth, making both my mother and the doctor flinch.

"Baby." My mother tries to console me, but I squeeze her hand tightly in response.

"There has to be something more we can do. We haven't even started the experimental treatments you were telling me about. There are still things we can do."

They both start speaking at the same time.

"I'm tir—"

"Your mother doesn't—"

I cut them both off and gently release my mother's hand, placing it on the bed. Then I face the doctor. "Can we speak in private for a moment, please?"

Dr. Mitch cuts a look at my mom, who nods, and I head into the hallway behind him. The scent of disinfectant and rubber makes me want to throw up because I always associated that scent with my mom being in the hospital. I *hate* it. Wrapping my arms around myself, I look up at the doctor. "If this is about money, I can get whatever we need to proceed, I promise, even if I have to quit school and get a job. I will do what needs to be done. Please don't deny her services just because we don't have insurance."

The doctor's eyes soften, and he leans closer. "This has nothing to do with the money. We have benefactors here at the hospital who can help. I think it's time to consider your options. Your mother is tired. She doesn't want to spend the rest of her final days fighting an inevitable battle. You need to understand that, even if it's not your wishes, it's your mother's."

I snap. "No. I don't care what she wants. Once it's over, she'll be alive and grateful that I stepped in and convinced her to do this."

He shakes his head at me. "I know this is hard, Maybel, but I do have to consider what your mother wants."

I suck a ragged breath into my lungs, but it doesn't even feel like I'm breathing. "I'll talk to her again. I'll convince her."

"You can try your best, but please remember your mother's wishes are important as well." I nod and blink back the tears forming in my eyes. I will not break down here. Not in front of him or my mother.

We walk back into the room, and I take my mother's hand again. "Mom, will you try this drug, this experiment, for me? What do we have to lose if you're..." I almost choke on the words. "Dying...anyway."

I need her to see how much losing her is hurting me. I'm not ready. I can't face this.

"Baby, we can't. We don't have the money for it, and I'm not letting you quit school for me."

"If I got the money without quitting school, then would you agree?"

She snorts, her eyes going hazy as the pump beside the bed administers another dose of medication into her IV. "You're not going to become a stripper, are you?"

I laugh. "Yeah, because everyone wants to see my pasty white body on display. I doubt there is a big demand for book nerd strippers out there." I shake my head. "No, of course I won't become a stripper."

Dr. Mitch steps up to the bed, staring at my mother. "Does this mean you want to proceed?"

She nods wearily, and I almost feel guilty, but not enough to take it back. She's all I have. Once the doctor leaves, I sit in the chair again and try not to let the panic I'm feeling seep into my voice.

"Don't worry, Mom, I'll take care of you, of this. We'll beat it together."

She turns in the bed, careful not to catch her IV tubing. "How are you getting this money? And tell me the truth, because sick or not, you're not too old to get a spanking."

"Tutoring, as usual. I'll just raise my fees, you know, for inflation. No one will think anything of it."

Her gaze has so much trust as she looks at me, and I will not balk from it. She's given me everything my entire life, raised me as a single mother and worked numerous jobs just to provide me with the things I needed. I can do this for her.

My phone vibrates in my bag, and I already know who is trying to get ahold of me. He can wait. Every person except my mother can wait. I settle into the chair and avert my gaze to the TV, enjoying this single moment with my mother for what it is.

CHAPTER 25
DREW

WHAT I HATE MORE than anything is being ignored. Now do I know with one-hundred percent certainty that she's ignoring me? No. What I do know is that she isn't replying, and to me, that's the same fucking thing. It's been a few days since she agreed to tutor me, and one more since she set this appointment, all via text. But now, she's no longer responding.

I'm barely keeping myself from going to hunt her down as I sit alone in the library, thirty minutes past when she said she'd be here. I grab my phone off the table next to my textbook and send her yet another message, this time, filled with more expletives than the others.

When she hadn't messaged me back for our last meeting, I checked the devices of hers I'd cloned from that time Jackie allowed me access to in her room. She went to see her mother in the hospital. That's the only reason I didn't press her.

But today, I know she's not at the hospital, so she has no fucking excuse to leave me sitting here waiting on her ass. Not when there are five hundred other things I could be doing. Like trying to figure out how to get my father back out of my business. Or figure out what the fuck is going on with Sebastian.

One of the football players walks by the table and nods, extends his hand for a fist bump, then keeps moving through the library. What is it about this place? It doesn't matter what day I come into this place. There is never any level of privacy. Why does my little wallflower like it here so much? I know she studies here often, even when she's not tutoring. I decide I'll ask her once I've punished her for keeping me waiting. Ten minutes later, she finally shows up. She slings her bag to the floor beside the cubicle I know she prefers, and then she claps her books onto the table, and a hard crack resonates through the room.

"Wallflower?"

She turns to glare at me but then sits with a huff and begins to dig into her bag.

I lean in and lower my voice. "What the fuck is your problem? You are the one who canceled on me, after taking my money up front for that matter, and then you have the nerve to leave me sitting here waiting, and once you finally deign to show your face, you give me an attitude. Start talking."

She sits up straight, and I have to pull back so my face doesn't smack against her shoulder.

"What do you want from me? I'm here, aren't I? Now, are we studying or not?"

I pull the edge of my book and let it slap against the table, not even looking at it, just keeping eye contact with her. "I've been here and ready to study, but you've been absent. I didn't realize I needed to fit into your calendar now that I'm your *client*. And I *better* be your only fucking client, or that money I gave you is going to disappear pretty fucking fast."

Something like panic enters her eyes now. "No, you're right. I'm sorry. I'm just having a bad couple of days, okay?

Let's just get to work, and I'll stay here with you as long as you want me to."

I slam the book shut again and lean toward her. "Excuse me?"

Her forehead crinkles as she meets my eyes. "What? I said I'll stay as long as you want me to." Her voice is gentle, placating, and it only pisses me off more.

I grit my teeth and continue to keep my voice low. "You fucking show up here and act like this, and what? You think I'm just going to roll over and lick your hand in thanks?"

Her eyes go wide, and realization seeps into her features. "Oh, look, this has nothing to do with you." Her attitude comes back in full force. "Not everything is about you, oh mighty football god."

"And now you're going to sass me. What the fuck, Maybel?" I hiss.

Her eyes go wide at my use of her full name. "What do you want, then?"

"An explanation, not half-assed excuses." Of course I know about her mother already, but I want to hear it from her. I want her to give me the truth, so I don't have to take it.

"I mean...I was busy."

"Busy?"

Her eyes narrow into slits, and she leans in so close we could almost kiss. "Yes, busy. Is that a vocabulary word we need to go over?"

I clench my fists, slide one over the back of her chair and angle so my chest is almost brushing her shoulder. "Watch it, wallflower, or I'm going to give you another introduction to punishment. And I know you don't want that to happen right here, right now."

Before she can react, I slide my hand under her skirt and cup it tight against her panty-covered cunt. "Or maybe you do want it. Maybe you liked how I used your body, and you're hoping to earn another punishment from me."

She squirms now, the anger in her eyes fanning to panic. "What...no...I never said I liked it?"

"Oh, you never said it. You never said it with the way that pretty little pussy milked my cock, or how you screamed for me as I did you? What's that saying, actions speak louder than words?"

She gulps hard, and I watch her throat working, wanting to wrap my fingers tight around the length of it. Watch her struggle as I cut off her air so that I'm the only reason she's breathing.

"Give me the real reason you blew me off, and I'll let you go," I whisper.

She squirms, and I can feel the heat of her pussy against my palm. My little wallflower wants me as much as I want her. She just hasn't accepted it yet.

"I..." she stutters. "My mom is sick. *Okay?* That's why I've needed the extra money, the extra time. She's sick, and I was spending time with her."

Guilt slices through me. "Why didn't you just fucking tell me that?"

"It's none of your business, and I don't want your pity!"

"My pity. You think I've been fucking you out of pity?"

There's distance in her eyes now, and I don't want it. I grasp her chin with my free hand and keep her eyes locked on me. While she's staring into me, I slip her panties to the side and delve two fingers straight into her waiting heat.

She hisses, and her eyes close.

"No, wallflower, open them. Look at me. Now."

The snap in my voice makes her open again, and she stares at me. "I want you to watch me while I make you come. So you know it isn't pity I see when I look at you."

"Someone might see us," she whispers.

I shake my head. "Don't worry about anyone else here. Trust me to take care of you. Keep your eyes on mine and stay quiet so no one else notices."

She nods her head, and I smile while curling my fingers inside her. "Good girl."

When I gently start pumping two fingers in and out of her, she bites her lip hard but keeps her eyes on mine like I've ordered. It's addicting to see this beautiful, intelligent woman succumb to the haze of lust just like the rest of us mere mortals. By the time I'm finished with her, she'll beg me to give her what she needs.

I lick my lips, drawing her gaze down, and then she remembers and snaps her eyes back to mine. The smile that curls my lips is genuine, and she jolts as if I'd stunned her.

"Stay still, flower." She shudders against me. "Do you trust me?" The look in her lustful gaze bleeds on the line of uncertainty, and I can't blame her. I hardly trust myself, but I've never hurt her or let someone else hurt her. "Slouch down in your seat so your ass is on the edge of the chair." She wiggles, inching forward, and I feel her thighs parting wider, giving me more access. Keeping my eyes trained on her face, I slowly insert a third finger and watch for any discomfort. "How much can you take like this? How much before you're coming and squeezing my fingers tight?"

Her entire body shudders, and the lustful haze fills her eyes. "I don't know..."

I pump my fingers a little deeper and love how she feels. So warm and wet. I'm hard, my dick pressing against the fly of my jeans, but this is for her, both a punishment and a demonstration. She wants me badly enough that she's willing to let me defile her in her precious library, while risking getting caught with my fingers inside her.

I move them faster and watch her squirm in the seat. "Careful, or you'll give us away."

She only shakes her head, her lust-filled gaze firmly on my eyes. I wonder what she sees there. No, it's probably better if I don't know the answer.

"Should I add another? Do you think you can take my entire hand?" She's more than aroused. My fingers are wet and slippery as they slide inside her again and again. Her pussy stretches around my finger, and I give her a grin and shift my hand enough that I fit my pinky inside along with my three main fingers. She tenses at the intrusion, and I move slow enough that she can adjust to the extra width. I definitely don't have small hands, so I can only imagine how it feels.

I lean in close so our mouths almost hover against each other. "How's that?"

She huffs, her chest heaving as she speaks brokenly against my lips. "You're only asking to tease me. It's not like you'll stop if I tell you it's too much."

Would I? I don't know. When it comes to her, there doesn't appear to be a rule, limit, or boundary I won't cross.

"You're right, flower, but for that sass, guess what? Let's see if you can take my whole hand up that pretty little pussy."

Another gulp, another flutter of her lashes, another thump of my heart as I watch her like this. It's the way she takes me, the way she pushes—it means nothing but a little challenge and a little fun. I move my fingers faster, pushing her closer to the edge. I twist my fingers together and add my thumb, slowly easing them all inside her. It's slow work and takes a bit of patience as she squirms and folds her lips together to keep from making a sound. Next time I do this, it's going to be in one of our beds so I can hear her moan and say my name.

"You're doing such a good fucking job. You feel so good around my hand like this. I'm so proud of you."

She gulps again, and her forehead falls against mine like she can't hold her body together anymore, and she needs me to support it while I drive her out of her mind. I so very slowly pump my hand inside her, flexing my fingers apart for a second with each pass. "Do you like being this full of me? What if I did this and took your ass with my cock. Do you think you'd survive, or would it be too much?"

This earns me a small whimper, and I smile. Her muscles start to flutter, and her fingers tangle in my shirt, gripping it tightly. She's not even bothering to keep the lust off her face, her pleasure written in every grimace and line there.

"Almost there, flower. Come on, I want to feel you explode. Come for me, now." As if on command, she breaks apart, and I slam my mouth against hers, swallowing her cries of pleasure. She clings to me, her orgasm ripping through her center, her chest heaving with every breath she takes. After a few more seconds, I break the kiss, and once she sinks into the chair, easing away from me, I gently ease my fingers out of her pussy. Lifting them to my face, I notice how shiny and wet from her cum they are, and I can't help but slide my index finger into my mouth to taste her.

"Mmm..."

She shoves at me with her hands, and a blanket of warm embarrassment climbs up her cheeks."Oh my god, I can't believe you just did that."

I grab the edge of her skirt and meet her eyes while wiping my hand on the floral fabric. "Did what?"

There's shock on her face and lust, and it's like she hasn't been paying attention to what I'm capable of this whole time. Now she sees me, and she's not sure if she's scared or if she wants more. I turn to face the book in front of me, the scent of her body wafting off my hands to make me even harder.

"Let's study, wallflower, or I'm going to drag you back to my house and fuck you over every flat surface I can find."

She lets out a strangled noise and scrambles for her books, her notebook, and then her pen. "Study, right? Let's study. After all, I better earn that paycheck."

CHAPTER 26
BEL

IT'S BEEN a long time since I could go to the grocery store for my mother and not worry about my debit card being declined. The couple of weeks I've been working for Drew, along with the ten grand he gave me before, has padded my bank account and made my life more stable. I, of course, won't say anything about it to him. He doesn't need the ego boost, but privately, I can be more than thankful.

My mom is out of the hospital, and outside of school and tutoring, I've been helping her at home. She's not very high-maintenance and hates that I'm doing it, but there aren't any other options at the moment.

I place the bags on the countertop and move around her kitchen to put things away. Soups, vegetables, high protein shakes. Things that are quick to eat and easy to prepare.

"Baby, you don't have to keep doing this. I can take care of myself," she calls from the living room, where she's lying on the couch.

I roll my eyes and then smile to myself. And she wonders where I get my stubbornness from. "Mom, no one said you couldn't take care of yourself. I'm your daughter. It's my job to do these things. Besides, I don't mind helping out, okay? You took care of me for twenty years, I can..."

"That was my job, and right now, your job is to finish school and take care of yourself."

With a sigh, I crumple the paper bag and toss it in the recycling bin. "Don't worry about it, Mom. When you're up and around again, you can take over your own grocery shopping."

There's a long pause, and I poke my head around the wall to check on her.

She frowns and meets my eyes. "Did you get the strawberry protein or the chocolate?"

I can't help the smile that slips out as I throw myself into an armchair across the couch. "Chocolate this time."

We sit in silence for a moment, and I take the opportunity to look her over. She's lost weight, and her face is all angles and lines. She's still beautiful, but she looks too thin, dry, and brittle.

A nurse comes in each week to administer medications, and do a quick IV with some pain medications, but I still want her to put on more weight.

I return to the kitchen and bring out one of the cold protein shakes. "Here, drink this."

She wrinkles her nose in disgust but takes it. I help her sit comfortably and shift the pillows around to support her. When I take my seat again, she's sipping the drink slowly, a little at a time. It will take her forever to get through it, but by then, the chocolate ones will be cold, and maybe I can force her to drink another one.

"Baby," she says, pulling me from the scheming in my head. "Where are you getting the money for all of this?"

It's not the first time she's asked me, but it's the first time she's been so direct, meeting my gaze, her forehead wrinkling in concern.

I sit back in the chair and sigh. "Tutoring, odd jobs, the same as always."

She tilts her head, her lips turning into a wry smile. "How are you tutoring when you've been here more than school? I know these protein shakes aren't cheap, so..."

I shrug. "What do you want me to say, Mom? I'm tutoring a high-profile kid at school. He asked for my services specifically, so that's what I'm doing. I charge more to just tutor him. It's basically almost a full-time income for less than part-time work."

"Why would someone pay that for your exclusive tutoring services? What does he *really* want from you?"

I throw up my hands and let them fall to my lap. "I don't know. He's rich. He likes his time to be private, and I don't know, maybe he's spoiled and thinks he'll do better if he has me all to himself."

Her eyes narrow. "So he wants—"

"To pass his chemistry exams, that's it."

Her gaze slides away. "Men like that...they expect things sometimes. Did you plainly have him spell out what he wants? Wait...what's his name?"

His voice in my head says, *"You. Belong. To me."*

I gulp and give her a wide smile. Maybe too wide. "He doesn't want anything but a tutor, Mom. I promise. Let's talk about you and the new drugs they are going to start you on. I want to make sure I'm here for you, whatever you need. Oh, and his name is Drew. Not that I think you'd know him or anything."

Her shoulders slump, just like they always do when I bring up the trial drugs. I can't stand the defeat on her face, so I stand, grab the dusting cloths from the kitchen, and start to run it over the shelves of knickknacks. "It's okay, Mom. It'll be okay."

I'm chattering at her and refusing to look at her. As long as she gets that look off her face, I'll be able to look at her again in a little bit.

I keep cleaning since I won't be able to hire a cleaning lady anytime soon. It's another thing that's easy I can do while she's recovering, focusing on getting better.

"Are you seeing anyone?" Her question comes out of nowhere, causing me to drop the cloth and the knickknack I'm polishing. "Maybe this Drew?"

"What?" I sputter as I snatch it off the floor. "Where did that come from?"

When I glance over my shoulder, her eyes twinkle, her smile showing teeth. She looks like Mom again, and my heart jerks hard against my ribs.

"I want grandkids one day. You have to meet someone to make that happen. A lot of women meet Mr. Right in college."

I snort and mutter under my breath. "More like Mr. Doesn't Take No for An Answer."

"What was that?"

"Nothing. No, I'm not really seeing anyone. Not permanently anyway. I went on a date a while back, but it didn't go as planned, so...yeah." She definitely doesn't need to know I was almost drugged...or worse.

"Well, maybe the next one will go better, but it's probably best to stay away from that boy you're tutoring. It's not a great idea to mix work and romance."

I finish cleaning and then turn back to face her. "I have to get back to campus. Anything you need before I go?"

She shakes her head. "I got it. Thank you."

"Seriously, if you want me to come back, just send me a text or call. I don't have a heavy class load at the moment."

Her eyes narrow a minute, but she gives me a nod and holds her arms open for a hug. "There are still some things we need to talk about, baby. I know you aren't ready, but it still needs to happen. We need to prepare, just in case."

It's on the tip of my tongue to deny and say no again, but if it makes her feel better to be prepared, then we'll do it. Then I'll say I told you so after the fact.

I hug her tight and head back to campus. Light traffic means I'm back in the dorm in record time.

My phone buzzes in my pocket, but I ignore it as I jog up the stairs into the suite.

Jackie is packing her bag at the table and freezes when I enter. "Oh! I thought you were with your mom all day?"

"She is already tired of me, so I decided to give her a little space. Apparently, there is a fine line between hovering and caring."

She sits at the table, and I avoid looking at the scarred wood so I don't remember how Drew's hands felt holding me down there.

I swallow hard and give my friend a smile. "Anyway, I should get some studying done."

She nods, her eyes soft, her smile gentle. "Do you want to talk about it? How is she doing?"

I throw my shoulders back and set my purse on the table by her bag. "She's fine. Weak from the meds and the illness, but she's doing better and will improve once we start these new meds."

"How does she feel about some experimental trial?" There's something in her tone that I can't pinpoint, and I don't want to even try.

"Well, she's tired. But she will be happy once it starts

working and she's still alive. Otherwise..." I can't say the words, a lump stuck in my throat. "Otherwise, we don't have much time left together."

She surges up and comes around to take my hands. She's a little shorter than me, so I'm staring into her eyes.

"Oh honey, it'll be okay. It'll all be okay."

I want her to promise. I want the world to promise that I'll get to keep my mom. She's the only thing I have left in this world, and I can't lose her too.

Instead, I sigh and squeeze her hands, then release her. "Yeah, it'll be okay. We start the new drugs and see how it goes. It *has* to be okay."

She returns to packing her bag, one eye on me and the other on her stuff. "Oh, I meant to ask if you're busy next weekend."

It's my turn to sit, and I tug my cell phone out of my pocket to check my calendar. "Lord Drew hasn't requested my presence yet, so I think so. Why? What's up?"

"I'm working with a temp agency to do some catering. Like serving, cleaning, that sort of thing. It's for a big law firm in town, and they always tip well for these things, especially if you are the one to keep the liquor flowing."

I snort. "And you always seem to come home with a couple of bottles of that overpriced liquor."

"I was thinking, if you were free, you might want to come? It'll be so much better with you there. The food should be good too. It's from that restaurant uptown neither of us can afford."

I'll likely be with Mom for the weekend, getting a head start on cleaning and prepping so I only have to stop by after classes. Still, I have plenty of studying I could be doing. "I shouldn't."

She braces her hands on the table and leans in. "Do you

know how much money I make at these events? More than I need for a month in one fucking night. You have to come, Bel."

One night for a month of pay does sound like a good idea. I could get a head start on money and maybe back Drew down on his studying if I need to. He won't take that news well, though.

"Please. It will be so much more fun if you are there. I'll even give you my tips. For your mom, of course."

I lay my head on the table. "Fine. Fine. I'll be there."

CHAPTER 27
DREW

THERE ARE days I don't want to see my father, and days I *really* don't want to see my father. The second I spot the idling limo outside The Mill, the day becomes the latter. With a sigh, I take my time picking up my boots, sliding them onto my feet, and grabbing a jacket. Drawing out the time I leave him waiting is dangerous, but it's really all the power I have in the relationship with him...*for now.*

One day, I'll get away from him, and make that bastard pay for what he's put Mom and me through over the years. Pay for the way he portrays himself as the perfect father and businessman. I know the truth, and eventually, so will everyone else.

Lee and Aries wander down the stairs into the foyer and eye me slowly while I'm tying my boots on the bench by the door. Sports equipment is scattered on the floor around me, so there's really only enough room for this one spot on the bench at the moment.

Aries rubs the back of his neck and leans to see the car idling in the drive. "Your dad?"

I grunt more than answer. Lee frowns, and they share a

glance before both of them direct their attention back to me. I sit up straighter, my back pressed against the wall.

"What?" I bark.

Lee speaks this time. "Do you want one of us to go with you?"

I almost laugh. Almost. And have my friends watch my father and his goons beat the shit out of me when I invariably say something sarcastic? *No, thank you.*

I stand and turn to the door with more urgency now so they don't force their way in. "No, thank you. I'll be back in a few hours. If I'm not, you know where to come looking."

"If you need anything, call us," Aries states matter-of-factly.

I nod, even if the chance of doing it is slim to none. At least they give a shit about me. Thankfully, neither of them try to stop me from leaving. The driver knows me and doesn't bother coming to open the door. I slide into the back seat, the leather creaking as I shuffle across the seat to sit on the far side.

There's a bar on the opposite side of the limo, and I snag the bottle of high-end whiskey my father keeps there.

He takes me to my father's office. A high-rise downtown with a nice view of the city. He owns the building but only uses a portion of it for his investment firm. He also has several apartments in the building, no doubt so he can keep his mistresses off our family estate outside of town. Once we pull up to the valet, I slow my pace, again taking my time before I get out and go inside. I didn't bother dressing up, wearing a pair of joggers, my boots, my university T-shirt, and my worn letter jacket. My appearance alone is going to piss him off. I know this, and somehow, I don't give a fuck. Maybe I have a death wish? Maybe I'm waiting for my father to end all of this for me?

My father meets me on the ground floor, which is... unusual.

He's wearing a wide fake-ass smile as he claps me on the shoulder. "Drew, my son. Glad you were able to take a break from school to come in for a visit."

His tone is just as fake as the smile he wears. It's all an act for his firm, for the security guards, everyone. From his slicked-back hair to the pair of leather loafers on his feet, every piece of him is a well-constructed image.

I know the part I'm supposed to play, but I just don't have it in me at the moment. "What do you want, Dad?"

His eyes narrow at my bite on the word, *Dad,* but he doesn't let his smile slip. "Come, let's go to my office. We have a couple of things to discuss."

My legs feel like there are cinder blocks tied to them. I already know where this is going to go, but I don't have another option. I can come willing or go by force, but I'll end up inside his office one way or another. Blowing out a breath, I trudge forward.

We get into the elevator, and I keep my distance, leaning into the shiny chrome walls.

"Want to fill me in on what's going on?" I ask, knowing the answer already.

"You'll find out soon enough. Patience, Son. It's an asset you'll need to cultivate when you follow me into this business."

We spend the rest of the short ride to the top floor in silence. *Thankfully.*

We exit the elevator together, and I shove my hands into my pockets as we walk through the lobby of his office. When we pass by a few cubicles and desks, his employees give me tight smiles, and my father makes a note, nodding to anyone and everyone who meets his eyes.

His hands come to my shoulder like he's the proud father escorting his son through his office. Showing him off like a prized cow at the state fair.

I cringe at the touch but follow along, knowing full well that if I make a show of dissent, the punishment will make me unable to play football for days. Hell, I probably won't be able to show my face at school for days. With that knowledge, I turn my grimace into a neutral line and continue my descent into hell.

It's a slight maze of desks until we reach the last area that opens into a line of offices with a view. Of course, my father has the best office and view.

I walk in, shaking off his hand. I recognize the lady from one of my father's parties. I saw him talking to her. She's the one with the daughter who wanted to climb me like a damn tree. I give her a nod and throw myself down into the leather chair in front of the desk.

She surveys me, not in the same way my father does when he checks to see if I'm wearing what he wants or if I've taken any injuries from the practice field.

Her assessing gaze reminds me of a shark, surveying the tastiest part of me to bite. I meet her gaze and hold it, eyebrow cocked.

Her red-painted lips curve into a smile. "It's nice to see you again, Andrew."

I can't agree, so I give her a nod.

"Manners, Drew," my father scolds.

With those words, I shift my shoulders back and let the mask slip into place. "It's a pleasure to see you again."

She turns her attention to my father, her hands on her hips, her black blazer framing the curve of her waist. A little old for my father's taste, but she's definitely not here for me. My father holds his hand out to shake hers. "It's really the best outcome for us all. It'll be a pleasure doing business with you."

She gives me one more creepy, assessing look and walks out of the office, her heels clicking off the marble floor. I watch her with caution until she's out of sight, then I put all my attention back on my father.

"What the hell was that about?"

My father sits behind his desk and clasps his hands on top of his desk blotter. "Nothing you need to worry about, at least not yet. In due time, it will all come together. I'll let you know when you need to know something. Speaking of, your attendance will be required at the next party that's coming up in December."

I let out a gruff sigh. "Really, and why is that? I don't exactly contribute to the proceedings." My father narrows his eyes and glances through his glass walls to the employees working tirelessly beyond. Then he flicks a button on a remote, and the windows glaze to frosted glass.

It's a threat more than a bid for privacy. Every muscle in my body tenses, and I meet his eyes. I'm not a little boy anymore. I have no reason to fear him, not in a physical sense, and I hate that he has that power over me still. "What do you want me to do?"

He shrugs. "It's honestly very easy. Wear the suit I send you. When you get to the party with your date, which I'll provide, you will be cordial and attentive. Hell, you'll get on your knees and eat her like Thanksgiving dinner if that's what the girl asks of you."

"You'll provide? I can get my own date. I don't need you to find one for me."

He pinches his lips and nods a few times. Obviously, his patience is very slim. *Shit*. He's pissed.

"I'm assuming you're referring to that little white trash

tutor you've been playing around with? I heard through the grapevine that you're spending a lot of time with her. That she's your *girlfriend*."

I tense and clench my fist in my pockets. I don't want her name in his mouth, and if I explode at him, it will only get worse for me. He'll know she's a weakness to me, and a man like my father only ever uses a person's weaknesses against them in the worst possible ways. Maybel doesn't deserve to have any more shit heaped on her.

"Not really sure what you mean. You know I don't date."

"Don't bullshit me, Drew. I know how you operate. You're not that different from your dear ole dad. A new girl every week, and you sure as hell don't keep the ones you run through that little play gauntlet of yours."

"Still don't know what you mean. Like you said, she's white trash. A white trash flirtation to pass the time as the season winds down. Nothing more than that, not until you told me to get a tutor, then she became my tutor, who I can fuck when the need arises. She's nothing more than a business transaction."

He nods once, but I can tell by his expression he doesn't believe me. *Shit.* I need to sell myself better. I lean forward and give him a smile. "Like you said when school started, it's the sluts at the bottom of the ladder who will do *anything* for money, and she definitely lets me do anything."

This sets a lascivious glitter in his eyes, and I try to keep my face neutral so he can't spot the relief there.

"Well, boys will be boys, I guess." He relaxes back into his seat. "The party will be a firm-wide event, with many clients in attendance, so I expect you to be on your best behavior. I even invited young Sebastian and Lee. Their parents are coming as well, being a couple of my top clients."

I switch the subject back to his demands. "I'll be there, but like I said, I can find my own date."

His smile slips. "And like I said, you will take the girl I tell you, and you will keep her satisfied for the entire night. No slipping off when the party gets going, no hiding out with your friends. You'll stay by her side and keep her happy and smiling."

I've lost this round, and if it keeps his gaze off Maybel, then I'll take whomever he wants me to take to his stupid little party. "Fine. Should I pick her up, or will I be meeting her there?"

The gloat on his face makes me want to punch him. "She'll arrive with her parents, and then you'll show her around the party and be the perfect gentleman, unless of course, she doesn't want you to be a gentleman."

I want to ask him how he can be such a motherfucker. How he can pimp out his own son for business, but it's not an argument I can win yet, so I don't even bother.

"Fine. I'll wait for the suit to arrive. I'll play my part as I always do."

Silence surrounds us for a moment, and I stare out the windows at the city beyond to keep from saying or doing something stupid. I can still feel his eyes on me, and I don't want to show him how much I hate his fucking guts. I have to wonder how I can hate my own father so much, but then I remember all he's done to me—all the pain, embarrassment, the guilt and regret. It makes me question how a father could live with himself after doing all he's done to me.

"Good. Don't fuck this up, Drew. I've warned you before of the implications of disobeying me. Don't make me do something that we both know I don't want to do. I know it doesn't seem like it, but every single thing I do is for your future, and I won't have you ruining all the hard work I've put in."

"I get it. No worries, Dad. I'll play my part. Can I go now?" I grit my teeth, asking for permission to leave. I hate the lack of control I have when it comes to my father. He nods, and I stand, ready to get the fuck out of this office, this building, except my relief is short-lived when I reach the door and hear the loud clearing of his voice.

Instead of turning to look at him, I just wait to hear what he has to say.

"Oh, and get rid of that little white trash whore before the party, or I'll do it for you. There's no reason for you to keep seeing her when you're going to be dating my client's daughter. We can't have rumors being started."

I grit my teeth, my jaw aching from the pressure. He never fucking said anything about dating this woman.

When he's done speaking, I head out. There's no reason to respond, not when I want to slam his head into the desk and pound out my frustration.

I don't bother keeping the scowl off my face as I walk to the elevator and down to the car. I walk right past the car and head uptown. I'll get an app ride back to campus. I don't want a goddamn thing from my father right now. Standing on my own means no life, no money, nothing. It means he'd actively work to destroy everything I've worked to build the last few years since I started at Oakmount.

I can't allow that. Not when his first target will be the only people I care about. My friends. My mother. Maybel.

I walk faster, using the burn of the cold air in my lungs to cool my boiling blood. If my father wants me to fuck this girl, fine, I'll do it, but I'm doing it my way. This bitch has no idea what she's getting into or better yet, who she's getting involved with.

CHAPTER 28
BEL

I SHOULDN'T BE AS EXCITED as I am to see Drew today. It's been a few days with the football game between, so I feel like it's been forever since I felt those penetrating dark eyes on me. A sensation I used to hate...but has grown on me now. Drew is smart. I'm not sure why his grades slipped, but it gives me a sense of accomplishment when he shares the news that he aced a test.

I shove some books into my bag and then eye the lip gloss on my desk. I don't know why, but it occurs to me to put myself together, to do my hair or makeup. Not that it'll dress up my hoodie, messy bun, or worn jeans. With an eye roll at myself for being stupid, I grab the ChapStick off the corner of my desk and swipe that on instead. Lip gloss would be wasted on Drew anyway, one way or another. He seems to stare at me no matter what I'm wearing or not wearing, for that matter.

I gather up my pens, highlighters, and other study materials and shove them into my bag. It's lighter now that I'm not tutoring twenty-five different people in ten subjects. I zip up the bag, throw it over my shoulder, and head to the kitchen. I grab a granola bar from the counter and an apple from the fruit basket, then head out the door. I've barely shut it behind me when I crash into a solid wall.

No, not a wall. *A person.*

I stumble backward, and big hands reach for me, circling my biceps and keeping me from falling over. My skin burns where he touches me, and his fingers gently press into my flesh. I look up at him, my eyes moving slowly over his fucking disturbingly handsome features: that sharp jaw and high cheekbones. Those penetrating dark eyes that will me to spill all my secrets or else. It's getting harder to tell myself I'm not attracted to him. I shake the thoughts away before I can get distracted further.

"What are you doing here? I thought I was meeting you at the library?" I attempt to take a step back, but I'm trapped between the door and him. The energy rolling off him makes me nervous. Did something happen? I'm ready to ask him, my lips parting, when he descends on me. His mouth slams against mine, and my brain momentarily short-circuits. Those big hands of his move from my arms to the back of my neck and hip, their path leaving a blaze of heat on my skin. A shiver ripples through me, and his tongue slips inside my mouth, tangling with my own.

I whimper as the kiss assaults me both physically and mentally. Holy *hell*, can he kiss. At his mercy, I clutch onto his jacket and let him devour me from the inside out. Drew terrifies me, not because of his actions, but because of the way his actions make me feel. In his arms, I'm so much more than the nerdy girl. I kiss him back with the same fever he kisses me with. The entire building could be burning to the ground, and I wouldn't notice, not with his lips on mine.

The spell breaks a moment later when he pulls back, leaving me dazed and limp. His other arm snakes around my waist to hold me in place. I peer up at him and notice the dilation of his pupils and how much darker his eyes are.

"I need you. Let's go inside."

His deep timbre reaches something inside me, and I stumble as he urges me forward but doesn't release me from his grasp. *What the hell is going on?* Inside the main room of the suite, my ass bumps against the dining room table, and he gives it a fond smile.

"Put your bag down. We aren't studying today. Just—" He pulls me into his arms again and steals another brutal kiss from me. This time, his searing kiss is harder, leaving my lips swollen and wet.

"What..." I'm a little stunned, and my eyes flutter open. "What's going on?"

Drew is breathless, his cheeks a soft pink, his gaze frenzied. He looks exactly how I feel. "Nothing. I wanted to see you."

"We were about to see each other at the library in like ten minutes. Why..."

Like an animal stalking its prey, he pounces on me and slants his mouth against mine. In a haste, he pulls my bag off my shoulder, and it falls to the floor with a thunk. I'm about to pull away and remind him how expensive textbooks are, but then his fingers grip onto the hem of my hoodie, and suddenly he's lifting it. I have to wiggle to make sure my bun doesn't get caught in the neck hole. With it out of the way, he tosses it across the room.

I hear some glasses tink together, but keep my eyes on him. It's dangerous to take your eyes off him when he's like this. A predator, ready to attack. His eyes drop to the tight T-shirt I'm wearing. It's got the school logo across the chest, worn and faded from too many washes.

"Fuck, you look beautiful. Have I ever told you that?" The words come out in a flurry.

I shake my head, feeling vulnerable with the way he's looking at me like I'm a piece of porcelain. This is different, and I'm not sure I like it. His hands smooth down the length of my body, stopping at the waistband of my jeans. "As sexy as you look with these jeans on, I'd rather see them on the floor and my cock stuffed inside your pussy. Fucking you will make me forget, make it better."

The lustful haze in my brain lingers, but the end of his sentence snaps me out of it. This isn't right. It's not just the sex part. It's the urgency, the deep-seated need. He's using my body to cope with something, using sex to forget. I wrap my hands around his wrists to stall him.

"Wait, Drew. What's going on? What's wrong?"

His expression shifts from abject need to cold indifference. I can see the walls coming up again. Every time I think I'm getting closer to seeing the real him, he disappears behind his mask.

"I don't pay you to be my therapist..."

I squeeze his wrists a little harder. "You don't pay me to fuck you either, so what are you getting at?"

The grin he gives me makes my stomach flip. "No, you'll fuck me for free, right? I'll bet if I slip my hand into your panties right this second, I'll find you soaking wet. I mean, you were practically begging me to fuck you out in the hall. The mind-blowing orgasm you get each time I fuck you is how you're paid."

His words make me flinch, and I try to pull away. Of course, he doesn't let me move, and pushing against him is pointless. Instead of releasing me, he presses closer, crowding me, forcing me to back away while also guiding me where he wants.

"Don't tell me you're objecting to me fucking you," he growls.

I don't even realize we're crossing the threshold into my bedroom until I spot my belongings out of the corner of my eye. "Wait, let me guess, you want to say no while I take you? Will it make you feel better to tell me how much you don't want it as your pussy milks my dick like it's the only thing in the world? Is that your fantasy? No control? No decisions? Nothing to care about but chasing the high? If that's what you want, we can do it. Don't pretend you don't want me. No matter how much you say no, your body betrays you every single time. We both know how this is going to end. The only question is, will it be with your submission or without?"

Why do his words shoot lightning bolts of pleasure through my body? Like the more he's a bastard, the more I want it. *No.* He can't keep doing this to me. He already admitted that he came here to use my body so that he could forget something. I don't want to be that to him. I want to be more. Sensing the defiance in me, he grabs the back of my neck again and tips my face up, capturing my mouth in another brutal kiss. It burns so *good*. His lips. His body. It hurts and rages and leaves me with a hunger I've never known.

Why does he make me feel this way? And what did I do to deserve someone like him? Karma isn't even that much of a bitch. Coming to my senses, I push at his chest and break the kiss, my heartbeat roaring in my ears.

"I don't want to be an object to you, not when I'm a human with real feelings and emotions."

"Oh, you're so much more than an object, Maybel." He bares his white teeth to me, and I shudder at the look in his eyes. Possession, deep-rooted desire. "Well, you might be human, but I'd prefer if you were my little pet, obeying my rules and giving me pleasure when I ask for it."

Anger like never before boils up inside me. "You chose the wrong girl, Drew. I need the money you give me for these tutoring sessions, but I'm not a whore. I'm not going to obey your every rule simply because you tell me to."

He presses against me, the whole length of his body, and I can tell this little sparring match is doing nothing to satisfy his hunger for me. If anything, it's turning him on more.

"For the attitude," he whispers against my mouth, his wet lips brushing mine in a smooth passing rhythm. "I'm only going to put myself inside you when you ask me for it. When you *beg* me for it, and I promise, you fucking will."

I tilt my chin, breaking contact with his mouth.

He smiles like I'm cute. Like my resistance is adorable.

And he pushes again until the back of my knees hits the edge of the bed, and I fall against it on my ass. Thankfully, I manage to keep myself upright.

Drew stares down at me with a feral hunger in his eyes. Then he steps between my open thighs and pulls at the tie on his joggers. He only pulls enough of the waist down to expose his rock-hard cock. His T-shirt lays over the root of him almost obscenely, and even if I should, I can't look away. My mouth waters, and the urge to taste him consumes me, but I stay still and slip my hands under my thighs to keep from reaching out to touch him.

Fisting his cock in his hand, he strokes himself hard while keeping his eyes trained on me. "Tempted to touch, my little wallflower?"

I bite the inside of my mouth to stop speaking and shake my head. Even if I want him, I don't want him like this. I want more. I want to be something to him. I don't want to be used and tossed aside until the next time. Sensing my desire and need, he taunts me.

"Fuck, you see how hard I am for you. I can already see myself sinking deep inside you, your tiny cunt struggling to take me on the first thrust, stretching around my thick shaft. It's okay if you want that because that's what I want too. I want to fuck you so hard, all you feel is the reminder of me and how I took you for days. I want you to be the good girl who takes my cock so fucking well, like it was made for you, but I need something in return. I need you to put your pride aside and ask nicely. Beg, really. And if you do it well enough, I'll stuff you full of my cum as a reward."

I blink and gulp. This is a game I'm going to lose, like always, but I'm nothing but a pushover if I don't put up a fight first. It's the fight he seems to enjoy anyway.

He tilts his head like he's resigned to work himself and strokes his length in one brutally tight grip. Precum beads on his head, and I can't take my eyes off him. I'm practically panting, my chest rising and falling so hard, I can see it in my peripheral vision while I watch him.

"Cat got your tongue, Bel? Or maybe you aren't ready to beg yet. That's okay. You can watch for now, but with your shirt off instead."

I shouldn't. I should deny him the opportunity, but seeing him this way makes me want to see how far I can take it. I blink and then do as he says. Why not? He told me he wouldn't fuck me until I asked, and removing my shirt and maybe my bra might take some of the pressure off my aching nipples. Gripping the hem of my shirt, I tug it over my head and toss it aside.

His predatory gaze sweeps over my body, down my lacy white bra, to my flat belly, then to the waist of my jeans. "Bra, too."

It takes seconds to remove that, and soon, my tits are bare to the chilled air. When I look at him now, there's fire in his eyes, not the cold indifference written into the grim line of his mouth. "It's really a shame you don't listen like this all the time. You're such a good girl when you want to be." He reaches for me and caresses my mouth with his thumb, dragging it across my bottom lip. The motion sends zings of pleasure straight to my core. I want him to fuck me. I want him to make me beg for it.

A whimper escapes me, and I can't even fucking help it. I'm so wet and achy for him.

"Anything you want to say?"

I shake my head. "No." But it comes out more like a question than a fully convincing statement. The smirk he gives me is deranged at best. He trails his damp thumb from my lips, down over my chin and neck, stopping once he reaches my stiff nipple. His thumb's warm, wet heat against the stiff peak makes me shiver, and I lean forward, wanting more. More sensation, more pleasure, more him. He meets my eyes for half a second, and then I look away, ashamed of how he can reduce me to my most basic instincts with nothing but the feel of his hands on my body.

Without warning, he pulls his hand back and then brings it down, slapping my tit hard. The sting of pain registers first, followed by a ripple of pleasure. A gasp escapes my lips, and I tug my bottom lip into my mouth, biting hard to stop myself from doing that again. Of course he hears and doesn't bother hiding his satisfied grin.

He repeats the action, this time on my other breast. Fuck. The sting hurts, but the pleasure mounts, and I swear I'm so wet from this that it's embarrassing. How does he do this to me every single time? The heat of him swamps me as he moves closer, my thighs spread open even wider. I feel the slightly wet tip of his cock as he glides it against my collarbone.

A whimper slips out of my mouth, the pleasure and need overriding me. He uses the tip of his cock to paint each of my collarbones with his precum, and I look now, needing to see him more than I need my pride. More than I need anything else at this second.

"Anything...on your mind yet?"

I swallow hard as my body clenches around nothing. Empty. Wanting. Needing.

"I want you." I say the words, hating the sour taste that fills my mouth upon admittance. The satisfied hum he makes shoots right through me, causing my pussy to clench and my hips to lift involuntarily. I hate the power he has over me and the way he reduces me to nothing. I wish I was stronger and could resist him.

"I'll let you in on a little secret," he whispers, pulling me to my feet by my arms.

I'm dizzy with lust and nearly trip over my own feet.

"I'd have fucked you without the request, but I love watching you break for me. Over and over."

A stupid retort sits on the end of my tongue but disappears when his fingers sink into the sides of my jeans. He drags them down my legs, including my panties, and tugs them off me. Bare-ass naked, I stand before him, his eyes inspecting every inch of flesh.

"I should mark you somewhere, brand you so you're always reminded of who owns you. Do you want that?"

I shake my head. "I don't belong to you, Drew. I belong to me. I'm just a hole to keep your dick warm, right?"

A feral growl rips through his chest, and he snaps. I'm not sure why my response angers him so much when it's the exact words he said to me. In an instant, I'm back on the bed.

Before I understand what is happening, his powerful hands latch onto me. He flips me onto my stomach and drags me up by my hips, forcing me onto my knees. My skin hums with the contact, with the anticipation. The head of his cock brushes against the seam of my ass, and my entire body tightens. *He wouldn't, would he?*

"I should fuck your ass just to punish you for being such a brat, but I don't have the patience to prepare you, and as badly as I want to hurt you, I don't want to break you, and I'd do just that if I did."

"Oh, how merciful of you." I roll my eyes, trying to keep my voice strong. I don't want to let him know that I'm already breaking.

"It's not mercy. It's making sure I can get my full use of you."

The words sting against my skin, and I don't know if what he's saying is true or not. I don't get the chance to ask him because a second later, he's sliding deep inside me, as far as he can. The thrust is so powerful that I'm knocked from my knees and onto my belly. His hands clench around my thighs hard enough to bruise as he holds me to the level he needs. Pleasure and pain mingle, swirling into one. I can feel each punishing stroke of his length, and even as wet as I am, there's still a sting with every thrust.

"Drew..." I whine into the sheets.

There's no finesse to how he fucks me, going deep and hard. My body takes the punishing pace and gives back more heat, more liquid. All I can do is groan as he punishes me, fucking me harder than he ever has before.

"This is what you get, flower. This is how I'm going to fuck you. Hard and fast."

I can barely keep myself upright, and at some point, I sag into the sheets, letting him use my body as he pleases. He grunts and moves faster, slamming himself into me, and with one hand holding me in place, he uses his other and places it against my head, forcing me to stay down. The angle he has me bent in causes me to feel every inch of his length inside me. An animalistic urge grips him, and he grabs me by the back of the neck, tugging me backward, my back flush with his chest.

With his cock nestled deep inside me, he thrusts upward, the head of his penis touching some special spot inside me.

"Oh my god." My gasp sounds nothing like me. The sound is deep, guttural, primal.

I can feel every indent of his fingers, every press of his own hips against my ass. His abs work overtime as he thrusts upward, balancing me on his cock. Forcing me to take every single inch. His hot breath fans against my neck, and my nipples harden. My fingers dig into his thighs, where I grasp on for dear life. He's fucking me so hard, I swear I can feel him in my stomach. My core tightens to the point of pain, and then I feel it, his teeth sink into the soft spot at the base of my shoulder and neck.

"Come on my fucking cock. Squeeze that tight pussy. I want to feel that hot cunt milk me dry. Do it."

It's like my body obeys his every whim, and I shatter, my legs shaking as every part of me clenches tight and then releases.

Ripple upon ripple of pleasure rolls through me, shooting me up with all the feel-good chemicals I've come to crave from him. He shoves me face-first onto the bed and continues fucking me all the way through my orgasm. A few more strokes, and he lets out a groan that vibrates through me. Then I feel it; his warm release spreads through my center, filling me to the brim. I feel the absence of his body against mine, and I nearly turn to ask him where he's going, but then he shifts me and settles into the bed beside me.

I watch him intently, noticing the tension in his jaw and his clenched fists across his chest. He's still dressed, and his pants are back up. Shame coats my insides, and I can feel tears stinging the back of my eyes. I fed right into his bullshit. I gave him what he wanted most, a warm hole to be used and discarded when done.

"I can't... We can't keep doing this," I whisper, almost as if I don't want to say the words at all. Drew makes me feel too much, but I don't have the same effect on him. I can't make him see something he refuses to see. Maybe this is why my brain put up such a tough battle when it came to him. Because it knew this could only end in heartbreak.

"What do you mean?" He blinks slowly, and I can't really read his face. "Do you mean tutoring? Or something else?"

"This." I motion between us and grab my comforter, covering myself up because I feel too exposed right now. "I can't keep doing this push and pull with you. Your hot and cold behavior is giving me whiplash, and I don't want to be a doormat for you to step on. You pay me to tutor you, not sleep with you. I know you're used to having random hookups and stuff, but I'm not. You're the first guy I ever... did anything with." I hate the tremble in my voice as I speak because what I'm saying is true. I can't keep doing this with him. "I need more, more than just sex. I want to feel wanted, cherished, valued. None of those things you can do. I hardly know anything about you. The only time we see each other is behind closed doors or in the library."

"I don't do that shit with anyone. It's not just you, Maybel, and I thought you hated me. It's starting to sound a lot like you've caught feelings."

I grit my teeth together, anger replacing the pleasure

endorphins. "What I feel or don't feel doesn't matter. You can't give me what I want, and even if you could, I don't know what a relationship with you would look like." I feel vulnerable as hell, but there wasn't any way around this. One way or another, we were headed here.

He laughs harshly but not in a way that says anything is funny. "Wait, are you trying to tell me you're finished with me? I thought I warned you before. I make the choices, and I'll decide when we're done. I don't care about what you want."

Looking into his eyes, I see no warmth, no joy. I see only anger and the desire for control. Maybe that's what brought us together. My desire to be free, and his desire to be in control. Too bad it didn't work out. Shoving off the bed, I wrap the blanket tighter around my middle. It hurts me to push him away, but I can't keep doing this. I can't keep fighting against something that isn't ever going to be.

"And that's the entire problem here." I shake my head in frustration. "Could you just leave, please? I'm not going to continue on this roller coaster of emotions. You've gotten your fill of me, and unless you plan to change your motives and direction, there is no place for me in your life."

He shoves off the bed and moves with lightning speed, his massive body crowding me. I don't want to be intimidated or bullied into compliance by him. I'm tired of feeling weak. I'm tired of being manipulated.

"If you think you can deny me what's rightfully mine, you're in for a world of hurt." His voice is low and deadly.

"I'm not denying you anything. I want to be free, and you make me feel free. You push me to my limits. You're selfish and want me to meet only your needs. I mean, you just told me you don't care about what I want. It doesn't get any more obvious than that."

"I don't need your permission, Maybel," he hisses through his teeth, and I can feel the anger rolling off him.

"You're right, you don't. You could take from me, rape me, hurt me, break me down until I'm nothing but a shell, but that's not what you want. You want me strong and defiant. You want me to agree because otherwise, it's not real. Otherwise, it's not good enough. You're many things, Drew, and while I have thought you were a monster a time or two, I'm starting to realize I might have misunderstood you."

My words must cut far too close to the surface because a moment later, he takes a step back, a look of disgust painting his features. Then another. My heart aches inside my chest, and I want to beg him to stay and talk to me, but he's not ready, and I'm not sure he'll ever be. I do know that I can't keep going down this road with him. With a shake of his head, he disappears from the room. The front door slamming closed makes me jump, and I climb back into bed, blinking back tears.

He makes me feel more than I've ever felt, and somehow, I can't make him see the destruction he's causing, what he's doing to me when I'm already so fragile. He can never build me back up in the way I need. He only knows how to destroy, and I can only take so much heartbreak before I shatter.

CHAPTER 29
DREW

YOU CAN ONLY RUN SO FAR from your circumstances. And my fucking circumstances have my balls in a vise that's threatening to pop them.

I walk quickly across the campus, needing the burn of the air to calm me down. To stifle the urge to turn around, go back to her, and fuck this need out of me. Until the itch for her stops. Fuck her until I no longer crave the taste of her skin against my lips.

It's an infatuation because my father wants her out of my life. All he's done is make her more desirable by making her off-limits.

A few students are running around the campus to different buildings, thankfully all giving me a wide berth. If any of them so much as look my way, I might explode and goddamn kill someone.

Anything to gain control of my life, for fuck's sake. That's all I want. Control. The ability to make my own choices, to make my own moves for what I want. Instead of what my father wants all the time. What the team wants, what my teachers want. All of it.

My life is always about what someone else wants. That might be why I don't go easy on my wallflower...she's the only thing I feel I have control of in my life. Fucked up for sure, but I don't care.

That's gotta be why I can still taste her and why all I can think about is having her again. She makes me feel like I'm in control for the very short time I get with her. But now, everything has changed. As much as I say she's mine, she's right. I want her fighting, spitting, cursing. I want her to fight back because it makes my control of her all the sweeter.

I jog up the steps of The Mill and touch the wood of the door. Home. At least my father isn't living here too. Inside, I get a moment of peace. If my friends aren't being dicks that is.

When I open the door, it's to Sebastian pacing back and forth across the foyer, kicking football padding out of the way with every pass.

He's wearing a button-down shirt and slacks like he just got back from a damn job interview. I stop short and close the door softly to avoid interrupting the conversation. He snaps out a word in French, and I catch a few curse words in the next guttural angry phrase.

He spins to make another pass across the entryway and glances up to meet my eyes. Another curse, and he cuts off the call and squeezes his phone in his hand. "What are you looking at?" he demands, locking eyes with me. There's real fury on his face, in the set of his jaw, the tense line of his neck.

"I don't know. What am I looking at?" I set my feet and cross my arms. I'm so close to the edge of something. Bel kicking me out, telling me things are done, has me primed for a fight, and it looks like Sebastian might need to take the edge off too.

We stare each other down, neither willing to put up with each other's shit.

He stalks forward until only a foot is between us. "What are you doing, man? You and that fucking girl?"

I tense, then clear my face to neutral. "What fucking girl?"

He opens his mouth, and I close the distance, going chest to chest with him. "Don't you dare say her name."

"You're going to choose some, some groupie, over us? Your friends, your team?"

He's close enough I can smell the whiskey on his breath.

"I don't have to make a choice. There's no need, so what the fuck is the problem here? Who was on the phone, and why do you feel the need to confront me about her at least once a week? She's my tutor, for the moment, and that's fucking it. Actually, no, I take that back. I'm already done with her. You and my father have gotten your way. She's nothing to me, really, nothing."

"Oh really? Is that why you smell like sweat and sex right now?"

"Get your head out of my ass, and you wouldn't need to worry about it, would you?"

There's a soft footstep on the stairs, and then a pause.

I glance over Sebastian's shoulder to find Lee, frozen, his hands on the rails. "Uh...what's going on, guys?"

I point and step back so I can keep them both in sight. "You want to weigh in too? The only person not riding my ass about Bel is fucking Aries. Maybe he's the only one who knows better!"

They share a look. Lee speaks up. "We only want to protect you, man."

"From what? If you clue me in, maybe we can stop this song and dance?"

Another shared look, and I'm done. I shove Sebastian

away from me. "You say you want to protect me? Keeping secrets isn't going to protect shit. Besides, you say I'm choosing her over you, yet you're the ones not telling me the truth. You can both fuck off."

Sebastian looks ready to charge me, and I stare him down. Lee takes a few more steps to come up beside Sebastian. "It's not like that, man. Come on. Calm down."

I take a deep breath because he's right. Not about the bullshit secrets, but the fact that I need to calm down. Another minute and I'll knock their heads together, and I might regret that later.

Lee pulls Sebastian back, and we all seem to calm down a little. All breathing, taking in the situation.

Lee takes the lead next. "You going to that stupid party of your father's?"

The question seems laced with more than what he's outright asking. But I can't pinpoint exactly what he wants from me. "Yes, I've been ordered to attend. My father said you two and your families will be there as well. Why?"

"Our fathers are two of your father's clients. We were told it's a family affair, and we have to show up. Same as you."

Something tells me they won't be pimped out to further their father's careers.

The thought pisses me off all over again. "Look. I'm tired. I'm going to go take a nap."

Sebastian stops me with a hand on my chest, and I freeze. "Get your hand off me, or I'll rip off your goddamn arm."

He drops his hand. "Just do what your father says. You've been spotted with the girl multiple times. People think she's unsuitable. I don't want to see you or her get hurt."

I meet his eyes now, letting him see the flint and fire in mine. "Are you threatening her?"

"For fuck's sake, no. Like I said, I just don't want to see you hurt."

There's another tense moment where we all stare at each other. "What do you want from me, Sebastian?" I turn to look at him. This is his fault. He's the one who instigated it all.

"Just watch your fucking back. That's all I'm trying to say, but you're too goddamn pigheaded to listen."

"I don't fucking need your advice or help. I never asked for it. "The words burst out as if my body can't contain them anymore. "Can't I have one fucking thing that is mine? MINE!"

The outburst echoes through the room, and they both stare. I've admitted more than I wanted to, and I hate that so much.

I shove at Sebastian, and his arm comes up before I can block it, his fist connecting with my jaw. My head is whipped to the side from the blow, pain shooting through my nerves and bones. It shocks me but also brings me back to reality.

Once I'm sure I won't kill the asshole, I meet his eyes. "Going my father's route to control me now? Nice."

This time, he lets me go with a look of shame flashing in his eyes. The rage builds with every step I take, and by the time I reach my bedroom, I'm ready to explode.

What the fuck is happening? What is my father doing to control my friends, MY friends?

I scrub at my face and turn circles around my room, trying to calm the fuck down. A tightness enters my chest, cutting off my air supply, and I bend over, gasping, just trying to draw breath for a moment. I know this feeling. I've felt it before, but it's been forever since I had a panic attack. The door to the bedroom opens, and a cool hand presses against the back of my neck. I smell the lemon verbena wafting off Lee, so I don't smack the hand away. Then a bag of ice brushes my fingers as he tucks it into my palm.

"For your face since we don't want to ruin your pretty boy image. Bastian didn't mean it, okay? He was just angry like you were. It was a misunderstanding."

I straighten, slump against the bed, and hold the ice to my face. "Yeah, the first time my dad hit me, he called it an accident too. He didn't mean to do it. I just made him angry. Look at us now."

Lee stares down at me a moment, then sinks to the floor, crossing his legs. "We just want you safe from him, from this whole situation. We all know if you keep him happy, that's one less day you'll come home with bruises. Besides, this isn't all about you. Something is going on with Sebastian too."

I meet his gaze and hold it. "At the cost of what? What's the point if I have to give up every part of myself to keep him happy? Once you take it all, what is left for me? What will be the point then?"

"I don't know, but no one wants anything to happen to you either."

I shrug because I don't care what happens to me anymore. "What's going on with Sebastian that makes him think he can kick my ass?"

Lee grins. "Again, I don't know. He's been yelling at his family and talking to this weird investigator guy. I've tried to ask him a couple times if he's okay or if I can help, and he gets snappy with me, so I stopped trying."

I freeze, letting his words register. "Investigators? For his father's business?"

Lee shrugs, then his shoulders sink, and he fiddles with some frayed threads on the throw rug underneath him. "I don't know shit, Drew. I feel like I'm trying to put fires out left and right. All I can think is keep your father happy now until we can figure out how to take charge of our lives again. Your life again. Then we'll do what we can for Sebastian too."

I lie back on the bed, so I don't have to look at him. "I'm not sure there's enough time for that. Right now, my father wants Maybel out of my life so he can marry me off for his career, for his own gain." I don't even bring up the fact that Maybel tried tossing me out of her life after our last fight.

Lee squeaks from the floor. "Marry?"

"Oh, whatever you're hearing from your fathers. They didn't tell you he expects me to entertain a date at this stupid-ass party. He told me, and I quote, to eat her like Thanksgiving dinner if that's what she wants."

"That's fucked up, dude. But not really shocking."

I don't bother replying to that. We both know how fucked up it is.

"Can't you like, make sure you only see Bel in private? Or maybe push her away for now until all this attention dies down?"

Remembering how skittish she is and how much fucking work it took to make her look at me like a person instead of a monster, I don't think so. Not when it all backfired, and she doesn't want me anymore anyway. "Probably not. She'll go back to hating me. And now that I see the lust in her eyes, I don't want to go back to that place. I can't go back there." It's more of a mantra. She's already given up on me, but I can't give up on her, not yet.

He sighs. "What if one of us pretends to date her instead and bring her to the house so you can see her?"

I snort. "She hates all of you fuckers way more than she hates me." I roll so I can see him again. "Besides, you all think it's better to stay away from her anyway."

"Dude. Real talk. I've never seen you like this about a girl before."

"She's mine," I whisper. "She's not special or important, but she's fucking mine. And I'm so goddamn tired of giving everything up for him. Mom. The house. Bel. Soon, he'll separate me from you guys, like he's already trying to do, then force me into his company to become a drone, his perfect carbon copy. Another body he can use to make himself more money. That's always what it's about for him."

I let the silence grow, staring at my friend. How did it come to this? We've always been so tight, impenetrable. This year, though, we are turning on each other, for what? I fucking hate this shit.

There's a knock on the door, and Sebastian enters, a permanent scowl etched into his face. He throws a garment bag across my desk chair. "This just came. And there's a note attached." He tosses it on top of the bag and stalks back out of the room.

Lee stands, graceful as always, "Let me try and figure this all out. I refuse to let anyone break up our brotherhood."

I nod and watch as he leaves just like Sebastian did. In the end, we've solved nothing. We've done nothing. I feel powerless, and I fucking hate it. I stand and grab the note, ripping it out of the envelope as if that small act of retribution will make me feel better. The creamy white paper is an embossed invitation. Scribbled on the back is a note in my father's messy loopy handwriting.

I expect you to be early, so you're here before your date.

I crumple the piece of paper up and throw it across the room as hard as I can. Fuck him and his orders. Fuck it all. And I almost laugh at myself because of how ridiculous it is. As much as I say that, we both know I'll be there. At least until I can find a way to get myself and my mom out from under his fucking thumb.

I'M STILL THINKING about what happened with Drew a day later. I feel raw, like a wound that hasn't healed. Part of me, the hopeless part, thought he'd have said something by now or at least tried to fix things. No luck, especially not when I haven't received a single text from him. I'm trying to figure out my tutoring schedule and who I can convince to come back and work with me. When I blew up this whole thing with Drew, the last thing I'd been thinking about was the money.

My phone vibrates beside me, and I snatch it up, hoping it's a client. The number for the hospital flashes across the screen, and I hit the green answer button and press the phone to my ear. "Hello?"

"Ms. Jacobs, this is Dr. Mitch. I'm just calling because your mother missed her appointment today, and she's not answering my calls now. I'm worried. I was going to send an ambulance, but I wanted to call and check with you first."

Time stands still. My heart is lodged in my throat so tight, I have to clear it. "What, what do you mean? I thought her appointment was tomorrow morning. That's what she told me. I was going to come with her."

"I'm afraid not. She was due to come in today. For the first of the experimental treatments she signed up for."

I sigh. *Mom, what are you doing?* Knowing how apprehensive in the beginning she was to do this, I'm not really surprised. She probably thought she could skip it without me knowing.

"I'll go check on her. Is it too late to show up for the appointment?"

"No, it's just a simple injection. You can come anytime. Please let me know if she is okay, though. I need to confirm."

"Of course. I'll be in touch soon."

I hang up the phone, grab my purse, and run out the door. Rushing to my car, I throw the door open, climb inside, and turn the key, bringing the engine to life. I back out of my spot and start toward the house. Part of me is angry. Why would she lie to me like that after all I'm doing to help her? But at the same time, fear gnaws at me from the inside that something is wrong, that something's happened to her. It will kill me if something has happened.

I race through town, watching for cops so I don't get pulled over and screech into my mom's driveway. I slam the brake in place and rush to the door. Of course, it's locked, and my fingers are shaking so bad, I fumble with the keys to unlock the knob and the deadbolt.

Inside, I spot my mom on the couch, eyes closed, completely still. My heart drops into my stomach. "No." It comes out in a rush of breath. I slide on my knees across the old carpet to her side. "Mom."

I give her a shake, feeling the warmth of her skin. "Mom. Mom. Please wake up."

She flicks her eyes open slowly, then focuses, rearing back. "Baby, what's wrong?"

Slowly, she swipes at the tears I didn't notice on my cheeks. I bow my head against her hands and let the tears fall, my whole body shaking. "I'm sorry I thought...the doctor called me, and I thought something had happened."

I sit back on the floor and wipe my face while she sits up. "Baby, I..."

"Why did you lie to me?" I demand. "I would have been here to take you. I need to take you to these things so I feel like I'm doing something. Like I have some kind of control over what's going on."

Her forehead wrinkles, and she tucks the blanket in around her tented knees. "I'm sorry, Bel. I don't know why I lied. I guess, I'm worried you're throwing away your life and all your future opportunities for me. For what, a chance that I'll live another couple of years at most? You heard how experimental this drug is. I don't want you to throw away your life for me, and then I die anyway."

I hate hearing these words from her lips. I hate them so much that all I can do is lash out in anger. "Stop. Stop saying you're going to die. Medicine has progressed since the last time you were sick. You can beat this. You just have to fight it and stop fighting me. I want to help you, but I can't if you refuse to listen to me."

We sit in silence for a moment, and I hate the scared, defeated look on her face. I ease up on the couch beside her and lean my head against her chest like I did when I was a little girl. "I can't lose you, Mom. I'll do anything to keep you with me."

She hugs me tight, her arms wrapped around my body. "That's what I'm afraid of, baby, you doing anything and everything and regretting it a few years down the road."

I sink into her, let her hold me, and enjoy the scent of her shampoo and the way she feels comforting me, like she's always done. Every scraped knee, every heartbreak, all of it— she's been there for me. Now, I can be there for her, and she keeps pushing me away.

I pull back and look at her. "I understand your apprehension, Mom, but I'll do anything to have another day with you. There's no regret in being able to have more time with a loved one. If you're up for it, the doctor says we can still go get your treatment." Standing now, I turn to face her. "Come on, I'll help you get cleaned up, and then we can go. Maybe stop for pancakes at the old diner while we're out."

She frowns and gives me a look of defeat. What am I doing wrong? Is there something I'm missing? That she isn't telling me? She's so determined to give up. It makes me think there is more than what she's shared. I help her up off the couch and then into the bathroom. Soon, I have her bundled into my car and on the way to the hospital.

I try to make small talk with her on the way, but she doesn't give me more than a few words or sounds.

At the hospital, I grab a wheelchair to make the long trek to the treatment room easier on her. Inside, the doctor shows up immediately with a smile on his face. "I'm so glad you girls could make it today, after all."

He sits across from us on a rolling stool and looks my mom over. "I'm glad you were okay. I was worried when you didn't take my calls."

My mom clears her throat and gives a wan smile. "I guess I slept right through them. I'm so sorry to waste your time, Doctor."

The doctor squeezes my mom's hand and shakes his head. "Don't you worry one bit about that. It's my job to take care of you, not the other way around."

Then just as quickly as he arrived, he spins on his stool, grabs the tablet off the counter, and makes a few clicks and swipes with his fingers. "Okay, we have you down to start a course of drugs today to treat your illness. I'm obligated by law to tell you there is no guarantee it will work and that you are participating in an experimental trial."

My mom tenses beside me but keeps her eyes on the doctor, who continues his spiel.

"Now, with today's hiccup, I need to confirm that you still want to participate, and you agree that I've told you the warnings."

There's a long moment while I look back and forth between my mom and the doctor. *Why isn't she saying anything?*

The doctor cocks his head to the side. "Ma'am?" He holds out the tablet with the legal jargon and a place to sign. "If you agree, sign here, and we can proceed. I promise, it's a painless procedure, just a quick injection, and you can go home and rest. I'll have the nurse print out side effects and questions that might arise."

After a moment, my mom lifts her finger and scribbles on the tablet.

The doctor smiles, nods, lays the tablet on the counter, and moves to a small refrigerator by the door. He punches in a code and then opens it, pulling out a small vial.

I watch him bustle around the room, grabbing a few more things and taking his seat again, then depositing his handful on a small rolling tray.

He moves my mom's arm to the side of the chair and rolls up her long sleeve. There are small scars from all the IVs she's had lately, and seeing them makes my stomach clench.

The doctor chats away about some upcoming early fall snow while he fills a syringe and cleans my mom's skin with an alcohol wipe.

I grab my mom's free hand and squeeze while the doctor gives the injection and then places a bandage over the tiny wound. Once she's finished, the doctor strips off his gloves, cleans up the mess, and sits one more time. His eyes move to me, and I almost flinch at the focus when I've been so glued to every twitch of my mother's.

"Now, she'll need lots of rest. Continue the high-protein, high-calorie diet we already discussed. If she starts feeling sick, I'll prescribe some meds to help with that as well. Just simple things that will make this all a little more tolerable."

Once he talks to us about the side effects, he leaves, and a nurse comes in to hand over some paperwork. We leave the same way we came in, and it all took only about twenty minutes. Even if it was a short trip, it's so monumental. It will keep my mom with me, so something in me feels like it should have taken longer; it should have left a physical impact, but it doesn't. We return to the car, and I bundle her up, raising the heat because she's shivering.

Mom opted to skip the pancakes. When we are back at her house, I get her settled into her favorite spot on the couch again. Then I bustle off to the kitchen to load her up with water and snacks. Once I have everything within easy reach, I sit on the floor by her side and hold her hand. Just to spend a few minutes with her.

"Are you okay, Mom? You've been quiet since we went to the doctor."

She rolls on her side and gives me a look, her eyes a bit hazy. There were some pain meds mixed into the shot, so I expected it.

"I'm fine, baby. Just don't tell your grandpa, okay?"

I freeze and stare at her. "Grandpa?"

She pats my hand. "He'll be so angry I left, that I ran away. But we're safe now, and I never got to tell him that."

"Grandpa," I whisper to myself. Then louder. "Who is grandpa? I thought your father was dead."

She makes a sleepy noise and snuggles against the covers. "Don't worry. They can't find you. He's dead too. No one can find you. But especially not your daddy."

Something old and bitter cracks open in my chest. "Daddy?"

Another noise, another slow blink my way. "Yes, he's dead too. Don't worry. There aren't many left."

All of this is news to me. Whenever I brought up anything related to her family or my father, she always brushed it aside. Told me they had passed away tragically. Now she's saying her father is dead, and my father is dead, but what does she mean about keeping me safe, then?

I gently shake her shoulder. "Mom. Who else is out there who would want to hurt us?"

There's no point. She's dead asleep now, her mouth already parting with a small snore.

I knew my mom kept secrets, as all parents do at some point in your life, but to keep a secret regarding our lives being in danger? Why would she keep that from me?

CHAPTER 31
DREW

MY FATHER WENT ALL OUT on this one. The ballroom at the estate is sparkling and gleaming, and I think good ole dad got a new chandelier installed. I stare at the crystals reflecting the soft candlelight bulbs throughout the room. Tiny rainbows spiral over the walls, and it's enough to calm me down for a second. To have a moment's peace from the hole in my chest where Maybel should be. It's not love. I'm not stupid enough to believe it's love. There's no such thing. But it's like she's taken something from me, something vital, and I fucking want it back.

Just as quickly, the panic returns. Is this where the money is going? Why he's pimping me out to a client's daughter? It makes me grit my teeth and drag my eyes to the already large crowd. It's packed in here, and the waitstaff circles with trays of food and drinks. At least I don't have to endure a formal dinner. I spot Lee's parents on the other side of the room and Sebastian's parents lingering near the bar. Not unusual for them. They'll stay there all night, probably. I snag a glass of something brown from a passing tray and throw it back in one huge gulp. It burns all the way down, but it's nothing more than an uncomfortable heat.

As I move to grab another, I spot my father on the other side of the room with his client and her daughter. The parents are talking, but the girl already has her eyes trained on me, locked and loaded. She knows what she wants, I'll give her that, but if she thinks she can just have me, she'll be mistaken.

I turn and head in the opposite direction, needing a little more time to put on my game face. The mask that saves me at these things. I spot a sulking Lee over in the corner, clutching a drink to his chest as he keeps his eyes open. If any of his father's friends are here, that explains his desire to hide. Which is for the best because he's gained twenty pounds of muscle this year, and I'm not sure he wouldn't kill one of them if they tried anything.

There's too much history there.

Sebastian is near the door, scanning the scene, assessing as ever, playing the part of dutiful son. It makes me roll my eyes. Fuck him and how easy he makes it look.

We still haven't talked about the fight. About whatever the fuck is going on with him. When I walked in the other morning, he'd been shouting at his phone. Something serious has happened, but he's not talking to any of us about it.

I shift my gaze and spot my father, his client, and my fucking date crossing the ballroom to my side. My father smiles and claps me on the back, and I barely contain the flinch his touch always causes.

"You remember my client and her daughter, Spencer?" He waves at the woman.

I smile, barely showing teeth, and turn to the younger woman. "Ahhh, yes of course!"

342

She looks pleased. "Oh, you do remember me. I wasn't sure you would."

Since she almost had her hands down my pants the last time we met, of course I fucking remember. Her mother beams down at her and then up at me. "You two go dance. It's a party, right? Get into trouble."

My father laughs. "Not too much trouble, though, am I right?"

I lead her toward the floor, but she winds her arm around my elbow and tugs me around the dancers. "I missed you."

Bullshit. I don't say that, though, giving her a noncommittal grunt instead.

Logic goes out the window, and she takes it as encouragement, just like her type does. If this girl joined The Hunt, she'd be training fodder for all the guys who love an easy catch. They'd take her one after the other and leave her in the woods to piece herself back together. They might let her come if she screamed prettily enough.

She snags a glass of wine, and I pull another whiskey off the tray. I'm going to need so much of this tonight. If only to keep the stench of her perfume from burning my nose.

My wallflower always smells so clean, like strawberries and coffee sometimes. I can't think about her here, not in this world. Not tainted by these assholes.

I let Spencer lead me along where she wants. Eventually, she stops, and I get a look at the gown she's wearing, green silk hugging tight to her tall, lithe frame, a slit that goes up to her fucking hip almost. I wonder if Spencer picked out her dress or if her mother did since she's wearing something similarly racy. It doesn't matter. I won't be taking it off her, even if that's what she thinks will happen.

She turns to face me and gives me a smile. "You want to dance?"

I hold my arm out, and she grabs my hand instead to place it against her lower back, almost at the curve of her ass. Goddamn, this one is needy. Not enough guys at her school to torment? My entire body cringes as I touch her, and I do my best to hide it. We linger at the edge of the dance floor so I can make a quick escape if I need to. She, of course, steps into my chest, her tits brushing against me with every move.

"It's hard to waltz with you so close to me."

Her tone tips as her eyes rake over my body. "Who says we need to waltz? Hold me close, and we can just sway."

"This isn't the fucking high school prom. Have some dignity."

She tenses in my grasp, and her eyes immediately brim with tears. "What, what did you say?"

I keep us moving as she barely shifts with the music now.

"You heard me. I get you find me attractive, and you want Mommy to buy me for you, but you should know I'm not for sale, and if you push me, I will make you miserable for it."

A few tears slip free of her eyes when she blinks, and I grit my teeth, wanting to tell her there are far worse things to cry about in the world, but I don't. Almost at the same moment, a hand clamps over my shoulder, and I recognize the hard grip immediately.

My father breathes into my ear. "Is there a fucking problem?"

I glance down at the girl, who still looks upset, but whose eyes are trained on my father now.

"Of course not. However, you're interrupting our dance."

"My apologies, but I'd like to have a word." My father's charming voice replaces the venomous one he just gave me, and Spencer smiles, taking a step back from me. My father whirls me around and leans into my ear. I already know what he's going to do. His goal is always the same. "You better get your shit together and do your fucking job, or there will be hell to pay. What about Mom's next barrage of drugs? You want me to accidentally forget the pain pill regimen the doctor has worked so carefully on?"

He wouldn't fucking dare hurt her to get back at me, and still, his face has never been more serious. "Don't believe me? How about you test me and find out."

I want to call him a bastard and elbow him in the face until a satisfying spurt of blood comes out, but acting out in violence wouldn't change what's already happened. He's not worth it. This is the exact reason I never fight him. Why I always stay in line like a little toy soldier. Any sort of rebellion ends up falling back on my mother, and when you love someone, you make sacrifices for them. I just don't know how much longer I can keep this up. I spin away from him and snag Spencer's hand, dragging her to the other side of the dance floor. We get back to dancing, and her hands are tighter around me now, but she leaves a few inches of distance between our bodies.

"I'm not a genius, but I take it you and your father don't get along?"

I peer down at her. "My father is my father. I do whatever he wants me to do."

"Including dancing with me?" she pouts. "You were so charming and sweet the last time we met. It's like you aren't even the same person."

Fucking hell, not only am I forced to be her personal fuck toy, but I have to stroke her ego while I'm at it. Of course.

"Don't worry about it. You want me to be the perfect date, then I'll be the perfect date."

Her frown deepens. "That's not what I want. I want you to want me, and not because you're told to want me."

"You can have one or the other, not both." I tug her closer, crowding her. "So what's it going to be?"

Her breath rasps out, and I catch sight of her nipples poking through the thin fabric of her dress. I guess that answers my question.

"Why don't we get a drink?" This time, I take her hand in mine and interlace our fingers. She lets me drag her along my side to the bar. The bartender approaches, and I order a double whiskey and a glass of wine.

We stand and sip our beverages for a moment while watching everyone else mingle. After a minute, she turns to me. "How is school going? Your little club?"

I grit my teeth and stare down at her. "Fine. It's all fine, of course."

She smiles back, tentatively. "Oh, I'm so happy to hear it." Her hand lands against my chest and climbs upward. When I don't remove it, she seems encouraged and leans into my side. She's a snake, slithering her way up my body. Across the room, my father stares at us, his gaze penetrating with the weight of ten concrete blocks. With his face growing redder by the second, I unclench my fist and force myself to wrap an arm around her body, clutching her tight to my side. Turning, she beams up at me with this awestruck look.

My stomach churns, the contents threatening to climb out of my throat and spill across the floor. I want to shove her away. I want to tell my father he can fuck off and that whatever he has planned will never happen, but I can't. There's too much hanging in limbo. My mom, Bel, any chance I might have at a future. Spencer reaches up to tug my hand into hers, then places her drink on a passing tray and pulls me toward the corner of the room to an alcove of curtains and privacy. I don't bother trying to stop her, not with my father's pensive gaze on us. Once we're out of sight, I pause, stopping her from pulling me any farther. I have no doubt what's on her mind, but if she really does want it, she'll have to start it herself, in the plain light of the room.

"What do you want, Spencer?"

She gulps. "Obviously you, silly."

It's nothing like Bel says, and I hate that I have to hear those words from another woman's fake-ass mouth. She doesn't want me. She wants my dick and what it will give her, not me. *Bel wants you. Bel gives a shit about you when she shouldn't.* I grit my teeth at the reminder of how shitty I've been to her. If I could, I'd leave her life for good, but I'm consumed by her. Her presence, scent, the way she looks at me, and those sexy glasses she wears.

Spencer seems to be encouraged by my lack of words, and she stretches up on her tiptoes to press a kiss to my lips. It's a gentle graze, and I hold tense, tight, not pulling her in, not kissing her back in any way. Her eyes are closed, sparkle coating the lids, but I keep mine open watching her. I don't want this. I don't want her. My stomach turns at the thought of her tongue in my mouth, and I have to clench my jaw as she goes for a second deeper kiss.

I can't stand the plastic taste of her mouth on mine or the way she whimpers like this tiny contact is turning her on, making her lose it. When I know damn well it won't.

Someone cuts in. "Oh, looks like you two are having fun."

Sebastian, the fucker, stands with a smile on his face. It's a soft, almost sweet one, something I've never seen on him. It's more unsettling than anything else tonight, by far. What is going on? "And who is this little dove?"

Little dove? I can't help it. I gape at him as she sinks back to her feet and stares at him. Of the two of us, he's the more classically good looking. Silky tan curls, bright green eyes. He's also the more brutal, not that she would know it.

He leans in and kisses her hand. "I'm Sebastian. Who are you?"

She giggles. Fucking giggles. "Spencer, uh, Spencer, yeah."

Well, shit. I guess if he's going to rescue me, I can't be a dick to him. He glances at me and smiles that stupid grin again, and I can't help but smile back with how dumb he fucking looks. In a flash, he turns his attention back to her.

"And what are you doing dancing with this reprobate, Spencer? Didn't they tell you that if you're going to date a guy from The Mill, it should be me, or maybe..." He taps his chin like he's thinking. "Only Lee is prettier."

She giggles again, and he points out Lee, who is still pouting in the corner.

"Should we go cheer him up, do you think? He looks like he could use a drink or two."

She turns her attention back to me, her body more relaxed. "Is he your friend?"

My smile is more real than fake now. "Yeah, I guess he is."

She follows Sebastian over to the other side of the room, and for the first time so far tonight, I feel like I can breathe.

Lee tenses when they approach but relaxes under Sebastian's pointed teasing of both him and the girl. I turn, intent on another damn drink, but the ground beneath my feet disappears. My eyes collide with another pair of pretty green eyes.

Bel.

She's standing behind the bar, her eyes wide, face as white as a ghost. There's no doubt by the heartbroken expression she wears that she hasn't missed a minute of what happened, including that kiss.

CHAPTER 32
BEL

IT'S like my body completely froze from the inside out. The tray in my hand shakes and threatens to topple, so I slide it behind the bar on instinct alone while the rest of me stays locked in place, staring at Drew over the high-top bar.

He whispers my name, and it breaks the spell, allowing me to move my legs and take one stumble backward.

His eyes stay on mine, and his hand comes up like he might reach for me even though we are several feet apart. No one else is in the room, and that thought scares me now. All I see is him, and on repeat in my head, the highlight reel of her kissing him, of her touching him.

What the fuck is happening?

The bartender moves my tray. "What the hell are you doing? The natives are getting antsy. Go circulate." The hard line of the tray hits my chest.

I take the weight and stare up at the large forty-something bartender as if he's speaking another language. "What?"

"Take this round and go. Come back when you need more. You're holding me up for custom orders."

I look up at Drew again, and he's closer now. Only the bar separates us.

"Bel," he breathes, and even with the music, the crowd, I hear it anyway.

It doesn't matter. I can't do this. I can't face him after what I witnessed. It hits me all at once that I know nothing about him. His grades, his schoolwork, how he feels inside me, but nothing real. Nothing substantial.

Has he had a girlfriend this whole time?

The thought shoots through me, and I can't face him. No. Not like this.

I turn, and I fucking run like the coward I am. Leaving the tray on a side table near the door, I race right into the service hall that runs along the ballroom. It's empty now, but it doesn't take long to hear the sharp tap of dress shoes on the linoleum chasing me.

"Maybel, stop."

He never uses my full name, and I hate him for doing it here. Now.

"Fucking stop, Bel. Damn."

I'm moving faster, cutting across another hall that leads into the kitchen to the other hallway that runs perpendicular to the main one. This place is a maze, but I will find my way out of here or die trying.

He continues to follow me, and I continue to ignore him. "You really want to do this here? Go ahead and run. It doesn't matter. I'll always find you. I'll always catch you."

I glare at him over my shoulder, still moving. He's slow, slower than I know he can move.

"Let me guess, you say that to her too? Did you chase her down and take her in the woods too? Claim her virginity and fuck up her life?"

He huffs and stuffs his hands into the pockets of his tux. A fucking tux he looks incredible in. "You sound desperate, little wallflower. If you stop, I can show you what I really think."

Fuck him and fuck this. "No," I snap and up my pace.

"You know I like it when you run from me."

His words make me want to stop and fucking deck him. Especially since I hadn't heard a word from him since he left my room the last time. The distance between us is so thick that I hadn't yet figured out how to breach it. I think that's on him, not me. If he's saving himself for some tall, willowy rich girl, me throwing him out means nothing despite his protestations.

When the next door comes up, I sweep through it and back into the party. It's all diamonds and big hair. All these people have far too much money and time on their hands. Drew follows me, pausing as he scans the crowd again. I grab a tray from a passing server and swing through the crowd into the big knots of people to keep him off my tail. He can't confront me in here, not in front of these people.

I stop short when a six-foot-tall giant cuts me off. He snags a champagne flute from the tray and stares down at me, a wrinkle in his brow. "You okay, my dear?"

I risk a glance at Drew walking up behind me and give the man a megawatt smile. "I'm fine, sir. Do you need anything? Are you comfortable?"

His eyes flick to Drew, who hovers behind me, waiting, no doubt, for the opportunity to sweep back in and drag me away. I pass the man who is still staring at me, a curious expression pinching his features, and move on to others, extending the tray, doing the job I'm being paid for. When I break out of the crowd, a hand grips me by the arm and drags me through another side door. Drew shoves me hard against the concrete brick wall adjacent to the door until my shoulder blades ache with the impact. *Shit.*

He's scowling now, his eyes locked on me as he pinches my chin between two fingers and tilts it up. "Now, you will listen to what I have to say because you don't have a choice, wallflower."

I stare deep into his eyes, making sure he can see and feel my defiance. He doesn't get the last say here. "That's where you're wrong. I always have a choice. Now tell me what you want so I can get back to work." The question drags up all the memories of us together, of all the times I've asked him that same question and never gotten an answer. Thinking about it, he probably wanted this with me all along. Someone to fuck with and play games.

This time, he leans in and whispers against my mouth. "We never made any promises. In fact, you are the one who told me to walk the fuck away. Remember?"

I jolt as his words sink in. That's what he wants to say when he's practically kissing me? I shove at his chest. "Get the fuck off me. You're right. We didn't make promises, except the second I even look at another man, you freak the fuck out. So...that tells me something is happening right, or maybe it doesn't go both ways? You can claim to all your friends that I'm your girlfriend, so they don't touch or mess with me. Meanwhile, you can see anyone you want, but I have to sit around until you decide to come to me?"

He huffs, his warm whiskey breath fanning my skin. "Bel..."

"No, you're right. We never made promises, but you sure as shit are going through a lot of effort to explain yourself if I mean nothing to you."

He finally steps away, and I feel like I can breathe again. It's not worth the effort as an ache forms in my chest from the fear, anger, and fucking betrayal. Why do I feel betrayed when we aren't supposed to be anything to each other?

This time, the words come out with all the weariness I feel. "What do you want from me?"

"Look." He gestures toward the exit door. His expression is earnest, pure, and I want to tell him to fuck off, but I don't. "That man you saw out there isn't really me. It's the act my father forces me to play. Or else..." His frustration bleeds into his words.

I blink and crane my head forward as if I'm listening harder. "Or else what? He'll stop with your ten-thousand-dollar weekly allowance."

His eyes go sharp and dark. "Watch your mouth, Bel. I don't give a fuck if you don't want me anymore. I'll still find a way to punish you."

"What are you going to do?" I demand, not caring if I'm yelling now. "You just said we never made promises. Fine. Then you have no say over a damn thing about me. If I want to walk out into the ballroom and kiss the first man I see and tell him to take me home and fuck the daylights out of me, then I will. You, Drew Marshall, do not own me!"

His fist comes out of nowhere, slamming into the wall above my head, and I flinch before glaring up at him. "I'll repeat myself, but only once. The man out there, with that woman, isn't really me. It's me doing what my father says, taking part in the family business. It's not what I want, Bel."

I cross my arms over my chest. "And that woman's tongue down your throat supports the family business, how?"

He cups my face as tears slip free from my eyes and trail down my cheeks. Fucking hell. I'm trying to stay strong here.

"You're the only one who sees me, Bel. The only person who sees the real me. That's what I want from you." His voice drops to a husky whisper that almost unmakes me. "I want you to be the one who tethers me to sanity. That keeps me from doing stupid shit. From ruining everything. Who doesn't just let me give in to my demons but fucking embraces them."

Tears are falling hard and fast now, and I'm relieved when they block his view slightly. "Please, let me go. I'm obviously not what your family wants for you if that, what did you call it, a show, was anything to go by. The heartache is too much. All of this is too much. "

His fingers tighten, and he dips his thumb under my jaw to tilt my face up. "I'll never leave you alone. Now cut the shit and listen to what I'm telling you."

I blink through the tears and wait, happy I'm at least not sobbing in front of him.

"You are what I've chosen for myself, Bel. That's why I'm stuck on you."

"What does that mean?"

He presses his forehead to mine. "Nothing and every-thing, okay. I want you, but I will never be able to keep you. For now, you keep me from making worse choices than the bad ones I'm already committed to."

"How romantic," I mumble, turning my face so his lips can't touch mine. There's still a splotch of pink on his mouth from her lipstick, and I don't want it touching me.

"I'm telling you in every way I possibly can that I need you."

I tug my face away, and this time, he releases me. There's no way I can give him the last word here, though. I'm raging mad, but more than anything, I'm hurt. "You need me, huh? That's a long way from even fucking liking me, isn't it? You like my pussy, my body, the way I scream for you, right? But not me. You say I see you. Well, you know what? You haven't even bothered to try to see me, have you?" The words hurt to say, but they are the truth. "Now let me get back to work. Unlike you, I don't have a daddy to hand me everything I want whenever I want it."

He blinks but takes a step back. Of course it's not a big enough one to allow me to leave without touching him. I wiggle between him and the wall until I'm free, then I stalk down the hallway, putting as much distance between us as I can. Drew follows—because of fucking course he does—and I keep splitting my attention between his brooding frame and the door at the end of the hallway. Paying more attention to him leaves me distracted, and I walk right into a broad tuxedo-covered chest. *Great.* I freeze on impact because this man is definitely not Drew, but he looks like Drew, just older.

He steadies me gently, grabbing me by the forearms. "Whoa, miss. Are you alright?" His tone drips money, and I stare up at him. I don't know if it's better or worse to know what Drew will look like in another twenty or so years. Drew's dad glances over my shoulder, and I turn to spot Drew rooted in place. He looks like a statue.

His father's gaze ping-pongs between us. Then he scans my features and down my body. It's not lecherous, but there's an edge behind his genial mask. Something close to surprise? He covers it with a smile that makes me nervous.

"Well, this is interesting. Young lady, why don't you head back to the party? I'm sure you have work to do."

His words are solicitous, but there's an edge to his tone I can't place. I nod and step around the man, staring at the door in front of me. Drew hasn't moved. His hands are still in his pockets as his dad crosses the space. *Do I leave him?* What a ludicrous question. The man is his father, after all. I have no reason to be concerned or be a part of whatever conversation they plan to have. Drew made it very clear to me many times over that his life is off-limits, and from the single look they exchanged with one another, this is a very personal matter.

The crowd's noise closes in around me, and I get back to work even though my heart aches inside my chest. I knew things would end this way. I called it from a million miles away, and somehow, I'm still shocked that we're at this point. The only person I have to blame for a broken heart is myself.

CHAPTER 33
DREW

I STEP toward my father and meet his murderous glare. His lip is curled as he stares me down, and I know he's about to punch me. The look on his face is always the same. "Be careful, Father. If you hit me here, there's really no way to hide it from everyone who's out there."

He doesn't care to listen and takes a small step forward, driving his fist into my gut. I should've anticipated the hit, but part of me thought maybe he wouldn't do it. I bend in the middle, pain shooting up into my ribs and chest. Before I can maneuver myself out of his way he lands a cheap shot, slamming his knee into my stomach. A sharp, stabbing pain fills my chest, and I gasp for air. I fall to my knees, my vision going blurry, my stomach threatening to dispose of the whiskey I drank earlier. I suck a ragged breath into my lungs, and the pain in my side intensifies. "I think you broke a fucking rib."

He tilts his head to the side, a smile ghosting his lips. "Guess we should get back to the party now, huh?" Uncaring to my pain or current condition, he lifts me under my armpit and hauls me up. Then roughly straightens my suit jacket. I

357

hiss through my teeth as my muscles protest at the movement. "We'll be having words after the party is over. Was that the girl you've been seeing? The trailer trash I told you to stay away from?"

I can hardly breathe, let alone speak, so I choose not to respond and follow him begrudgingly back out to the party again because I don't have a choice. He stops just inside the doorjamb and leans into me. I want to punch him, to hurt him like he's hurt me, but not here. Not right now.

"Speak to her at all, and I'll make sure she's punished, and then you'll be watching it before you get your own. And I promise you, I won't be gentle with her."

I grit my teeth, wishing this night was over. Wishing that I could take Bel away from all of this. If I have to kill this man to protect her and my mother, I will. I'm tired of playing his games. Tired of pretending for the sake of pretending.

I scan the crowd, looking for Bel, and find her serving drinks across the room. I follow my father to where his client and Spencer wait.

She greets me with a smile and immediately loops her arm into mine, tugging me tight against her. "I missed you. Where did you go?"

I answer, trying my best to hide the pain and still keep my eyes on Bel, who continues to move about across the room. "Just had to step out for a moment. School stuff, you know?"

She nods, and I cup her waist as my father sends an icy glare my way. "Do you want to grab a drink?"

Her hand runs down the length of my chest, and I flinch. Of course, she doesn't notice, leaning her head against my shoulder. "Yeah, let's get something to drink."

I tug her to the side of the crowd and move in the direction of the bar. My father calls my name, and I pause, my back to him.

"Come back soon. The speeches are going to start soon."

I barely restrain myself from lashing out at him and pull Spencer toward the bar in the corner, as far from both my father and Bel as I can get. She orders a glass of wine, and I order a double whiskey. Something to dull the pain in my rib that is climbing up into my arm now. *Fucking hell.* It's hard to focus on playing my part when the only thing getting through right now is pain.

Once I down the whiskey, I face the room. It's impossible for me not to seek out Bel in the crowd. Even in a work uniform and slightly sweaty, she looks better than the woman at my side in diamonds and silk.

Spencer chooses that moment to interlace our fingers, and I have to actively not pull away from her even though every fiber of my being screams at me to shove her away. Not just because of Bel but because I hate that my father has basically sold me to the highest bidder. She tugs me by the hand to the corner alcoves again, and I know she'll push for what she's wanted all along.

I sit on a bench trying not to cringe as I do, my side throbbing and on fire. She plops down beside me with a sigh.

"This is the best party ever. Does your dad do events like these often?"

"No, only a couple of times a year."

"Do you attend all of them?"

She sips her drink, and I stare down at her. "No, only the ones I'm ordered to attend."

"Ordered?"

How can she be so damn stupid? "You don't remember the conversation with my father? The only reason I'm here is because he ordered me to be here." My response doesn't sink in at all. She places her glass on the floor by the bench and leans up to kiss me. Like the first time she tried to kiss me, I don't move under her mouth.

When she swipes my lips with her tongue, I'm forced to end this charade, and I grab her chin, stopping her. Her eyes pop open, and I see heat there, not fear. Maybe she'd do better in The Hunt than I thought. There's a tap of crystal, and the music cuts out. I stand and extend my hand out to her. "That's our cue. We should get out there, or we'll be missed."

Her lips form into a pout that makes me want to punch something. "We could skip it and stay here instead. It would be the perfect time to get to know each other better while everyone else is distracted." I don't need to ask her what she means by the perfect time or getting to know each other better. She wants my cock, and that's too damn bad.

More gently than I feel, I tug her out of the alcove, and we return to the party. Upon our reappearance, my father spots us immediately, a smug smile on his face. Everyone gathers in a small circle in the middle of the room. He ushers me over with a wave, and I force a smile, walking slowly toward him.

"Now that my son has joined us, we can start the speeches."

He waves at the client to his left and lets her talk about stocks or some shit. I tune it out and keep my eyes on Bel as she circles the edge of the room. It's not like I need to pay attention. It'll be a year, at least, until I can start at my father's firm anyway. Spencer watches her mom speak about mergers and investment, and when she claps, I clap.

The lights dim, and I peer around the room, confused. *What the fuck is happening?*

My father surveys the crowd. "As many of you know, my wife has been ill for some time." There's a murmur of sympathies from the crowd, and I clench my fists so hard, my knuckles ache. How dare he bring my mother into this fucking sideshow? "It's why I'm so thrilled to make the next announcements. It's a wonderful thing for our families, and it's even more important because of the new investments that will be made in the company."

I try to slink back into the crowd to escape this madness, but his eyes land on me. One single look, and I know if I make another move, I'll pay dearly for it. "Son, come here and bring your lovely girlfriend with you."

Girlfriend? What the fuck? My lips press into a thin line, and with zero choice, I move us closer to my father, giving him a vicious smile. All teeth and no heart. Spencer blushes beside me at the attention we garner. Everyone gushes and makes comments about how beautiful of a couple we are. If only they knew the truth.

My father grips me by the shoulder hard and turns to the room as if he's looking for something. "Ah, young lady, please bring your tray over. We need to make a toast."

I realize he's motioned to Bel, and she looks like she'd rather be anywhere but here. Regardless, she weaves through the crowd and extends the tray to my father. She keeps her eyes on the floor, refusing to look at me. I can't say I blame her. My father gives her a grateful smile and passes flutes of champagne to me, Spencer, her mother, and then takes one for himself.

"It's my pleasure to announce the engagement of my son, Drew, to Ms. Spencer Kelly. With their marriage, we'll join our two great firms and become an unstoppable powerhouse."

There's a pause before the crowd applauds, but I hear nothing and see nothing. Nothing but Bel's horrified expression. Every single part of me wishes to reach for her and explain that it isn't what she thinks, but I can't. I can't fucking fix it, not here in front of everyone in this room.

Spencer grabs my hand, and my father comes over to shake my other hand, pressing something hard into my palm. "Do it. Now."

I glance down to find a velvet ring box. *Is he fucking kidding me?*

Spencer pulls me back to her side, and I feel like a Ping-Pong ball with no control over my landing. A familiar ache in my chest threatens to drown me. No. I can't do this. When I don't hold out the ring, Spencer opens the box for me and gasps.

I stare down at the glittering diamond and band that has to be at least two carats. Of course my father would spare no expense on my fake engagement ring. Spencer slips the ring onto her finger and waves it out in front of the crowd. Holy shit, she is even crazier than I thought. This is merely an act. She can't actually think that I'll marry her, right? She turns to face me and lifts her chin like she wants a kiss. My father squeezes my shoulder, and once again, I'm stuck between them. I lean down and brush her cheek with my lips. It's not really a kiss. It's not real, either way.

When I stand again, Bel is in my vision, and I freeze. She looks...broken. Turned inside out. This is my fault, and causing her this kind of pain is something else entirely from the pain I enjoy causing her. She takes a wobbly step back, and I spot Sebastian in the crowd. He's directly behind her now, and for once, I'm glad to see them together. At least he can get her out of here, save her from me, and what I might do if I get her alone again.

The crowd simmers down, and my father continues to speak, but I'm done listening. I'm pinned between the betrayal in Bel's eyes and the way Spencer grasps my arm tight against her body. There's nowhere to go, and I've never felt more powerless in my fucking life.

Sebastian leans down to whisper in Bel's ear, and again there's no surge of jealousy, nothing but relief that he's here for her.

Lee cuts through the crowd, a smile on his face as he grabs my hand from Spencer's, shaking it vigorously. "Man, I'm so excited for you."

Then he leans in and whispers into my ear, "What do you need? What can we do?"

It's as if he can tell I'm on the edge. Of breaking open and killing my father, maybe? Of walking away from this room and never looking back?

"Let's go get another drink to celebrate," he suggests, tugging me back toward the bar. Sebastian holds Bel's arms, and I can see the fresh tears on her cheeks.

Fuck. This goddamn hurts.

When we reach the bar, Lee casually turns to me so my back is to the rest of the room, nothing but Lee in my face. "What do you need? Want me to get you out of here?"

I shake my head. "It's pointless. He'll just hunt me down and make me pay in another way for embarrassing him or our family name."

I clutch my ribs, and he eyes me up and down. "Wait, did he already hit you? That fucking bastard."

My father's discipline has never been a secret among my closest friends. They try to help, but they can do nothing except save me from the destructive warpath I go on afterward.

He grabs me by the shoulders and gives me a little shake. "Snap the fuck out of it, man. This isn't you. You control the school, The Mill, all of it. You don't bow to the whims of one damn asshole. Get yourself together and take care of this. Or are you going to let your father continue to humiliate your girl?"

I turn and find Bel had been beckoned once again to pass out drinks. There's a spotlight on Spencer's glowing face as she shows everyone within six feet the fat princess-cut diamond on her finger.

I'm hopeless. "There's nothing I can do. Not yet at least. Once this is over, maybe there's something, but you guys aren't going to like it."

He snorts and takes a swig of a beer. "We don't like throwing ourselves in front of three-hundred-pound line-backers to save you either, yet we still do it."

My father seeks me out in the crowd, his pensive gaze on me, and I let out a sigh of defeat and walk back out to the floor. It's all a circus act. My father may be the ringleader for now, but he can't hold the crowd's attention for long. I just have to wait until he passes the baton. And when he does, I'm going to fucking destroy his pride and joy, his company, his entire fucking world from the top down.

CHAPTER 34
BEL

ALL I CAN DO IS STAND HERE like a fucking lawn ornament and offer people drinks. I wonder if he's been engaged the entire time he's been...well...fucking me. A slimy feeling coats my insides. I feel sick and duped. He was right before when he said we never made any promises. He made demands, and I acceded to him. He doesn't owe me anything, and I don't owe him anything. If that's true, then why does it feel like my chest is caving in? Like he put his big foot inside and stomped all over my damn heart?

I circle the group, keeping my eyes locked on the tray. I countdown the seconds until I'm out of drinks so I can run away to safety. I'm desperate to get out from under the scrutiny and judgment of all these fucked-up people. Or hell, even worse, their indifference. They don't think I see it, but I do. The way their noses tick up at me as I pass by. I'm nothing more than a walking drink dispenser to these fucking people. I keep my distance from Spencer and the sparkling symbol of my stupidity on her finger.

There's no way he wasn't at least fucking her and me at the same time. God, please explain to me how I missed this.

How could I have been so stupid? Engagements take time. Commitment. All the things he wasn't willing to give me, clearly since I was nothing more than a secret fuck.

Perfect for fucking in a dusty library but not bringing home to Daddy. My heart races in my chest, and yes, I know I should've expected this since things like this are the entire reason I refuse to date or do anything with a man, but I thought... I thought Drew cared, at least a little bit. He told people I was his girlfriend. Yes, it was only to keep people away, but it had to stand for something.

When the last glass is plucked from my tray, I make a beeline through the crowd to escape. I'm standing smack dab in the middle of the party towers, everyone wanting to congratulate the couple, so it takes a moment of fighting, using my tray to practically shove people out of the way. My vision blurs, my lungs ache as I hold my breath, and panic bubbles up in my chest. It's been a long time since I had a panic attack, but this feels just like all the other times. I need to get out of here, away from him, these people, this damn room.

When I finally reach the end of the room, I can breathe a little easier, but that breath is stolen from my lungs when an arm snakes out of nowhere and latches onto me. I'm seconds away from punching the person in the face when I realize I'm not in any danger.

It's just Jackie. A safe harbor in a wind-swept sea. She has no idea how much I need her right now. All the broken pieces I've been holding over the past few minutes push me over the edge, and I immediately break down, letting out a horrendous sob on her shoulder. She doesn't say anything. Then again, she doesn't have to. Holding me tight against her chest, she turns us so my back is to the room and lets me release all the tears I've been holding back.

All the pain, sadness, and heartache spill out of me and onto the floor like I've been cut open. After a few minutes, she finally speaks. "It's okay, Bel. It's okay. Let it out, and then march back into that room with your head held high. Don't let him see you breaking down. That's what he wants."

I know that, but it's harder than you'd think to see someone you thought gave a shit about you hold hands and dance with another woman who you just discovered he's been with for a while since he's now engaged to her.

"I just don't know how I missed it. Clearly, they've been together for a while... and if they have, then..." The words barely squeak past my lips as another sob rips through me. I don't know what to believe. All the rumors said he didn't date. Even Drew himself admitted he wasn't boyfriend material, yet here he stands with his future wife wrapped around his arm. It was all a sham.

How could I have been so stupid? My brain feels like it's been put into a blender. The tears refuse to stop falling. I don't know how long I stand there crying. How long it takes for my eyes to dry. It's pathetic, I know.

"Shhh, it's okay." Jackie's soothing voice helps to bring me back to the present. Even with the heavy weight of pain pressing down on my chest, I know I can't let him win. I can't leave the party and let him see how much it hurts me that he's with someone else. That's what he wants. I need to be strong and push through the pain.

Once I can draw a full breath into my lungs without letting out a sob of defeat, I pull away. "Thank you, Jack."

"Of course, that's what friends are for. Now tell me what the hell happened out there? I thought you and Drew were like, a thing? He's uber possessive over you. Now it looks like he's engaged, and I didn't even know the guy was dating someone."

I snort and swipe at my damp cheeks. I can only imagine how much of a hot mess I look. "Well, apparently, the way he feels about me is very different from the way he feels about her."

"I know it hurts, but you'll get through it." She holds my tray up, and I hug it tight to my chest like it's a shield that can save me from this nightmare of an evening. "Look at me. Why are you here? Why are you doing this?"

"To work."

"No. Wrong. You're here for your mother, remember that. This is a job, and you're here to earn money, to pay for her treatments, and to put food on the table. You're not here for him. This isn't about him."

Another sigh passes my lips, and my shoulders seem to ease with the reminder of why I'm here and doing this at all. "You're right. I'm here for my mother. To help her."

"Exactly, and if you go back out there and make any kind of scene, they will kick you out of here, and this whole night will have been for nothing. We have over a thousand dollars in tips accumulated for the night. I'd hate to see you lose all that over one stupid guy."

Per usual, she's right. She's always right. I tug her into another quick one-armed hug, the tray trapped between us. "I'll pull it together. I can always lose my shit later."

She leans back and winks. "And I'll steal one of these pricey bottles of champagne to help with that breakdown. Emotional crises always feel better with some good alcohol."

A laugh escapes me, and I turn to face the bar. More drinks, more endless circles. Only a couple more hours, and I can go home. All I have to do is make it through the rest of the night, and I'll never have to see him again. Jackie gives me a hard smack on the ass as I walk away, and I turn to glare at her over my shoulder, playfully.

"Go serve those drinks," she calls, and I shake my head.

The bartender and his assistant load my tray, and I make the rounds again. I keep my gaze averted, reminding myself that I'm here to make money, but then I catch a glimpse of Sebastian out of the corner of my eye. It feels like he's hovering at my back, but he's not doing anything wrong so I don't bother confronting him. I notice that he's got his phone pressed to his ear, and there's an uncanny expression etched into his features. I haven't seen him wear this expression before. It's not...sadness, but something deeper. Usually, he offers the world nothing but a fake mask, but whatever is going on, on the other line of that phone must be wavering enough for him to forget to keep it in place. Feeling his eyes on me, I look away and continue serving drinks. I don't want to draw any more attention to myself.

My feet are starting to ache, the pain mirroring the one in my chest, but quitting isn't an option. Not for me. I make another circle around the room, and as I'm about to turn and head back toward the bar, I'm cut off by another one of Drew's friends. His hulking frame blocks my path. I look up at him, ready to tell him to kick rocks, but the words stick in my throat. In his eyes, I see great sadness and pain. The fake smile I've worn all night slips away.

"Please move. I have drinks to serve."

"I will in a minute, but I want you to know this is nothing more than an act. A way for his father to make connections. He doesn't give a shit about that woman. You're the only thing that matters to him."

The pity in Lee's tone only angers me further. I don't want his pity. I don't want anything but a paycheck from these assholes. "I don't give a shit. If I was the only thing that mattered, he would've given me a heads-up, a warning. It doesn't matter now. He's still a dick. He's always been a dick, and I realize now that I was stupid and blind for getting close to him, but no worries. I understand my place now. But, just to keep things interesting, tell him if he wants to continue tutoring, I'm doubling my fee. Let's call it asshole inflation."

I shove the last drink on my tray into his chest and slip past him, walking away with my head held high. Now that the speeches are over, some of the partygoers start to funnel out, and the people inside thin out. It's tempting to skip out early, but I can't risk it, not with so much money on the line. Which sucks when all I want to do is run. It's hard to ignore his existence when he's standing across the room, his eyes tracking my every move.

The petty urge to grab one of his friends and take them into the corner and kiss them flits through my brain, but I let it pass. There's no need to start a fight, at least not until I get my tips. Time trickles by slowly, but I push on. I keep an eye out for Drew, his friends, and his father and maintain my distance at all costs. Any minute now, I'll be able to walk out of this place and never have to look back to this terrible fucking night.

On my last trek to the bar, I notice Drew's father standing by the back door leading out to the service hall. Something is wrong. I can feel it. Drew saunters up behind him, and I cut my gaze away from them. It's none of my business. *He's not my business.* He made that very fucking publicly clear. *Then why the hell do I care? Why am I wondering if he's okay? If something is going on?*

Despite trying my hardest not to glance back at that door, I do. I can't shake the bad feeling that's intensifying in my gut with each passing second. I catch a glimpse of Drew's dad holding him by the back of the neck, pulling him into his side. Pain pinches Drew's features.

What the hell is going on?

My eyes dart to his father, and I stop cold between a few guests. That look I recognize easily enough. I've seen it on Drew's face plenty of times. It's rage. He's pissed at Drew. Shit. What is he going to do? I shouldn't give a shit. Whatever happens to him is on him, but that's not who I am.

I skirt the crowd and head that way slowly, not drawing attention to myself. Every muscle in my body is wrung tight and tense, and prepared for a fight.

Sebastian and Lee stand by the bar, not paying attention to me, or to Drew and his father. When they disappear into the door, I turn and face the other end of the room. *Shit*. The only way to get into that hall without being seen is to go the other way, the long way, and even then, the sterile lighting might give me away.

But which of these assholes pays attention to servants anyway?

I duck into the door and press against the wall at the farthest end. Voices carry down the long hallway, filtering into my ears. Peeking around the corner, I catch a glimpse of Drew's father as he grabs him by the throat and screams into his face, spindles of saliva flying.

"What the fuck did you think you were doing out there, mooning over that fucking server. She is trash, garbage, the dirt beneath your feet. Is that what you want for yourself? Our family legacy and namesake is on the line, and all you can think about is some white trash pussy? Does anything mean a goddamn thing to you?!!!"

I place a hand over my mouth to stop myself from reacting. His father's words sting as if he slapped me with them. When I chose to attend Oakmount, I knew I was attending a university for the rich and elite, but I also knew that no matter what or where I went, I would never fit in. I guess I never anticipated my financial status to become that big of a factor in my life.

Drew makes a small noise and mumbles something that I can't make out. My emotions are wavering and conflict brews deep in my gut. *What the hell do I do?* I force air into my lungs and try to remind myself that this isn't my problem. Like Drew told me many times, I should keep my nose out of other people's business.

I shake my head, my heart clenching tightly in my chest. This isn't my business. It's not my job to protect him from his family or anything really, since it's clearer than ever that I was never anything to him.

"I can't believe you! You almost ruined everything, every single fucking thing I've worked for, and guess what? I think it's time you start paying for it. I warned you. I told you what would happen if you disobeyed me, but you think you're smarter than me, don't you?"

The venom in his father's tone makes me shiver, but I remind myself that Drew is a goddamn quarterback, that he's the bully who steamrolls everyone in his way. He can take care of his father if he needs to, right?

Besides, what would me getting in the middle of it all do anyway? *Nothing.* That's what, and still my heart refuses to let me walk away, even with the knowledge that he's getting married to someone else and that he probably has been sleeping with us both this entire time. Who cares if his friends and him claim it's an act? None of this has been an act to me.

I continue peeking around the corner. My phone vibrates with a text, and an idea hits me. What if I record this? A rich asshole who puts on a fake smile to the rest of the world. What would happen if everyone found out it was a lie? I tug the phone out of the apron and peek around the corner, with nothing more than the camera part angled down the hall. I hit record, and watch the phone screen intently. Yeah, I want to beat Drew till he's black and blue, but his father... his father shouldn't want to hurt him.

A pain-filled grunt fills the space, and I glance up from my phone screen to see Drew slide down the hard concrete wall before slumping to the floor. I have to help him. I take a step forward, nearly giving myself away, but then I freeze. *How am I going to help? I'm no one.* This isn't like when I stuck up for that guy in the library against Drew. This is different. I can feel it in the pit of my stomach. I can't help him in the same way I helped that kid, so even if I want to run to him, I can't. I need to stay here, hidden.

His father moves closer, pulls his leg back, and lands a harsh kick to his stomach. A scream threatens to escape my throat, but I press my palm to my lips to hold it in. Tears build behind my eyes. *How. What...*

All the old aches, the new ones too, seem meaningless against this assault. No one should have to endure abuse like this from their own parents. Not even an asshole who makes me regret the majority of my choices over the past couple of months.

I have to do something. I step back and turn to peer back through the door that leads into the party space. Lee is on the other side, casually standing, acting as if he knows nothing about what is happening on the other side of that door.

How can they call themselves friends? No, there isn't anything I can do to help, but they could. They're rich and powerful. Money can buy you anything you want, right? Rage drives me forward, and I march right up to them. I push any and all fear aside and press a finger into Lee's expensive suit jacket.

"How can you consider yourself to be a friend when you know he's getting his ass beat right on the other side of that door, and you aren't doing a damn thing about it?"

The look he gives me at that moment should have me

tucking my tail between my legs and running for the hills, but if I've learned anything, being quiet doesn't always get you what you want. Sometimes you have to get loud, you have to make noise.

"Don't look at me like that. I asked you a damn question." I give him a shove, and his expression changes in an instant.

He drops the pretty boy charm, and the lethal shark, ready to attack at any given moment, steps into place. Those pearly white teeth of his gleam in the light when he snaps at me.

"Word of advice, Drew might play nice with you, but I won't. Don't talk about shit that you know nothing about. He doesn't want us involved, so we help how we can and pick up the pieces afterward. That's all we can do."

Furiously, I shake my head. "That's fucking bullshit, and you know it."

Maybe I'd be scared of him under different circumstances, but not today.

"If he wanted us to help, he'd tell us. Now run along because as smart as you appear to be on paper, you sure as hell don't know when to leave well enough alone."

Flickering flames of rage burn deep inside my chest. I clench my fist tightly, wanting to lash out and inflict pain on this idiot. *He's not a friend. He's nothing.* Even as the urge to wipe the pointed look of annoyance off his face rips through me, I know he's not worth it. Not even a little.

"Smarts have nothing to do with being a friend. I hope the guilt of doing nothing eats you alive. Maybe you can stand to sleep with that, but I can't. If you won't do something, then I fucking will. Where is Sebastian? Maybe he'll listen to reason."

"None of your business. You'd have to have a conscience to feel any type of guilt, sweetheart. Drew's been enduring this shit much longer than you've been around." His dark tone is a warning. "Don't assume I don't give a fuck about my friend. It might lead you to find yourself in a world of trouble."

"Fuck off," I growl and spin on my heels, stalking back to the other entrance.

I'm not going to waste any more time sparring with that asshole. I notice as soon as I cut through the hall that it's empty. My pulse spikes, and I barely catch sight of the kitchen door swinging open.

Shit.

I rush down the dimly lit corridor, not bothering to stay quiet. I can't hear much of anything except the heavy beating of my own heart and the ragged breaths entering my lungs. My adrenaline spikes once I reach the end of the hall, and slowly I peek around the corner and into the kitchen. I catch sight of Drew's father holding him down by the neck against the counter. The room is empty, though I imagine there might be someone guarding the door on the opposite side of the room.

Of course a rich man like him wouldn't want anyone to discover the truth, to see the real monster beneath the perfectly painted mask. His father leans down and whispers something into his ear. Drew's entire body goes still, a statue cast in pain and anger. Whatever his dad just said hurt him far more than any of the punches.

It's a good thing I don't give a fuck about any of their rich asshole bullshit...

CHAPTER 35
DREW

BITTER COLD SWEEPS THROUGH ME, a numbness if you want to call it that. Though I can already feel the bruise forming on my cheek from where I hit the wall. There's a table beneath me, but I don't feel it. All I hear are his words ringing in my ears.

"Did you take a good look at the girl, Drew? She looks like someone you know, doesn't she? She certainly looks like her whore of a mother, but maybe you recognize someone else there too. I know I recognized it when I saw her back in that hall."

What the fuck is he implying? I try to push against his hold, but it's iron. "What are you talking about? How do you know Bel's mother?"

Then it hits me...like a twenty-pound anvil on my chest. The illness she's been dealing with her entire adult life, according to the medical records I glimpsed on Bel's laptop. It's the same kind of illness my mother has. The doctors have always documented it as cancer or something akin to it.

Leaning into my face, a sickening look fills his eyes, and

when he speaks his words, they shatter my existence, the existence he's been trying to break for years. "She's your half sister."

No. That can't be true. No. This is another one of his fucked-up games. It has to be. My stomach twists into a tight knot. Except the eyes. The sparkling green eyes of hers that she hides with her cute little glasses. We both have green eyes; my father has green eyes. I try to tamp down the terror and heartbreak threatening to consume, but I can't. I'm drowning in it.

No. NO. *No.*

I slide to the end of the table, and bile rises in my throat. This can't be true. This can't be.... before I can even attempt to stop it, I'm vomiting off the side of the counter. All the whiskey I drank earlier to keep myself in check and make the night easier pours across the shiny floor. It's by the grace of God that I remain standing, that and Father's hand still clutching me tight.

When the puke splatters across his shoes, he releases me with a curse. I crash into the wall, barely keeping myself upright. "Pull yourself together, Son. It's sickening, I know, but lucky for you, I saved you from doing something stupid. Like getting that whore pregnant."

"Don't talk about her like that," I growl as the copper tang of blood fills my mouth.

I know reacting is nothing more than pouring gasoline on the fire, but I've spent my entire life taking his shit. I can't bear to stand here and listen to him speak so ill about someone he doesn't even know. The world goes quiet, and I can't be bothered to move or try to block his attack, so I let him hit me again, his fist slamming into my already tender and swollen ribs. The pain is nothing but a dull ache. It's like

I can barely feel it as I sink into myself and forget, float away, try not to focus on anything until it's all over.

After the damage is done, I'll feel it, but I've learned that if I crawl deep inside that secret place in my mind and simply endure, it's easier. My father's image blurs in front of me, and I feel his fingers digging into the back of my neck. He drags me back to the counter and slams my face against the cold marble. My cheek throbs, and fire blazes up the side of my head and into my temple. Warning signals go off in my brain, but I ignore them.

"I should've had your mother abort you. I swear you've been nothing but a stain on this family since the day you were born, yet you're the only heir I have that's worth anything." He digs his fingers into the back of my neck, squeezing, and then repeats his action from moments ago. Maybe this is where it all ends? I can hear my heartbeat in my ears. *Thump. Thump. Thump.*

The world around me goes silent, and more blood fills my mouth. It's all I can taste. Without warning, I'm moving, flying through the air as my father tosses me across the kitchen like a rag doll. With blurry vision, I look down and realize I'm on the floor now, barely missing the spot of vomit.

I want to crawl deep inside my mind and hide there. Wait for this to be all over. No one can save me. *Save yourself.* A voice echoes through my mind. *Protect them. Fight for them. Bel, your mom. Protect them.* That voice gives me enough hope, enough strength to climb out of that dark spot in my mind, and even as my body protests against me, I stagger to my feet, anger overriding the self-imposed calm.

My eyes are nearly swollen shut, and my head throbs, a wave of dizziness threatening to pull me back to the floor, but I clench my fist and straighten my spine. "I can't believe you have the audacity to call yourself a father. You're nothing to me or her. I wonder what all your friends would think if they discovered the real person beneath the mask? If they found out you sold me to the highest bidder and pimped me out to your client's daughter just because she's a spoiled brat who has never heard the word no in her life."

As I stand there, another jolt of abject fear hits me. What would he do if he got his hands on Bel? A woman to throw around and sell to his friends to be used, abused, and discarded. He's never given a shit about me, and he raised me, but her...he's spoken five words to her. If this is how he treats someone he supposedly loves, I can only imagine what he will do to her. I have to get a grasp on the situation. Spin it. Keep his focus on me and off her. Just like I do with Mom.

My father sneers, and I hate seeing myself in every twitch of his face. Will this be me one day? Taking out my pain on the rest of the world? Hurting those I love for the hell of it? God, I hope not.

"Your only goddamn job is to listen and obey me!! Now fucking listen." He crosses the room in a flash, his hand circling my throat, his long fingers digging into my flesh. For an old man, he's strong as shit. "AND OBEY!" He screams the words into my face. I don't so much as blink at the rage he expels upon me.

"What do you want?" I grit out, barely able to draw enough breath to speak. I have to do what I can to keep them safe until I come up with another plan, something better. A way to get rid of him.

"I just told you." He shoves me again, and I crash against the stove, barely catching myself. We stare at each other, and I know that things will get progressively worse if I don't obey him. There's no saying he wouldn't keep me here and send one of his stupid goons to attack Bel, and then we'd all be fucked. I'd be forced to watch, to feel the guilt of bringing her into my life.

"Okay, but leave her out of this. If you want someone to hurt, I'm right here. Hurt me."

My father pulls his cuffs down and straightens his bow tie. "How poetic, even with the truth sealing your fate, you still want to protect her." He shakes his head. "Let me help you understand something. What I do or not do with her is none of your fucking business. I don't answer to you; you answer to me. I thought you were coming to understand that, but it turns out I was wrong. I'll take care of that."

In the back of my mind, questions linger, and I want to know who is feeding him this information. My mind flashes back to the memory of Sebastian on the phone yelling in French. It's the only other language my father knows outside of English. Was Sebastian spying on me for my father in the name of protection? My body flashes red hot for a moment when I remember how Sebastian hovered around her after the announcement. How he's been pushing against me lately. He's always thought The Mill should have gone to him to lead. Not me. Is this payback years in the making?

We've been friends since we were kids, and I hate that I'm actually considering the fact that he's betrayed me and to my father, no less. I had assumed all my friends hated him. I shake my head in disbelief. *No. No.* He wouldn't do this to me. Not after everything we've been through over the years. Lee would never say a word against me, nor would Aries. The only one who's been different lately is Sebastian.

"Who told you about her?" I force the words out.

"Curiosity killed the cat, Drew. I'd tell you, but it's not really any of your business. Just assume I know everything and work off that. You should've known better. You couldn't hide this from me, not even if you wanted to, and with the way you were fucking her all over campus, being possessive and shit, that tells me you really didn't want to anyway."

Shit. How can I keep her safe from him if he has eyes on me and her. There are no other options available, no other way to fix this that doesn't end in heartache. The mere thought makes my stomach churn. I want to vomit all over the fucking floor. *Again.*

My father props himself on the edge of the counter, sort of leaning. "Listen, Drew. You're my son. My only son. The only child who will carry on my legacy."

I don't trust the new soft tone or lower volume. It never bodes well for me. It's more like the calm before the storm.

"Look at this whole marriage thing as a business transaction. It's a contract, a merger, for example. It means nothing, really. It's more of a pretty party and a legally binding contract that will line our pockets and get us the necessary connections. Nothing in that contract says you have to stay faithful. I'm not asking you to be a doting husband. Marry the brat, sign the contract, and you can go find another piece of trailer trash to warm your bed until you're sick of her. I went through one of those phases, too, you know, but I grew out of it pretty quickly."

I blink, letting the words sink in. *How dare he?* How the fuck he dare talk about my mother that way. Not the white trash part—she's always been rich—but the fact that he'd never stayed faithful to her. I'm fucked in the head in so many fucking ways, but cheating, that to me is the worst possible thing. It shouldn't really come as a surprise, he's always been a dick to her, and her illness has only intensified that assholeism. *Her illness.*

"Leave her out of this."

"Your little library girl? Fine, if you do what you're told."

I shake my head. "No. Mom. Leave her out of this shit between us. She shouldn't be punished for my wrongdoings."

He rolls his eyes and clasps his fingers over his knee. "I don't give a shit about your mother. I keep her around as a way to control you. I'm surprised it took you this long to figure out. Word of advice: never show your weaknesses, Son, because they will always be used against you."

Suddenly, the threat of violence, of fucking torture, is no match for the burning inferno of rage inside. I've dealt with his shit for so many years. I've endured his beatings and beratings. I've stayed in line and been his punching bag. I'm done. I launch myself at him, taking him down to the floor. With both hands, I grab him by the head and slam him against the tile floor, then I tighten my fist and punch him in the face.

I only get one good shot in before a set of burly arms wrap around my middle and pull me off him. I don't need to look to see who is grabbing me. I already know. My father's goons. There's two of them with him tonight. Roscoe secures me around the chest, his hold tight so I can't move, while Baxter helps my father to his feet.

Once standing, he swipes at his face with the back of his hand and spits a wad of blood onto the floor before looking at me. It's so fucking satisfying to see his teeth stained red and a trickle of blood trailing down over his lip from his nose. Looks like I broke it, and I don't even give a fuck. I'd kill him if I could.

I'm losing my fucking mind. A bubble of manic laughter escapes me, and Baxter steps forward upon a wave of my father's hand and punches me hard in the gut, forcing me to double over the best I can while still being held in Roscoe's iron grip. Still the best moment I've had in a while. And if he puts me in the hospital, it will mean I have something to enjoy as I dream. At least I know he won't kill me. He needs me far more than I need him.

My father grabs a towel and some ice from the freezer and then approaches me slowly, his eyes gleaming as he studies me like an animal in a cage.

"I had high hopes for you, Son, but now I see you need a little more preparation. All those beatings you endured over the years didn't do shit to toughen you up. Looks like we'll be starting over, and this time, I won't stop. Not until I fucking break you and piece you back together as I see fit."

I recede into the darkest confines of my mind when Baxter steps forward and throws the first punch. *Pathetic.* He's not even going to hit me this time; he'll just have his goons do it while he watches. Typical lazy asshole. He gets his hands dirty well enough, but sometimes, he likes to let someone else do it since they know how close to take me to the edge.

I keep my eyes trained on him as he leans against the counter and wraps his knuckles in the ice, simply watching as Baxter lands hit after hit against me. I feel each one, but the pain is muted this far back in my mind. No one can reach me here, and it's for the better. Something warm splatters down my chin, and I hear my father's order from far away.

"Stop."

I fall to my knees, then my stomach. A bright red liquid pours out of me onto the sparkling tile below. *Is it blood?* My entire body feels numb, a coldness creeping up my limbs and into my core.

"Goddammit, look what you made me do, Drew. If you had just behaved, then I wouldn't have had to resort to these methods. There's blood everywhere...sit up and look at me. This mess is all yours." I roll to my side, but it takes me several minutes to move into a sitting position so I can meet his gaze. I don't know why I bother or even try.

"Now, tell me what do I expect from you, and please get it right so we don't have to do this song and dance anymore tonight."

I lick my swollen busted lip and croak out the words that make me sick. "Marry the girl and fall in line."

It's not about marrying the girl of his choosing anymore. It's about protecting Bel and my mother. It's about destroying him and watching him burn in the aftermath of his own doing. Reaching out with the same hand that has given me countless injuries, he pats my cheek, and I wince from his touch. "Good. Now stand up. I'll have the guards carry you out the back and get you home. I'm sure one of your friends can find a bandage or two to fix you up."

It's hilarious how nonchalant he is about my friends' knowledge of the way he abuses me, yet no one will ever say anything or do anything because of who he is, what he does, and who he works with. He thinks he's invincible, but I will find a way. I will end this motherfucker, even if it costs me everything. I sputter and cough, my chest aching as I spit more blood onto the floor. I shake my head. I can't stand, not yet. The room spins each time I try.

"Are your ears broken? I said to get the fuck up." Dragging me up off the floor, he delivers another quick punch to my face. The world spins all around me like I'm on a Tilt-A-Whirl, but thankfully, I land against the counter, catching myself. It's better than the floor. Now I just have to get my legs to fucking work.

It's at that moment that a scream pierces the heavy fog clouding my mind. It comes from somewhere, somewhere that is still far away. Slowly, I grasp onto reality, sinking my claws deep into that space. There's a scuffle and movement to my left. With substantial effort, I lift my head and turn, looking up just in time.

I try to speak, but the words are lodged in my throat. *No.* I know I hurt her, and I know this whole thing is fucked up, but I won't let my father, *our* father, now touch her. I have no time to cringe at the thought. It's Bel. She's here, and I need to make sure she leaves unscathed to the best of my abilities. My father takes one long look at her, one that forces me to stand despite every cell in my body protesting.

No, I won't let him hurt her. Not to get back at me.

I have to keep her safe. This is my fault. All of it.

I step forward, wobbling, an arm wrapped tightly around my middle like it can keep my lungs from spilling out the holes and fractures in my rib cage. "Please... leave her alone. She doesn't deserve this." I move between them, shielding his gaze from her.

He sneers at me. "What are you doing?"

"Stopping you from doing something stupid. She's just a girl trying to earn some extra money for school. That's it. She has nothing to do with our world."

His eyes narrow once more. "She has everything to do with our world, Son. More than you can comprehend at the moment. That's why we need to get rid of her."

Get rid of her? His words seem so final, and there's no way he would actually kill her, right? He's crazy and fucked up, but surely, he's not a murderer?

I take a step back, forcing Bel to take one as well. From experience, I know she's not going to let him break her. Not like he's broken me over the years. Bel is stronger than I'll ever be. Caught up in my thoughts, I don't notice one of my father's men moving in on us, not until it's too late. A thundering crack echoes in my ears, and the world catches up real fucking fast. I twist around just in time to witness with horror as Bel's head is forced to the side, her fragile features absorbing the impact of Baxter's hit.

Something inside me snaps, and I charge forward, my shoulders slam into Baxter's stomach, and my feet don't stop until we crash into the wall. I pull my arm back and land a punch against his face, the sound of bone cracking fills the space.

"Don't ever fucking touch her again." I seethe, barely standing on my own two feet. Baxter snarls his lip at me but doesn't move. My father chuckles from the other side of the room, and I slowly walk back toward them. Every step takes significant effort, and I take even shallow breaths to stop the pain from swallowing me whole. "Father, stop. Let me take care of this. Let me prove myself. I'll do whatever you want me to do. Just don't... please."

I've never in my entire life begged my father for a single thing, but I will do it today if it means I can save Bel. He stands proudly like he's won the battle. He has no fucking clue that this war has barely begun. "Fine, if that's what you want. Deal with her, but I expect her to be out of the building and away from here in the next ten minutes. That, or she will be coming back to the main house with us. There is plenty for her to do there."

I nod and turn my attention to Bel. Her face is a mask of confusion and hurt, and when she looks up at me, those two emotions morph into something softer, sweeter, something only she shows me. I hate that hurting her is the only way to protect her, but it's what must be done. Someday, she'll understand. I know she will.

Leaning forward, I skim a finger across her cheek and down the side of her neck. She trembles, her eyes darting between my father and me. *I'm sorry, Bel. I'm so fucking sorry.* I can feel my father's gaze hot on my back. He's watching every move I make, and I need to make this as believable as possible.

When she nuzzles her face against my hand and relaxes into my hold, I slice my fingers through her hair and twist her long braid around my fist. Then I slip the mask of fury and rage into place. "What did I say about minding your own business, wallflower?"

Her eyes are frozen lakes of fear, and I think—no, I know this—this is how he will break me for good.

CHAPTER 36
BEL

HIS HAND TIGHTENS in my hair, and I jolt. This isn't like it has been in the past. This fucking hurts. My entire scalp is on fire. I claw at his hands, but his fist is anchored in my braid like a fucking vise. "Let go of me." I whimper. "I only came here to help!!"

He leans in closer, his swollen face giving him an even dark edge. "What the fuck makes you think I need someone like you to save me? You're nothing."

His words sink through the painful haze, and I drop my hands. Yes, he can be mean, a downright dick at a multitude of times, but he's never been this cruel. Even at his most rageful, there have always been cracks of light shining through in the darkness. There's always been a softness that he seems to carry just for me. I'm so confused. His friends tell me it's all an act, but this isn't an act.

"I don't understand what's happening..."

He grabs my chin with his other hand and clenches my jaw shut, and I swear I see a flicker of guilt in his eyes before the rage overtakes him. "Shh...when I ask you to open your mouth, it will be for me to put my cock in it, and that is it. Do you understand?"

One of the goons behind us snickers, but I can't move. Hell, I can barely breathe as I stare up at the cold, hate-filled rage in Drew's eyes. This can't be real. He's acting again. I can't truly believe this is how he's felt all along. I think back to the times he's shoved me away, keeping me at arm's length, refusing to let me get too close. The way he used my body and walked out that last time. It makes sense, and the pieces align perfectly, but my heart, it doesn't want to believe it.

"No." I hate myself for how small that protest sounds. "No. You're lying. I know you care about me. I know I'm more to you than this."

His grip grows tighter, and it feels like he's going to rip my hair out of my head. A scream rips from my throat, and I claw at his hands and kick at his legs, but he's had practice fighting off women in his precious psychopath games, so I'm easily subdued.

"Not so fast. You're staying right here until I say you can fucking go."

I shake my head, the terror inside me ramping up with every second that passes. This isn't him. I refuse to believe it. He told me everything at these parties is an act. Is that what he's doing? Acting the part to keep his father from doing worse. That's what this is. It has to be. The thought gives me a glimmer of hope. A useless, mostly guttered thing, but I've lived on less.

"Stop, please. Don't do this, Drew. You're more than this. Don't become your father."

He sneers, and there's not a hint of the man who drove me up sheer cliffs of pleasure and threw me off, only to catch me at the bottom. This isn't him. His face moves closer to mine, and even though I want to push away, I can't move. His lips are so close to mine, I could touch them. I look into those emerald depths and see nothing of the man I've come to care for. The Drew I caught glimpses of is nowhere to be seen. It's almost as if he never existed at all.

"See, that's going to be a problem because, as it turns out, I am my father's son. It's not my fault you refused to see the real me this whole time. That you romanticized something that never existed. I need you to understand something, and I know you're smart, so lock it away in the confines of your mind. You're nothing to me, Maybel. Nothing but white trash with a nice little cunt that I enjoyed fucking for a short time. The icing on the cake was taking your virginity. Perhaps that's what got you twisted into thinking I gave a shit. I don't really know, and I don't really care. Now my duties to my family and name are the most important thing to me, and while your pussy strangling my cock was nice, I need to fulfill my obligations by getting married to someone suitable. Someone worth being seen with. Though, maybe, if you're a good girl and don't make a fuss, I'll give you my dick one more time after the wedding."

It would've hurt far less had he ripped my heart out of my chest and stomped on it. I don't think all I can do is react. I pull my hand back and slap him hard across the cheek. The smack rings through the room, the burn of it enveloping my palm. Silence settles over us until all I hear is his heavy panting above me.

"Is that all you got, wallflower? If so, then you're fucked." He shoves me backward, and I lose my balance, my body tilting sideways. Horror flashes in his eyes, and I watch in slow motion as he reaches for me, his fingers missing me by a breath. It's like a car accident happening right before my eyes. One moment I'm standing, and the next, my head collides with something hard and unforgiving. Red-hot pain stabs through my skull. The world spins around me, my stomach churning and threatening to empty onto the floor as I land on my hands and knees. I fight through my blurry vision to look up and find Drew's father staring down at me, a cruel smile on his lips.

"Well done, Son. Now send her away so we can continue this discussion."

I don't know how I ever trusted him, how I ever thought he gave a shit about me. If this is an act, then he deserves an Oscar. When Drew stalks forward, my only thought is to escape. I no longer know this man nor do I trust him not to hurt me. My head feels heavy like it's a fish bowl, but I don't let that stop me. I skitter backward like a crab on my hands and feet to keep him from touching me again. When I hit the wooden door behind me, I know I'm trapped. Trapped between him, the door, and every shard of syllable he's slicing me open with. He crouches down in front of me, and the memory of when he did that same thing in the woods pops into my head, the scent of earth and damp forest all around us.

"It's time for you to leave, Maybel. You can take the trash out yourself, or I can take you out. Either way, this ends tonight. You're nothing to me, and you never were. Nothing more than a warm hole to sink into every once in a while. Now get up and get the fuck out and let us men do our talking."

I don't know why, but my heart forces me to cling to some type of false hope. I can't possibly believe any of this is real, not when I know what I felt. "This isn't you, Drew." I shake my head, fighting back tears. Every single fiber in my body tells me to believe his words, but my heart, my heart tells me to look deeper. To notice the little details.

He shakes his head as if he can't believe I'm questioning

him and reaches into his pocket. Tugging his wallet out, he thumbs through it and pulls out a wad of cash. The dollar bills rain down on me. "I forgot to pay you for the last time we were together. That should be enough, right? If you need more, stop by The Mill. I'm sure one of the guys will be happy to let you suck them off for a little more. You know...for your mommy."

My heart collapses into my stomach. His words are salt in a never-healing wound. "She has nothing to do with this or any of you assholes! You don't even deserve to speak about her."

His lips twist up into a heart-breaking smile. "Oh, there she is. I was afraid I might have put out your fire. Nice to know you're still in there. Now do you want to keep fighting, kitten, or do you want to go home with whatever remaining fucking pride you have left?"

I slowly push off the floor, using the stationary door for support to gain my footing. A wave of dizziness hits me, and I take a slow breath into my lungs, steadying myself. When I meet Drew's gaze, I swear I see concern, but when I blink, it's gone. All that's left is his stupid smug smile.

"You're a disgusting, self-righteous prick, and I can't believe I ever thought there was a single ounce of good inside you." I want to hurt him. To stomp on his heart the way he's stomped on mine, but I don't know that I can. Not when I'm not even sure there's a heart inside him.

He doesn't appear affected by my lashing of words. "The apple doesn't fall far from the tree. Isn't that what they say?"

I look back and forth between him and his father. "I guess not. Not surprising, really. You're just like him. I thought I had witnessed the real monster that night in the woods, but it turns out he never really showed me his face. Not until today."

393

He takes a step toward me, and I shield my face with my hands, afraid he might hit me, but he doesn't. Instead, he grabs me by the wrists, my skin burning where he touches me, and using the weight of my own body, he shoves me backward. He pushes me hard enough to dislodge the swinging door behind me. The doors fly open with the weight of my body while I spill out onto the floor ass first.

Pain registers in my mind as my tailbone throbs from the fall, but instead of sitting there like a damn statue, I scramble off the floor and onto my trembling legs.

"I hate you! I hate you, and I hope that when you realize how much you've messed up, you experience the same pain I am right now. I hope you see that I was the only one to give a shit about you."

"I don't need you to give a shit about me, Maybel. I'll find another tight cunt to keep my cock warm. That's all you ever were to me anyway, a nice warm hole to fuck."

Those are the final nails in my coffin. There is no point in me continuing this conversation or trying to understand. I'm only prolonging the inevitable. I turn to leave, my eyes full of tears, making my vision blurry. My first reaction is to run, but I don't. I won't let him run me out of here. I thought...I don't know. I don't know what I thought. Whatever we shared or whatever semblance of what we shared has been shattered and blown into a million pieces. It doesn't matter. I lived without him before, and I'll do it again. Fuck him and this whole fucking world.

When I make it to the door on the other side, I pause. Anger threatens to swallow me whole. He doesn't get to throw me out like trash when he's the one with the secret and the shitty family. This is not on me. It's on him. I turn and stare down the long hallway, watching as a woman comes through the back of the kitchen. She's in a server's uniform like me, and I think maybe she's going to tell them someone called the police or to break up the argument, but she walks straight into Drew's father's arms.

My gaze travels back to Drew. He's clenching his fists as his father leans in and kisses the woman passionately. It's at that moment when he sinks his fingers into her hair, and she lets out a terrible giggle that I recognize who she is. *Jackie.* The ground beneath my feet shifts. I can't be seeing this correctly. The world spins, and I feel bile rising up my throat. *No.* She wouldn't do this to me. Jack is my friend, my best friend, she'd never. The betrayal cuts through me like a dull knife cutting through meat. How could she?

What the hell is going on? You know what? It doesn't matter. None of this matters. Not Drew, not this fucking family, or the money. Tears fall hot and heavy, making tracks down my cheeks, but I don't feel them. I continue forward, but the door on the other side swings open the second I reach it, and I almost walk into...someone.

"I'm so..." I sniffle and duck my head, trying to hide my red face and tear-filled eyes. "Sorry."

Gently, as if I'm made of glass, the person grabs me by the shoulders. I lift my head and stare into a pair of eyes that have never shown an ounce of concern or care for me. *Sebastian.* This day keeps getting more and more fucked up.

"Come, Bel. Let me take care of this." Why is he looking at me like that, and what is he talking about? What is there to take care of?

I try to shrug out of his hold, but his grasp is ironclad. "There is nothing to take care of. I'm done with him, and I don't give a fuck if I ever see him again."

"I understand that, but they don't get to treat you like this. To toss you out like trash. You're not trash. You're fucking royalty."

I'm so confused by his words that I have no response. Instead, I find myself staring at him. His cheeks are pink, his curls tousled and shoved away from his face. His bow tie is undone as he surveys my face, and I swear I can feel his eyes penetrating the spot on my cheek, the bruise already forming from where that stupid goon hit me. The concern melts into red-hot rage as he takes in my entire face, clearly seeing something that angers him.

He releases my shoulders, his huge hand circling my wrist instead. "Come," he orders, gently tugging me down the hallway back toward Drew and his father. I must've hit my head harder than I thought because nothing about this man, the care of my body, and being safe should ever be used in the same sentence, but that's how I feel with him by my side. If anything, I should be running in the opposite direction, not letting him lead me back into the lion's den. I know better than to trust someone who is friends with Drew, but this is so out of character for Sebastian that I can't do anything but follow him and see what happens.

Sebastian walks into the room, his head held high, his eyes blazing, but the rest of his face is impassive, like a prince staring down at his subjects. I use every single inch of willpower in my body not to look at Drew. Each person stands as still as a statue, their eyes bouncing between him and me.

Drew's father is the first to speak, his gaze narrowed to slits.

"Can I help you, Mr. Arturo?"

Letting bravery lead the way I stare up at Sebastian. His hand still grips my wrist, anchoring me to the ground, keeping me sane. I watch him intently as he takes in the scene. Drew, his father, Jackie. All of it in one quick analytical survey. His sharp jaw tenses, and he squares his shoulders as if preparing for war.

When Sebastian doesn't respond, Drew's father presses. "Can I help you with something? I didn't see your grandfather out there." His gaze ping-pongs back and forth between Sebastian and me, a wrinkle of confusion forming between his brows.

"I'm not here to answer any of your questions. The only one who will be asking anything will be me, and my first question is: who did this?" His voice cuts through the air like a knife. I'm unsure of what he's talking about until I feel something wet and warm trailing down the back of my neck. I wipe at it with my free hand, and when I pull it back, I notice the streaks of blood on my fingertips. This must've happened when I hit my head on the edge of the counter.

My knees threaten to buckle beneath me. The weight of everything suddenly becomes heavier. My body sways, and I'm about to go down, but Sebastian catches my shoulders and adjusts me, keeping me in a vertical position.

Drew chooses then to take a protective step forward, a grimace on his face. He looks like he wants to help, but Sebastian, keeping me upright, shakes his head slowly in warning.

"Whoever did this to her, they'll pay. Consider this your only fucking warning. If any of you come near her again, I'll destroy you, piece by fucking piece. I don't care who the hell you are, whether you're my friend or what your last name is."

My brain must be fried because it can't compute what I think it is. Sebastian is sticking up for me, threatening his own friend?

"Sebastian, where is your grandfather? I'm sure we can figure this out together. Our families have been friends for years. You don't even know this girl. It seems a bit irrational to make such rash statements when you haven't the first clue on who it is you're defending. That girl is no one. She fell all on her own and probably has nothing more than a concussion." He lets out an anxious laugh, his gaze sweeping the room.

"You're right." Sebastian's grin resembles that of a shark. "I don't know her, but as of right now, she's under the protection of the Arturo family."

Yup, my brain is leaking out my ears because what he's saying doesn't make sense to me. Protection, what does that mean? What the hell is going on?

"Protection? Sebastian, you don't even know this girl, and what happened here today has nothing to do with you or your family. I think you'll find this entire thing is being blown completely out of proportion. The girl is simply upset that Drew is moving on."

"Oh, I'm sure that's what it is, and perhaps I'd believe you if I didn't know the real piece of work you are. Don't fuck with my sister again, or I'll skin you alive with my own fucking hands. There are few things in this world that I give a fuck about, but I won't have you disgracing her. Touch her again, and we will have a fucking problem."

Sister? I'm so confused. I'm still staring up at him, trying to understand the words he's said when, like a puzzle, the pieces move to align in my brain. The conversations with my mother, the things she said that appeared to be a riddle now make complete sense.

"My mom. Is she... Did she call you?"

Sebastian's expression softens but only a hair when he looks down at me. "No, she didn't call me. I only found out the truth an hour ago. I was coming to find you because your mom was admitted to the hospital. They called me after she wrote a note telling them what to do if things took a turn for the worst."

Took a turn for the worst?

"What...what do you mean? What happened?" I shake my head, backing away, tugging loose from his grasp. None of this is real. It can't be. Someone please wake me up from this horrible nightmare. It feels like my chest is caving in, every breath more labored than the next. My legs buckle beneath me, and the room spins. I can't lose her. I can't.

Sebastian grabs me, his hands gripping firmly onto my arms. I flail, trying to fight him off, but he refuses to let go. "Bel, listen to me," he growls, and when I continue to struggle, he gives me a shake that rattles my brain back to reality. "I know you're hurting, and the last thing you want to do is believe another asshole in this room, but I need you to believe me."

"I can't believe anything or anyone. I don't know what's real or fake anymore."

Sebastian nods like he understands, and then he grabs me by the back of the neck, his meaty fingers pressing against the pressure points there. "I'm sorry, Bel. I can explain everything later..." He whispers into my ear, and I struggle, but only for a moment when he presses harder, and my vision becomes black. I sink deeper into the darkness, praying when I wake up, this will all have been a nightmare.

Thank you for reading. I hope you enjoyed part one of Drew and Maybell's story. Please consider leaving a review on the retailer you purchased your copy from. Part 2: The Wildflower is available for preorder and will release March/April. If you're looking for something to read in the meantime, check out my other series with

similar tropes: Blackthorn Elite, Worse Than Enemies, and North Woods University.
Keep up to date with all things JL Beck by signing up for my unapologetic newsletter.
Sign Up Here

ABOUT THE AUTHOR

J.L. Beck writes steamy romance that's unapologetic.
Her heroes are alphas who take what they want, and are
willing to do anything for the woman they love.
She loves writing about darkness, passion, suspense, and of
course steam.
Leaving her readers gasping, and asking what the hell just
happened is only one of her many tricks.
Her books range from grey, too dark but always end with a
happily ever after.
Inside the pages of her books you'll always find one of your
favorite tropes.
She started her writing career in the summer of 2014 and
hasn't stopped since.

She lives in Wisconsin and is a mom to two, a wife, and likes to act as a literary agent part time.

Visit her website for more info: www.beckromancebooks.com

Stay up to date on sales, new releases, and freebies by signing up for her newsletter

ALSO BY J.L. BECK

Torrio Empire Trilogy

Blackthorn Elite Series

Moretti Crime Family Series

King Crime Family Duet

Worse Than Enemies

Doubeck Crime Family Series

North Woods University Series

Dark Lies Series

Devil Duet

Made in the USA
Columbia, SC
19 April 2024

34615633R00224